MEET ME IN MIAMI

Patricia J. Parsons

MOONLIGHT PRESS | TORONTO

MEET ME IN MIAMI

This is a work of fiction. Unless otherwise indicated, all the names, characters, businesses, places, events and incidents in this book are either the product of the author's imagination or used in a fictitious manner. Any resemblance to actual persons, living or dead, or actual events or businesses is purely coincidental.

ISBN 978-1-998358-03-8

For information or permissions:

Visit www.moonlightpresstoronto.com
Or email moonlightpressinfo@gmail.com

This book is for Art.

My muse, my inspiration, my guide.

"Life can only be understood backwards, but it must be lived forwards." ~ Søren Kierkegaard

"... when we really delve into the reasons for why we can't let something go, there are only two: an attachment to the past or a fear for the future." ~ Marie Kondo

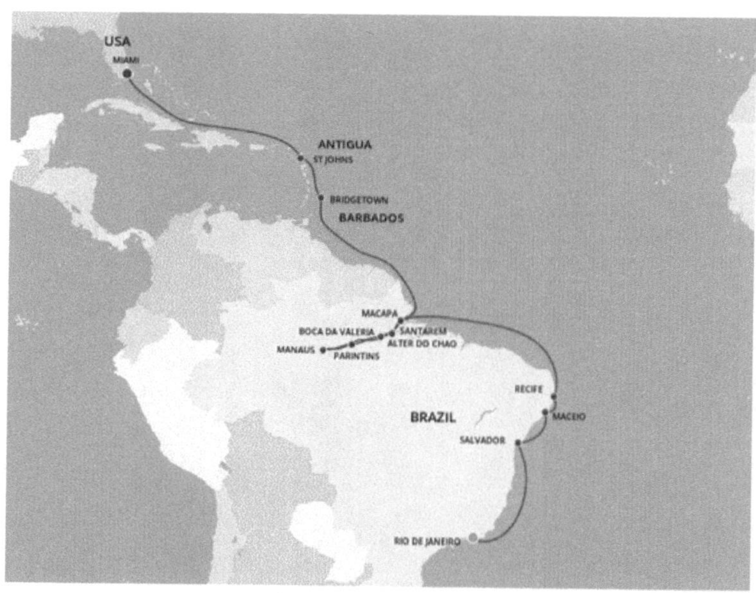

WHERE WE BEGIN...

MANAUS, BRAZIL, THE AMAZON RIVER

IN EVERY ORDINARY MOMENT, there is an extraordinary illusion. It's the illusion that what you see is real. You get up every morning and look out your window. What do you see? I don't mean do you see skyscrapers or a meadow, the ocean or your next-door neighbour drinking coffee on his deck in his underwear. I mean, what are you really seeing?

Is what you think you see real, or is it all just an illusion? Can you be sure that it's not some kind of fantasy? At best, a mirage? At worst, a deception? But perhaps the most puzzling question of all is this. Is anything in life real at all?

I know how crazy this sounds. It sounds just as crazy to me. The truth is that I'm an inveterate pragmatist, rarely given to pondering deeply about the meaning of life or questioning the way things are. I see what's in front of me, and I deal with it. But here I am, considering how I could possibly have gotten to this moment and contemplating these things for the first time in my life. And perhaps you would, too, if you were standing at the railing on the deck of a cruise ship staring down into the murky water of the Amazon River in Brazil, wondering how you came to this moment—wondering how the past ten days could possibly have gotten so out of control. Yet, here I am.

I'm so far away from home in this strange place. I'm looking at an odd phenomenon in the water below me. It's the place where you can see a clean line in the water dividing two rivers that flow alongside one another for six kilometres, never mixing—at least that's what we're told. Anyway, I can't help but think the two rivers are like two people whose lives seem to run in parallel, never really overlapping. Until they do. Here in the Amazon, they call it the "meeting of the waters" because the black water of the River Negro meets the brown water of the Amazon River. One river is cool; one is warm. One is fast; one is slow. One is opaque; one is clear. Like two people who are so close and yet so different.

I'm starting to feel like I'm one of those rivers—so close to the other one and yet so different from it. At the same time, I'm wondering what would happen to that line between the two rivers if I jumped in. If, right this minute, I climbed over the railing like we're told never to do and jumped in because it occurs to me that such an impulsive act might be just what the doctor ordered. What would happen to that clear demarcation between the two rivers then? Would the waters mix for just a moment, then flow alongside one another, parallel once again or would it make a significant difference? Where would I end up? And I suppose you might well ask, why would I even think about such a thing—jumping off a cruise ship?

Well, I recently heard someone say that mapping out your life might be the dumbest thing we do—that things happen to shape our fate in a way that's far outside what we could have imagined. I hear a sigh and realize it's me.

With the heavy mantle of humidity and the stultifying, unrelenting heat pressing down on my head and shoulders, I'm seriously wondering what I'm doing here. But then, how could I have known what would happen? The past ten days hadn't gone at all as I'd hoped. This was not what I had imagined when this whole thing started. But if I know anything at all, I now know this: things don't always turn out the way we expect them to. Perhaps life would be a lot simpler if we all just lowered our expectations. Or maybe even stopped expecting things at all. But there were still ten more days to Miami.

ONE

Eliza

SÃO PAULO, BRAZIL

I COULD SEE THE OUTSKIRTS OF THE CITY coming into view as I raised the sunshade on the window beside me in seat 2D on Delta Airways flight 227, fifteen minutes from touchdown in São Paulo, Brazil. It had been a supremely comfortable ten hours since I settled into my pod as we took off from JFK, taking me on an adventure that had seemed like such a good idea at the time.

I finished sipping the dregs of the champagne I'd had with my breakfast. It was helping me to keep the nervousness and that speck of doubt I was still having at bay while I considered how this all started. It was eight weeks ago in a snowstorm on an island in the North Atlantic, at the edge of my world. So very far away from where I was at this moment. But just like with any story, you have to recognize where it really begins, and that wasn't it.

It started even before that—three months ago, just after I welcomed my first grandchild, my granddaughter Mary-Catherine (a very un-Jewish name, I know, but that's a long story), forcing me to recognize that being just north of fifty years old did not make me too young to be a grandmother. Although, I still can't shake the feeling that twenty-one was too young for my daughter, Izzy, to be a mother. Anyway, it is what it is, as the saying goes.

I'd been waiting for the birth to be over before embarking on a task I'd long recognized had to happen. I had to tell Jake, my husband, that our recent separation was about to become permanent. I was going full speed ahead with the divorce we so badly needed to get on with our lives while he dragged his feet, moaning and whining. He must have learned that from his mother, Esther.

I sat back and closed my eyes, listening to the sound of the landing gear as it locked into place somewhere underneath me, and I remembered the events that unfolded that day I decided I had to tell him about my decision.

My daughter Izzy—Isabel—had moved back to New York from California earlier the previous summer and into the home the three of us had shared for years on the upper west side of Manhattan, and little Mary-Catherine was born in October. On the afternoon in question, Izzy had taken tiny Mary-Catherine to meet Astrid, Izzy's best friend. Since I had kicked him out a few months earlier, Jake was living back home with his parents in their palatial residence not more than ten blocks from us. He was coming over because I had told him we needed to talk, and I had promised him we'd revisit the separation thing after the birth of our granddaughter. I had wondered if he'd be bold enough to use his key when he arrived that afternoon, so I sat in the living room, waiting.

I was surprised when the doorbell rang. I suppose I expected Jake to act in a far more proprietary manner since, after all, as he had pointed out to me some months earlier, his parents owned this house before us. It was after that little pronouncement that I'd had to remind him that despite their previous ownership, as a result of his father's accountant's tax and legal liability advice (I didn't even want to know the details at the time—perhaps I should have asked more questions), it was now solely in my name. In addition, over the years, I had made more than a significant contribution to the household, both financially and otherwise. Anyway, there was no sound of a key in the lock. I got up and went into the foyer to open the door when I heard the doorbell chime again.

There stood Jacob Cohen, a man I'd met within weeks of moving to New York City the first week in that fateful September 2001. He was practically hidden behind the most enormous bouquet of flowers I'd seen since my mother's funeral five years earlier. What in the world was he thinking?

"These are for you," he said, thrusting the pile of white roses, baby's breath and ferns at me. At least he remembered that white flowers were my favourites.

I took the flowers as he walked past me into the foyer, where he shook off the droplets of rain beading down his Burberry raincoat.

"Things look good here," he said, hanging his coat in the closet as if he had just walked in from a day at work and hadn't been absent from the premises for almost two months and counting.

"How did you expect things would look?" I said as I passed by him and made my way down the hall and into the kitchen at the back of the house to find a vase. I doubted we had one large enough. I thrust them into a copper pot that I retrieved from the large selection hanging above the island's work surface before heading back out to get on with the afternoon's planned activities. I had an agenda, and I had an objective that I intended to achieve.

By the time I arrived back in the living room, Jake had already poured himself a scotch from the selection on the sideboard and was sitting with his feet up on the coffee table, loosening his tie. I have no idea why he was wearing a tie on a Saturday afternoon, but perhaps there had been an emergency meeting at Bluestone Pharma, his family's business. After all, they were currently facing at least three lawsuits and had brought one against a whistle-blowing doctor. There was always drama in the Cohen clan.

"Why don't you just make yourself at home?" I said, sarcasm dripping from every word.

Jake ignored me and said, "Why not? It is, after all, my home."

I could feel my jaw tightening and realized I had to get on with this and get it over with. So, I told him.

"Jake, I'm filing for divorce. This separation has been just the distance we needed for us to see that there is no future in our marriage. My attorney will be sending the papers over to your office, and you can sign them there and courier them back."

Jake swirled his Baccarat crystal glass—one of the many his mother had given us over the years in her attempt to make me appreciate every expensive thing she worshipped—then sipped his scotch thoughtfully and leaned back with his free arm stretching across the back of the sofa. He swallowed and then looked over at me, where I was now sitting on the facing sofa. "No." That was all he said before taking another sip. I waited. Nothing.

"No?" I said. "What do you mean, no? No isn't an answer, nor is it an option."

"No, Eliza. No. No, I will not let you divorce me. No, I will not sign the papers. No, I will not be Eliza Houlihan Cohen's ex-husband. Just no."

I could feel the fury rising. "I suppose your mother told you to come over here and say that to me, didn't she?" As you may be beginning to understand, I loathed Esther Cohen, the family matriarch whose own husband was a high-powered business tycoon by day and a toadying husband by night.

"No, as a matter of fact, she didn't. Just so you know, she called you a gold-digging *shiksa* and that I'd probably be better off without you in my life. Although, I suppose it might be a tad difficult for her to explain to her mahjong friends how her successful son could possibly be getting a divorce. Good thing she won't have to." He sipped his scotch meditatively once again. "I suppose that might well be the first time I've ever defied my mother." He seemed so pleased with himself.

I don't know what made me angrier: that Esther Cohen called me a *shiksa* when I was, at that moment, a far more ardent Jew than the man sitting in front of me or that her son, Jake, had chosen that moment to develop a spine in the face of his mother's many loathsome opinions.

I was jolted back into the present moment by the plane's wheels hitting the runway at Guarulhos International Airport in São Paulo, the first stop on what I hoped would be an adventure of a lifetime, not to mention the kind of break with reality that might make one believe the illusion, no matter how temporary. I had left the divorce papers on my desk in my office at home. Mine were signed. I knew Jake's were not.

~

"Bom dia, Senhora Cohen. Bem-vindo ao Brasil!" The young man standing at the top of the jetway was holding a tablet with my name on it as I disembarked. I was momentarily dazzled at the sight of this stunningly handsome, dark-haired Romeo

with a spectacularly sparkling smile. "Hello, *Senhora* Cohen. Welcome to Brazil!" He was wearing a navy-blue suit with a crisp, open-collared white shirt. For a moment, I thought, *If I were just a decade younger …* Then I remembered why I was even in Brazil.

He introduced himself as Carlos. "I will be happy to be your guide from this moment, through immigration and on into the city. We will then go on to your hotel, where you will have a lunch meeting with the esteemed *Senhor* Ribeiro. I am certain you will enjoy his company." His broad smile flashed a set of the whitest and most perfect teeth I'd ever seen this side of a Hollywood screen. Dental care must be a big thing here in Brazil.

As tired as I was from the long flight, I was enchanted by this young man. I told him I was delighted to meet him, smiled my best older woman smile, and let him guide me smoothly through immigration to the shiny black Suburban waiting in the parking garage. It reminded me of the truck-like vehicle I'd spent an odd week in with my extended family just last summer on a road trip on the island of Newfoundland. As I considered this for a moment, I realized that the trip I hadn't even wanted to go on (who wants to spend a week with extended family members you can barely tolerate?) was where this Brazilian trip began in the first place. If I hadn't gone to Newfoundland, I wouldn't be here in Brazil. Anyway, that's a long story, but it made sitting behind the driver by myself as we wended our way through the traffic in this astonishingly mega city that was home to twenty million people feel peculiar.

I had lived in New York City since 2001 after fleeing my home in Canada (fleeing from my family, to be truthful), but it seemed almost quaint now in comparison with São Paulo. I had only one day to spend in this vast metropolis before I had to be in Rio de Janeiro to get on a cruise ship. In Rio, I was meeting a man named Peter O'Brien, a man I hardly knew yet but who was the reason I was even here in Brazil. Indeed, he was the cause of the apprehension I felt as I sat there, knowing I'd be seeing him again in mere days. So, I was going to have to make the most of my single day in this fascinating city. Why, you might reasonably ask, was I in São Paulo when I was supposed to be in Rio? Good question.

The unexpected invitation to embark on this expedition to Brazil came at Christmas, two months ago, when I'd been in Newfoundland (twice in one year!) because my paternal grandmother had inconveniently died several days before the Christmas and Hannukah festivities were about to kick off. While I was there, I once again bumped into Peter, whom I'd met and spent a few days getting to know during the previous summer during that odd family trip to Newfoundland. I was newly separated from my husband, Jake, to whom I'd been married for almost twenty-five years. I suppose I was bound to find an exceedingly handsome, rugged doctor attractive. And the fact that he seemed to find me utterly fascinating was intoxicating for a fifty-year-old woman who had recently joined the ranks of the grandparent brigade. What woman in my situation wouldn't have been flattered?

By Christmas, Jake and I had been separated for almost two months, and I was proceeding with a divorce, so when Peter suggested I join him on this bucket-list trip to Brazil and the Amazon, as unhinged as it should have been to say yes to a trip with someone I hardly knew, I hesitated for only a moment. A few weeks later, while having a regular catch-up telephone conversation with my long-time editor and friend, Margot Talbot, who had been with me through thick and thin as I developed my reputation as a sought-after cookbook author, I may have mentioned it—several times.

Margot had been bewildered, to say the least. "What about Jake?" she had said. I could hear the confusion in her voice.

What about Jake? I thought. Then I realized I'd probably not told her that Jake and I were separated. So I did.

"Separated? Eliza, hun," she had said in her usual I-used-to-be-British way, "are you sure you know what you're doing? Husbands aren't disposable, you know."

As I reflected on that possibility, I thought, yes, husbands like Jake were, indeed, disposable.

"Hun," she had continued, "I'm just thinking." I could picture her there in the middle of her chaotic office, trying to wade through the masses of paper that always surrounded her. "I'm trying to remember what just came across my desk."

If anything had "come across her desk," I had no doubt that it would take months and an excavator to find it.

"By George, I've found it. Yes, I thought I remembered something. As it happens, our Brazilian publishing partner," (until that moment, I had no earthly idea we had a Brazilian publishing partner), "yes, Ribeiro or something like that. Anyway, they are just now doing a translation of your latest book. You must know this, Eliza. Surely, Helen told you about this."

Margot was referring to my agent, Helen Becker, who had been my literary representative ever since I'd started writing what was now a series of bestselling cookbooks. She might have mentioned something, but I suppose I yawned when hearing tell of anyone who spoke Portuguese being the slightest bit interested in a cookbook that introduced the basics of Jewish cooking to the Jewish-curious and culinarily challenged among us. I had a vague memory of a brief conversation to that effect.

Now, I could hear the excitement in Margot's voice as she told me that she would start making arrangements for me to meet with *Editora Ribeiro*. Of course, though, they were not located in Rio, so I'd have to make a stop on my way to fun in the sun, as she put it. That, and the fact that I couldn't get a non-stop flight into Rio, was the reason I was here by myself in the megalopolis of São Paulo with the ravishingly handsome Carlos as my driver and guide.

"We go first on a little tour," Carlos was saying as I came back to the present moment. "You know, *Senhora*, we like to say that our city is the beating heart of our country. So, when you get to Rio, do not let anyone tell you that the heart is there. It is here." I could see Carlos pound his right hand over his heart. He continued. "The city is so very modern in some ways," he pointed to the skyscrapers I could see up ahead, "but wait, and I will show you the more traditional aspects as well." He turned slightly to address me while I watched the traffic ahead and hoped he'd soon turn back. "I would love to take you to our *Mercado Municipal* to offer you to sample exotic fruits and to share our famous mortadella sandwich for lunch, but I must take you to your hotel where you will lunch with our esteemed leader."

"So, you work for *Editora Ribeiro*?" I'd assumed that he was a regular chauffeur for a car service company and thought it was odd that a publishing company had its own car and driver, but perhaps they were even bigger than the New York branch.

"For the moment, *Senhora*. For the moment," he said, turning his attention to the traffic once again.

For the next two hours, Carlos drove me around the city past modern buildings, colonial buildings, parks and more heavily fortified apartment buildings than I had ever seen in my life. Every building was surrounded by a high fence and a locked gate. He told me it was just the norm. By the time we drove up in front of the Renaissance Hotel in the Jardins District of the city, I was starting to fade. I had managed a few hours of sleep on the flight, but I still always found travelling exhausting, and then there was the anxiety and excitement I was feeling about the trip itself. I really wanted to check into my room, take a shower and a nap. Since there was essentially no time difference, I wasn't worried about jet lag. I was only concerned about looking my best by the time I met Peter in Rio the day after tomorrow. The moment that notion crossed my mind, I mentally slapped myself. *Get a grip. You're a grown woman. You're fine.* At least, I hoped I was fine.

"I will assist you with your baggage, *Senhora* Cohen," Carlos said, opening the back door to let me out.

"No need, Carlos, "I said. "Thanks, but I think I can manage. You have been terrific."

I saw what looked like a cloud passing over Carlos's sunny demeanour. "Please do not mention to *Senhor* Ribiero that I did not assist you."

I thought that was an odd request, but I promised him that I would not, and thanked him as a member of the bell staff took my suitcase for me.

"Oh, yes," Carlos said, "I will pick you up at nine o'clock tomorrow so that we can make our way to Rio."

"You? You're going to be my driver?" I could have flown to Rio, but when Margot mentioned travel arrangements, I told her that the thought of a commuter flight in a country where I didn't speak the language might be less attractive than a five-hour drive between the two cities. And besides, I thought it might be nice to see some of the country while I was here. I thought Margot had arranged for a day trip driver.

"*Claro*, of course. We will not leave you to the *caprichos* of the drivers of Brazil." I must have looked confused as he seemed to be searching for a translation, although I could guess the meaning of the word. "Whims perhaps in English?"

I nodded, although I have to admit I was amazed that the publisher was going to such lengths for me. A day-long trip with a handsome, well-mannered young man didn't sound like the worst idea I'd ever heard.

"Remember, you are having lunch with *Senhor* Ribeiro in the restaurant here at two p.m.," he said as I waved. How could I forget?

~

As I approached the amiable front desk staff, I was momentarily mesmerized by how beautiful the three desk clerks were. All under the age of thirty-five or so, each one was different, carrying off the chic grey suits that were their uniforms in their own way. One young woman was dark-haired and olive-skinned with beautiful teeth (there they were again), perfect make-up and thick eyebrows that seemed to work above her sultry eyes. The second young woman was blonde and just as stunning. Then there was the young man—all dazzling smile and perfect dark hair. All of them seemed genuinely happy that I'd told them I was checking in. Then, it was my turn to be happy. My room was ready.

An hour later, after freshening up a bit, I made my way down to the hotel's restaurant to meet the mysterious *Senhor* Ribeiro. From what Margot had said, I expected he would be a gruff old-time publisher, although I wasn't sure she had ever met him in person.

Another beautiful young woman led me to my reserved table and, in impeccable English, informed me that *Senhor* Ribeiro had called to say he would be fifteen minutes late. That he had called ahead seemed the height of good manners to me. So, I ordered a glass of wine (perhaps not a good idea under the circumstances, but well) and settled in to people-watch.

The Terraço Jardins Restaurant was a sunlight-filled greenhouse of a dining room crammed with greenery. It lined the windows in massive planter boxes, spilled out of pots on shelves that stood in for room dividers and reached toward the ceiling from pots on the floor. It really was like sitting in a hothouse, although the air conditioning was perfect. I sipped my glass of local chilled chardonnay contentedly.

Precisely fifteen minutes after our arranged lunch time, the young hostess approached the table. "*Senhora* Cohen," she said, "*Senhor* Ribeiro has arrived." Before she stepped aside so that I could meet *Senhor* Ribeiro, she said, "The champagne will be here momentarily."

"I'm afraid you must have made a mistake. I didn't order champagne," I said as she stepped aside to reveal *Senhor* Ribeiro. I looked up into a pair of dancing, smiling dark eyes.

"I am so sorry, but it is my fault, *Senhora* Cohen. I hope I have not overstepped. But I have ordered a bottle of my favourite champagne to welcome you to Brazil and to *Editora Ribeiro*." He extended his hand. "I am Alexandre Ribeiro, and I am truly delighted that you have agreed to have lunch with me."

I offered my hand, which, instead of shaking it, he immediately took to his lips and brushed it gently. "*Boas-vindas calorosas, Senhora Cohen*. My very warmest welcome."

I was speechless. The perpetually verbose Eliza Houlihan Cohen was struck dumb. Have you ever met someone whose aura immediately seems to overwhelm you? As someone who is decidedly in the camp of disbelievers when it comes to people's auras, I can tell you that at that moment, I became a believer.

Alexandre Ribeiro wasn't a tall man, perhaps only a few inches taller than my five-foot-seven inches, but he stood tall, shoulders back, projecting confidence and self-assurance. He also had the kind of presence that envelopes you like a cloud of expensive-smelling cologne. I managed to mutter how I was delighted to meet him and permitted myself a few moments to recover while he busied himself with the sommelier who had arrived with a bottle of—dear god, was that Dom Perignon? I loved a glass of champagne, but I knew that this was the most expensive bottle they had. I knew this because I'd seen it on the wine menu when I'd selected my single glass. I always read wine menus in their entirety. Who doesn't? However, it did beg the question of how a cookbook author could be worth so much to a Brazilian publisher. I certainly wasn't worth Dom Perignon to my erstwhile husband.

I looked at his dark, impeccably tailored suit and his open-collared blue shirt. Above the collar was a handsomely rugged face whose precisely clipped beard didn't even take away from his looks. And if I could say that—I who abhorred facial hair on any man—this must have been an elegant man. But it was his eyes that drew me in the most. They were dark and smouldering. I took a deep breath and caught a hold of myself. I'd met many handsome men in my life and had often found them to be vapid and self-absorbed. I hoped he would be different.

"We shall toast to a very favourable future between the famous Eliza Cohen and *Editora Ribeiro,*" he said as he reached for his glass that the sommelier had just filled halfway.

"I am looking forward to working with you and your team, *Senhor* Ribeiro," I said as I lifted my glass. He was staring into my eyes, and I suddenly wondered where I'd met him before. Perhaps he had been a famous actor in his life? Maybe I'd seen him in an old movie on Netflix?

"Please call me Alex. May I call you Eliza?"

"Of course," I said, hoping the familiarity would stop the pounding of my heartbeat. What was wrong with me? Had I been so suppressed by being unhappily married for at least the past decade that I'd flutter like a schoolgirl at the sight of a handsome man? I took a sip of the extraordinary champagne that I'd had only twice before in my life despite the wealth of the Cohen family into which I'd married, not to mention my own success. But my mother-in-law, Esther Cohen, was always of the opinion that if something expensive could not be flaunted in front of other people, like a Chanel handbag or a Hermes scarf, then it wasn't worth the money. Champagne, which is meant to be savoured as an experience living only in memory, was one of those unnecessary things. So, if Mother Esther said it, then her son, Jake, would be only too happy to go along even when she wasn't around. As I felt the warmth of the bubbles caress my throat on the way down, I realized that this was a pivotal moment. That was the moment when I decided that this trip would be different. I decided that I'd be in the moment and enjoy whatever happened. Then, I wondered how long that decision would last.

Alex began by telling me that my book, *A Schmear on a Bagel: Jewish Cooking for Everyone Else,* was destined to be a big success in Brazil with its Jewish and Jewish-curious population, something I'd never considered a part of the Brazilian culture. He told me their marketing department had several tie-ins planned for the launch later in the year, and then he came in for the kill.

"When *Senorha* Talbot told me you were coming to our little city, I could have kissed her through the telephone line," he said, lightly touching my arm. I almost snorted champagne out my nose as I thought about how wild-haired Margot and her wife would react to such a gesture. He didn't seem to notice my near-gauche behaviour. "I wish to invite you to be our guest here at the launch and to conduct several cooking classes. I also would like you to consider writing a cookbook about Brazilian cooking. We wish to market our wonderful cuisine to the world, and you have the reach we desire. I do not expect an answer yet, but please tell me you will consider a cookbook based on your upcoming travels. *Senhora* Tabot has told me that you will be cruising up our Atlantic coast and into our Amazon River. That is exciting and the very best way to do research."

Did the man ever take a breath? I was half listening to him but still wondering where I'd seen him before.

"Tell me, Alex, have we met before? Perhaps at a New York literary event?"

He shrugged. "Perhaps I have, as they say, one of those faces."

I doubted that. "No," I said. "It's as if I've met you."

Suddenly, he began to laugh. "Of course, you would feel that way. I should have realized. It is as if you have met me, or so everyone says. He does look very much like me, does he not?"

"Who?" Was the champagne going to my head that quickly?

"Well, Carlos, of course," Alex said, laughing. "I am flattered that a beautiful woman such as yourself believes a fifty-year-old man may look like his twenty-three-year-old son."

It suddenly clicked. "Oh, I am so sorry. I thought Carlos was an employee."

Alex's laughter suddenly became a wry smile. "Ah, yes, but he is an employee, after all. He should be at university as we speak, but there you have it. I am saddled with a son whose choice it is at this moment is to be my driver instead of studying so that he can take over the family business." He sipped his champagne and continued. "I do not suppose anyone can understand the situation unless they have been in it, but to see one's highly intelligent son leave university because it isn't fulfilling his needs is … how does one say it in English? Gut-wrenching."

"Oh, Alex, but I do know." And suddenly, I found myself telling this stranger the details of the past year of my life.

As I told him about my daughter Izzy deferring her acceptance to medical school to pursue fulfillment in a yoga studio or chakra centre or whatever it was in California, Alex patted my hand. As I told him about Izzy's return to New York with the news that she was having a baby and that she had no intention of telling us who the father was, he placed his hand over mine and said, "What you have been through."

Then, for some unknown reason, I told him about my situation with Jake and how I was taking a massive leap of faith to come on this trip to take a cruise with a man I hardly knew. At that, he squeezed my hand and then sat back, staring at me.

"Eliza, you are a most amazing woman. All of this and now a grandmother. I cannot believe that this ravishing woman in front of me is a grandmother. And this Peter of whom you have told me is a lucky man. We must have more champagne."

Ravishing? Me at age fifty? I wasn't at all sure I could handle any more champagne, but having someone call me ravishing was certainly reason for celebration. When the cork flew out of the second bottle, I nudged my glass a bit closer to the sommelier. Tomorrow was another day, but today was the present.

TWO

Eliza

SÃO PAULO TO RIO DE JANEIRO

ALEX AND I WERE ALREADY ON our second bottle of champagne when the server arrived with our lunch orders. No matter how much I've had to drink, I am never far away from my persona as a cookbook author. So, I retrieved my ever-present notebook from the depths of my large handbag.

I had deferred to Alex's familiarity with the menu to order since the menu at this upscale restaurant was more unexpectedly local than I might have expected at a hotel. He suggested we order several starters to share, and now, as the server placed them on the table, Alex began to explain them to me.

"We start with a local fried croquette," he said, pointing to the first dish. "It is made from meat, corn and homemade pepper sauce. Then we have baked Benzinho cheese with Guaraipo honey and organic cornbread. Delicious. Please." He gestured for me to start.

The cheese looked a bit like Brie to me. I took a piece and put it on the cornbread. It was creamy and luxurious with a nutty, slightly tangy flavour. I was going to love sampling food and recipes in this country. Perhaps his idea that a Canadian-turned-American, Catholic-turned- Jewish cookbook author really could handle a project about Brazilian food wasn't so daft, after all.

The rest of the lunch was just as delicious as the starters. I chose the sea bass, which was the fish of the day, with a side order of something called crumbs. As it turned out, these crumbs were exactly as you might expect. They were like breadcrumbs made from cassava flour and vegetables, toasted and served with a large spoon. This dish was clearly another dish I'd have to explore while I was in Brazil.

By the time we finished, I realized we'd spent the entire afternoon eating and talking. I was stuffed (stogged, as my late Newfoundland grandmother might say). I realized that there would be no need for dinner. So, when Alex looked at his watch and said, "What a wonderful afternoon, Eliza, but I am afraid that my wife will be expecting me for a drink before our dinner out with friends this evening, so I must be off," I was amazed to think that this svelte man would even consider another meal out today.

As I got up to say goodbye, I found myself being drawn into a bear hug. "We will be in touch, Eliza. And I thank you for sharing some of your story with me. I believe we have a great deal in common, and I would welcome the opportunity to work with you in due course. But if I may be so bold as to offer you some Brazilian wisdom." We drew apart, and I told him that it would be most welcome. "Our great Brazilian novelist Paulo Coelho once wrote, 'Be brave. Take risks. Nothing can substitute experience.' And if I might add what I have come to know to be true in my life, we have only our experiences to keep with us at the moment of our deaths."

~

The following morning, as I dragged my suitcase through the lobby to meet Carlos, I was still thinking about what Alex had said about taking risks. I was thinking about the fact that this entire escapade was a risk. I felt like I was on the edge of a cliff, looking over the precipice. My monkey mind was racing through all the possible outcomes, trying to predict what might be coming, yet I knew I could only find out by stepping forward. It was at once exhilarating and terrifying knowing I would have to let go of the familiar and embrace the thrill of the unknown—at least, I hoped it would be thrilling.

I remembered that as I lay in bed the night before, it had occurred to me that what I was doing was so out of character for me. I was someone who planned things. I liked to consider every possible contingency. Jake had once told me that he thought I was an over-thinker. I considered that to be a compliment. He did not. I had fallen asleep alone in the luxurious king-sized bed, wondering if it would be possible for me to spend the next three and a half weeks going with the flow. I had hoped I might wake up with one of those revelations other people seem to have, but I had nothing, and I was still contemplating this when Carlos spied me as he came in through the front door. The moment he saw me, he smiled broadly and hurried over to take my suitcase for me.

"*Bom dia, Senhora Cohen*! Good morning, good morning. I hope you slept well."

This morning, I supposed, in preparation for a day-long drive, Carlos was not attired in the business suit from yesterday. Today, he was wearing a very preppy-like outfit consisting of knife-pleated khakis, a peach-coloured polo shirt with the collar slightly popped (as the fashion people like to say), a white sweater tied around his neck and suede driving shoes. He looked like a Brooks Brothers advertisement.

"I have polished the car just for you, and there is cold water for your pleasure. Please," he said, leading the way to the car parked right in front of the door.

Once I was settled into the back seat, Carlos gave me the run-down for our trip to Rio. "And I have a little surprise for you along the way. We do not go directly to Rio. We will take a little detour up into the mountains so that you might see where some of our families spend the summer holidays."

That sounded interesting. "How much time does it add to our drive?"

"Oh, let us say about one and a half hours, but it will be worth it."

I wondered if Alex had arranged this little junket as a way to see if I could sit back and just enjoy the experience. He had to have recognized the control freak in me—a control freak who needed to get from point A to point B in as direct a way as possible to avoid having to consider contingencies. I sighed.

As Carlos maneuvered the big vehicle out of city traffic and onto the highway, I said, "You didn't mention that *Senhor* Ribeiro is your father."

Carlos turned his head slightly back toward me, but I couldn't see his eyes behind the reflective aviator sunglasses that he wore so well. "I try to keep that a bit of a secret, *Senhora* Cohen. I do not like to be accused of—how do you say it in English when a family member gets special privileges?"

"Nepotism?"

"*Sim! Sim!* Yes, just that." He returned his attention to the road ahead.

"But it must be difficult to keep that a secret since you look so much like him." I saw him shrug.

"Yes, you may have noticed the family resemblance." That was an understatement. "And I suppose you and my father may have spent a moment discussing the issues of being a parent."

"We did, Carlos. And you'll be happy to know that I have a daughter who also didn't continue her education in the straight line as her parents might have hoped. That doesn't mean it's the wrong way to do it, though. I'm certainly not judging you."

I could see his smile. "You are a wise woman, *Senhora* Cohen. I tried to study the courses he suggested so that I might wish also to have a life of letters as my father does, but I wish to be an engineer, a path he does not understand. So, I decided to take a gap year as the British say. You see, it is very difficult to be the son of a man who is so devoted to his books. And may I ask if my father offered you one of his words of wisdom from one of his favourite Brazilian authors that he enjoys so much?"

"Indeed, he did, Carlos. And I was grateful for it. Does he offer you words of wisdom?"

"You have no idea, *Senhora* Cohen. You have no idea."

I sat back, thinking that perhaps I did have an idea. "May I ask you something, Carlos?"

"Of course. Anything."

"In all your years of listening to your father's wisdom, is there anything that rises to the top of your memory? Something he said that you really do find useful?"

"*Senhora* Cohen, are you familiar with the great Brazilian writer Clarice Lispector?" I told him I was not. "She was a great woman who wrote her first book at the age of twenty-three, the same age I am now. When I was sixteen years old, my father suggested that I read her book *The Hour of the Star,* which she had written just before she died. I did not listen to him then. At Christmas last year, my girlfriend, who studies literature and creative writing, gave me a copy, and I felt obliged to read it."

"You didn't read it when your father suggested, but now you read it when your girlfriend gave it to you?" I knew I should be quiet and listen, but as a frustrated parent myself, I couldn't let that go.

"Yes, I am sorry to say, *Senhora* Cohen. That is just how I was with my father. But now I understand. So, to answer your question, it was not so much words of wisdom my father told me; rather, it was words of wisdom from an author he told me I should read. In that book, Clarice wrote, 'Everything in the world began with a yes. One molecule said yes to another molecule, and life was born.' I had never considered this before. But now I know that nothing happens if I do not say yes."

Nothing happens if I do not say yes, I thought. Perhaps it was time to rethink my approach to life.

~

I was getting hungry as Carlos pulled the car off the main highway and headed north into the mountains toward a place he called Campos do Jordão. The road had changed from a divided four-lane highway to a two-lane road that twisted and turned upward. As we drove up the winding road, the lush greenery and rolling hills began to surround us, conjuring a serenity that was absent in the city we'd just left, and if I didn't miss my guess, probably in the city that we were heading toward. I watched in astonishment as we drove into a thick fog on one side of the mountain and around out into the bright sunshine on the other. As we neared the outskirts of the town, we were back in the brilliant sunshine. It became increasingly clear that this was unlike any town I might have expected to see in Brazil. By the time he pulled up into a parking spot, I felt as if I'd been picked up and dropped into the Swiss Alps.

As I got out of the car, Carlos told me he'd made a lunch reservation at one of the outdoor cafés that lined the main square. I had expected the elevation to mean that the temperature might be cooler and crisper. I could not have been more wrong as I noted an LED sign that told us it was a sweltering thirty-five degrees Celsius. As I walked along the cobblestones, lined with what appeared to the naked eye to be quaint chalets and timber-framed houses, I started to laugh at the incongruity of it all. What the eye could see said I should be wearing a sweater, perhaps even a quilted vest. What I felt was telling me that I should have worn shorts. It was like walking into an illusion or perhaps a movie set—maybe they're the same thing, after all.

After lunch at one of the countless restaurants (was the place nothing but restaurants?), Carlos and I walked back to the car so he could take me for one more stop before we set out once again for Rio. He took me up to the peak of the mountain that formed the backdrop for the town. On the way, he pointed out an enormous white house perched on the side of the mountain with a gated driveway.

"That, *Senhora* Cohen, is my family's summer house." It turned out that the tourists in this town were rarely from outside the country. Instead, it was the playground for the locals, many of whom clearly had boatloads of money. The Ribeiros seemed to be among them.

As I stood on the viewing platform above the town, taking in the vista of mountains and chalets, I laughed at myself. What in the world was I doing here? I guess I'd soon find out.

~

I had fallen asleep in the back seat as we motored along the highway, approaching Rio de Janeiro. I awoke just as Carlos was looking for a spot to pull off the interchange for a moment. Dusk was gathering, and we were smack in the midst of bumper-to-bumper rush-hour traffic, which included motorcycle after motorcycle roaring by, squeezing their way between cars, trucks and vans. Every driver seemed to be looking for a way to get to where they were going faster. I'd lived in New York for two and a half decades, visited Los Angeles on several occasions, and weathered the traffic trying to get into Paris, and I had never seen anything like this.

"Why are we pulling off?" I said once I realized what he was doing.

"I am changing my maps. I have been using Waze to find the best and fastest way, but it will take me through the favelas. I do not wish to go there, and I do not wish to take such a lovely lady as yourself into the favelas. We will be stopped by the local gangs for sure to see if we are harbouring police."

I shivered slightly as I looked over to the other side of the interchange, where I could see the favela Carlos wanted to avoid. There, clinging to the side of a hill, was an immense conglomeration of houses, each one blending into the next. I had heard about the favelas, but this was the first time I'd ever seen one. The density of the houses made it look overwhelming. Most of the houses were several stories high and seemed to have been built from anything the builders could find— bricks, concrete blocks, clapboard, metal sheets. From where I was sitting, I could see masses of electrical wires that seemed not to have any rhyme or reason or even safety. When I asked Carlos about them, he told me the residents plugged themselves into the grid wherever they could and never paid for electricity. I was astonished.

"They are free of the urban planning, as we like to say," Carlos said wryly.

Once Carlos had ensured we would not be traversing any favelas this evening, he pulled back into the traffic, and we continued until we finally emerged onto the Avenida Atlantica, the broad street running parallel to Copacabana Beach and the location of my hotel. Darkness had descended, but the lights on the beachfront sparkled and glowed in welcome.

"Welcome to Copacabana, *Senhora* Cohen."

A few minutes later, we had pulled up in front of my hotel which looked out over the beach. "It has been such a pleasure, *Senhora* Cohen," Carlos said as he handed my suitcase to the bell staff. "You are a classy lady, and I believe you understand my plight. I would like to offer you one more quote I have always remembered from Clarice Lispector's book that I have told you about. She said, 'I want the true absurdity of life to be felt.' There is one thing I learned in that year I spent studying that which I did not want to study. It is that if the opposite of to be absurd is to be sensible, I will choose to feel the true absurdity."

Carlos shook my hand and went around to the opposite side of the car, leaving me to wonder how I'd managed to meet two of the most remarkable men I'd ever met in my life in less than twenty-four hours in this country. I suppose I was beginning to feel that true absurdity.

~

Once I was settled into my room overlooking the lights of Copacabana Beach and had considered what I'd wear to meet Peter when he arrived the following day, I wandered out into the crowds that milled about up and down the street. I was hungry, so I found an outdoor café that was serving, of all things, French-style hamburgers with frites. I couldn't pass that up.

As I sat at a curbside table, relishing the sultry heat after the cold New York February slush I'd left behind, I once again had the odd feeling of unreality. Sitting here alone sipping a lovely French Bordeaux at a café in Rio de Janeiro seemed like the height of madness for someone like me. There isn't a soul in this world who would consider Eliza Cohen to be impetuous or in any way unrestrained. And yet, it felt right. The thought lasted mere moments until I was brought back to reality by the pinging of a text from my phone that was ensconced in my tote bag under the table.

Snowstorm delay here in Toronto. Likely to miss my Rio connection in Miami. I think there's another connection I can make. Meet you on board the ship. Cannot wait to see you. Peter.

Oh, no, I thought, *what if he misses the ship's departure?*

Our ship, the S.S. Damona, was scheduled to depart Rio at ten o'clock the following evening. Peter and I had planned to meet at my hotel in the early afternoon after I finished my private tour of the highlights of Rio, have a late lunch and then board the ship together. What else could I do? I texted him back that everything would be fine and that I was looking forward to seeing him, too. This was not one of the possible scenarios I had planned for. I seemed to be losing my contingency planning touch, and I was beginning to feel the seeds of self-doubt start to cloud my otherwise competent persona. Was I doing the right thing being here to take a cruise with a man I hardly knew? I guess I would find out.

Suddenly, the twinkling lights of Copacabana weren't quite so alluring, and the people were just people. Even my wine didn't seem to taste as good as it had. What was wrong with me? I had hoped that by this time in my life, I didn't need someone to make things all better for me. I had to do it myself. Perhaps young Carlos had been right. Maybe a bit of absurdity was what I needed to experience.

I called the server over and ordered another glass of wine along with a serving of warm madeleines for dessert. I decided that after my tour tomorrow, I was going to go to Ipanema and buy myself a Brazilian bathing suit. That should be the height of absurdity.

~

My head was pounding from all the red wine I'd imbibed the night before as I waited in the lobby for my private tour guide early the following morning. I was checking my booking to find my guide's name when I heard someone calling to me.

"*Senhora* Cohen?" I looked up and nodded some kind of acknowledgement. "I am Michael. Are you ready to see Rio?"

I was indeed ready to see Rio with yet another ruggedly handsome man, this time in shorts and a singlet.

"We go first to see Christ the Redeemer," Michael said as we settled into his car, whose backseat contained the biggest child's car seat I'd ever seen. "It is early, and we get there before the crowds. Today seems like we might even see it."

"What do you mean?"

"He so often covered in fog, *Senhora*."

I had never considered that possibility.

Have you ever seen a photo of something somewhere in the world and thought, *I have to visit that place before I die*? I remembered the first time I'd seen an image of the statue of Christ the Redeemer in Rio when I was in elementary school. We had been studying South America, and my teacher showed us slides. I was awestruck. Yet, in all the years I'd been married to Jake and all the places we'd been lucky enough to travel in the world, we had never been to this city, and I had never visited this statue. I guess someone might even say it was on my bucket list. Today would be the day.

As Michael drove me through the city, it was as if I could feel the beats of the samba and bossa nova. I was excited as he parked the car, and we made our way to the ticket booth. One of the perks of a private guide was that we didn't have to wait for a boarding time later. We walked right onto the tramway train car that was waiting on the rail to take us to the top of Corcovado Mountain, home to this impressive and iconic statue.

Michael was still a bit concerned as we made our way to the top that it might, as it had been in recent days, shrouded in fog. We were lucky that day. The massive face of Christ moved in and out of the mist as we walked around, taking in the extraordinary Art Deco icon from every angle. It was very atmospheric. If I thought being in Rio was an illusion, being at the foot of Christ the Redeemer made it feel very real.

Despite the early hour, the crowds on the top of the mountain were already beginning to gather. So once I had my fill of fulfilling my fantasy, it was time to get back on the tramway train and go back down. Then, we would make our way to the top of the other icon that makes Rio so recognizable in photos: Sugarloaf Mountain.

Getting to the top of Rio's Sugarloaf is a two-stage trip on two gondolas. If I had not been with a private guide, I would have missed the stop halfway up. Instead of immediately boarding the next gondola, Michael took me on a walk through a lovely garden. It was like being suspended between the earth and the sky, with Rio laid out below and the top of the mountain still towering overhead. As I walked along the suspended pathway between the masses of greenery swaying in the breeze, I was suddenly confronted by an odd tree right in the middle of the walkway. It looked like a two-pronged fork reaching up toward the sky. Michael told me I should not walk around it; instead, I should walk through it.

"It is the Wish Tree," Michael said as I hesitated. "You walk through it into a world where you may have your wish. Do not walk around it, *Senhora.*"

I looked at the sign on the tree, which said, *"Árvore dos desejos,"* and lifted my leg as high as I could to step over and between two thick trunks that made up the single wish tree. I closed my eyes for a moment and wished for joy.

We continued along the pathway that eventually led us back to the gondola, where we boarded another one that transported us to the top of the mountain. I felt like a pilgrim hoping for clarity, trying to reach the guru at the top.

It was incredible to be at the summit of Sugarloaf Mountain, a natural monument that had graced so many travel brochures and movies over the years. I took out my phone and busied myself taking pictures of everything in sight. I could see the shimmering water of the bay below, framed by the lush green mountains surrounding it. I could see the long, languid crescent shape of Copacabana Beach. Although from this distance, the people on it were like so many pebbles. I could also look over and see where we had already been this morning. The statue of Christ the Redeemer stood across the bay, its outstretched arms seeming to embrace the entire city.

Once back at sea level, Michael suggested another "must-see." He called it the *Escadaria Selarón,* which turned out to be a set of steps covered with tiles. I had no idea what this was, so I went along. It turned out to be a hot, crowded tourist attraction consisting of a set of outdoor steps covered with colourful tiles. I found the whole thing seriously underwhelming, but I didn't bother to mention this to him. He seemed to think tourists would love it.

Our last stop was the Metropolitan Cathedral of San Sebastian. Michael thought I might enjoy seeing a church that wasn't at all what I might expect to see in Brazil. He was right about it being unexpected but perhaps not so much about how much his client might enjoy a church. I had memories of visiting countless churches as Jake and I made our way through Europe one time until we finally had to say to our tour guide, "Enough!" European churches are immensely impressive, but after a while, even the finest Rococo designs become overwhelming, and they all begin to blend into one another. This one was different.

The edifice was an enormous modern cone-shaped structure with a stained-glass cross on the massively high ceiling. I could appreciate its uniqueness, but since churches aren't really my thing, I could have lived my life without ever having seen it. It was time to return to the hotel.

I had arranged for a late checkout, initially expecting to have lunch with Peter before getting a taxi to the port. Since he wasn't here yet (his plane had finally left, but he was still in jeopardy of missing his connection), I got a taxi to Ipanema a short drive from my hotel on Copacabana Beach.

The first thing I noticed as I tried to decide where the driver should drop me was that the street fronting the beach in Ipanema was almost entirely residential, unlike the myriad bustling hotels and restaurants along Copacabana. The beach itself was smaller but with much more wave action. I could see bronzed surfers walking along the beach, surfboards at the ready and the tiny dots that were the surfers out in the waves. There were lots of people, and although there were plenty of bikinis, I didn't see Jobim's girl from Ipanema—at least not the way I'd pictured her from listening to the music.

Finally, the driver dropped me at a cross street and told me the shops were tucked in behind. I wandered from one to another until I found one with just the bathing suit I thought I needed.

It was a one-shouldered beauty with risqué cut-outs held together with translucent plastic rings. I put it on and could not stop laughing. I looked closely. Could I get away with this? I decided I could and bought it quickly before I lost my nerve. Eventually, I'd have to find the right moment to wear it. I then took a walk along the beach before flagging down a taxi to return to Copacabana.

Once back at the hotel, I had only half an hour to finish packing before I headed to the port by myself, hoping that Peter would make it on time. Just as I was zipping up my final bag, my phone rang. *Finally,* I thought, *news from Peter*. Except it wasn't.

"Hi, Mom, how's the trip going?" It was my daughter, Izzy.

"Izzy, what's wrong? Are you okay? Is the baby okay?"

"Chill, Mom. We're fine. I just wanted to catch you before you got on that ship in case the internet isn't so good. I just got off the phone with Grama Esther—"

"What did she want?" The hairs on the back of my neck started rising ominously.

"Mom, it's okay. She just told me I could use the condo, so I can meet you in Miami when the ship gets there in a few weeks."

"She isn't going to be with you, is she? She's still planning on that reunion trip, isn't she?" It was hard to keep the panic out of my voice at the unwelcome prospect of seeing my soon-to-be-ex mother-in-law in Miami or anywhere else for that matter.

"No," Izzy said, laughing. "I'm just about to book tickets for Mary-Catherine and myself, and I wanted you to know first in case you want to cancel your hotel reservation and stay with us. Unless…" she trailed off.

"Unless what?"

"Unless you want to stay at a hotel with that dishy doctor you're going on the cruise with. How is Peter, by the way?"

It was a surprising relief to me how easily Izzy had accepted that I was going on a cruise with this man we both hardly knew so soon after her father and I broke up. But I was grateful anyway.

"I think I'll just keep my Miami hotel booking for now," I said. "And Peter hasn't arrived yet."

Izzy was momentarily horrified, thinking I'd been stood up. Once I explained the situation to her, she asked me to keep her in the loop, and then I said goodbye so I could get down to the lobby to meet my taxi.

It took the taxi half an hour to wend its way through the city and along the bay to reach the passenger cruise terminal. As I paid the driver and gave my luggage to the valet who was waiting, I looked up at the brilliant white ship sparkling in the sunshine. *Well,* I thought, *time to throw caution to the wind. What's the worst that can happen?* We can never know the answer to that question, can we?

~

I was just settled into my gorgeous suite on deck eleven and had gratefully accepted a glass of champagne from my butler, who introduced himself as Rakesh, when my phone rang. This time it was Peter. He had just landed and would be on board in an hour. My heart started thudding.

An hour later, I meandered down to the atrium to see if I might be able to be there the minute he stepped on board. As I waited, ostensibly examining the premium wines on offer, I saw a woman I thought I recognized. I stared at her, but she didn't turn around fully, so I was left with a feeling that I knew her, but I couldn't be sure.

Just then, Peter waved from the gangway. Show time.

~

Peter had settled into his own suite (smaller than the one I was in), and we were sitting at a bar with a martini before dinner. "I can hardly believe we're actually here," I said, smoothing my skirt and wondering for the millionth time how I looked. What was wrong with me?

Peter's eyes shone in that way I'd come to know during the five or six days we'd spent together with my family last summer when we'd met. It was as if you could see the joyful little boy behind the quite proper and responsible emergency room doctor. "I can," he said. "I just knew this was going to work out."

I could feel a warm glow spread over me as we clinked glasses.

"How's your daughter?" he said.

"Oh, I forgot to tell you. She's going to meet me in Miami when the ship docks."

Peter's eyebrows raised. "Wow. That's really strange. I had a call from Liam while I was waiting for my delayed flight in Toronto. He and Fiona are planning to be there, too. It seems Liam's on study break, and Fiona is on a break between performances." Liam and Fiona were Peter's children. Liam was a law student, and Fiona was a ballet dancer. I'd met Liam briefly at Christmas when I was in Newfoundland, but Fiona lived in Toronto, and she hadn't been there for Christmas because of *Nutcracker* performances with her company, The National Ballet of Canada.

"That *is* strange. So, I guess we'll have to make the best of the next three weeks," I said, laughing.

"I'll drink to that," Peter said, gesturing to the bartender for another round. Then he looked at his watch. "Maybe we should go up on deck. We're about to sail away. Rio must look spectacular from this vantage point at night."

"Absolutely," I said.

At that moment, the image of the woman I'd seen earlier in the atrium floated to the top of my consciousness and I remembered why she looked so familiar. I hesitated to even mention it since I didn't want to ruin the moment.

"You know, Peter," I said after some consideration, "I saw a woman in the atrium just before you arrived. She looked a lot like Claire."

"Claire who?" he said as he contentedly chewed on his last olive.

"Claire, your ex-wife?"

"Geezus, Eliza, Claire is the last person in the world I want to think about on this trip."

I had to agree with him. After just one encounter with that woman last summer, I had no desire to be in her presence again. But there was something about that woman.

THREE

Claire

RIO DE JANEIRO, BRAZIL

MY DIVORCE WAS AN ACCIDENT. Perhaps, dare I say it, even a mistake. For other people, their *marriages* are a mistake. I am so not like other people. I never make mistakes, but my divorce might just be the exception that proves the rule. As I think about it now, perhaps it wasn't a mistake so much as an oversight. A lapse. But oversights and lapses could be corrected, and I intended to do just that.

It had taken a chance meeting with that dreadful Eliza Cohen woman in the ladies' room at that tiresome birthday party for that obnoxious old woman—her grandmother—last summer to realize that I could not, under any circumstances, let her get her claws into Peter. He was too good a man (my good man), and she was, as I had discovered in my online research, a Canadian-turned- American cookbook author of all things. She was clearly unsuitable for a man of Peter's intelligence and status and even more unfit to be around my children. Of course, I realized that I might have a bit of difficulty getting him over my slight indiscretion. From the moment I'd told him about the situation, it seemed to me that he considered it to be far more important than I did, and really, there were extenuating circumstances in my view.

What almost-fifty-year-old woman wouldn't be flattered by the attention of a gorgeous, brilliant (at least according to his press) thirty or forty-something fellow panel member at a conference? It had only happened once—or at least only for a few days while I was in Los Angeles—but Peter just couldn't seem to see it the way I did. He said it was a symptom of a failing marriage. I might have agreed for a moment or two at the time, but when I met that woman last summer, I knew I would have to take action. So, you can understand that when my daughter, Fiona, told me Peter was taking a cruise with her, I was close to apoplectic. I knew what I had to do.

Fiona was spending a few quality days with her mother (me) over New Year's when she let it slip. She wasn't one to drink much, but it was New Year's Eve, and she was spending it with her mother, so who could blame her? We were sitting in my living room in St. John's, Newfoundland, watching a movie. It was one of those inane romantic Christmas movies that pea-brained young women seem to like so much. I was only half paying attention, but I had noticed that it was called something like "The Christmas Cruise."

Suddenly, Fiona said, "Oh, it's set in Miami. That's where Dad's cruise ends." Then, she hiccupped and immediately clapped her hand over her mouth.

"What are you talking about?" I said, my antennae rising. "There is no way your father would ever go on a cruise alone." Peter hadn't actually wanted to go on the three cruises we'd gone on together. I looked at Fiona carefully as she busied herself with pouring another glass of wine. "He *is* going alone, isn't he?"

It didn't take too much needling to get her to tell me that he was, indeed, not going alone. He was going with that Eliza Cohen woman. After my initial shock at such odd news, I began seething. I kept my thoughts to myself, though, as I continued to probe for details. Where they were going, what cruise line, when, etc. She had all the details. I told her what a lovely thing that would be for her father while recognizing that I'd have to do something about this situation. I just didn't know what it would be yet. I even suggested that she and Liam might enjoy meeting their father in Miami after the cruise and that I would even pay, but she had already tuned back into the absurd movie. I'd get back to that as I hatched my plan.

A few days later, after Fiona had left to go back to Toronto, where she was currently living, I dragged myself to the gym. It was Saturday morning, and if it had been June instead of January, I would have been in Bowring Park walking or running with my only girlfriend, Lisa Pinfold. I had never been a woman who collects girlfriends, but Lisa and I had known one another since before we both went to medical school. We were both uber busy women, so we didn't have time for mundane female companionship other than one another. I had been a year ahead of her in med school. Then, we both eventually went into pediatric specialties—she into pediatric cardiology and I into pediatric surgery—so we both worked at the Children's Hospital and saw one another regularly both at work and outside. Running or walking together several days a week had become a ritual for us. That morning, Lisa was already sitting on one of the many stationary bikes when I walked in and took a seat on the one next to her. I just sat there, leaning on the handlebars, not moving my legs an inch.

"Claire Barrett, what's eating you this morning?" she said, not even slowing down the pedalling.

We had known each other for so long that Lisa could tell when I wasn't quite myself. I started pedalling slowly. "Lisa, do you remember me telling you about that woman I saw with Peter at that party last summer?"

"Not this again. Claire, let it go. You and Peter are divorced. Move on."

I should have known how Lisa would react. She had never really liked Peter for all the years we were married, and there were few people in the world who didn't like the charming Dr. Peter O'Brien. Right from the start, she had maintained that he was too good to be true. Peter was always composed and level-headed (it went with the territory—he was an emergency room physician) and never had a bad word to say about anyone. He also had a wicked sense of humour. Lisa's husband, Derrick, was a Jungian psychologist and had opined, on more than one recent occasion, that Peter never showed his shadow side but that everyone had a dirty corner, as he put it. The general consensus was that Peter had to have one. Lisa had told me that she agreed. I happened to know that Jungian psychology was a load of crap and that Peter was one of those truly good people. I was willing to admit that I was his shadow from time to time, but he was the real deal. And he and I had always been good for one another. That was the moment when I decided that I had to remind him about that.

I told Lisa about Peter's upcoming trip.

"It sounds to me like he's moving on, Claire." She took a sip of water from her bright pink water bottle. "Derrick and I have a friend—"

"Please don't start that again, Lisa. I have no interest in dating at my age."

Lisa stopped peddling, wiped her forehead with the towel she had flung over the handlebars and turned to look at me. "At your age? You're barely fifty, Claire, as am I. You have your whole life ahead of you."

I sighed. "Lisa, you know that is so not true. Just look at us here, desperately working out so that we can stave off the vagaries of aging."

"What are you afraid of, Claire?'

"Afraid? Me? You know very well that I'm not afraid of anything."

"Much too defensive, Claire. I think you're afraid of what the future might hold. You're afraid of getting your heart broken, so you continue to focus on the past. Peter is in your past. At the risk of sounding like a broken record, it's time to move on."

"Peter knows me and all that I've accomplished. He understands me. I should never have allowed him to have that divorce."

"Are you saying you made a mistake? The perfect Dr. Claire Barrett, world-renowned pediatric surgeon who flies to far corners of the world to teach her innovative techniques for fixing tiny bodies, has made a mistake? Well, I suppose that's something for you, Claire."

"Call it a mistake, a blunder, or simply a misstep. In any case, I have every intention of fixing it."

Lissa sighed loudly and stopped pedalling. "Do you really think you can get him back?"

"Watch me." I started pedalling as if my life depended on it. Because, on some level, I knew it might.

~

A few weeks later, I had myself booked on the same cruise Peter would be taking, despite my misgivings about Brazil and the Amazon. I forced myself to submit to a yellow fever shot and got my prescription for the anti-malarial pills that were recommended. Then I bought a boatload of DEET-fuelled insect repellent against the mosquitoes I expected to encounter and got on a plane. It was my secret, though. I told my department head I was going to a conference and would take some of my accumulated vacation along with it. I didn't even tell Lisa about it. I couldn't bear another lecture about moving on. I'd tell her about it when I succeeded in accomplishing my goal, and I'd be able to gloat a little.

So, here I was in Rio de Janeiro, boarding the S.S. Damona for a three-week cruise up the coast of Brazil, into the Amazon and then out to the Caribbean, ending in Miami. If all went according to plan, my little family would be having a much needed reunion in Miami in three weeks.

"Welcome on board, Ms. Barrett," my butler, who said his name was Rakesh, said as he passed me a glass of champagne. I was checking out my suite. My head snapped back toward him and the proffered champagne. "It's *Doctor* Barrett," I said. Why could they never get this correct? I had been very clear about my title on all my cruise documents. Anyway, what I really wanted was for him to go so I could get unpacked and get on with my project.

After showing me how to set the thermostat (surely any moron could figure it out), offering me a choice of bath products (Bulgari or L'Occitane, both equally unsuitable) and explaining the pillow menu (a truly pretentious offering in my view), he finally left me alone. Before I unpacked, I perused the suite.

It had a spacious living room with a large sofa and two chairs, a credenza topped with an odd glass sculpture and a massive coffee table. There was also a dining room with a well-stocked wet bar, presumably for all that entertaining the usual guests in these suites did, a media room, a good-sized bedroom, a walk-in closet and two bathrooms. Of course, I didn't need all that space just for me, but I thought I'd treat myself under the circumstances. And since my plan for my onboard project was still a bit fluid, I thought it couldn't hurt to have options for entertaining. Oh, yes, it also had a large veranda with a jetted tub. I'd make good use of that during that Amazon River part of the cruise. Perhaps by the time we floated into the Caribbean on the home stretch, I'd even have company in it. *Hold that thought*, I said to myself.

Thinking about the Amazon River made me wonder why Peter was really doing this. It must have been that woman who had chosen the itinerary. I could never even once remember Peter mentioning that he was interested in this part of the world. When I thought about the Amazon, it conjured images of a boundless, untamed wilderness teeming with exotic wildlife and perhaps even hidden mysteries. Then there was the potential danger—venomous snakes, mosquitoes bearing the delights of malaria, yellow fever and dengue, to name only three. Peter had always been so danger-averse, so calm and calculated in his decisions. This behaviour was so not like him.

Anyway, at least it was ending in Miami.

When I heard that, I had my first brain wave and implemented the first plank in my as-yet fluid plan. I offered Liam and Fiona the chance to spend a week in Florida, all expenses paid. I told them it would be a wonderful surprise for their father to be able to spend some time with his kids, if even for only a few days at the end of their week after the ship docked. Since Liam was on study break at precisely the right time and Fiona would have just finished one production with some time before rehearsals began for the next one, it was perfect timing. Of course, I didn't breathe a word to them that I also was planning to be on that cruise. I would leave that as a delightful surprise when we could all be together as a family at the end. However, I told them I'd be on a work-related trip to several different places during the weeks preceding their vacation in case they looked for me and wondered why I wasn't at the hospital where I generally spend the better part of twelve hours, five days a week and a few hours each day on the weekends. Yes, I am a workaholic. So, sue me. I'm very good at what I do. And I am the best in the world if I do say so myself. I also love what I do.

I hadn't always wanted to be a pediatric surgeon. In fact, when Peter and I were in med school, I'd wanted to be a radiologist because I figured that of all the medical specialties, radiology involved the least amount of patient contact, a part of medicine that didn't suit my personality. However, after a rotation in pediatric surgery, I realized that the challenge of putting tiny bodies back together would allow me to focus my perfectionism. That I wasn't really a fan of children wasn't an impediment. I could feign warmth and interest for the small amount of time I actually spent with my patients when they were not lying on my operating table under anaesthetic, and I avoided their parents as much as possible. As my career developed, I began to realize that parents loathed me, but since I was the best there was, they were willing to tolerate me. That was just the way I liked it. I worked best alone. I didn't need parents' opinions on their children, and I didn't need anyone else to have an opinion on my evolving plan.

I had spent the night before embarkation at a hotel in Ipanema and had already started to become acclimatized to the heat as one must, but the ship was cold. Too much air conditioning, in my view. We almost never needed A.C. in St. John's, the city in Newfoundland where I lived and besides, I had always considered air conditioning to be unhealthy. Give me an open window to let in the fresh air any day. I locked my passport, wallet and jewelry in the suite's safe, picked up my very lightweight cashmere shawl from where I'd laid it on the bed and set off to explore the ship a bit. My plan was starting to gel, and I knew I'd have to arrange some way to get the inside track on the activities onboard. My first order of business would be to introduce myself to the cruise director.

~

The daily ship chronicle that could be expected to arrive every evening for the duration of the trip had been on the bed in my suite when I arrived. It held the list of what would be happening on board on this embarkation day. It also introduced essential people on the ship's staff. One of those essential people was the cruise director.

I studied the photo and the bio of someone named Rebecca Bebbington-Hughes who hailed from Manchester in the north of England. She looked about forty in her photo, but I knew from experience that anyone in this kind of job was likely to offer a photo that showcased her at her best, so I was likely looking for a slightly older, more tired version. She had begun her cruise ship career as a cabaret singer and worked up to the cruise director position from there. If we could become, if not pals, then at least well-acquainted, she could be a great source of information about what, where and especially who was on board for the next three weeks. The principal role of the cruise director is to be the primary entertainment coordinator, ensuring that all guests have a memorable time—memorable in a good way, I might add.

I knew from past cruise experience that a successful cruise director would be talkative, bubbly and enthusiastic. They usually displayed that kind of over-the-top ebullience that the average cruiser loved. I was not the average cruiser any more than I was the average woman. I often found their excitement about every group activity, every bingo, every port of call, every everything exhausting. Their constant positivity, even in the face of adversity—like cancelled port stops and at-sea medical evacuations—left me feeling that their everyday optimism was just a tad bogus. But that was just me. Despite it all, I knew Rebecca could be my greatest ally, even if she were unaware of her role in my little pageant, and she would *definitely* be unaware of her role.

I wandered into the massive, crystal-festooned atrium later in the afternoon to see if I could effect our first brief encounter. I'd been on board for a couple of hours, but the latecomers were still arriving. We weren't scheduled to set sail until ten p.m., so they were still streaming in. Although the ship billed itself as a small one, the twelve hundred passengers made it seem huge to me. Our previous cruises had all been on ultra-luxury ships that carried under five hundred passengers. This one was upscale premium, but with so many passengers, it could hardly be considered luxury, as it liked to call itself. But I digress.

I was standing at the edge of the grand atrium, scanning the crowd, when I noticed a familiar face across the vast space near the premium wine display. It was that damn Cohen woman. I immediately recognized that sunken-eyed, black-clad, overweening minimalist New York style that she embodied. I peered around, but Peter was nowhere to be seen. I ducked behind a pillar since I hadn't yet decided when I would make my presence known. Then I saw her wave in the direction of the gangway where passengers were embarking. It was Peter.

So, I thought, *they haven't even flown to Brazil together. This is good. They haven't had time to bond yet.*

Peter looked good, as he always did, if a bit tired. He looked like he might just have come from a flight. *Cutting it a bit close,* I thought. *Perhaps he isn't as enthusiastic as he thought he'd be at the idea of a few weeks with the uppity Ms. Cohen.*

They were approaching where I was hiding, so I ducked behind a group of people who were laughing and chatting in front of a large display that said, "Welcome Members of the International Zen and Tonic Connection—Where mindfulness meets hedonism." What in the world? It seemed to be an onboard conference for some kind of oddball group. Then I looked at the large placard to the right of the main table where people seemed to be checking in. I almost choked.

It was a giant poster leaning on an elaborate gold-coloured easel. It said, "Introducing our Main Stage Speaker." Then, there was an enlargement of the cover of a book called *I Am a Creative Genius* that was unmistakable. I had seen it before. Beside it was a headshot of the author's smiling face. I could feel the hairs rising on the back of my neck as my heart rate started to increase rapidly. Was it too late to get off the ship?

FOUR

Claire

LEAVING RIO

I NEVER THOUGHT I'D HAVE TO LOOK into those eyes again. I never thought I'd ever have to think about that face again. I thought that was all in the past. It was possibly the worst thing that I could encounter as I embarked on this project. My indiscretion was staring me in the face, and his name was Jeffrey P. Montgomery. The memories that I'd pushed to the back of my mind flooded back.

I had been in Los Angeles for only three days, and I had no idea how an American celebrity psychiatrist with a bestselling book and a world-renowned pediatric surgeon could possibly have anything to say on the same subject. But there we were on a panel devoted to something about mechanical medicine, evidently, the argument I was representing versus conscious medicine (whatever that meant), which Jeffrey was spearheading. However, I had agreed to do it for a spot as a keynote speaker at this conference. Everyone has their price.

After the panel, Jeffrey lingered while I gathered my purse and briefcase.

"That was fun," he had said.

Fun was not precisely how I would have described it, and I told him so. That started him laughing after which he proceeded to ask me to have a drink with him. I remembered looking at his laughing eyes and thinking he reminded me of Peter when we had first met. After almost two decades of marriage, it was a Peter I hadn't seen in a long time. It jolted me. I threw caution to the wind, but never in my wildest nightmares did I ever expect to lay eyes on him again. And he was evidently on this cruise.

After a moment of panic, I backed away from the poster-sized headshot beaming out at me and stared at it for a moment. I considered the possibility that I could see this as a great opportunity rather than an obstacle. I remembered how upset Peter had been when he found out, which only happened because, in the throes of an argument one evening, I told him. However, I didn't share the identity of the object of my indiscretion. Had I detected jealousy at that moment of truth? Perhaps I had, and jealousy could be made very useful in support of my project goals since Peter had no idea who Jeffrey was. Maybe I wouldn't flee yet.

~

I slipped away from the crowd, deciding that this might not be the most opportune moment to introduce myself to the cruise director. As I looked over at where she was standing with several officers, looking smart in their white uniforms, I studied her for a moment. I might not have been someone who liked to work with people, but I considered myself quite a good judge of character and personalities. In my view, you can tell a lot about a person from their external presentation.

Rebecca Bebbington-Hughes was, as expected, more than a tad bit older than her headshot in the daily newsletter might have suggested. She was tall, even if she hadn't been wearing three-inch platforms, with a mass of long, curly hair that I felt she was too old to carry off well. This choice suggested to me that she was trying too hard. That piece of information could be useful to me. She was wearing a floral wrap-around dress that pulled a bit too tightly across a thickening middle, which further suggested she was closer to my age than she liked. That could be another point of connection. She and I could see eye-to-eye on many subjects, or at least I could make it seem that way. She didn't really look like the sort of person Dr. Claire Barrett would be chummy with—not an insurmountable obstacle to a temporary pseudo-friendship. I then observed her behaviour for a few moments.

Rebecca seemed to relish the attention of the guests as she greeted them and welcomed them on board. Every once in a while, she smiled at the tall man standing to her left in his whites. They seemed to know one another very well. I peered at the epaulets he sported on the shoulders of his uniform jacket, trying to identify his role onboard. I could see three gold bars with red stripes between them. I tried to remember what that meant, but its significance eluded me, so I whipped out my phone and did a quick online search. I still had good cell service since we were still at the dock in Rio.

There it was. The man she was so friendly with was the ship's doctor. Bingo! We now had another point of connection.

So, I was right about our Rebecca epitomizing the generally demonstrated traits of the average cruise director. She would probably also be only too happy to accommodate a passenger in one of the larger suites on board. It was not lost on me that the bigger the suite, the greater the attention. This project might actually be fun. I headed off in search of a bar.

Since it was mid-winter at home and I'd noted there was another snowstorm approaching the city I'd left behind, I thought the best thing I could do was to get outside in the heat of the early evening. I soon found myself sliding onto a stool at the Waves bar, mere steps from the swimming pool. The bartender, a young, smiling Filipino man, handed me the bar menu and poured me a glass of ice water.

I spent a few minutes perusing the offerings. It always amazed me how people on cruises seemed to lose all sense of respectability, quickly succumbing to oddball activities and even more screwball drinks. I wondered if the cruise line had some kind of contest every year to see if the bartenders could come up with the most puerile cocktails they could possibly conjure. This bar menu did not disappoint.

On it were things like the "Don't Run for Rum" drink featuring various types of rum as well as elderflower syrup and both orange and lime juice. I thought that one might make me gag. There was also something called "The Top of the World" that caught my eye because of its name, I suppose. It was a concoction of black rum, peach schnapps, more elderflower syrup and several juices. I thought I might pass on that one as well.

I kept running down the list. "Tropical Sunset," then the ever-popular cruise drink, "Piña Colada," then a "Raspberry Infusion." At that point, I thought it might be safest to have a glass of wine. But what fun would there be in that? This was not meant to be a cruise for safety. It was a cruise to embark on a risky adventure on so many levels. I went back to the first drink on the list.

"I'll have the 'Spicy Passoin Caipirinha,' please," I said, recognizing a local drink if ever there was one—with a cruise ship touch. I knew that the caipirinha was Brazil's national drink, fashioned as it was from their local liquor, cachaça, a Brazilian liquor similar to rum but earthier. This one also boasted passion fruit purée, sriracha (hot chili sauce), and fresh lime.

"Great choice, ma'am," the bartender said as he turned to find his ingredients.

As he mixed my drink, I swivelled my seat to get a better view of the swimming pool. Cruise ship swimming pools are notoriously small, and I had never understood the allure. You couldn't help but bump into people, both literally and figuratively. It was so not my thing.

I watched as people splashed in the pool or sat in the shallow water edges, chatting amiably, no doubt exchanging cruising stories. People generally seemed to be constitutionally unable to sit and be with themselves, a situation I'd noted was especially loathsome on cruises. Every time you slowed down anywhere, someone was bound to strike up a conversation. Cruisers seemed to like nothing better than to tell others all about all the wonderful places they'd travelled and how many days they'd sailed. I'd observed this on the few cruises Peter and I had taken in the past.

I swivelled back toward the bar just as the bartender placed the lavishly decorated, footed plastic glass on the bar in front of me. I thanked him and wrapped my lips around the straw. I closed my eyes and sipped. I don't know what startled me most. Was it the sudden aroma of the deliciously spicy liquid or the voice in my ear?

"My god, it *is* you. What the hell are you doing here, Claire?"

FIVE

Eliza

Leaving Rio

AS PETER AND I MADE OUR WAY up onto the upper deck to view Rio in all its nocturnal glory, I couldn't shake the image of that woman I'd spotted earlier. When I mentioned to Peter that she looked like his ex-wife, he had shuddered and moved on. But she sure looked familiar, although I could not for the life of me believe that there would be such a coincidence as to have Peter's ex-wife on the same cruise. What were the odds? Infinitesimal, in my view. And yet ...

It was last summer. I had known Peter less than a week, but I knew that he was divorced, and I also knew there was something about him that was at once different and riveting. I wouldn't normally have even paid him a second look, but I seemed to be under the bewitching influence of the island of Newfoundland that I hadn't even wanted to visit. I wouldn't have been there, either, if not for my grandmother Nora Houlihan's summons for the family to attend her one-hundredth birthday. Then, there was the unresolved Jake situation hanging over my head.

Peter and I were both attending my grandmother's birthday party in her and Peter's hometown of St. John's on Canada's east coast. My father had been brought up on the island but had left to go to university and never returned to live, so I hadn't spent much time with my grandmother. However much time it had been, it had been more than enough. There was little love lost between my exasperating grandmother and her far-flung family, but she had insisted on everyone being there for her centenary. At some point during the birthday dinner, I noticed a fiftyish blonde woman wearing what appeared to be a head-to-toe cream-coloured Chanel tweed suit staring at me from across the large room. I thought her behaviour was a tad rude when I noticed, but then I forgot about her until some time later when I happened to encounter her in the ladies' room. I wasn't in the habit of chatting up people in restrooms, but I couldn't avoid her. However, since I'd observed that it was kind of a Newfoundland thing to be friendly to strangers, I was getting used to it. I was not, however, prepared for her attack.

The woman had said something to me that seemed so odd at the time. It was something about seeing me sitting with Peter and wondering what my "intentions" were. I don't suppose I often hear things like that. It sounded like something my mother-in-law might say. It was at once anachronistic and menacing. Have you ever met someone and immediately know that you dislike them? That's what happened. At the time, I didn't know she was Peter's ex, but later, when I asked him who she was, he might have used the word "bitch" to describe her. I couldn't disagree. And now, just when I was beginning to feel like I was doing the right thing by taking a risk on this adventure of a lifetime, I seemed to be seeing her here or her doppelganger. Even her doppelganger was unnerving. But I couldn't shake the feeling that Claire Barrett might actually be on board this ship, as bizarre a coincidence as that would be. Surely, it was just my mind playing tricks on me. But I didn't believe in that kind of illusion. To my way of thinking, either something was real, or it wasn't, and I never used to believe in coincidence. Now, I wasn't so sure. What I did know, however, was that I wasn't going to let a nagging worry about a phantom woman drag a dark cloud over my sunshine. I turned my attention back to the present moment up on the deck with Peter and the city we were departing.

"Wow," Peter said. "I really wish I'd gotten to Rio earlier. Now I have to be content with seeing Christ the Redeemer from afar."

"You do have to admit it looks pretty spectacular," I said, gazing at mountain's peak where the lights bathing the statue against the maroon black of the night sky made the icon look like a star in the distance. The ship glided smoothly away from the dock, into the bay and then out to sea.

Anyone who visits Rio de Janeiro and doesn't get to see the glimmering lights of the city from this vantage point is really missing out. Sure, I'd enjoyed that moment when I stood at Christ's feet the day before, looking down over the city and its beaches, but this was something special.

The waterfront lights reflected shades of white, yellow, red and green in the undulating water as we sailed slowly by. Then, as we passed first the crescent of Copacabana and then Ipanema beaches, I could almost feel the nighttime throbbing of the ubiquitous samba. I closed my eyes for a moment and realized that the ship was playing Brazilian music softly from the speakers, adding to the atmosphere. For a moment, I even forgot we weren't alone on this deck. The feeling was one of magic, an ethereal feeling that was new to me.

After we had put Ipanema in our rearview mirrors, Peter said, "Ready for dinner?"

I was ready, although I realized with some horror that I was feeling a bit of trepidation about having dinner with this man. It had been over two decades since I'd had a non-business-related dinner with any man other than my husband. I was starting to feel like a high school girl going on a first date. I thought that I'd left that Eliza far behind. I realized that she was still me—or one part of me, anyway.

We descended from deck fourteen to deck six to find the Grand Dining Room. We gave the hostess our suite numbers, and she asked us if we'd like to join others for dinner. We declined. I figured we'd be in the company of others often enough over the next few weeks. Besides, this was really the first opportunity for us to get to know one another. As I followed the server to our table, I realized that Peter and I had not really spent a moment alone since we'd met. It was a thought in equal measures thrilling and terrifying, thus the feeling of a first date.

Once we were settled into our table for two, holding the enormous dinner menus, I looked around. A woman standing at the door, who I'd seen earlier in the atrium greeting passengers, was talking to the hostess. The woman was probably close to my age, with masses of long hair and a bubbly sort of personality. The two of them looked over toward us, and they both smiled. The woman waved and started walking in our direction.

"Good evening, Ms. Cohen," she said as she approached. "I do hope I'm not intruding on your dinner. I am so delighted to have you on board. I'm Rebecca Bebbington-Hughes, the cruise director."

The moment she opened her mouth, I recognized the northern British accent and the voice as the one emanating from the loudspeakers earlier, telling us first about the required muster drill (so we could know what to do in the event of a need to evacuate the ship at sea) and then to provide a run-down on the evening's activities. I wondered why the cruise director was introducing herself to us, of all people. I didn't have to wait long.

First, she turned to Peter, who introduced himself. Then she turned back to me. I seemed to be the object of her approach. "Ms. Cohen, I am a great fan, perhaps your greatest. I own all your cookbooks and even keep them on board in my cabin when I'm on contract. When I'm home in Manchester on a break, I always make it a point to learn something new from them. I also have a set of your cookware and your wine glasses."

"I'm so happy to hear that you enjoy my work," I said. This was peculiar. I had occasionally been unmasked by someone, usually in a grocery store, but this was gushier than I'd experienced to date.

"Please do tell me that you're working on a new cookbook," Rebecca said.

"In fact, I am. I did some travelling on the east coast of Canada last summer, and I'm working on a new cookbook inspired by that experience."

Rebecca smiled broadly, showing a set of less-than-perfect teeth that seemed to suggest years as a smoker. Since this was a nonsmoking cruise, I could only surmise that it was a thing of the past. "Well, I won't keep you much longer from your dinner," she said, "but I do have a proposition for you."

I wasn't sure I liked the sound of that. I was, after all, on vacation.

"The moment I knew you were on board, I made some inquiries and took the liberty of setting things up in the hopes that you wouldn't turn me down."

I had no idea where she was going with this.

"What I'm trying to say is that I—we—would love it if you would agree to do one or two presentations while on board and perhaps even run a cooking session in our teaching kitchen for our guests. Then we could do a book signing. Our guests would love it. You know that we're known for our culinary arts on this ship, so there are just so many guests who would appreciate your insight and style."

I didn't quite know what to say. "How could we do a book signing when surely there are no copies on board?" Why did I ask her about a book signing when what I really wanted to say was no, I wasn't interested in or prepared to be a cruise ship speaker?

"You just leave that to me. I have already inquired about having copies of your book awaiting us when we dock in Salvador the day after tomorrow. I had a lovely chat with someone at a Brazilian publishing house called Ribeiro something or other—"

"*Editora Ribeiro*," I said.

"Yes. Just so. I left a message, and a few hours later, a lovely man named Alexandre Ro-somebody..."

"Ribeiro," I said, imagining how delighted Alex would have been to hear this odd request.

"Yes, that was him. Sounded absolutely divine with that brilliantly sexy accent of his." Rebecca seemed momentarily flustered. "In any event, he assured me that he could have as many of your books as we needed brought on board in Salvador. He also mentioned that I should say hello to you for him."

I looked over at Peter, who was smiling and shrugging.

"Please say you'll do it, Ms. Cohen." She was practically begging.

"Please call me Eliza," I said. I turned to Peter, who was pretending to read his menu. He seemed to be enjoying this awkward moment I was experiencing.

Peter glanced up. "Don't look at me. It sounds like fun."

So, I agreed not only to prepare and deliver not one but two presentations. I also agreed to run one of their onboard cooking classes.

Rebecca clapped her hands like a schoolgirl. "That would be brilliant, Eliza. Now, before I go, I want to invite you," she turned to look at Peter, "and this devastatingly handsome man to attend a little cocktail party with the captain and the ship's officers tomorrow evening. It starts at six p.m. sharp in the Horizons lounge on deck fifteen, forward. It has a lovely view, and I'm sure you'll enjoy meeting the other special guests on board. I'll leave you to enjoy your dinner and see you tomorrow." She practically skipped away.

"You've seen me at work," Peter said, referring to the one unfortunate night in a snowstorm in Newfoundland at Christmas when I ended up in his emergency department, "and now I'll get to see the famous Eliza Cohen in her element. I am truly looking forward to that."

Peter's face was a mask of childish delight. I almost felt like giggling.

~

After a surprisingly good dinner, Peter and I took a walk on deck in the moonlight. Is there anything more romantic than the image of walking in the moonlight on the deck of a ship as it glides smoothly through the ocean? The only sound is of the swishing of the water against the hull—and the engines, of course.

Peter had done well in not lagging this evening. He had flown from Toronto to Miami (a three-and-a-quarter-hour flight), then waited hours after he missed his connection before boarding the eight-and-a-half-hour flight from Miami to Rio. Then, he had spent the evening with me. It was hardly surprising when, as we stood looking out at the moon's reflection on the waves, he started to yawn. I reluctantly said goodnight and insisted he get a good night's sleep. Yes, of course, the idea of spending the night with Peter had crossed my mind, but truthfully, I didn't think I was ready for that yet, and I didn't want to blow this. It was, after all, our first date. I also wanted to spend a few more minutes on deck alone before heading back to my suite and figuring out what I might talk about to a group of cruisers.

After ten more minutes, I strolled back to my suite three decks down and opened the door to find that it had been meticulously set up for the night. The bed had been turned down; there was a single rose on the pillow; the pillows I'd selected were on the bed, their pristine white covers gleaming in the dimmed light. There were two chocolates on the pillow, and slippers had been set beside the bed. All in all, I felt like I could get used to this. Then, a ping from my phone shattered the solitude. *Probably Izzy,* I thought as I reached for it from the clutch that I'd taken to dinner.

It was not from Izzy. It was from Jake.

Tried to get you at home. No answer. Tried your cell earlier. No answer. If you get this text, please confirm. Are you out of town? I need to talk to you. I miss you. J. 😦

He missed me? What nonsense was this?

The only thought on my mind at that moment was, thank god Izzy hasn't told him where I am. The second thought was what to do about this text. I could ignore it and hope he would get the message, or I could respond. But If I chose to respond, what in the world would I say? I could hardly say that I'm on a three-week cruise to the Amazon River with a gorgeous doctor that I barely know. Or could I?

SIX

Claire

EN ROUTE TO SALVADOR, BRAZIL

I ALMOST ASPIRATED MY DRINK the moment I heard the voice. I didn't need to look up from my caipirinha to know that Jeffrey P. Montgomery, celebrity psychiatrist and would-be cruise speaker, was standing over me, casting a shadow larger than he should.

Before I had a chance to say a word, Jeffrey slid into the empty stool next to me. When the bartender asked him if he could get him something, Jeffrey looked at my glass and said, "I'll have whatever the lady is having."

He placed his oversized, reflective aviator sunglasses on the bar and his left arm beside them. I could see that he was still wearing his silver Cartier Santos watch with its navy blue alligator band, which I'd noticed the first time we'd met. At the time, I'd considered this a bit of quiet luxury for a man who I would otherwise have expected to be wearing a blingy Rolex. I soon learned that Jeffrey never made a choice on a whim. His every move was calculated for effect. He always had a reason. "So, what *are* you doing here?" he said.

"I am on a cruise," I said when I finally got control of my breathing. I had no desire to spend much more time chatting with Jeffrey until I had a plan for how I would deal with him.

"Well, I can see that, Dr. Barrett," he said as the bartender placed the drink in front of him. He raised it and said, "To old friends and shocking surprises."

"To shocking surprises," I said, wondering how to get rid of him as quickly as possible. Then, it occurred to me that I could use this opportunity to figure out his precise role on board in case it came in handy for me.

"You still married?" he said suddenly. A complete *non sequitur*.

"As a matter of fact, I'm not, but I'm surprised you even remembered that I had been." I took another sip, this time very carefully. "Are you?"

He shivered. "Certainly not. Tried it once and hated it. That will never happen again. I must have told you this when we met."

Perhaps he had, but I seemed to have forgotten. "Maybe you just married the wrong woman," I said idly, then immediately regretted it. He might misinterpret me.

"Maybe," Jeffrey said. "But I consider re-marriage to be the triumph of hope over logic."

"So bitter."

"Not at all. I carry no bitterness at all. You should know that. I am the truest of the romantics. I see love as powerful and transformative."

"Have you ever been in love, Jeffrey? I mean, really in love?"

He got a faraway look in his usually steely eyes. "I have, Claire."

"What happened?"

"I woke up one day, and it was gone."

"It was gone, or she was gone?"

He laughed, but it was that wry, ironic, mirthless laugh.

"That was then, and this is now. I don't have to spend my life in love to know that our experiences transform us in ways we haven't even thought about yet. I have a wonderful chapter about the transformative nature of love in everyday experiences in my new book. Have you read it?"

I frowned. What in the world would make anyone think that Dr. Claire Barrett, a surgeon and a scientist, would have the time or the inclination to read something about the transformative power of love, whatever that meant? As Tina Turner once asked, "What's love got to do with it?"

"No, Jeffrey, I have not read it. And, by the way, what exactly are *you* doing on this cruise?" I, of course, had a general idea, but I needed him to explain it to me.

"I'm the featured guest at a group meeting that's taking place on board."

"Yes, the Zen and Tonic Connection?" I snorted. "Seriously? There's a group with that name?"

"Don't be so fast to judge, Claire. You might find that you have more in common with them than you think. They believe in hedonism tempered with a splash of the transformative power of meditation."

"Transformative power of meditation? Didn't you just say that love is the transformative power?"

"There's no one thing, Claire. In a couple of days, I'm also doing a general presentation for the guests who aren't members of the group called 'Life: Illusion or Reality?' A surgeon like you might find it," he stopped for a moment and smiled at me, "transformative." I didn't think so. He continued. "I have an idea. Why don't you be my date tomorrow evening?"

I couldn't think of anything more awkward, but a little voice inside me whispered that I should go with the flow—at least for the moment. So, I said, "A date? For what?"

"There's a cocktail party for all the onboard special guests tomorrow evening. The captain is the host. It should be fun. And I'd love to have a beautiful woman on my arm."

How could I refuse?

~

The late great Nora Ephron once wrote, "Never marry a man you wouldn't want to be divorced from." From where I now sat, I had to respectfully disagree with her. I believe it should say, "Never divorce a man you should be married to." Of course, since I'm not an average woman (and Nora Ephron was well known for speaking to the average woman among us, which is most women), her *bon mots* don't apply to me. I was thinking about this the following morning as I sat on one of a dozen exercise cycles in the well-appointed onboard gym, surrounded by the kind of people who can't go a day without their workout, even when on vacation. I would call us the driven crowd with not a moment to lose in life. I had to admit that the view from a floating gym was more gratifying than one on dry land. The gym's location in the bow of the ship on a high deck afforded it an incredible view looking out the front of the ship into the unexplored ocean ahead. As my legs pumped around and around, I was considering how my plan was unfolding.

My first order of business was to figure out how to control when and where I ran into Peter and that Cohen woman, although I would have preferred not to run into her at all. I knew that wasn't going to happen. I decided that a standing date with an exercise cycle in the gym every day early in the morning would be a good place to regroup and evaluate my interventions. I figured that for a Jewish cookbook author from New York, the gym was the last place on board I'd ever bump into her. And I'd been married to Peter long enough to know that he abhorred early morning workouts. So, this would be my safe public space and time. I could think and plan.

On the top of my mind was how to meet the cruise director. When Jeffrey asked me to attend the party with him later today, at first, I was going to decline (for so many reasons). Still, on second thought (that little voice in my head that suggested I should go with the flow), I realized it would probably be the perfect place to meet the cruise people and get my plan rolling. So, on this day at sea, while the ship made its way along the Brazilian coast and slightly north to the city of Salvador, where we'd dock the following day, and other guests lolled on the pool deck or played bingo or whatever other things they did, I expected to get my entire strategy worked out. But first, I had a spa appointment. I wasn't going to "unexpectedly" run into my soon-to-be-not-ex-husband without looking my very best. Being brilliant only got you so far.

~

"You look amazing," Jeffrey said as I walked into the bar called, oddly, Martinis at five o'clock for a drink before drinks.

"I do, don't I?" I did look amazing. I believe that if a woman doesn't think she's amazing, she can hardly expect anyone else to think so. I was also well aware that although my plan at that stage was to make myself known to Peter the next day (I still had a few details to work out), I was acutely aware that it was possible I might run into him inadvertently. To minimize the possibility that this would happen, I was on the alert every time I turned a corner.

As I sat down at the small table where Jeffrey had taken up residence, I noticed his drink. "That looks like a negroni."

"My favourite drink, as you might recall from our four days in L.A." I did not recall, and it was only two and a half days, but who's counting? I didn't correct him.

The server came over as I was selecting a glass of wine from the (rather limited) selection. One thing I knew about my generation was that we adored our quality wine and Peter and I had spent considerable time researching and tasting it during our marriage. I noticed that they had a bottle of 2017 Château Pichon Longueville Comtesse de Lalande 2ème Grand Cru Classé from Pauillac, France, for $260. I asked for a glass of that.

"Ma'am," the server said, looking alarmed, "we do not serve that by the glass."

"Of course, you don't, and I don't expect you to. Please pour me a glass and send the rest of the bottle to our table later in the Grand Dining Room for dinner."

The server nodded and scurried away.

Jeffrey picked up the wine list and looked at the page I'd been reading. "Wow, Claire. You have expensive taste in wine. I hardly know my white wines from my red wines."

I seriously doubted that. "How old are you, Jeffrey?"

"How old am I? Didn't you ask me that when we first met?"

"I did, but I didn't receive a satisfactory answer."

"What does it matter?" he said, lifting the negroni to his lips.

I stared at the vibrant red liquid swirling around in his glass. "Well, you seemed to suggest a long career that escorted you to your current celebrity, leading one to believe you were not that much younger than I am. By the way, I'm almost fifty." He nodded and raised his glass to me. "However, I had a feeling you were actually quite a bit younger."

"I'm not sure what you're getting at."

The sommelier arrived at our little table pushing a wooden cart carrying my bottle and a crystal decanter. "Please just decant one glass now," I said. He looked disappointed that I'd clearly ruined what he expected to be a performance. "And thank you." Then I turned back to Jeffrey. "Jeffrey, what I'm getting at is that I believe you're a bit of a fraud." His eyes widened, but before he could say a word, I continued. "Don't worry, I know you're a board-certified psychiatrist in two states. Of course, I researched you."

I had found it odd that his (quite extensive) Wikipedia page didn't include his date of birth or the dates when he graduated from undergrad or medical school. Mine did.

"You researched me? I think I'm flattered."

"Don't be too flattered. I do it for everyone I meet. It took me a long time and hard work to build my reputation, but I believe you've taken a rather shorter route. I think that your online presence is an intentional part of a strategy." And I knew a thing or two about intentional strategies. I was an expert. "I'm also convinced that you've developed your popular theories and written your books, expecting them to be embraced by people who believe you to have considerable life and career experience. I don't believe you do." By the way he was clutching his glass and waving the server over to order another one, I got the distinct impression he was trying to keep his cool.

"The lack of exact dates in my online biographies isn't exactly sinister, Claire. I don't think it suggests some kind of scheme. Anyway, I really have no idea why you think I'm younger than I seem—although I suppose I should take that as a compliment."

"As you wish. Anyway," I said, "as regards evidence, first, there's your drink of choice. I've worked with enough younger colleagues at this point in my career, which, by the way, I built brick by brick over two decades, to know that cocktails like that are the drink of choice for millennials. And millennials seem to harbour a distinct disdain for my generation's apparent wine snobbery. That would make you, at the most, forty-three years old today if you were among the oldest millennials. But I'd be willing to bet that you're younger than that. Am I getting warm?" Was he squirming?

"I suppose if I am that much younger as you suggest, that would make you a cougar." He smiled, swaggering just slightly.

"Touché," I said. "However, that doesn't bother me at all. I'm more concerned about your credibility as a pop psychology guru."

"Pop psychiatry and personal transformation," he said by way of correcting me, I suppose. "Although I dislike the 'pop' thing. It seems so down market—a bit 1980s. And no one wants the 1980s back, right?"

I laughed and took the first sip of the astonishingly good wine. With a base of 70% Cabernet Sauvignon, 23% Merlot, and a touch of Cabernet Franc and Petit Verdot, the deep dark liquid had a silky mouth feel with a burst of fruitiness that was almost orgasmic. Almost.

I let the topic of his age go, and Jeffrey told me about his upcoming lectures. When I had finished my wine, Jeffrey looked at his watch. "Time to meet the captain. Shall we?"

~

As we stepped off the elevator on deck fifteen and turned the corner toward the entrance of the lounge, I could see a small receiving line. The very first person in the receiving line was the cruise director. Bingo! I was in luck. My plan was about to begin.

I took Jeffrey's arm, and we walked toward the entrance. I turned to smile at the people who had gotten off the next elevator and were rounding the corner into the corridor outside the lounge when I heard a familiar voice.

"What the actual fuck are you doing here?"

SEVEN

Eliza

AT SEA, EN ROUTE TO SALVADOR, BRAZIL

I HAD SPENT A WONDERFUL DAY relaxing on deck in the South American sun with Peter. We drank those delicious vacation-conjuring cocktails called sea breezes and ate potato chips. I don't know if it was the copious amounts of grapefruit and cranberry juice that played a supporting role to the vodka in the sea breezes, but I found Peter even more compelling than I remembered. He was just as funny and disarming as he had been when I first met him last summer. This situation was completely different, though, since I now had him all to myself. I was also feeling sanguine since I'd chosen not to respond to Jake's text at all. I would have to respond eventually, but right now, I didn't want to engage with anything that would remind me that Jake hadn't yet signed the divorce papers, and, technically, despite the separation, we were still married. I wanted to feel free for a few weeks. The rest of it would work out.

When Peter knocked on my suite door to pick me up so we could attend this captain's cocktail party for onboard special guests, I felt like a high school kid—again. I was wearing a silver-sequined dress I'd worn to an atrociously pretentious cocktail party with Jake's friends earlier in the year. I hoped I could imbue it with better memories since it had cost me an arm and a leg, and I liked it. So, by the time we stepped off the elevator on deck fifteen, I was actually looking forward to this soirée that had seemed so unnecessary when Rebecca mentioned it. I took Peter's arm, and as we rounded the corner, I stiffened. I could see that same head of bouncy blonde hair I'd seen in the atrium the day before. Then I felt Peter go rigid and so did I. It turned out I hadn't been seeing things.

I had never heard a four-letter word emanate from Peter's lips before. But the moment I saw those eyes as they turned toward us, smiling at first and then frowning, I heard myself say, "Oh fuck."

That was the moment the man beside her turned, presumably to find out the source of the lack of verbal imagination. I don't know what happened, but the moment I saw those eyes, I melted a little. *Dear god,* I thought. *Who is that beautiful man? And why is the wicked bitch woman hanging on his arm? And isn't she too old for him?*

"What? Well, what a surprise!" Claire Barrett looked at her ex-husband with the wild eyes of someone who had been caught in the act. The question was: What was the act?

And seriously, what the actual fuck *was* she doing here?

Peter looked around as if to ensure no one could overhear us as we edged toward the receiving line. "I mean it, Claire. What are you doing here? And don't tell me this is a coincidence."

"Well, you took the words right out of my mouth. A coincidence. Who could believe this kind of a fluke could happen? You'd never believe it if it were in a novel!" She giggled, which I thought looked odd on her.

I could tell that this was a woman who did not giggle. Ever. To tell you the truth, she looked a bit flustered to me.

The beautiful man whose arm she was clinging to seemed to click into the situation. "Wow, Claire, what are the odds you'd run into someone you know on board."

She turned, and I'm sure she glared at him. "Jeffrey, this is Peter O'Brien." She stopped for just a beat. "My ex-husband."

A light seemed to dawn on Jeffrey's face. He smiled, nodded knowingly and extended his hand. "I'm Jeffrey P. Montgomery," he said. "I'm delighted to meet you." Peter didn't extend his hand, so Jeffrey P. Montgomery dropped his hand and continued. "You know, Claire, I don't believe in coincidence at all. This is a demonstration of Jungian synchronicity."

"What in god's name are you talking about?" Claire said. She was clearly in the coincidence camp.

"Synchronicity. Jung said synchronicities are meaningful coincidences that we can't explain by simple cause and effect. If two events happen at the same time, they must be logically related. There's no such thing as a simple coincidence."

"I know what synchronicity means, and I know all about that Jungian nonsense," Claire said peevishly. She smiled through what appeared to be gritted teeth.

At that moment, I remembered where I'd seen his name before. He was on the list of onboard speakers that Rebecca had provided me, along with the written invitation to this cocktail gathering. I remembered wondering what the "P" stood for and why he used it, but I hadn't had the time or interest in researching him. I might have to rethink that decision. I was still reeling from the realization that I was captive on a ship off the coast of Brazil for three weeks (three weeks!) with Peter's ex-wife. I had no idea why that terrified me, but it did. Perhaps it had something to do with the terrifying and actively intimidating personality that Claire Barrett had in spades.

However much progress I'd made over the past year with my evolution to grandmother and almost-divorced-independent woman, I hadn't completely shed my own bitch personality. I still had only one employee—my assistant Mary-Lou—who wasn't terrified of me. I decided that no matter what Claire thought she was doing on board this cruise ship, interfering with my holiday wasn't going to be one of them. I took Peter's hand.

Just as I did so, Claire looked at Peter as a frown began to create ugly jagged lines across her forehead (okay, perhaps they weren't that ugly). "By the way, this is a private cocktail party. What are you two doing here?"

Peter's eyes were shooting daggers at Claire, and before either of us could answer, Claire moved ahead as the queue reached the receiving line. Any further discussion of coincidences versus synchronicities or why we were attending this cocktail party would have to wait. I watched Claire as she approached Rebecca, taking her hand as Jeffrey introduced them and then leaning in to chat. Suddenly, Rebecca and Claire both looked in our direction. Claire glared at me, then composed a smile and turned back to Rebecca. I supposed she now had her answer to the question of why we were there.

It was now my turn to greet Rebecca, who was then introducing one and all to Captain Guilio Lombardi, a tall, broad Italian man with a handlebar mustache and a jolly laugh and on the captain's other side, the ship's doctor, another Italian, Dr. Antonio Ricci. I smiled, and they said the usual things one might expect, "Welcome aboard," "Have a wonderful voyage," and "So happy you agreed to be a part of our onboard activities." This last greeting was from Dr. Ricci, causing me to wonder why he was interested enough to know who I was at all.

After we'd finished with the receiving line, we retrieved a drink from the silver trays that white-gloved servers were passing and found a table far from the centre of the room, back against the windows. I saw the doctor and the cruise director together. It might not have been clear to everyone, but it was clear to me. There was something more than collegial intercourse going on between the two of them. I briefly wondered about the cruise line's policies on fraternizing, if they had one at all. I also watched as Claire and Jeffrey took seats as close to the front as they could manage. At least we weren't stuck with them—at this point, a fate worse than death, in my view.

"Why the hell is that woman here?" Peter said, quickly finishing his first glass of champagne. It was almost immediately replaced by a second one.

"Peter, maybe it *is* just a coincidence," I said. "Maybe she and that man are a thing, and he invited her on board." Peter was staring at the back of their heads. If looks could kill, there would be holes bored through both of them. "They do look very chummy." I looked at Peter and considered his reaction. "You aren't jealous, are you?" Why the hell did I ask that?

The moment I said "jealous," Peter's head snapped back toward me. "Jealous? Are you kidding me? I hope he knows what he's doing."

Why wasn't I entirely convinced? I decided to let it go for the moment and consider Jeffrey, Claire's companion. He was, in a word, hypnotic. It was almost as if you would believe whatever he said, no matter how preposterous it sounded. There was something about his eyes that drew you in and held you there. The other peculiarity about him, as I saw it at that moment, was that he appeared to be younger than Claire—a lot younger, if I didn't miss my guess.

"Did you ever think that your ex-wife was a cougar?"

"A cougar?"

"Yes. You know, it's that term that means an older woman having a relationship with a much younger man." I sipped my champagne. "Funny, there's no corresponding word for when much older men have relationships with much younger women."

"Cradle-robber?"

I snorted a bit of champagne up my nose, which caused Peter to smile. I was delighted to see him smiling once again. I had started to worry that this turn of events might drag a dark cloud over the sunshine of our journey of getting to know one another.

"Fuck it," he said finally, reaching for an hors d'oeuvre from the plate of delicacies a server was currently offering. I almost smiled, hearing Peter say that again. From the way the server flinched, I had to assume she'd heard Peter's, uh-hem, slang. He popped the tiny piece of blini with caviar into his mouth and turned to me. He took my hand and said, "Who cares? It's a big ship. We can avoid them for the next few weeks. Anyway, it might be fun for Claire to see that I've moved on."

So, he had moved on. Interesting.

~

We were having dinner that evening in the ship's Asian restaurant. Since there were several dining venues, I hoped like hell that we'd chosen one where Claire and Jeffrey might not be eating. We were in luck, managing to spend the rest of the evening without running into them even once. Things were looking up. When it was time to call it a night, Peter and I said good night in the atrium and went our separate ways. I kept second-guessing myself, wondering if I was being too standoffish—if Peter was going to think that I wasn't interested in getting closer to him. However, he hadn't given me any reason to believe that was his conclusion. I wondered how long this would go on.

Once back in my suite, I slid out of the sequins and into an oversized, fluffy bathrobe so kindly provided by the ship. I then sat down to do a bit of research about this Jeffrey person. I was startled when my phone rang. With no cell service, I figured it must be good wi-fi.

"Eliza? It's Abigail. I'm sorry if I woke you, but I've been trying to get a hold of you. Are you out of town?"

"Abigail, what a surprise. Yes, I am out of town. Is there something wrong?" Abigail Zimmerman was my attorney. She was handling all the issues related to the divorce that seemed to be stalled.

"Not wrong, exactly, but you had mentioned you wanted this divorce behind you as soon as possible, and I hadn't heard from you. I wondered if you'd had second thoughts or if you wanted to rework any aspects of the agreement."

I thought about the divorce papers that Jake had refused to sign. "No second thoughts, Abigail, only a husband who refuses to sign the papers."

"Jake is refusing to sign the papers? Why didn't you tell me?"

I sighed. "He says he won't let me divorce him."

"Eliza, he can't do that, you know."

"That's what I tried to tell him. However, if there is one thing Jacob Cohen believes about himself, it is that he can always get his way." Just thinking about it made my head hurt.

"No, Eliza, I mean it. He can't do that. He cannot refuse you your divorce. We live in New York state."

I had no idea what she was talking about. We had drawn up the papers, Abigail had one of her employees even officially serve him the papers at his office, and I had a set at home that I had hoped I could get him to sign since he hadn't signed his copy. He wouldn't sign.

"Eliza, you don't need Jake's signature to get a divorce." Abigail then went on to explain that we lived in a state where there was such a thing as a "no signature required" divorce, something I'd never heard of, but it did sound terribly modern. "Since he failed to respond within twenty days, your divorce papers can be processed even without his signature on them. We can get on with it, and you can be free. How long will you be gone?" I told her I would be gone for almost a month. "Okay. Can you arrange to have the papers you signed sent over to my office? That way, we can get on with it."

I told her I'd have my assistant get them to her within a day or two. I sat back, unable to believe the good news I'd just heard. Then, I came back down to reality. "Abigail, how does the asset allocation happen if he doesn't sign the papers?"

"I'll get the papers processed, and a judge will follow what we call the rule of equitable distribution, although there's no statutory requirement for a 50/50 split as there is in other states with community property laws. But in my experience, the judges do a good job. Given the issues Jake's business has been having, the judge might even be sympathetic to a wife who wants nothing more than to get away from such a family." She laughed. "Anyway, since yours is the only name on the deed to the house and other assets, as I recall, the judge will consider this to be what they call separate property, so that will be yours anyway, regardless of other allocations."

I was starting to feel a glimmer of what I could only describe as glee beginning to bubble.

I had to clap my hand over my mouth to stifle a giggle and told Abigail to go ahead and let me know the minute the papers were processed. I didn't care at all about any other property settlement, and I wasn't looking for alimony. However, Abigail suggested I might be granted it anyway since we had more than ample evidence that Jake had been sleeping with his secretary (and possibly others) for a considerable length of time.

When I got off the phone, I sat back on the pile of pillows on the heavenly bed. I had forgotten all about the incident earlier in the evening at the cocktail party, or at least it had melted back into obscurity from whence it had emerged. And I realized one thing. Until now, I'd been keeping Peter at a distance. I still considered myself a married woman and had harboured the fear that if I got closer to Peter, Jake might somehow find a way to use it against me. That was all over. I didn't plan to spend much more time alone in this suite.

I got up to brush my teeth just as my phone pinged. I smiled, hoping it was Peter texting to say goodnight. It wasn't. It was Jake.

EIGHT

Claire

SALVADOR, BRAZIL

THIS WAS NOT HOW I HAD PLANNED IT. Not. At. All. Although I have to admit that I did look amazing—amazing enough for an unexpected encounter. I had wanted to be the one to approach Peter first. I had wanted to be the one who with great delighted surprise, asked him what *he* was doing here. Instead, when I heard that familiar voice say, "What the actual fuck are you doing here?" I realized I had mere seconds to consider how to play this.

I glanced at Jeffrey as I composed myself. At least I had the great advantage of not being alone, and Jeffrey was an impressive-looking man. That was the moment I realized that the universe had sent him to me to be a prop despite my usual lack of faith in such things. I just had to figure out a way to avoid having Jeffrey mention at any juncture that he was the subject of my little indiscretion—that he was the one I'd slept with at that conference. I didn't think that would go over very well.

I managed to suggest to Peter that it was quite an unbelievable coincidence that we should run into one another while I took stock of that Cohen woman who was clinging to his arm. What in god's name made her think that a woman her age could get away with silver sequins? I could never understand the tackiness of New Yorkers with money. I knew she had money because I'd done my research. I had discovered that her husband and his family were uber-wealthy. (By the way, what had happened to the husband? Another piece of information to tuck away for later use.) However, in the decades that I'd known Peter, I had never gotten even the slightest impression that money was a major driving force for him. He wasn't attracted to money. He was a dedicated professional who was attracted to brilliant and elegant women. That was where I came in. I just had to be able to use Jeffrey long enough to get Peter's attention. Yes, Jeffrey.

At the moment Jeffrey began to go on about synchronicity, I had the distinct urge to slap him. The last thing I wanted was for Peter—the logical and practical man he was—to begin to believe there was more to this than mere coincidence. There was no need for him to consider even for a moment that there had been some planning involved or that I might have been the one who had done it. Thank god the receiving line pulled us ahead, leaving me to continue to wonder why they were here at this private event this evening.

Finally, I arrived in front of Rebecca Bebbington-Hughes, the cruise director. Jeffrey introduced me, at which point I began to tell Rebecca how wonderful she looked and how much I was looking forward to getting to know her. Then I mentioned that I'd just had the uncanny experience of running into my ex-husband. We both turned, and she said, "Oh, that lovely man with the incredible Eliza Cohen is your ex? How delicious."

I didn't think it was at all delicious, and I especially didn't like the tone of her voice as she referred to that Cohen woman as incredible.

"Dr. Barrett—"

"Oh, please call me Claire." At least she had paid attention to the "doctor" part. That's all I ever asked.

"Claire, you really must attend the cooking class Eliza has agreed to conduct. She is quite a marvel. Are you familiar with her books?"

A cooking class? Dear god, it was worse than I could even have imagined, but it did explain why Eliza (and Peter) were here at the party. This scenario was not going as I had planned, but I was nothing if not practiced in the art of the pivot.

"Cooking class? That sounds like marvellous fun," I said, still maintaining my smile.

"I shall put you down for attendance." Rebecca turned to Jeffrey. "Dr. Montgomery, darling, shall I put you down along with Claire?"

"A cooking class with a famous cookbook author sounds like a lot of fun," he said, "as long as you can get her to attend *my* lecture."

"I shall try," Rebecca said as she turned her attention to Peter and Eliza, who were approaching, while Jeffrey and I made our way into the lounge. Jeffrey led us to a table at the very front of the lounge on the edge of the dance floor in front of the band. There was a microphone on a stand where I presumed Rebecca would soon introduce the special guests, Jeffrey included. As I considered the bubbles in my champagne flute (they weren't as lively as they ought to have been in my view—had the bottle been open too long?), I wondered if I'd have to sleep with Jeffrey (again) to keep him on board, as it were, as long as I needed him. Truthfully, it wasn't the worst prospect.

~

I dined with Jeffrey in the main dining room after the cocktail reception. I didn't expect him to spend all his free time with me, but if he went on the prowl, there were any number of women on board, both younger than he was and older, who would probably kill to spend time with him. Although that particular turn of events wouldn't bother me, I didn't want Eliza or Peter to begin to think he wasn't totally devoted to me—at least not yet. Again, I considered that perhaps I *would* have to sleep with him to keep him on a short leash.

When we had finally finished dinner, Jeffrey and I said good night and headed off in our separate directions. He did ask me to have dinner with him once again the following evening, but there was no mention of activities during the day. We would be docking in the city of Salvador in the morning, and I was booked on what the cruise line called a shore excursion. These activities were arranged for groups of people to go ashore together with a guide to see the sights in and around ports of call. Although I wasn't a fan of group activities, I thought it might be a good way to learn something, an added advantage of this itinerary.

The following morning, after an in-suite breakfast provided by my butler, Rakesh, I sprayed some DEET-filled insect repellent on the bare parts of my body, grabbed a sun hat and my nylon Tumi bag and made my way to the lounge as my ticket instructed. There, I would meet the group so that we could all go ashore together.

I was soon boarding a bus that was parked in a row of similar buses on the pier. Everyone else seemed to be part of a pair. This state of affairs was hardly surprising, I suppose, since cruises are notoriously filled with happy—or pseudo-happy—couples mainly of "a certain age." I might have been fifty, but "a certain age" was so much older on this journey. I considered the fact that I was alone among a sea of couples. It wasn't as unappetizing as I might have thought, but the alternative—Peter once again back where he belonged—was even more delicious. I settled myself into a window seat halfway down the bus's aisle and prepared for what I expected to be a boring lecture from a tour guide with a weak grasp of the English language. The guide, however, turned out to be a forty-something man with impeccable English who began his narration with a few fun facts about this area of Brazil known as Bahia, of which Salvador was the capital.

I don't know what I had expected of Brazil's Atlantic coastline, but cities of two-and-a-half million people were not on that list. Despite living in a city of less than a hundred and twenty thousand people, I considered myself cosmopolitan since I travelled so much. Whenever I returned home to the island of Newfoundland, where I was a big fish in what I recognized as a small pond, I always felt grounded. So, I suppose I had expected the cities up the coast of Brazil to be more like what I was used to. I was willing to admit that this was something of an education for me.

Our first stop was in the historic centre of the city. We slowly clambered off the bus and were like the children following the Pied Piper as we crept along at the speed of the slowest among us (something I detested). The cobblestone streets wound past vibrantly coloured colonial buildings in shades of pale yellow, blue and pink, with small second-story Juliet balconies of black wrought iron in many cases. Street musicians filled the air with their Afro-Brazilian rhythms. Until the guide pointed it out, I had been unaware that this part of Brazil was so closely associated with its African roots.

I shuffled along with the group, getting increasingly hotter and sweatier as the day progressed. I had realized that it would be hot here, but it was beyond what someone who spends her life in Newfoundland in the North Atlantic is used to, and I expected it might only get worse as we neared the Amazon River itself. As I stood in the shade of one of the (many) Spanish Baroque churches we visited that day, once again waiting for the slowest among us to exit the latest specimen of papal opulence and fanning myself with my hat, I again wondered why Peter had to choose Brazil, of all the places in the world he could have selected for a trip. In the more than a quarter of a century that we'd known one another, he had never once mentioned a burning desire to visit the Amazon (or at least if he did, I hadn't noticed), so I had to believe it was Eliza Cohen's influence. And yet, I had no idea how they could have gotten to know one another so well in such a short time.

Before I booked myself on this cruise, I had tried not to pepper Liam and Fiona with questions after Christmas. There was no point in alerting them to the fact that their mother was the slightest bit interested in their father's current activities. However, when Fiona let it slip about her father's trip, I had nudged her to see if she might give me, her loving mother, more information. It seemed there was little to tell, or at least her father hadn't shared much with her. To me, that meant that whatever was between Peter and Eliza was nascent, at best, the ideal time to slide a wedge in. As I got back on the bus after the final stop of the tour, I realized that the time was now, and I was ready.

As we drove back to the port, I gazed out the bus windows at the favelas rising in layers on hills overlooking the central city. I couldn't even imagine what it must be like to live in one of those hovels. I was astonished when our guide mentioned that he would love to live there so that he could have his own house rather than living in an apartment. I was struck by the differences in our value systems in different parts of the world and the frame through which each of us sees our life. I suppose I already knew this, but occasionally, the contrasts are put into sharp relief. This was one of those times.

~

I had managed to spend my entire time ashore without running into Peter and company. Of course, I realized that with every activity I embarked on, I ran the risk of seeing him. However, I was now ready, so I didn't feel like I had to hide any longer. I now knew that my best strategy would be a two-pronged approach.

The first prong involved using Jeffrey. I would cultivate the illusion that Jeffrey was madly in love with me, thus causing Peter to realize what he'd missed. The second prong relied on my own ability to stand out in a crowd, something I excelled at most of the time. I would plan to highlight the stark differences between that Cohen woman in all her New York glory (not) and me. I could see that she would be a formidable opponent but make no mistake. She may have the aura of a confident New Yorker, but I knew her father was born and raised right in the small city that I called home, so there was just something a bit implausible about her persona. I was going to find the real Eliza Cohen and hold it up in front of Peter so he could know how to make the right choice. All roads would lead back to me.

When the shore excursion came to its hot and sweaty end, all I could think about was taking a shower and enjoying a cold drink. Once that was accomplished, I sat in my living room and picked up the daily newsletter. I was reviewing the times and locations for the musical entertainment on offer when my doorbell rang. It was Rakesh.

"Dr. Barrett," he began, "a gentleman asked me to give you this note." He smiled and nodded as I took the small envelope from him.

I hoped it might be from Peter. It wasn't.

"Dearest Claire," it read, *"I'm hoping you'll join me this afternoon for the film they're showing in the theatre. It's an old one I've been dying to see, and it's very appropriate.* 😉 *And it was filmed here in Salvador. Hope you don't mind subtitles. I'll arrange popcorn and champagne and meet you there at four. Kisses, JP."*

It seemed as if prong one—the Jeffrey P. Montgomery prong—might be easier to pursue than I thought. It was almost too good to be true. I knew I'd have to be careful. I picked up the daily newsletter and looked at the activities again. The movie was called *Dona Flor and Her Two Husbands*. What the hell was Jeffrey on about? I wasn't sure I wanted to see a movie while on a cruise ship at all, and I was even less sure about seeing one about a woman with two husbands. What was Jeffrey trying to say? I sighed, threw the newsletter on the sofa and wondered what I should wear.

~

Rebecca was doing her cruise director thing outside the theatre, smiling and greeting everyone when I arrived on deck five just before four. She was standing beside a colourful movie poster that sat on an easel.

"Oh, hello there, Claire. Dr. Montgomery told me I could expect you. He's already inside." She looked at me as I peered at the poster. "Have you seen this one?"

I told her I hadn't. It was clearly an old movie, as Jeffrey had suggested. Judging by the illustration on the movie poster, it was filmed in the 1970s, if I didn't miss my guess. The image was of a smiling woman lying in bed with each of her arms around a different man.

"What's it about?"

"Ooh, I shan't give it away. It's a bit of a spicy romp, and I'm sure you'll enjoy it."

I wasn't as convinced. "When was it released originally?"

"I believe it was 1976, based on a famous Brazilian novel from a decade earlier, so it's something of a vintage find. It was filmed here in Salvador, you know. I was so thrilled when I found it and proposed it as our daily feature while in port."

I wasn't going to get any more information about it from her. I'd have to see it for myself. I said goodbye and went into the theatre in the direction Rebecca had indicated I'd find Jeffrey.

As promised, he was already there, a bottle of champagne on the floor between two seats and champagne flutes and bowls of popcorn on the small pull-out table in front of him. I looked around and was surprised at how many people had opted to sit and watch a movie on a sunny afternoon. However, given the excessive heat, the air-conditioned theatre was probably a relief. As I settled myself in, I noticed the backs of two familiar heads four rows in front and just to the right of where Jeffrey and I were sitting.

"I see you've spotted them," Jeffrey said, following my gaze. Just then, the lights began dimming. The movie was starting. "We do need to chat about this, Claire. It's too amusing a story to ignore."

Amusing? I had no idea what story he was referring to.

NINE

Eliza

En route to Recife, Brazil

AS I SAT IN THE SHIP'S DARKENED theatre that afternoon with Peter by my side, I started to ruminate about the text I'd received from Jake the evening before. I'd managed to push it out of my mind all day as I toured the city of Salvador, Brazil, with Peter. Now, in the dark, it floated to the top of my consciousness again.

`Please don't do this. Please let's talk about this more. You have been the centre of my universe for so much of my life. Remember that fateful month we met?`

First, the centre of his universe? The Jacob Cohen I knew (and probably loved at one time) would never say such a thing. Was he getting someone to write his texts for him? I sincerely hoped not.

Then, he referred to the fact that we'd met in New York the week before the 9/11 attacks. In more recent years, I'd wondered if that tragedy didn't provide us with an illusory sense that we were closer than we really were. Didn't tragedies tend to do that? Remember all those World War II love stories where they fell in love amid the chaos all around? It felt a bit like that. The text continued.

Don't forget all the good times, Eliza. We used to be good for each other. I know we can be again. We need to talk.

Were Jake and I good for each other? Was there a time when that was how I viewed our relationship? Was I the one who had changed as we drifted apart? I've always believed that it takes two people to make a marriage work and two people to make it fall apart. I was willing to accept that I had probably changed over the years, becoming less and less enamoured with his attachment to his family and other people and things. I had also become increasingly alarmed by the business practices involved in Bluestone Pharma, the generic drug company his family owned. When the business's legal counsel determines that certain personal assets would be best protected if transferred to uninvolved spouses, you know there is something not quite right about whatever is going on. There were so many times I'd buried my head in the sand, and now I wondered if I'd made a mistake. In the end, though, it was Jake who drove the final stake through the heart of our marriage by his behaviour, namely his affair with his secretary or assistant or whatever it was they called her these days. That spoke volumes to me. I had to admit, though, that there had been good times. And now we shared a granddaughter. I sat there, hoping the movie would distract me.

The movie was an oddball one. According to Peter, who had done a bit of recognizance, the film, released in 1976, was based on an earlier novel. In the years since then, it had evidently become one of the most iconic Brazilian films of all time. It was set in 1940s Salvador, the city we'd just visited. The first thing I noticed as I sat in the dark watching a movie when I should probably have been outside in the sun was that I realized we'd walked through some of the squares where this fifty-year-old movie had been filmed. The places looked astonishingly similar to what we'd seen today. Little seemed to have changed over the decades. We could have been walking through the movie's set. But it was the story. The story was the thing.

The film's main character, Dona Flor, a breathtaking Brazilian beauty who happened to run a cooking school, was married to a philandering, irresponsible *bon vivant* (dear god, this was feeling familiar), whose main attraction for Flor was that he was an astounding lover, especially for a girl who had been sheltered by respectability her whole life. Their mutual lust was a new feeling for her. When Vadinho, the negligent husband, dies unexpectedly while partying without her, she is the only one who mourns his death. She remarries a man who is the complete opposite of Vadinho, a dull but very respectable, responsible pharmacist who is most assuredly not a great lover. The hilarity mounts when the now-dead Vadinho reappears, a nude ghost of sorts, in a scene where the new husband is trying to make love to Flor. He then tags along with them everywhere they go and during everything they do. Flor is the only one who can see her dead, nude husband whose love-making skill she sorely misses.

I wasn't sure what to make of the whole thing. Then my monkey mind kicked in, and I wondered, *Is Peter respectable but dull? Is he the unexciting lover?* Geezus, I hoped not. I swatted the thoughts away as quickly as they had arisen and took a deep breath as the lights came up.

"Well," Peter said, smiling, "that was interesting. You and Flor have a lot in common."

I was momentarily startled, wondering how he could have read my mind.

"You both teach cooking and then there's the husband thing." His eyes danced with teasing mischief.

"I suppose you want me to tell you that Jake was the madly passionate lover."

Peter shrugged amiably. "I hope not. That might make me the respectable but dull health professional."

So, he *was* considering himself to be a potential lover. I hadn't put him off yet. Things were looking up. At least things were looking up until we turned, and there, four rows behind us, were that odious Claire person and that strangely compelling young man, Jeffrey. Jeffrey caught my eye and nodded while Claire seemed to be deliberately ignoring us. I still wanted to know how she managed to find herself on the same ship at the same time as Peter—and me.

~

After another night of luxuriating in the king-sized bed—alone—I opened the drapes to discover that we were already docked in Recife, Brazil, up the coast from Salvador. Peter had asked me to meet him at the gangway at nine a.m. (he acted very secretive when I asked him where we would be going). So I showered, sprayed on my bug spray, had breakfast in the dining room and arrived just on time. Peter, who was already there, standing at the open door to the gangway, told me he had a surprise planned. He led me out onto the pier to a waiting taxi. Standing beside the cab was a guide who said his name was Manuel Pinheiro.

Manuel shook my hand vigorously and told me how happy he was to meet us, and then he said he was delighted to show us *his* corner of Recife, whatever that meant. As we pulled out into city traffic, Manuel began to tell us about his city, which he was proud to call the Venice of Brazil.

"You see, we are at the meeting of the Capibaribe and Beberibe rivers, and we have these many bridges and what you might say are little islands." He then spoke quickly in Portuguese to the driver, and we swung onto a street away from the water, eventually coming to a stop in front of a yellow colonial-style stucco building with multiple archways filled in with red doors. The sign on it said, "Sinogoga Kahal Zur Israel." Of all the things I might have expected to see in a country settled by Portuguese Catholics, a synagogue was not one of them.

Manuel led us from the taxi and into this historic building, which had astonishingly been established by Brazil's first Jewish immigrants in 1636. It was now a museum. While we were visiting the museum, I was thinking about my meeting with Alex Ribeiro in São Paulo and how odd I thought his idea of a Brazilian Jewish cookbook had been when Manuel suddenly said, "And now for food."

What? It turned out that Peter had managed to find a guide who was going to take us to his mother's apartment for a Brazilian Jewish cooking lesson. I was all in.

Manuel's mother lived in a surprisingly modern grey stone apartment building fronted by a forbidding-looking gated entrance. Judging from what I'd seen in Brazil so far, this was the norm rather than the exception. Every building seemed to have a security surround that would rival Fort Knox. We took the elevator to the fourth floor of the eight-story building, and Manuel opened the door to a very modern apartment. I suppose I thought an apartment in Brazil might be a bit more—well, a bit more Brazilian, whatever that was in my imagination. In any event, Dona Maria, his mother, was a tall, dark-haired woman in her late sixties who, I could tell, had been a great beauty in her day. She reminded me of what an older version of Dona Flor from yesterday's movie might look like as she aged.

Dona Maria led us to her sparklingly modern kitchen with its quartz countertops, gas range and cream-coloured cupboards. She had already set out the ingredients for several recipes she wanted us to make with her. Then we would eat.

First up was something called Almoronia, which consisted of layers of chicken, onions and eggplant seasoned with nutmeg, cinnamon and a touch of honey. Despite our obvious language difficulties (Dona Maria spoke no English, and I did not know a scintilla of Brazilian Portuguese), we managed. At the same time, Peter and Manuel drank the caipirinha's that Manuel taught Peter to make.

Once we had that in the oven, she turned her attention to something called Dafina, a slow-cooked stew, which, according to Manuel, they had almost every Friday for Shabbat dinner. Of course, because it would have to be cooked a long time, I was disappointed that I wouldn't be able to taste it, but Dona Maria came to the rescue. She had made one the day before for just such an occurrence. I was ecstatic.

I had come across Dafina in my research for Jewish foods for a previous cookbook and knew it originated with Moroccan Jews. I was surprised when Manuel told us that there had been a small influx of Jewish immigrants to Brazil from Spain and Morocco in the nineteenth century, so this became a staple dish. It was basically a stewed beef roast with sweet potatoes, chickpeas, and barley, seasoned with turmeric, cumin and cinnamon. Before very long, I had my notebook out (I never travelled without it, even on a day trip) and was making copious notes. I hadn't even come close to finishing my current cookbook (which I should have been at home in my office working on at this very moment) on Newfoundland food, but this might very well be the next one.

By the time we left Dona Maria's apartment (I was still wondering how a Jewish mother could have ended up with the name Maria, although I did have a tiny Jewish granddaughter named Mary-Catherine), I didn't think I'd be able to eat again for a week. However, when we arrived back onboard the ship, and Peter asked me to join him for pre-dinner cocktails, I could only wonder if we might continue our conversation from earlier. You know. It was the one where he intimated that he didn't want to be the dull, respectable man. That one.

TEN

Claire

EN ROUTE TO THE MOUTH OF THE AMAZON RIVER

I DIDN'T BOTHER GOING ASHORE in Recife. From what I could tell, it was more of the same as we had seen the day before in Salvador—cobblestones and churches mainly. Besides, I had other priorities. I wasn't on board this floating hotel for a holiday. I was on a mission, so I planned to spend the day at the spa or, to be more precise, the spa and vitality centre, according to the staff.

I wonder why more people don't realize that on a day when the ship is in port, the spa is heavenly. There are few guests and lots of staff to pamper you, catering to your every whim—for a price, of course.

When I arrived in the spa lobby, I was immediately struck by the calmness it exuded. It would have been difficult to feel stressed there among the myriad scented candles, the soft blue of the upholstered furniture and the softly glowing bamboo lanterns (of course, all the candles were of the battery-operated variety).

I booked myself for something called "aroma stone therapy" to begin my day at the spa. The brochure said it used Balinese stones (presumably, there is something magical about stones from Bali; I had no idea) that are bathed in body oil and worked deep into the muscles. Of course, as a surgeon, my idea of something deep in muscles did not resemble in the slightest anything remotely relaxing, but I suppose we see things through our own lens. I just had to trust that they knew their business as well as I knew mine. The brochure promised "sparkling vitality" as the result.

I have to admit that I was feeling pretty mellow when the therapist finished rubbing the large, smooth, oily stones all over my back, legs and feet. I slid off the table and into my robe before heading for my facial appointment. I would take a shower later after the oil had a chance to do its work on my skin. I felt like a slime creature slithering out from the primordial ooze, but I did as they suggested.

Facials were something far more familiar. I was a proponent of regular facials for women my age and had a standing appointment at one of our local spas. I may have lived in a very small city by world standards, but we didn't lack anything in the realm of health and beauty.

As I lay there with my eyes covered with sweet-smelling cold compresses and the facialist massaged my shoulders with lavender-scented cream, my mind started considering the movie Jeffrey and I had watched the day before.

By any standard, it was an odd movie for me. To be truthful, though, I wasn't much of a movie fan at the best of times. When it was over, Jeffrey leaned over to me and asked, "Are you Dona Flor?"

I had no idea what he was trying to say. Did he think that Peter was the roguish, super-lover sex god that Dona Flor's first husband was supposed to be? I hoped Jeffrey didn't think that I thought he was the dull, respectable second husband. First, there was nothing even marginally dull or respectable about Jeffrey. Second, and even more to the point, was that Jeffrey being my or anyone's husband was too funny even to consider.

I remembered what he'd said about remarriage being the triumph of hope over logic and remembered that Oscar Wilde had once written that "marriage is the triumph of imagination over intelligence. Second marriage is the triumph of hope over experience." I had to agree, although in my view, re-marrying your first husband didn't count. I might not believe in getting redoes in life, but I did believe in second chances.

After my facial, I had a hydrotherapy session, a manicure and finally a pedicure. By the time I strolled dreamily back to my suite, I needed to lie down for a few moments before getting ready to have dinner with Jeffrey. He'd been invited to dine with the cruise director and several of the ship's officers and possibly even the captain and he had asked me to be his plus-one. Things were going very well. First, though, we were meeting in the bar for a pre-dinner drink.

~

"Wow," Jeffrey said, standing to greet me when I arrived in the bar later, "you slayed the memo this evening, didn't you?"

Who said things like "slayed" these days? Then I remembered. It was a favourite expression of the so-called millennials. Dear god, how young was he? Anyway, he was right. I did slay (not sure if that needed an object; did I have to slay something in particular, or could I just slay? Whatever.). I looked around at all the grey and silver hair and the floral chiffon things wafting in the air-conditioned breeze. I realized I was hotter than ever in my black Dolce and Gabbana sheath dress that I'd added to my wardrobe on a recent trip to lecture in Chicago. With a sudden jolt of apprehension, I realized I might have looked as if I were channelling a New Yorker. I shuddered a bit.

The server brought me a perfectly stirred Vesper martini—gin, vodka, and I could tell he'd used a touch of Cocci Americano instead of Lillet Blanc. I was delighted since I was a bit of a martini snob. Of course, the very best bartenders (and their customers) these days prefer Cocchi Americano over traditional modern lillet because it more closely resembles the original flavour profile that James Bond's creator, Ian Fleming, would have encountered when he invented the cocktail. In case you don't know, the original recipe, featured in *Casino Royale* in 1953, called for "Kina Lillet," a French aperitif wine with quinine, giving it a subtle bitterness alongside its sweetness. Unfortunately, the lillet of the twenty-first century isn't the same. Modern Lillet Blanc lacks the pronounced quinine bitterness that characterized Kina Lillet, making it milder and less complex. Cocchi Americano contains quinine and has a closer flavour profile to the original Kina Lillet. I prefer to think I'm sharing an experience with James Bond. I savoured another sip while Jeffrey stared at me.

"Claire, let's get down to it, shall we? Why are you *really* on this cruise?" Jeffrey said as a first and unexpected volley.

I sipped my Vesper thoughtfully for a moment, then said, "Why? I suppose I'm here to get a much-needed vacation."

Jeffrey raised his eyebrows.

"Why am I getting the impression that you don't believe me? You're here to give presentations and I'm here to luxuriate in all this floating hotel has to offer while at the same time enriching my understanding of the larger world."

Jeffrey snorted. "How long did it take you to memorize that one?"

I was insulted. "I have no idea what's gotten into you."

"Oh, don't worry, Claire, I'm not going to ruin your plans or out you, but I do think you should come clean with me. When I mentioned that it was more than a coincidence that you should run into your ex-husband on this trip, you were adamant that it was that and nothing more. As you may have figured out, I don't believe in coincidences, and you know what Shakespeare said. 'Me thinks thou dost protest too much.' You are protesting way too much. If I have this figured out correctly, the only synchronicity about this is me. I'm the meaningful coincidence that you're going to exploit."

"Now, Jeffrey, just a minute," I said.

He waved his hand as if swiping away my response. "The way I see it is that you, Dr. Claire Barrett, are here to figure out a way to get your ex back. And now that I'm here, I make a terrific foil for him. I'm young, accomplished, and far better looking than your ex, even if I must say so myself, and I have the great distinction of being your former lover." He narrowed his eyes and peered at me. "It's still former, isn't it?"

I sat back, draining my first martini while Jeffrey waved to the server for another round. "I don't know what makes you think that you have this all figured out."

"I may be a celebrity now, but you seem to forget that I'm first and foremost a psychiatrist. I'm trained to figure people out."

"First and foremost? I thought you were, first and foremost, a television personality."

"And a TikTok influencer. Don't forget my two million followers on TikTok."

Dear god, he *was* a millennial—and massively more of an egotist than I remembered.

"You know, Claire, I might be able to help you."

I hope so. Dear god, I hope so, I thought.

~

Rebecca Bebbington-Hughes was standing in the centre of the dining room beside a long table that was glittering under the massive crystal chandelier. She was chatting with the Greek man I recognized as the chief sommelier. They were pointing to various pieces of stemmed glasses that were set by each place. As Jeffrey and I neared the table, Rebecca saw us and immediately waved us over.

"Dr. Montgomery," she said to Jeffrey, "welcome! We're destined to have a brilliant time this evening." Then she turned to me. "Dr. Barrett—Claire—I'm delighted you're joining us as well. Please," she said, gesturing to two places across the table, "have a seat, and the sommelier will pour the champagne while we await the rest of our jolly group." She actually clapped her hands. "It's going to be a massively terrific evening." Then she turned her attention to two of the ship's officers who were heading in our direction. I recognized one of them as the ship's doctor. I presumed they were joining us, but they stopped to chat with Rebecca and two other guests who had just arrived.

I followed Jeffrey around to the other side of the table, where we peered at the engraved place cards indicating where we were to sit. No sooner had I begun to pull out my chair when a white-gloved waiter rushed to help me. Jeffrey settled himself beside me and thanked the sommelier for the champagne before looking around at the rest of the places.

"Well, isn't that great," he said, apropos of nothing that I could see. He then lifted the place card from the table in front of the seat next to him.

I peered at the letters, which very clearly said, "Ms. Eliza Cohen." Could I not get rid of this woman for even one evening? Suddenly, I had a thought. If Eliza's place was next to Jeffrey, Peter, who no doubt was accompanying her, would likely be on her other side. I would simply move the place cards so that Peter would be sitting beside me. I started to ask Jeffrey to help me with the bit of rearrangement when I was interrupted by Rebecca.

"I believe you all know each other," she was saying as I looked up.

There, standing across the table from me were Peter and Eliza. Eliza was, as I should have expected, attired in head-to-toe black. Was that a jumpsuit? Dear god, did she think she was Stevie Nicks? She looked like an aging rock star who was trying too hard. And that brooch. Who wears brooches? I should have wished that I'd decided against wearing black, but I realized that I looked better than she did, and that made me, if not happy, then at least smug. Rebecca was pointing to their appointed seats. So, it seemed that Jeffrey would be spending the evening chatting to Eliza, and I would be stuck with—I looked at the place card next to me—the ship's doctor. Would the hilarity never end?

~

Dr. Antonio Ricci, the ship's doctor, was a slickly charming Italian with what I could only describe as a lascivious nature. I based this on my observation of the way he looked at the women who passed by him. I might even call it leering. Just before the captain arrived (I hadn't been sure he'd be joining us), Dr. Ricci walked around the table, kissing the hands of every woman already seated, and then sat down beside me. He grabbed hold of my hand, kissed it and then sat there holding it while telling me how utterly delighted he was to meet me. He then peered at my place card that very specifically (and correctly this time) said I was "*Dr.* Claire Barrett."

"What is this?" he said with what sounded like mock concern. "How is it possible that *la donna più bella,* the most beautiful woman I am privileged to dine with, should be a doctor? How is it possible that one person can be endowed with both great beauty and great intelligence? This dinner promises to be a far more exhilarating experience this evening than the many captains' tables at which I have dined over the years."

Even I was starting to gag, and I loved nothing more than being praised for both of these features. Sure, I'm a bit vain, but then, when you have that incredible combination as I do, how can you not be? I was considering my options when I noticed Rebecca staring daggers at me from her seat, which she had taken near where I now realized the captain would be sitting when he arrived. As it turned out, this was the proverbial "Captain's Table."

The table itself was long and wide, thus effectively preventing much conversation other than with those seated on either side, so I didn't expect that she would verbalize her annoyance with me any time soon. I remembered seeing Rebecca with Tony (he asked me to call him Tony, and I told him to call me Claire) in a tight tête-à-tête a few days earlier. I was willing to risk her possible jealousy because as I sat there feeling the dry warmth of his hand as it almost imperceptibly caressed my palm, an idea began forming. Perhaps spending the evening chatting with Dr. Antonio (Tony) Ricci wouldn't be as annoying as I thought it might be.

ELEVEN

Eliza

EN ROUTE TO THE MOUTH OF THE AMAZON RIVER

THE INVITATION TO DINE with the captain indicated that I could bring a plus-one. Of course, that would be Peter, as Rebecca had demanded. The problem I had when I arrived back in my suite after meeting Dona Flor on the silver screen was that I had so many food-related notes I wanted to organize that I almost forgot I'd have to decide what to wear.

The dress code for the evening was formal. I had no problem with the concept of formal. After all, I had attended more than a few tedious formal galas in New York in support of one or the other of Jake's business and charitable endeavours over the years. (Make no mistake, though. Jake and his family's charitable endeavours were all in support of their business endeavours. There is no more charitable individual than a wealthy person with a business that can benefit from the adulation it will receive for being so charitable.) Yes, I had much formal experience and I had brought along two formal outfits for this trip after reading their online brochure indicating that people who typically travel on this cruise line dress according to the mandated dress code. I just wondered how formal dress would be interpreted by a group of passengers who hailed from such widespread places as England, Canada, Australia, France, Japan and, of course, the

U.S.A. And I not only had that dilemma, but I was even more concerned that I look beyond terrific this evening.

I put away my research notes and concentrated on dressing. I finally decided that black was always appropriate, even if we were in Brazil. I'd noticed that Brazilian women embraced bright, lively colours that were obviously inspired by their tropical flora and fauna. I probably should have embraced something a bit outside my New York comfort zone and gone with yellow, blue, or even red, but I knew I looked good in black. So, I dressed in my flowy black jumpsuit, accessorized with jewelled shoes and handbag, and a brooch the size of Rhode Island on my left shoulder. It was a giant Swarovski crystal ladybug. I concluded that its tiny orange crystals gave me that pop of colour the outfit needed. I was ready.

I went down a few decks to Martinis bar to meet Peter as planned before dinner. As I stood in the entrance, letting my eyes become acclimatized to the dim light, I saw two familiar heads leaning together at a table on the far right by a window. I rolled my eyes. *Those two again*, I thought.

Claire and Jeffrey were deep in conversation and didn't notice me. I hoped that Peter had steered clear of them, given the possibility that we might not be able to avoid them at dinner. Just then, I saw a wonderfully handsome man attired in what appeared from this distance to be a midnight blue tuxedo standing beside a table far to the left of the large room that had the benefit of pillars hiding one part from another. He was waving me over. Peter looked wonderful, and for a moment, I wondered how many formal events he attended in Newfoundland. I felt a frisson of excitement as I made my way across the room between tables of highly energized, formally clad drinkers in conversational clutches.

When I arrived, he gathered me into a bear hug. "You look utterly amazing, Eliza. By far the most beautiful woman on this ship."

As flattered as I was, I couldn't stop myself from saying, "Don't let Claire hear you say that."

He stepped back. "Why the hell not? It's true, and I don't give a flying fig about what she thinks."

I smiled at his use of "flying fig," an expression my father used to use. I suppose it went with the territory. They had both grown up on the island of Newfoundland. I would have said I didn't give a fuck, but that's just the New Yorker in me. In any case, I hoped I hadn't set the evening off on the wrong foot by invoking Claire's name.

We sat at a small, dark table in the corner where we could see but not be seen very easily and ordered drinks. The possible awkwardness of my remark seemed to have been forgotten.

"So," I said, "have you ever dined with the captain of a cruise ship before?"

He said he had not. I told him the story about the one time Jake and I had been invited to the captain's table on one of our few cruises. It had been in the Mediterranean, and the weather hadn't been ideal. The boat rocked and dipped the entire day before the scheduled dinner, so much so that the dining rooms were all empty at lunch—everyone was holed up in their staterooms, no doubt with their heads hanging over toilet bowls. I'd always thought of seasickness as a slow-motion rollercoaster, taking you slowly up one side of the track to the pinnacle where all you can see is that drop below before it begins, gathering speed as you can no longer stop yourself from hurling. Yes, that's how everyone felt that day. Since Jake and I were seasoned sailors who rarely got seasick, we were among those who had spent most of the day feeling only slightly off. As the evening approached, however, we were feeling less and less self-righteous. We decided to attend anyway, hoping it would be an early evening.

There we were, all ten or so of us, dressed in our finest formal wear, faces sporting assorted tones of green as we sat quietly awaiting the captain's arrival. The whispered news from those who had been at these before was that the captain generally arrived just before service began, drank nothing and left before dessert. We could do this.

The captain, whose name completely escapes me, arrived as expected just before the dinner service began but insisted on walking around the table to greet everyone personally. He then sat down and ordered his complete dinner—including dessert and wine. I hoped the first officer (or the duty captain) was up to the task at hand because before the dinner was over, the captain had consumed most of a bottle of wine and a glass of cognac and had savoured every morsel of every one of the four courses set before him. We, on the other hand, like the rest of our fellow diners, ordered plain grilled chicken with rice and spent the evening moving it and a few lettuce leaves around our plates. When the captain finally wiped his mouth with his massive linen napkin and arose, saying he was sad, but he must go, we all rose at the same time. The minute his heels cleared the dining room door, we all bid our table mates good night and rushed off to our respective staterooms to lie down—presumably after a little puke.

"So, you can see why I'm hoping this evening will be different," I said as I finished my tale.

By this time, Peter was laughing uproariously. Then, without warning, a cloud seemed to move across the sunshine of his laughter.

"I suppose that dreadful Jeffrey will be at the table this evening, won't he?" he said.

I said I expected he would since it seemed to be yet another event for us "special guests."

"The table will probably be long, and likely it won't be possible to engage with anyone who isn't sitting right beside you, so we should be fine," I said, grasping as I said this that the hellish possibility of sitting beside them did loom.

"What are the odds?" he said, sipping his drink.

What odds, indeed?

~

Our cruise director, Rebecca, was standing in the middle of the dining room, waving us over as we arrived half an hour later. A tuxedo-clad, white-gloved server offered me his arm, and Peter followed behind as we were led to the huge, rectangular table in the middle of the dining room. This anachronistic ritual of the woman being led by a server and the man following behind seemed especially pretentious in these surroundings, where everything is an overblown pomposity. It felt a bit odd, but I played along. As we approached the table, I stiffened so much so that the server glanced at me in alarm. I shook my head gently and continued our approach. Of course, I'd spied Claire and Jeffrey already ensconced at the table.

"I believe you know each other," Rebecca was saying as she directed the server around to that side where it appeared we were, indeed, sitting with none other than the famous Dr. Jeffrey P. Montgomery and his sidekick, Claire. At least he said he was famous. How would I know? Pop psychology or whatever it was they called his claim to fame these days was so not my thing. And yet, here I was, imprisoned beside him for the foreseeable future, or at least the evening. At least I didn't have to sit beside Claire, and neither did Peter, who was on my other side.

Just then, the ship's doctor arrived and took his seat beside Claire. He was followed by an older couple who sat directly opposite us. The large man, clad in a white dinner jacket that was pulled tightly across his rather ample mid-section, leaned across the wide table and then stretched out his hand.

"It's a pleasure to meet y'all this evening," he boomed as his portly wife, wearing peach-coloured sequins and chiffon, looked at the lot of us stiffly and nodded as she sat down opposite me. "Name's Randall Parker, and this here's the little woman, Dixie. But you can call me Randy."

Little woman? Who in god's name said things like that in the twenty-first century? All I could think about was that if he moved the conversation toward making America great again, I'd have to leave. Really. This evening was certainly turning out to be more colourful than I had expected. Perhaps even a bit too colourful. It suddenly occurred to me that dinner conversation with Dr. Jeffrey P. Montgomery might be the lesser of two evils.

The captain arrived, as expected, just before the dinner service began. We had all chosen our four-course dinners in advance, so the service was seamless and required no one to spend any time puzzling over the extensive menu. I had decided to start with oysters Rockefeller, followed by lobster bisque, and then Moqueca (Brazilian fish stew that I was dying to sample). For dessert, I had carefully chosen the Brazilian dessert they were offering. I wanted to avoid the usual cruise line suspects of carrot cake, the ubiquitous cheesecake and the peculiarly popular flourless chocolate cake. I had never figured out why such a thing was popular since, on every occasion that

I'd tried it, the cake had tasted like sawdust. I was having Quindim. I had seen photos of it when I'd done some Brazilian food research and saw pictures of a bright yellow donut-shaped cake with a glossy surface that was supposed to have a coconut flavour—coconut, sugar, butter and egg yolks were among its ingredients, so I knew I couldn't go wrong. At least the food would be memorable, even if the company were not. I hadn't bargained on a charm offensive from the young Jeffrey.

"You are quite an impressive woman, Eliza Cohen," Jeffrey said as I sipped my champagne after downing my first oyster. I actually preferred plain oysters that I could season with a bit of lemon juice and let slide down my throat, followed by champagne. Oysters Rockefeller were, in my opinion, a dish created primarily for people who couldn't stomach the unadulterated truth of an oyster. Perhaps it was a metaphor for the unadulterated truth of our lives. *Oh, dear, I'm waxing philosophical*, I thought. *Not at all like me.*

I was so surprised by Jeffrey's implication that he knew anything about me at all that I almost choked on my champagne. I cleared my throat and dabbed my lips with my napkin, trying carefully to avoid transferring lipstick to it in the process. "And what precisely impresses you about me, Dr. Montgomery?"

"It's Jeffrey, Eliza. If you must know, I'm a bit of an amateur cook myself, and I love nothing more than a great cookbook."

Why did I get the feeling that he might be exaggerating just a bit? But I was willing to play along.

"So, then, Jeffrey, you're familiar with my cookbooks?"

"As a matter of fact, I am," he said. Then, he began to drop the names of one after the other of my recipes.

I listened for a few moments, basking in the adulation that was clearly intended when I began to notice a pattern. Most of what he mentioned was contained in the samples of my books that were for sale in the online bookstores. So, I asked him if he liked a specific recipe that I knew was in the middle of my most recent book.

"Have you ever tried making my recipe for chocolate chip Babka?" This dessert was a favourite in our household. Both Izzy and Jake lunged for it every time I made it, although, in recent years, I'd been too busy to cook much of anything for my family and left it up to our housekeeper, Marina, who was a terrific cook herself. I was particularly proud of this Babka because it was a bit of a twist on a cherished traditional Jewish dessert recipe.

"Oh my god," Jeffrey said, "how did you know it was one of my favourites? I'm an expert at the yeast bread stuff. I find it so relaxing to spend a Sunday afternoon getting my hands into a dough, kneading and stroking."

I was staring at his hands as he kneaded and stroked, and all I could think about was what kind of lover he must be. I had to swat away that thought. Why in the world would I be thinking about sex in relation to a man who was probably young enough to be my son or at least my younger brother while I was aboard a cruise ship with an extraordinary, accomplished man my own age? Perhaps it was because Peter and I were still on friendly (very friendly) but almost platonic terms. Anyway, I suddenly clocked in that Jeffrey was, indeed, talking about his kitchen prowess, and he was listing off other recipes of mine that he'd actually tried.

"Hey, Eliza," he said as I came back to the present moment. "I bet you thought I was pulling your leg when I said I was a fan." He laughed. "I can tell when someone is trying to trip me up. I deliberately mentioned recipes you know I could get just by googling you. But I gotcha! The truth is that I really am a fan," he said. He whipped out his phone and swiped through a few photos. I tried to sneak a peek at them but only glimpsed what appeared to be photos of women or perhaps a single woman—a flash of a smile here and a whisper of a hat there. "Look at this," he said, holding out a photo of a kitchen. "See that shelf over there? It's my collection of cookbooks." He told me that it was his new house in Boston.

"You're not married?" Why did I say that? I didn't care if he was married, and the fact that I would even think that an unmarried man couldn't be the sole owner of a collection of cookbooks in an impressive cook's kitchen just put me into the category of the older woman who doesn't understand the new generation. It made me a dinosaur.

Jeffrey just laughed. "Guilty as charged. But I used to be—for a very short time. Not that she ever did much cooking."

I sipped my wine, and the server put my lobster bisque in front of me. I didn't say anything, hoping he'd simply continue. He was interrupted by the server, so that gave me a chance to break away from our conversation. I turned to see Peter's gazpacho just as it was being placed in front of him. I had noticed that Peter had been monopolized by a conversation with Randy across the table. It was hard not to notice since Randy was so loud, giving Americans (like I was, after all) a bad name. The only reason Peter could even hear him across the table was because of the sheer volume of his voice that seemed to carry through the dining room—I knew this because I saw occasional diners at other tables look over and shake their heads. Peter was too much of a polite Canadian to tell him to tone it down, but I might have to intervene if Randy had any more to drink.

"You okay, Peter?" I said, concerned he thought I might be spending too much time chatting up Jeffrey.

"Of course," he said, lifting his soup spoon. "I'm actually finding it mesmerizing that Randy isn't at all shy about telling us all about his thousands of acres of tobacco farms and his stake in several big tobacco companies."

"Have you mentioned that you're a physician?"

"No, and I don't think I'm going to. I bet you didn't think there was any more revolting kind of big business to be in than big pharma, did you?" Peter was, of course, referring to Bluestone Pharma, the mega generic drug company that Jake's family owned, as I mentioned. They always found themselves on the downside of the moral high ground in lawsuits that were becoming ever more frequent in recent years. Yes, I did tend to think that drug companies were moral bottom-feeders, but big tobacco? Was there a lower place on the moral mountain?

Peter smiled as he tasted his gazpacho. "Delicious. And you? How's old Jeffrey there?"

I told him that Jeffrey was something of a cooking fan. Peter laughed just as Randy boomed across the table. "You're one of those Canadian fellows, aren't you? Can tell by your manners. But really, y'all are just gagging to be Americans, aren't you?"

I thought I'd leave that one to Peter. After all, I was hardly a shining example of a Canadian happy to be just who she was.

"How's your dinner, Eliza?" Jeffrey said as I finished my bisque. I told him it was fine, and we proceeded to our main courses.

I chatted a bit with Peter on one side and then Jeffrey on the other. Randy, thankfully, didn't talk much while he was inhaling his massive steak and the largest baked potato I'd ever laid eyes on. Then, just before the server picked up our plates, Jeffrey leaned over toward me and said, "Do you believe in love, Eliza?'

Who the hell didn't believe in love?

TWELVE

Claire

APPROACHING THE MOUTH OF THE AMAZON RIVER

AS DINNER WITH THE CAPTAIN progressed, I tried, without much luck, to overhear Jeffrey's conversation with Eliza. I hoped that he was doing his job of making Eliza believe that he and I were in a hot and heavy relationship. She would then be bound to tell Peter. I hoped Peter might even be listening, but every time I tried to lean closer to Jeffrey to listen surreptitiously, I heard only snippets about cooking. Damn that Eliza and her cooking. She was monopolizing the conversation. And every time I thought I might be able to insert myself into their conversation, Tony inevitably pulled me back into his orbit. He was very persistent.

"*Mia cara Claire,* my dear Claire, you really must come to visit me in the ship's infirmary. I would very much like to show off my equipment to a fellow physician." Did he smirk just a bit and wiggle his eyebrows? Jesus, Mary and Joseph, as my mother used to say. His *equipment*?

I sighed and resigned myself to leaving Jeffrey to do his part while I capitalized on the opportunity that presented itself right here and now. I had a handsome (like Peter, only greasier) physician (like Peter, only less impressive) right here in front of me, practically begging for my attention. This situation would surely be at least enough to begin a little itch of jealousy in Peter, or so I hoped. I decided to go with the flow for once and see where that led.

Finally, the servers were bringing out dessert. I didn't usually eat dessert, but it seemed polite to at least remain at the table until dinner was over, and I could hardly leave without Jeffrey, who was still in some kind of deep conversation with Eliza. What could a young psychiatrist and television personality have in common with a middle-aged cookbook writer? I rolled my eyes at the very thought of the mundaneness of their conversation. I would have to debrief him later to determine how far he'd gotten in making Eliza believe we were mad about one another and if he had managed to ensure that Peter knew about it.

I had chosen the cheesecake, a safe choice in my view. I glanced over at Eliza's plate and noted that she was eating the Brazilian dessert that had seemed a bit much to me. Then I noticed that both Jeffrey and Peter, on either side of her, had made the same choice as Eliza. What was it about this woman?

"That looks interesting," I said in Jeffrey's general direction. He was so engrossed with Eliza that he didn't even acknowledge me for a moment. I picked up my fork and glanced at Tony's gelato.

Jeffrey then turned and looked at my cheesecake. "You know what Lemony Snicket said about cheesecake?" I wasn't even sure I knew who Lemony Snicket was. "He said, 'Some people think destiny is something you cannot escape, such as death or a curdled cheesecake, both of which always turn up sooner or later.' Destiny and curdled cheesecake. Such a great metaphor, don't you think?" At this point, he turned back toward Eliza, and he, Peter, and Eliza began discussing the finer points of Brazilian desserts.

I sighed and turned back to Tony but was interrupted by a voice booming from the opposite side of the table.

"Well, look there, little lady. A terrific looking piece of cheesecake." Was that overbearing, over-stuffed specimen of American excess actually referring to me? Little lady? He continued. "We all love a bit of the great American cheesecake in our neck of the woods, don't we, Dixie?"

Both he and Dixie looked like they'd seen more than one too many slices of cheesecake in their lives, a thought I considered voicing but thought better of it.

Eliza's head turned as she seemed to tune into the conversation—if you could call it that. She frowned. "Actually, Randy," she said, "I believe you're mistaken. The first cheesecake was created over four thousand years ago in ancient Greece. It's not American at all."

Randy looked stunned for a millisecond, then started to laugh out loud. "You had me there for a moment, little lady." Another little lady? "I know you're pulling my leg there."

Eliza sat up straight. "No, I'm not pulling your leg. And as a matter of fact, the very first English cookbook in the year 1390 included a recipe for cheesecake."

At least being a cookbook author provided you with some trivia that came in handy at a dinner party. I had to give her that.

"Well, there you have it then. American."

I saw Eliza actually roll her eyes. I must say I agreed with her here. Was this man as obtuse as he was corpulent?

"I hardly know where to begin," Eliza said. "English as in England or the fact that in 1390, the only people in the U.S.A. were the local indigenous tribes. They weren't writing cookbooks."

Randy looked nonplussed. I don't think he had the slightest idea what she was getting at. I stifled the laughter that was beginning to bubble up.

"Well, all I know is that this little lady here," he pointed to me, "is having cheesecake, and that's American enough for me."

I could stand it no longer. I jumped into the fray. "First, sir," I said, "I am not an American, thank you very much. I am a Canadian. Second, I am not a little lady. I am a doctor—a surgeon, to be more precise."

Was that a smile I saw erupting on Dixie's face? Was she enjoying this little exchange that made her husband seem like the buffoon of the year?

"Well, is that a fact? You're a doctor, are you? A surgeon, you say. I am impressed. I suppose they do let ladies into medical colleges these days, especially in the frozen wasteland of your country. I prefer my woman in the kitchen or the bedroom." He laughed. "Otherwise, they get so stuck up they're fixin' to drown in a rainstorm." He laughed at what I suppose he thought was a joke.

Eliza jumped into the conversation. "I might remind you of something Gloria Steinem once said, Randy. 'Men should think twice before making widowhood women's only path to power.'" Then she looked over at Dixie, who was laughing while holding a hand up in front of her face.

Randy just looked confused. I don't think he had the slightest idea who Gloria Steinem was. We all went back to our respective desserts.

Before the evening was over, I told Tony that I would love to visit the infirmary and see his equipment. We made a "date" for the following afternoon after Jeffrey's first presentation, which I planned to attend. I wasn't at all interested in whatever it was he had to say, but damned if I was going to let Peter see that. I'd have to suck it up and go. Tony was, in a word, ecstatic. Me, not so much, but one does what one must under challenging circumstances.

~

The following morning, Jeffrey texted me to say he'd look forward to seeing me later this afternoon in the audience at his first onboard presentation. I had no idea what he was doing in the morning, and I didn't really care. As we left the dining room the evening before, when I'd asked him about his conversation with Eliza, he had been oddly evasive. I asked him point-blank if he thought she (and Peter) were beginning to see that we were engaged in a mad affair. He shrugged and said nothing. I was furious. Then he'd said, "I guess if she falls for *me*, then you can have Peter all to yourself."

Jeffrey and Eliza? The thought made me feel slightly nauseated. I wasn't at all happy with the prickling sensation of something that I never thought I'd feel. Was that jealousy? I had a sensation that I didn't want Eliza to have Jeffrey—or Peter.

I was still thinking about his remark as I wandered into the specialty coffee shop called Baristas on deck fourteen, just off one of the sun decks where people were already lolling on lounge chairs, roasting themselves in the heat. I had to walk across the deck to access the coffee shop and had begun to sweat the moment I set foot outside the door. Did I mention the heat? As we neared the mouth of the Amazon, the sweltering heat of Rio seemed to be morphing into a sweat-soaked sauna. Would it get any worse? I guess I had yet to find out. In any case, I was in search of a latte.

As the automatic doors opened and drew me into the air-conditioned cool of the café, I breathed a sigh of contentment when I saw there was no line-up. As the smiling Filipino barista made my perfect latte (I knew it would be perfect because he'd made me one the day I boarded the ship), I selected a pastry to go with it. Yes, it was quite an indulgence, but this cruise wasn't all work. I chose a mille-feuille, which people sometimes call a Napoleon. I loved how the delicate layers of crisp, buttery puff pastry crackled as I bit in. Then, it would be a split second before the cream filling would ooze out. Vanilla and caramel were two of my favourite flavours, and together, they were dynamite on a plate.

I picked up my latte and my pastry and turned to find a vacant table. In the far corner, I saw a familiar head bent over what appeared to be a tablet, a steaming cup of coffee next to him. What was Peter doing here alone?

I almost hesitated and turned to find a table on the other side of the café. Peter had made his displeasure at seeing me on this cruise perfectly clear, and I hadn't prepared myself for an encounter this morning. It was too early in the game to expect the prickling of jealousy to have begun to bubble to the top of his consciousness. Any encounter at this point could go badly. Just then, he looked up.

"Claire. I see we've both been ditched this morning."

I smiled and still hesitated.

"Why don't you join me? I promise not to bite. We're both adults, and there was a time when we actually enjoyed each other's company. No need for recrimination at this stage of our lives." He was probably thinking that it would be rude to see me and pretend I wasn't there. Peter was polite like that, and he did have a point about the two of us and our past.

I did think that it would be foolish if two people who had shared two decades of their lives, not to mention two children, couldn't even have a coffee together. So, I placed my coffee and pastry on the table and sat opposite him.

"I see you still love those Napoleons," Peter said, smiling in that way I missed so much.

"Almost as much as Liam likes them," I said. Liam had developed his love of pastries from me despite my years of trying to avoid them. "Where's Eliza this morning? I thought you two were joined at the hip." I hoped I didn't sound as catty as I felt.

Peter laughed, but it was a bit hollower than I might have expected. "I'm surprised you don't know. She's with Jeffrey. Well, the two of them are at some kind of meeting for the entertainment staff. Funny to think of them as entertainers, but I suppose they are in this case."

My mind was racing. I had that monkey mind that I hated so much as I tried to catch a thought here or there. I had to make use of this encounter. Then, as suddenly as it started churning, my mind calmed itself down, and I was left with one set of thoughts. Be conciliatory and amenable. And if I could manage it, compassionate and even empathetic.

"You didn't happen to notice how well they seemed to be getting on last evening at dinner, did you?" Peter said as I took my first bite.

I almost choked. Was Peter jealous of Jeffrey? Jealous of Jeffrey's possible interest in Eliza rather than me? As odd as Jeffrey's behaviour the evening before had made me feel about him, my thoughts turned to annoyance that Peter might be feeling jealous of Eliza but *not* me. My first thought was that this was not going according to plan at all when I began to wonder if this situation could work to my advantage. Jealous men were not to be trifled with, as far as I was concerned. Perhaps it wouldn't matter where the jealousy began.

~

By the time I arrived in the theatre for Jeffrey's lecture, I found myself in the unexpected and annoying position of having to search for a seat. What in the world were all these people doing here? How could Jeffrey's lecture be this much of a draw for cruisers? Of course, it was another sea day, and they were looking for something to do, but I'd expected most of them to stay on deck, basking in the equatorial sun or sitting at a bar drinking the cocktail of the day (yes, there was a cocktail of the day, every day). So, I stepped over people who hogged the aisle seats and finally settled myself in a seat dead centre.

The theatre was at least planned well enough to afford even the worst seat in the house a good view of the stage. At any rate, that was true unless you were sitting behind a pillar of which there were at least six. I was wedged in between two rather large men, one of whom was fanning himself with the daily program and the other who was already asleep. The sleeping giant was listing ominously in my direction, snorting disgustingly, and I didn't relish the thought of his head falling on my shoulder. He looked like he would drool at any moment. I proceeded to try to place my purse under my chair, a move that required a lot of leaning and moving this way and that, resulting in the need to (inadvertently?) nudge my seat companion. He woke with a start and a rather loud snort. Of course, being the polite Canadian that I have always been, I apologized profusely. Sorry, not sorry, you know. Once I was finally convinced that I wouldn't be acting as a pillow for my next-door neighbour, I focused my attention on the stage.

The set-up was sparse. It consisted of a podium with a microphone stage left or right. I can never remember which is which, but it would be on Jeffrey's left as he looked out at his adoring fans. The rest of the stage was empty, except for a massive screen that took up all the space behind him as if he were about to embark on a TED talk. On the screen was what I supposed was the first slide of an inevitable PowerPoint presentation. On one half of the slide was a blow-up of the cover of Jeffrey's book that had greeted me when I first embarked.

The cover illustration was an image of undulating stripes in shades of light blue and grey, evoking the thought of waves. In the middle, three rocks balanced on one another. Over the rocks, in enormous letters, were the words "Creative Genius." These words were preceded by the word "I" in an equal-sized but different colour font. Between them, the words "am a" in letters so tiny you could hardly read them were wedged. It was clearly designed to give the impression of "I" being the genius. Clever, I suppose, if you like that kind of obvious imagery intended to hammer home a point to the seriously symbolically challenged.

The sub-title was "Creating Me." It occurred to me that the notion of "creating me" was more than a bit of a nod to 1990s narcissistic navel-gazing. I did, however, think that Jeffrey might be eminently qualified to wax poetic on how to create one's persona. He was, after all, very experienced. I mean, just look at that cover. What do you see first? Of course, you see "I" and "creative genius." Jeffrey certainly did consider himself to be a genius, and I knew this because he had told me in those and other words. He had actually referred to himself as a virtuoso, and later in our conversation at that infamous conference where we'd met, as a wizard. A wizard? I wondered how the publisher had gotten away with making Jeffrey's name so small on the cover. I hoped the presentation wouldn't be either too snooze-inducing or too cringe-worthy. After all, I still planned to be seen in public with him over the next couple of weeks or as long as it took to get Peter back into my bed. I knew that if I could get him back into my bed, he'd also be back in my life. There were a few things we'd always gotten right in our two decades together.

On the other half of the slide were two quotes.

"We must be willing to fail and to appreciate the truth that life is not a problem to be solved, but a mystery to be lived."
~ M. Scott Peck

"Life is terminal, but suffering is optional."
~ Jeffrey P. Montgomery

Good lord, I thought, *he's comparing himself to that bestselling pop psychiatrist who wrote that book The Road Less Travelled back in the 1970s. Is there no end to the conceit of this man?* If there was one human trait I despised, it was conceit. My belief has always been that people really do need to get a better grip on their limitations.

I looked at my watch and saw that it was five minutes past the scheduled start time, and there were still people coming in. Why couldn't people get to events on time? I sighed and then sat up straight as I saw Peter stand up at his seat a few rows from the front to let a latecomer in. Naturally, beside him was Eliza. I wondered how the rest of his day had been going after our conversation this morning in the café. That was the moment when the lights dimmed, and Rebecca walked onto the stage with a hand-held microphone.

"Good afternoon, one and all," she began. "If I have not yet had the pleasure of meeting you, I am Rebecca Bebbington-Hughes, and it is my great privilege to be your cruise director. I am beyond thrilled to have the pleasure of introducing our speaker for this afternoon. He came on board to be the featured speaker of a wonderful group we are delighted to be hosting on board during this cruise, The Zen and Tonic Connection."

There was a smattering of applause, presumably coming from the members of the group who couldn't get enough of Jeffrey. There was an equal level of what sounded suspiciously like snickering, presumably from those on board who found the whole idea of people being in a group with a name like Zen and Tonic to be a bit of a joke. Perhaps I wasn't as alone in my opinions as I thought.

"Now, ladies and gentlemen, at the end of the lecture, please stay in your seats. I will be drawing for signed copies of an exceptional book." She winked and nodded toward the photo on the slide as if we couldn't tell what she was talking about. "Without further ado, it is my extraordinary honour to welcome to our stage the world-renowned expert on transforming your life, Dr. Jeffrey P. Montgomery."

Dear god, I thought. *A tad over-blown. World-renowned?* Oh well, fame was fleeting. At least in the world where I was world-renowned, it would go on for generations.

I watched as Jeffrey walked onto the stage, demonstrating both humility and charismatic self-knowledge in equal measure. The applause was surprisingly deafening. He was good. He walked to the podium and immediately took off his suit jacket, which he handed to a minion waiting at the side (choreographed, of course). He rolled up his sleeves as if he were about to get to work. He was then ready to pick up the microphone from its stand on the podium and walk out in front, closer to his adoring fans. He peered out as if trying to make eye contact with as many people as he could, even if he probably couldn't see them in the spotlight. As they say, he had done this before.

"Do you believe in love?" he said.

And once again, I had to invoke the erudite Tina Tuner. What's love got to do with it?

THIRTEEN

Eliza

AT THE MOUTH OF THE AMAZON ON THE EQUATOR

THERE IT WAS AGAIN. Jeffrey's question to me. "Do you believe in love?" I had no idea that he would be talking about this in his lecture today. I thought he was a "personal transformation" guru. Anyway, I hadn't answered the question when he posed it to me because I was immediately offended that he would even have any reason to ask me. Of course, I believed in love. Isn't it a fundamental part of being human? Doesn't it provide emotional fulfilment? Aren't loveless people dry, empty shells? Yet, the question had hung in my mind, and despite my knee-jerk response of wondering who the hell *didn't* believe in love, I have to admit that it did make me stop and consider what it meant to be *in* love.

"Ladies and gentlemen, I am here today because I believe that love is the driving force behind creative personal transformation."

After my conversation with Jeffrey at dinner the night before, I would never have gotten the idea that this is where his thinking went. He seemed to be utterly concrete to me, and yet this. Love is the driving force behind personal transformation? What the hell was that all about? And yet …

"Let's begin at the beginning—before love. We can't talk about love yet. We have to get there. Let's begin with your life.

Is your life an illusion, or is what you're experiencing and calling life something real? Because we can't talk about love until we know the answer to that fundamental question."

I could hear murmurings all around, mainly on the side of reality as far as I could decipher. This type of presentation might have been a bit too deep for people on an Amazon cruise, but it was something to do on a hot afternoon.

"I can hear you. I know that most of you consider life to be something real. You might even believe the definition of reality is the way things actually are. But have you really considered that the way you believe things to be might very well be only the way you see them? Here's the thing. Life is a series of experiences. Agreed?" There was nodding. "Well, then, how can something that you experience in the moment only to live on in your inner self be anything but an illusion?

"What, you might ask, is an illusion? Is it a mirage? A fantasy? Or is it a deception? Is it a point of view? Experiences can't deceive. They can do nothing more than fill your memory with the only things that you will take to your death. You will not take your car, your money, your house, your family—only your memories. They will be all that is left to you. So, life is a series of experiences, and experiences are illusory. They're like shadows on a wall, cast by a flickering flame, holding their shape for only that split second of now. Then, the shadow can be rearranged or even wiped away by changing how your creative mind remembers it. So, we have to begin with the premise that your life is illusory. And if love is a part of those experiences, then it, too, is an illusion."

Dear god, love is an illusion? What had I been thinking all my life? Didn't I believe love to be something concrete? Something to be sought, cherished and given away? I suppose I had considered it to be a reality. But if Jeffrey was even close to being right (and I wasn't convinced), and love is only an illusion, then how can it be such an essential part of our lives? I wondered what Peter was thinking, but I have always considered it rude to chat during someone's lecture, so I decided we could debrief after this—whatever it was—was over.

Jeffrey continued. "Now that we've established that we live an illusion," more murmuring, "let's consider how often we fail to realize that our unconscious, another illusion, influences us. As I've encountered more and more people throughout my career, there is one thing I know to be true. Those among us who fail even to notice the extent to which our unconscious thoughts and feelings influence them are the ones *most* influenced by them. They are the ones who are the most likely to act in accordance with that which they fail to understand is a part of them."

Even I was getting confused now.

"So, now to love." He walked across the stage, catching people's eyes. "Being *in* love is a metaphor. It is not a reality. It suggests that we're using our physical spaces, the state of being *in* something, like a box, for example, to define something that is distinctly not physical. Of course, unless it is."

Jeffrey stopped and looked around at his audience as if trying to determine if they were still with him.

A hand shot up right in front of where Peter and I were sitting. "Dr. Montgomery, I must respectfully disagree with you on this. The English word 'in' has a variety of definitions. Just because one of them suggests physical 'inness,' for lack of a better term, does not convey metaphor. Now, if you were to say, 'Love is war,' then that would be a metaphor and perhaps one with which many people in this audience could identify." There was a smattering of laughter.

Just as the audience member questioning Jeffrey said, "Love is war," Jeffrey smiled as a series of slides flashed up behind him on the stage one after the other.

Love is war.
Love is a journey.
Love is madness.
Love is sex.
Love is a fragile flower.

Jeffrey smiled. "Of course but being *in* love is also a metaphor since you can't literally be *in* love like you can be *in* a car, or *in* a house, or *in* a choir. You are *in* the illusion." He turned and walked back to the centre of the stage and said, "You know there's an old Elvis Presley song that says love is a banana peel. It's something you slip on and fall." More laughter. "And, of course, Leonard Cohen said love is fire." He looked around. "If love is all these things, how can love just be love? It can't. Because there's no such thing. It's an illusory experience you can use to transform yourself."

I sat back, staring at Jeffrey up there on the stage, my mind racing. Did I just want that feeling of being in love again? What was it about love that I thought I was missing? I wondered if I was missing the part of love that is the quiet comfort of knowing that there was one person in the world who wanted to be with you no matter what. Or was it the breathless excitement of something new? Did I think I deserved a second chance? Then I thought about Claire and wondered (not for the first time) why she was *really* on this cruise. Maybe that's all she was looking for, too.

~

"He's a strange one, isn't he?" Peter said as we managed to detach ourselves from the crowd, which was now streaming out of the theatre.

My mind was still back there, thinking about being in love and the illusion of love and wondering what part of it was real.

"I wonder what Claire sees in him," Peter said.

I looked at Peter, who was shaking his head. "You mean other than the fact that he's younger, wildly successful and superbly good-looking?" Now, why did I say that?

Peter looked startled. "You think he's good-looking?"

"Well," I said, considering the situation, "he's probably a good fifteen years younger than we are, so that gives him a bit of a youthful advantage. And Claire likely loves the attention."

He stopped and looked at me. "What about you?"

"What about me?"

"You seemed to be basking in Jeffrey's attention last evening and likely this morning when you were together at that meeting. You're the same age as Claire, give or take a year or so. Are you loving the attention, too?"

I felt a touch of annoyance begin to creep up my neck. Was Peter jealous? We hadn't even managed to consummate our relationship yet (can you say that if you're not married?), and it looked like it was destined to stay that way at this rate. I decided to turn the tables.

"Peter, how do you really feel about seeing Claire on this cruise? Didn't you mention that the two of you had coffee together this morning?" Yes, what was that all about?

He shrugged. "We have a history."

"Jake and I have a history, too, but that doesn't mean I want to have coffee with him."

"Jake isn't here, Eliza."

Thankfully, that, at least, was true. I shuddered at the thought of Jake showing up unannounced as Claire had done. We continued walking in the general direction of my suite. Before we turned down into the corridor, Peter said, "I think I'll go up on deck for a bit of air before dinner."

Geez, I thought. *What air? We're in the Amazon basin. You can cut the humidity with a knife*. However, I decided now was not the time to voice my opinion about meteorological phenomena. He clearly wanted some time alone.

"See you later at dinner, then," I said as breezily as I could manage. I turned down the corridor and was swallowed up in the air-conditioned bliss.

When I got back to my suite, I flopped down on the sofa. I reached for my phone, as one does, and turned it back on. Despite the spotty Wi-Fi service on board, I saw that I had missed messages. They were all from Jake.

Miz-day-en, I thought. It was the only Yiddish word I'd ever heard my sister-in-law, Allegra, say. It was one of her favourites. Yes, fucker. She said it a lot.

~

By the time I noticed that it was time to get ready to meet Peter for dinner, I'd had a couple of hours to myself. Time alone always seems like such a good idea at the time, but when you come right down to it, all that solitude can be dangerous. I had time to consider all sorts of possible scenarios and all kinds of ways this cruise could end. And not all of them were pretty. I'd also had time to ruminate about Jake's texts. Perhaps more precisely, I'd had time to ruminate about Jake. What the hell was going on with him anyway?

The first text I'd missed was cryptic, to say the least.

Eliza darling. Can something change and still remain the same? The parts might not be what they were but the whole of it is what it was. Think about it. Please.

I read it three times and still had no idea what he was getting at. I'd never known Jake to think deeply about much of anything. No one would have ever said he was philosophical. If there wasn't a spreadsheet involved, he floundered. Change and yet remain the same? I had no idea. I had no more luck with the second one.

Where are you? I miss you so much. I had no idea what I'd be missing. I know I have to make a choice, or I'll starve to death. I can't have both.

I was about to give up. It was clear that Jake had been reading something, and I suspected that he had misinterpreted much of what he'd read. He was going to starve to death? Then, when I read the third one, the Jake I'd always known (and loved, it has to be said) reemerged.

What the hell? That Zimmerman woman just sent me a letter. No, there will not be a judge involved. No judge. No divorce. You and me. Together. J.

So, Abigail, my attorney, had finally touched base with him, or at least the long arm of the civil legal system had done so. I supposed my divorce was now inevitable, despite Jake's alarming suggestion that he and I should stay together. The thought made me sit back and think for a moment. This was what I wanted. Of course, it was. And now I was moving on. I had Peter in my life (at least, I thought I did), and I was reaching out into a sometimes terrifying, potentially exciting future. What more could I want? And yet, it made me feel sad.

I suppose anyone would feel a bit sad when their marriage comes to an end.

FOURTEEN

Claire

BOCA DE VALERIA, AMAZONIA, BRAZIL

ONE THING I HAD NOT EXPECTED to experience at Jeffrey's lecture was someone in the audience asking a question merely to prove his own intelligence. Oh, yes, that's what it was. When that man's hand shot up, and he told Jeffrey he had to "respectfully disagree," I knew it was for only one reason. He wanted to show everyone in the audience how smart he was. I know about these people because there was always one in every lecture I'd ever given. And when Jeffrey put him in his place by flashing those slides, I was proud of him. You always had to know just how to handle those people. Having said that, I wasn't sure I believed much of anything that emerged from Jeffrey's mouth, presumably having originated in his brain.

I remembered that Jeffrey and I had a brief discussion about love on the first day on board the ship after he asked me if I was still married. I had then asked him if he was currently married. He said he wasn't, and he'd never get married again. Of course, I then had to ask him if he'd ever been in love. He had said yes but then said he woke up one day, and it was gone. When I asked him if *it* was gone or *she* was gone, he changed the subject. At the time, I couldn't help but notice the wistful look that transformed his usually lively blue eyes into something akin to dark clouds. I hadn't given his response much thought at the time, but it was now crystal clear to me that someone must have broken his heart. I wondered what kind of woman could have had such an effect on the Jeffrey I knew. Perhaps he wasn't as much of a playboy as I'd thought. Now, though, it seemed his work (or at least his new book) was focused on that very thing. I was convinced that his experience had inspired it. I also wondered what the hell someone like him thought he had to offer others about love. His hubris was mildly amusing, though.

After the lecture, I didn't have much time to continue my reflection on Jeffrey P. Montgomery. I had more pressing matters to attend to, the first one being visiting Tony in the ship's infirmary. As I left the theatre, I felt a hand on my arm. I turned. It was Rebecca. *Oh-oh,* I thought. *Is she jealous of the attention I've been getting from Tony?* I had figured it would only be a matter of time before this green-eyed monster reared its ugly head.

"Dr. Barrett," Rebecca began oh-so formally, "may I have a word?"

Given I could feel her fingers pressing into my arm, I decided I didn't have much choice but to have that word with her. I'd thought, perhaps, that since I was a guest, she might just back off. That no longer seemed a likely scenario.

We moved away from the crowd that was spilling out the doors and along a corridor leading past the ship's boutiques.

"Please excuse my forthrightness, Dr. Barrett, but I do believe we have a situation that bears discussing." She pronounced every syllable of "situation" very carefully.

I was all ears but decided to say nothing yet.

"It is not without some trepidation that I approach you on this subject, but needs must," she said.

I had never understood the expression "needs must" that the Brits are so fond of, but I was beginning to get a sense of it.

"It is of a delicate nature."

I had never considered jealousy to be delicate at all. I had always thought of jealousy as more like a heavy chain, weighing you down, or perhaps even a gnawing worm, but never anything delicate. Still, I suppose the nature of her reaction might well be delicate, given that she was a cruise line employee, Tony was a cruise line employee, and I was a guest—a guest in a large, expensive suite, I might add.

"You see, Dr. Barrett, it has not gone unnoticed that Dr. Ricci is lavishing attention on you."

Not unnoticed by whom, I wondered? I suspected only by Rebecca. "Rebecca," I said, "you seem like a lovely woman who is good at her job. I believe Dr. Ricci and I may have overlapping professional connections. In fact, it occurs to me that as an employee, you might consider your own relationship with him. I'm sure the cruise line has some kinds of rules around fraternization between employees."

At first, she frowned as if considering the meaning of my words. Then I saw what appeared to be a lightbulb go off in her head, and she smiled. "Dear god, Dr. Barrett—Claire—we do seem to be at sixes and sevens on this."

"Sixes and sevens?"

"Sorry, a very British expression Americans don't have in their vernacular."

I huffed a bit at that. "As you are aware, I am not an American. I am a Canadian, which is decidedly not the same thing."

"Oh, of course, Claire, I apologize profusely. However, I don't think it's in the Canadian vocabulary either." Her smile faded. "We do need to get back to the matter at hand."

"Yes, the matter at hand," I said, my annoyance increasing. I still needed to use Tony's attention to my advantage, and I didn't need some petty jealousy impeding my plan. "The matter is your personal desire to keep Tony to yourself. Might I remind you—"

Before I could remind her that I was a (high) paying guest, she interrupted me, waving her hand around dramatically. We were standing in front of the window display in the jewellery boutique where the couple next to us, staring at a piece of gaudy jewellery, began to pay attention to our discussion. We moved down the corridor to a more private place, and Rebecca continued.

"Sixes and sevens for sure," she said. "What I mean is that the situation is somewhat confused. Indeed, you and I are not on precisely the same page, although I do have to admit it might take us to the same conclusion."

She was entirely correct on one point. I was very confused.

"Claire," she said, patting my arm lightly, "I am not the slightest bit interested in Tony, fraternizing as it were. I consider him to be a bit of a slimy Cassanova, if I might be so blunt. However, my sister thinks differently."

"I'm not following you," I said.

"As we speak, my sister is tending house and her confounded vegetable garden in a small villa in the town of Anzio just south of Rome. In fact, she is expecting a baby, which, in point of fact, is due in a month."

"What does your sister have to do with this?" I was starting to lose my patience. "Could you please get to the point, Rebecca?"

"I am so sorry, Claire. Of course. What I am trying to say, and clearly doing very badly, is that Tony is my brother-in-law. My sister knows what a rogue he can be, but she seems to love him anyway. I was simply hoping to inform you of the situation and ask that you put some distance between yourself and Tony—for my sister's sake and yours as well."

I started to laugh. "Rebecca," I said, "do you have time for a quiet cup of coffee with a guest?"

I realized I had finally found an ally.

~

By the time I arrived in the ship's infirmary an hour later, Rebecca and I were fast friends. As I'd hoped at the outset, she was just the collaborator I would need to achieve my goal—always up for a bit of fun, she said. Once I told her that my divorce from Peter had been unintended (I still hated to think of it as a mistake), and that I had a specific goal for this cruise, and that we could pull one over on Tony at the same time, she had begun to clap her hands in apparent glee.

"Two birds with one stone, as it were," she said. "This is too rich, Claire. You get Peter back, and Tony gets stung as he deserves. Just let me know how I can help."

As I alighted from the elevator on deck four, I found myself in a different world. The below-decks area for employees looked completely different from the corridors that housed staterooms, suites and amenities. Gone were the fancy carpets and sconces. In their places were a bright white utilitarian floor and fluorescent lighting. I found the door to the infirmary halfway down the deserted hall. As I opened the door, I was greeted by a receptionist wearing green scrubs, sitting behind a small, white reception desk. The place looked like the tiniest emergency room I'd ever seen—and the least populated one in my experience.

"You must be Dr. Barrett," the pretty, dark-haired woman said. "Dr. Ricci told me to expect you. He's just gone for coffee, so you can wait in his office. I'm just about to go on my break. Is there anything you need?"

I told her I was fine and then wandered into Tony's cramped office with its tiny porthole not far above the ship's water line. I took the opportunity to look around to see if I could figure out what kind of man he was. Any information might help me with my plan. The first thing I noticed was a shelf with photos. The largest of the framed pictures was of someone accepting an impressive-looking trophy for what appeared to be some kind of road race. The person receiving the trophy was standing beside a Ferrari. That person was Tony, and a buxom blonde was kissing him. *Well, well, well,* I thought, *a doctor with a penchant for race car driving. I wonder if that's his wife.* I didn't have to wonder long because tucked in a corner behind a trophy was an elaborately gold-framed wedding picture, and the buxom blonde most assuredly was not Tony's wife, Rebecca's sister. He looked decidedly uncomfortable standing beside his bride, who looked like a wholesome English country girl in a long white dress with eyelet lace sleeves and tiny flowers scattered in her hair. I gazed at the photo for a few seconds, then heard the infirmary door open and close.

"In here," I said, placing the photo back where I'd found it.

"Ah, mia cara dottoressa Barrett - Claire. Sei affascinante come sempre. You are as captivating as ever," Tony said as he came into the office bearing a tray with coffee and what appeared to be muffins.

It was all I could do to stop myself from a bit of eye-rolling. I only hoped I could pull this off. Tony was so not my type.

After clearing off a spot, Tony placed the tray in the centre of his desk. I wondered how he managed to get anything done with such a mess around him. I was meticulous when it came to my office and my patient-related paperwork, not to mention my publications and presentations. He then took my hand and kissed it. "So, you have come to see my equipment." Did he actually wiggle his eyebrows as he said that? This was going to be harder to do than I thought.

I smiled and said, "I am ready for the tour." And hoped I struck a balance between sounding enthusiastic and earnest—without too much of either.

We toured the small infirmary. Tony boasted about the fact that they had four in-patient beds and a section with stretchers where he could see two other patients. He told me that, generally, cruise ships had one inpatient bed for every one thousand passengers. Since this ship had only twelve hundred passengers, the number of infirmary beds was impressive, although I wondered if they had enough staff should they actually ever need them all. I was impressed with the array of emergency equipment they had and wondered if Peter had ever considered a stint as a ship's doctor. His credentials as an emergency physician would have made him the perfect fit.

I conveyed to Tony what I considered to be a suitable degree of enthusiasm, after which he put his arm around my shoulder and leaned in. "*Mia cara,* Claire, you are a lovely woman, but I am sure you know this."

I did, in fact, know this, but I needed him to think he was the first to tell me this. I did my best impression of a coy woman—eye fluttering and all—which almost made me vomit, but we do what we must. Suddenly, I realized I had to get ready for dinner. Jeffrey was waiting, but I refrained from mentioning this to Tony, hoping to leave him with the impression that I would be looking forward to future encounters.

I told him how impressed I was by his infirmary and his equipment, thanked him for the tour and fled.

~

When I met Jeffrey later for dinner, he asked me what I'd thought about his lecture. I couldn't exactly tell him that I felt much of what he talked about was pure nonsense, so instead, I told him that I thought he had an interesting perspective.

"What metaphor do *you* use to describe love, Claire?" he said as we sipped the last of our wine with dessert.

"I've never given it much thought," I said. And to tell you the truth, I did not have a single reason to ever think about it. For me, love was love. Nothing more and nothing less. Right? I was not a metaphorical kind of woman. I had once read something about metaphors that I thought captured them perfectly. I was trying to remember what it was. Oh, yes, someone once told me that they are the Swiss Army knives of language—handy for everything but occasionally getting stuck in the corkscrew of misunderstanding. I figured the next thing I knew, he'd be comparing love to a kitchen appliance. But he wasn't to be deterred. He kept prodding me. I had to think fast.

"I suppose love is a river, isn't it? It flows inexorably onward." I was grasping at straws here (a metaphor, perhaps?), but being on the Amazon River gave me my inspiration. Honestly, though, I had no reason to believe it or any other metaphor for love, but it sounded good—at least to me.

"Interesting," he said. "A river, you say? Flowing, changing, unpredictable? What about dangerous rapids and thundering waterfalls?"

"Yes, all of that," I said, thinking how smart I was. Why were we talking about this, anyway? I was on board this ship for a concrete reason. Metaphors be damned. I then busied myself with finding a server for another glass of wine, and we moved on to other, more mundane topics to round out the evening. Thank god.

~

The following morning, we anchored in what appeared to be the middle of the Amazon River. If I'd expected this spot to look any different than what had been flowing past our windows for the past two days as we cruised slowly along the river, I would have been wrong. Since we'd turned left from the southern Atlantic Ocean into the mouth of the Amazon River, it had been monotonously consistent.

The sandy brown of the river moved slowly past the ship's hull for kilometre after kilometre as we made our way slowly toward the city of Manaus, fifteen hundred kilometres from the mouth of the river and the last stop for a vessel of any size. Beyond that point, the river is too small for anything larger than a riverboat. At least, that's how it looked from the satellite image I'd seen. Then, along the river's shores, all we could see was the top of the tree canopy that made up the upper layer of the Amazonian rainforest. It was long, low and monotonous. And then there was the heat.

The moment we entered the estuary of the river, the skies had darkened, and the rain had pelted down. It was an unrelenting rain that flooded the ship's decks. I had never seen anything like it. When the rain stopped, the sky remained leaden, and the clouds seemed almost to envelop us. Then there was the humidity and the heat. Stultifying, unforgiving, suffocating heat pressed onto our heads and shoulders, making even walking across the open deck past the pool an excursion not to be taken lightly.

When we were approaching the mouth of the river, the cruise staff sent out a communiqué that I'd initially considered a bit over the top. There were new rules about water conservation, presumably because there was nowhere for a large ship to take on water for the next week. There was a particularly strongly worded edict to keep all veranda doors closed at all times. I did notice that when I had the occasion to open my door to take a walk out onto the veranda, the windows inside immediately began to steam up. Of course, humidity and the essential functioning of the air conditioning system on the ship were only two of the open-door problems. There was another, perhaps even more pressing issue. One word: mosquitoes.

Do you know that mosquitoes carry about one hundred diseases that affect humans? That was a piece of medical trivia I thought would stay back in my course on infectious diseases that I'd taken years ago in medical school. Now, as I travelled through an area where mosquito-borne diseases are endemic, it began to take on a whole new meaning for me.

I'd never been one to worry much about my health. I'd always taken it for granted. Before this trip, though, as I mentioned before, I did roll up my sleeve for the recommended yellow fever shot to prevent one of the nastier mosquito-borne diseases prevalent in the Amazon basin of Brazil. I also brought along anti-malaria pills. But that covered only two of the many nasty consequences of a mosquito bite—or, to be more precise, a bite from a mosquito carrying one of those nasty problems. Not all of them did, of course, but they hardly carried tiny signs around their necks to tell us which ones were infected and which ones weren't—and if they did, the signs would be so small as to be unreadable!

Mosquitoes in Brazil also carry dengue fever, and Brazil is the world capital of the dengue fever mosquito. Of course, you won't likely die from dengue, but you'll feel awfully miserable as diarrhea spills out of you for several days. Anyway, the more I thought about the cruise line directives, the more I realized they were probably wise, and my best bet was to slather on the DEET-filled insect repellent. That's what I found myself doing that morning as I looked out onto the sameness of the river where we were anchored off a place called Boca de Valeria.

I met Jeffrey at the door leading outside to the tender deck, where we boarded a ship's tender (actually one of the enclosed lifeboats) with a crowd of other guests. As I sat in the cramped, airless space, I thought about what it would be like to be on board one of these during an actual ship evacuation. We would be cheek to jowl, as they say, and there wouldn't be any more air than there was at that moment—for what I supposed might be hours and hours. I shuddered at the thought. I was grateful that the tender ride was less than ten minutes long.

When we pulled into the tiny dock, we disembarked with the tide of humanity, all trying to get a breath of air. Judging from the chatter around us, they all seemed to be heading for a ship's excursion. It sounded like a guided forest trek. I shuddered and thought about the mosquito quotient among the trees. Jeffrey and I were on our own.

As we disembarked the tender, gulping fresh (if tepid) air, we walked down a boardwalk and immediately found ourselves in a small riverside village. Village children, indigenous Amazonians, crowded around us, holding out their pet toucans and sloths, all hoping we might ask them to guide us through their village or at least pay them for a photo op. We did the latter. Jeffrey used that universal sign language of pointing and eyebrow-raising until one of the children realized Jeffrey wanted him to put his toucan on my arm. The kid shrugged, and I hesitated, but Jeffrey was determined to have the photo. I held out my arm, and the colourful bird stepped lightly onto my arm.

I held it away from me as far as I could. I have never been a big fan of birds in general, and I certainly had never had one on my arm. My experience with birds was primarily based on the pigeons in the city, which I hated, and the seagulls that swooped and soared everywhere at home on the island of Newfoundland. I looked at the black feathers, the long curved yellow beak with a big black splotch near the end and the button-like eyes that seemed to be smiling at me, or perhaps they were laughing at me. I held my breath for a moment, lest the thing smell, but when I couldn't hold it any longer and breathed, I realized it had no odour at all. Still, I was uncomfortable, hoping Jeffrey would stop laughing and get his photo. Finally, Jeffrey seemed satisfied with his cheeky moment, and I gratefully transferred the bird back to the child's arm.

Jeffrey and I continued walking along a dirt path past a dozen or so wooden houses on stilts. I imagined what this village would be like when the river was high, as it would be in some seasons and some years. It wasn't very high now, so there was even space for a line of colourful wooden canoe-type boats to be pulled up in the grasses lining the river. As we walked past the houses, the church, which occupied the higher ground, and the schoolhouse, Jeffrey and I didn't talk. I was thinking about the lives of these children. I suppose I might have had a tendency to think of them as underprivileged, but what did I know? Isn't the concept of privilege a relative thing? I was comparing their lives to the lives of my own children and the children who had the privilege of having me operate on them every day. This was their life. Then I thought about their parents.

I wondered what it would be like to marry and raise a family in these conditions. It occurred to me that happiness isn't attached to the level of creature comfort that we perceive. It's attached to the people. That's when I thought again about Peter and what I'd given up. It wasn't over yet.

FIFTEEN

Eliza

Boca de Valeria, Amazonia

AS A WOMAN BORN AND RAISED on Canada's east coast and now a proud New Yorker for more than two decades, I wasn't used to such hot, humid conditions. I was thinking about this as Peter and I boarded the tender to go ashore the following day while the ship was anchored in the middle of the river just offshore from our first Amazonian "port." It was a tiny village called Boca de Valeria. We had waited until guests who were going on excursions had left, hoping to avoid the crowd. We had figured that the tender might be a bit more comfortable if we weren't armpit to armpit with the rest of the unwashed masses aboard our ship—AKA other guests. We were right.

By the time we boarded the tender, we had the boat to ourselves. Other than the crew consisting of the captain and the crewman who maneuvered ropes and helped us off and on, we were alone. Still, it was hot—so hot we had to stick our heads out the open doors on the sides of the small vessel for a breath of air. As we approached the village, I could see a row of houses on stilts and lots of children. It seemed that they were the greeters, guides and photo ops for the port call. I looked at them as I walked along the boardwalk from the little dock and thought I could read contentment on their faces. There are so many different people in the world and so many different kinds of lives. This place might not have been where I'd like to live, but I suspected that few of them would relish Manhattan. I was suddenly grateful that we were all so different. Wouldn't it be a boring world if we were all the same?

Peter and I walked past the short string of houses along a dirt path, feeling the slow, rhythmic pace of life along the river. It felt like life here was somehow attuned to the flow of the Amazon itself. I looked around, observing people and signs of life, like lines of colourful washing and vendors sitting out of the sun under houses on stilts where handmade jewellery sat on blankets in the soft dirt alongside T-shirts made in China. I felt like I was looking through a lens that had misted up around the edges. It was like a photograph that had been manipulated to be a vignette with soft edges encroaching on the centre. Behind the houses that were lined up like charms on a bracelet was the rainforest itself, dark and shadowy. I wondered what exotic creatures lurked beyond the edges. It was clear what kind of critters populated the light.

All around us, children were trying to get us to either hire them as guides through their village or pay them for the privilege of taking a picture with their pet sloths and birds. At first, I wanted to pass right by, and then I remembered how much fun it had been last summer when I was on vacation on the island of Newfoundland to let go of some of my proper ways and creature comforts and go with the flow. I was thinking about the afternoon I spent watching the puffin colony offshore. I remembered watching my cousin, who was a former journalist, snapping photo after photo.

I took a few myself, but most of them were unfocused and too far away to be good, but that didn't seem to matter. The memory of one of the most unforgettable days of my life to date was cemented in my mind's eye. That's when I saw Claire and Jeffrey up ahead.

Claire looked decidedly uncomfortable, standing there with a child's pet toucan on her outstretched arm. I had to stifle a giggle as I observed the look on her face that seemed to be a mixture of alarm and distaste. For a woman who herself had been born and raised on the island of Newfoundland in the North Atlantic, Claire seemed to me to be a tight-assed prig, something I saw no evidence of among the inhabitants of her home province during my last vacation. She must have been something of an anomaly, and given how down-to-earth Peter was, I wondered how they had managed twenty years of marriage. Then it struck me. That was me just a year ago. I had changed.

At that thought, I turned to Peter. "Shall we get a few photos with sloths and toucans while we're here?"

Peter had seemed a bit off for the past twenty-four hours, which made me wonder what was going on, but he brightened up when I mentioned photos with sloths and toucans. I gestured toward a little boy in a red-striped T-shirt cradling a brown furry sloth like one might carry a baby on a hip. I had a brief moment of panic about the potential insect load this tiny animal might be harbouring, as well as the personal habit situation of such creatures. I was reminded of a trip to Australia years earlier, where I was cautioned against holding a koala because doing so might well result in it peeing on me. Throwing caution to the wind, I quickly discarded such thoughts. "How about you take my photo while I hold that sloth?"

Peter looked skeptical. "Maybe try a toucan. I had a patient who worked in a zoo in the ER one time when I was a resident. He'd gotten quite a bite, and for such small animals, sloths have enormous teeth that they'll use if they're frightened or disturbed. I can tell you that my patient's sloth bite wasn't pretty."

I looked at the cute little creature and considered whether the child might have drugged it in some way, although I knew that sloths were known to be, well, slothful. But on balance, I felt I should listen to the expert, and we settled on a colourful toucan offered by a little girl with dark, saucer-like eyes. I thought the little boy would be disappointed, but he just shrugged and seemed to take it in stride as he went in search of someone more inclined toward a sloth.

As the girl in her blue T-shirt and faded denim shorts slid the bird onto my arm, I glanced across the expanse of grass and sand toward Claire, who hadn't yet seemed to have noticed us. She had just given her toucan back to a little boy and was now proceeding to brush herself off. I had no idea what she might have to brush off unless it was the whole experience. I turned back to Peter and smilingly posed for the camera. Why was I beginning to feel like I was in a competition?

~

After our trip ashore to mingle with the toucans and the locals, Peter seemed much more relaxed. He and I laughed and joked in the corner of the tender boat while we watched Claire and Jeffrey across on the other side. We hadn't arrived on the same tender as they had, but we left on the same one. I noticed Claire adjusting her hat and fanning herself with one of those battery-operated fans that menopausal women are so fond of. You might well remind me that I am one of those women, but neither I nor anyone I knew would be caught dead with one of those little plastic rotary fans. Claire and I were, after all, quite different. Once back on board our floating hotel, I was so hot and sweaty that I couldn't even consider a drink until I'd showered. Peter and I planned to meet in an hour.

When I arrived at Martinis bar at the appointed time, Peter hadn't yet arrived. I was feeling much fresher and more optimistic about where Peter and I might be heading. I truly enjoyed his company and especially his sense of humour, something Jake seemed to have left in his past a decade or more earlier. I'd been so focused on my own career that I'd forgotten how important it is to laugh. Last summer's holiday, when I met Peter, had taught me the value of laughing—and often laughing at myself.

Since Peter seemed to be running late, I decided to order myself a drink. I was taking my first sip of what the bartender had called a "Porn Star Martini," a lovely concoction of vanilla vodka, passion fruit liqueur and lime juice topped with brut champagne with a side of champagne to add to the bubbles as they dissipated. I was thinking about the possibilities of a cookbook that included cocktails as sides when I looked up to see Jeffrey standing above me.

"Looks delicious, Eliza," Jeffrey said as he sat down opposite me in the seat that I had expected Peter to take. "Seems we've both been left to our own devices for a bit."

"I'm just waiting for Peter," I said. "Where's Claire?" I didn't really care where she was, just as long as she wasn't in my line of sight.

"I'm not sure. She said I'd see her later, but she didn't elaborate on what she was doing. Maybe she's gone to the spa. By the way, Eliza, when's your cooking class? I'm really looking forward to taking it."

"The day after we leave Manaus." That was three days hence.

Jeffrey looked at his watch. "Mind if I join you for a drink—at least until Peter arrives?"

I told him I didn't mind. There was something about Jeffrey that I actually liked. It was beginning to feel like an older sister thing. I would have said mother, but I didn't feel the least bit motherly toward him and suspected that Claire didn't either.

"So, Eliza, how long have you and Peter been together?" Jeffrey said as the server left with his drink order.

"We aren't really what I'd call a couple," I said. "We've only known one another for a few months, and this is the first time we've had a chance to spend any time together."

"So, you've been married before, too?" He glanced at my left hand, where I wore a platinum band with three rows of diamonds. I suppose it might have looked like a wedding ring, but it wasn't. It was a ring I'd bought myself years ago when my first cookbook hit the *New York Times* bestseller list. I suppose it was imbued with the memory of success and independence.

I nodded as I poured some more champagne from the tiny crystal pitcher into my coupe.

"Children?"

"A daughter. In fact, I also have a granddaughter," I said as nonchalantly as I could manage. I raised my coupe to my lips and sipped, savouring the sweet-tart flavour as it slid over my tongue.

Jeffrey's eyebrows raised noticeably. "You don't seem old enough to be a grandmother if I might be so bold as to say, Eliza."

I was inexplicably flattered by this.

The server arrived with Jeffrey's negroni. Jeffrey thanked him, raised his glass in a toast and said, "To new friends." We clinked glasses. "So, Eliza, you're not a wine drinker? Claire is a bit of a wine snob, you know."

I didn't know, but it didn't surprise me. "If you must know, I can fall into that trap, too. You know—people our age." Now, why did I say that?

"Your age? Do you mean as in the older generation?" Jeffrey was laughing.

I put my glass down on the napkin on the table in front of me and looked at him pointedly. "How old *are* you, Jeffrey?"

"I'll tell you if you'll tell me."

"I'm fifty and proud of it. Now, your turn."

Jeffrey looked around, then leaned in as if he were trying to avoid being overheard. "I'll tell you if you promise not to tell a soul." I agreed. "I'm thirty-four."

I almost spluttered a porn star out my nose. "Thirty-four? You really are a millennial, aren't you?" He shrugged. I was thinking that he was closer to Izzy's age than mine. Now, I *was* beginning to feel motherly toward him. "You've had something of a meteoric rise to fame, haven't you?"

"What can I say? I've been in the right place at the right time with the right idea."

"And your charismatic personality doesn't hurt, either, does it?" Before Jeffrey could say anything, I heard a text ping from inside my tiny clutch bag that was on the table beside me. "Sorry. I should see who this is." I was hoping it wasn't Jake. That would ruin all the fun. As I reached for my bag to retrieve my phone, I glanced at my watch and noticed that Jeffrey and I had been chatting for half an hour. Where in the world was Peter? I didn't have to wonder long.

Sorry to have missed you for a drink. Called to the infirmary to consult with Dr. Ricci. May have to miss dinner. 😨 P.

"That's peculiar," I said as I tapped a response, telling Peter I hoped the situation wasn't dire. Then I told Jeffrey where Peter was.

"That does seem odd. I'm also wondering where Claire is."

I looked at him closely. "Well, Jeffrey, it's highly unlikely that Claire's in the infirmary as well unless she's trying to impress that Dr. Ricci. They seemed to be in a cozy clutch the other night at dinner. Are you and Claire really a couple?" Since he'd been asking me about my situation, I thought it only proper to return the favour.

He didn't answer right away, as if he might be trying to figure out his answer. "To tell you the truth, Eliza, she and I only met briefly a few years ago at a conference in L.A. We were on the same panel. I had no idea she'd be on this ship. We just ran into one another again."

I was thinking about the two of them meeting at a conference. Something rang a bell in the back of my mind, but the sound was faint. "What kind of a conference was it? It seems odd that the two of you, being in different medical specialties, would be at the same conference."

"I know. I found it odd myself when I got the invitation from an esteemed national group of pediatric surgeons to be a keynote speaker at their conference that year. It seems that my essay in the *New York Times* earlier that year had inspired them to add something a bit more esoteric to their usual line-up of speakers on the newest techniques for one thing or another."

I racked my brain to remember ever reading anything in the *Times* written by Jeffrey P. Montgomery. I was drawing a blank. I told him I read the *Times* religiously and didn't remember his essay.

He seemed surprised. "I'm kind of disappointed you don't remember it. The piece got quite a bit of media coverage at the time."

"Do you mean *social* media coverage?" He nodded as I continued. "Then there's the difference between a fifty-year-old woman and a thirty-four-year-old man. Anyway, tell me about it."

He laughed. "I suppose you're right."

Jeffrey then went on to explain that he wrote the essay as an update of something that an earlier psychiatrist had written in his own bestselling book. That book was called *The Road Less Travelled,* and the psychiatrist in question was someone called M. Scott Peck. I vaguely remembered seeing that book on my father's bookshelf when I was a child and a quote that Jeffrey had used on a slide during his lecture.

"Wasn't that published in the 1970s?" I said, trying to remember if my father had ever mentioned what it was about.

"It was published in 1978, to be exact. The book was something of a game-changer for many people at the time. It's hard to believe there was a time when the idea of self-help was unknown. It was in its infancy then, and his book suggested that the only way to make your life better was to do something about it yourself."

I sighed. "That's certainly a message more people these days could use." I'd never been on the self-help wagon train, so that kind of book wasn't exactly a cultural touchstone for me.

He laughed. "You are so right. But it wasn't that message that I focused on in my essay. Peck also wrote that 'we are often most in the dark when we are the most certain, and the most enlightened when we are the most confused.' I brought this assertion into the twenty-first century, and that was what the conference organizers were interested in. They wanted to make the point that when surgeons are most certain, that might be the time for them to step back and take a closer look."

"That must have gone over like a lead balloon with the esteemed Dr. Barrett."

Jeffrey laughed. "I suppose you could say that. After the panel session was over, we continued our argument over a glass or two of wine. I even humoured her in the wine selection issue and drank what she ordered. Anyway, one thing led to another ..."

"And?"

"Do I need to spell it out for you?"

He did not. I poured the last of my extra champagne into my martini glass and sipped it thoughtfully. I was stuck on the fact that they had met at a conference, and one thing had led to another. And it had been several years ago, presumably while Peter and Claire were still married. The lightbulb finally blinked on in my head. Or more to the point, and at the risk of mixing my metaphors, I could hear that formerly faint bell in the back of my head clanging loud and clear. Claire's indiscretion. Jeffrey was her indiscretion. I tried to hide my sharp intake of breath.

"Does Peter know who you are?"

"What do you mean? Who I am?"

"About you and Claire. They were still married then, you know."

"Oh, I do know that. Claire made that point crystal clear. But, no, I'm pretty sure Peter doesn't know that she and I had a brief fling at a conference."

"He knows she had a fling with someone."

"You're not going to tell on me, are you?" He got that puppy-dog look on his face, the kind of face that could melt a woman's heart.

"I can't promise you anything on that front, and, anyway, it's not really my story to tell," I said, wondering if it was, indeed, my responsibility to tell Peter what I knew. But how could that benefit anyone? Except, maybe, me. As I put that thought away for later consideration, Jeffrey's phone, which was face up on the table beside his now empty glass, lit up.

He reached for it and said, "Speak of the devil. A text from Claire."

I was considering ordering another drink since I'd enjoyed that one so much, but I decided to wait to hear what Dr. Barrett might have to say. Perhaps she was "consulting" in the infirmary as well.

"Well, that's a bit cryptic," he said. "Anyway, I don't know what's keeping her, but it seems I'm at loose ends for dinner. Care to join me?"

Since Peter didn't seem to be able to make it for our dinner plans, who else was I going to have dinner with?

~

After very nearly finding ourselves having dinner with the odious tobacco farmer Randy and his charming wife Dixie, who were awaiting a table when we arrived in the dining room, Jeffrey and I slipped into a table for two in a far corner where no one else seemed to want to sit. My observation of the guests on this ship over the past week was that everyone seemed to be looking for someone else other than their spouse to talk to. Everyone was interested in group activities. I realized that I was not like them at all, and I was suddenly grateful that Jeffrey wasn't, either.

Once we had settled into our table and agreed on a bottle of wine (even a millennial will drink a good wine when eating dinner, it seems), I returned to his description of the *New York Times* essay he'd written, which I had every intention of looking up at my first opportunity.

"Tell me again what that line was that prompted you to write that essay for the *Times*."

"Peck said, 'We are often most in the dark when we are the most certain, and the most enlightened when we are the most confused,'" Jeffrey said. "Why? Does it resonate with you?"

"I suppose it does." I wasn't sure I wanted to tell him that if M. Scott Peck and he were right, I should be very enlightened, indeed, since I was very confused. "I'm probably comparing myself to Claire. She seems to be certain about everything."

Jeffrey laughed. "I do have to say that she's one of the most self-assured women I've ever met." I couldn't argue with him there. "I've observed that she always seems absolutely certain about everything—her work, her life, her wine choices."

I laughed. "Claire does appear to be one of those people. I suppose we share some of that certainty in common, but I'd like to think that I have evolved enough to recognize the uncertainties in my life and use them. Why do you think Claire is so much like that?"

"Are you asking me to put on my psychiatrist's hat and diagnose her?"

I hoped he would. "Why not?"

"Okay," he said. "Here's what I think. I believe Dr. Claire Barrett suffers from imposter syndrome."

I'd heard of it and thought I understood it, but it didn't seem to describe the Claire I had glimpsed. I needed a bit more, so I prodded him to continue.

"Imposter syndrome develops when someone who, by all objective measures is a high achiever, doubts her abilities, skills, or accomplishments. She feels like a fraud despite very real competence and success."

I thought about that for a moment and realized that, without a doubt, no one could say I suffered from imposter syndrome. I firmly believed in my capabilities and how I'd built my success and reputation brick by brick, and I deserved every accolade my work brought to me. I asked him to tell me more. I guess I was hoping to understand Claire better. Why would I want to do that, you might reasonably ask? The word "competition" once again bubbled to the top of my consciousness. I tried to tamp it down.

"Well," Jeffrey said as the server brought us our first course, "people with imposter syndrome are perfectionists. I have to admit that was the first thing I noticed about her. She was so perfect. I guess, in some way, that immediately attracted me. I know for a fact that anyone who is so apparently perfect has a few dirty corners, and I wanted to find hers."

"I guess you accomplished that," I said as I sipped my lobster bisque.

He laughed and continued. "They also fear failure and constantly compare themselves to others. Claire does that *ad nauseum*. She always needs to be built up. And the truth is that it happens most often in women who are in male-dominated fields. Surgeons are still largely male. After I met her, I looked it up and, in the United States, even in pediatric surgery, only twenty-one percent are women."

So, this was what Peter had been contending with for his entire married life. It must have been exhausting.

By the time we'd reached dessert, my phone pinged again. I usually hated it when people reached for their phones while socializing, but these circumstances were different. It was Peter, of course.

`Sorry I missed dinner. Grabbed a snack and coffee in the café. Gone back to the infirmary. I hadn't intended for you to be left by yourself. Talk tomorrow?`

I texted back that I would look forward to that.

When Jeffrey and I finally called it a night, and I started back to my suite, I had an idea. I'd drop by the infirmary and say goodnight to Peter.

I made my way down to deck four and found the infirmary. When I pushed open the door, I saw that no one was sitting at the reception desk. I could hear hushed voices coming from the interior room. I walked in and stood by the door, where I saw a curtain pulled around what I assumed was a hospital bed. I was about to announce myself, but the familiar voice stopped me. And it wasn't Peter's. Or Dr. Ricci's.

SIXTEEN

Claire

ENROUTE TO MANAUS

"YOU'VE ALWAYS BEEN THERE for me, Peter. I know in my heart I can always count on you," I said, pulling the sheet up just far enough for it to lay languidly across the top of my naked breasts. Of course, it had been so much easier to get the cardiac leads on my chest without wearing anything on top. "I don't know what I'd have done without you today. I was so scared."

"Don't worry," Peter said, patting my hand. "I'll be here with you. I told Dr. Ricci I'd stay the night so he wouldn't have to be here."

Stay the night. It was music to my ears. The fact that I was lying in a cruise ship hospital bed and Peter was sitting on a chair beside me mattered not in the slightest. I was making progress.

I shifted my left arm that Peter had expertly splinted based on his diagnosis of a sprain. The splint was slightly uncomfortable, possibly a tad too tight, but nothing was ever accomplished without a bit of discomfort. Then, when I'd had that little "spell," and he had to catch me in his arms, I knew that it was all worth it.

"Claire, you look so pale. Do you want me to call Fiona and Liam to tell them about your situation?"

My situation? Hardly. "No, let's not worry them. I'm sure I'll be perfect in a day or two." I knew I would be.

Peter looked so concerned that I wished I could reach up and hug him, but I thought better of it. Peter then took my hand, and I could feel that old spark that we always had between us when we both had time to get together. It wasn't dead. I knew it. Only a few more planks in the plan, and we'd be getting off this ship in Miami hand-in-hand. And the kids would meet us there. It was going to be perfect.

Dr. Ricci came back to check on me an hour later. After all, he was still responsible for the patients in the ship's infirmary, and I happened to be the only one in residence, thank god. Things were going very well, very well, indeed. I even let Dr. Ricci—Tony—give me a mild sedative. When I woke up the following morning, I opened my eyes to see Peter asleep on the chair beside me. I felt a bit of a heart flutter at the sight of his handsome face next to me in the morning. I had taken that for granted for too many years in our marriage, throughout those years when we were both building our careers, and we had two small children. We had drifted apart, but we were coming back together. This cruise had been a brilliant idea. Now, all I had to do was get rid of that damn Eliza Cohen. She was not suitable for Peter even if I were not in the picture, which I certainly was.

~

Peter stirred in the chair beside me. I pretended to be asleep so that when he stood up and bent over me (which I knew he would, being the doctor that he is), I could sleepily open my eyes and see him there with concern written all over his face. However, I fell asleep again, and when I woke up again, Peter was gone. I could hear voices outside the patient area by the reception desk. As hard as I tried to hear the specifics of the conversation, I couldn't make it out, but I did recognize Peter's and Tony's voices. Then I heard the infirmary door open and close, after which Tony appeared at the end of my bed.

"Tony—Dr. Ricci," I said, "I'll just get dressed and get out of your hair." I was gagging for a shower and a cup of coffee.

"But, no, my dear, of course, you cannot leave just yet."

"I feel so much better, and now that Peter has splinted my arm, everything should be perfect."

"But the pain. We will have to manage the pain here for a day or two."

This was no longer going as well as I thought it should. I was not going to be held prisoner in a cruise ship infirmary against my will, so I had to make Tony understand that no matter what he might say, I was not staying. I pulled the fellow-physician card, that I was well aware of what I was doing and convinced him that I was leaving anyway.

I dressed quickly and made my way back to my suite, hoping that I wouldn't run into anyone before I'd had a chance to take a shower. After showering and changing, I set out for the café for a latte and a croissant. As I sat in a corner seat, gazing out at the shore of the river in the distance as we glided by, making our way toward the city of Manaus, Rebecca spotted me.

"Hello, lovey," she said breezily, then she sat down opposite me and leaned in as if she might be a co-conspirator. "How'd it go with your two favourite doctors?"

I laughed. "I'm getting a bit tired of this, you know. I thought a bit of cloak and dagger might be fun, but that's not really who I am. But in answer to your question, I believe it went well."

Rebecca looked at my splint. "How long will that be on?"

I looked at it and shrugged. "I haven't decided yet. I'll give it a few days, I suppose."

"Well, love, must go. Bingo to call!"

And she was gone, leaving me to my thoughts. A picture of Jeffrey floated into my mind. I have to admit feeling a bit annoyed at myself for how I reacted when I saw how cozy he was with Eliza. I wasn't really interested in Jeffrey in terms of a relationship, and he'd made it abundantly clear that he had no such thoughts. And yet, I didn't want Eliza to get her claws into him either, although that would certainly make it easier to convince Peter that we were meant to be together. I was exhausted, though.

I could work a twelve-hour shift at the hospital, doing three complicated procedures and come out feeling invigorated in the end. This objective I had to get my family back together, though, was draining me in ways I didn't know I was even subject to. As I sat there gazing into the dregs of my latte in my cup, for the first time, I wondered if I was doing the right thing.

"Well, well, well, if it isn't the lady doctor." The voice boomed from across the sparsely populated café.

I looked up, and to my abject horror, Randy from Texas and his charming (not) wife, Dixie, were heading in my direction with plates piled high with what looked from a distance like chocolate croissants. I could see that Randy was eyeing the empty seats at my table. Why hadn't I sat at the counter? That would be because I wanted to be alone at the back of the space where only tables for four sat.

"Hello, Randy, isn't it?" I said. Well, what could I do? I could hardly pretend I didn't see them.

"Mind if we join you?" Randy said, placing his plate on the table and pulling out a chair before I even had a chance to say a word. Then, before he sat down, he turned to his wife and said, "Where in the hell are my manners?" He then pulled out Dixie's seat. She nodded to him and sat. "Well, just look here," Randy said, lifting a croissant dripping with chocolate to his mouth. "I'm so hungry, I could eat the north end of a south-bound polecat." Then he laughed and took a massive bite, causing flakes to begin tumbling to his plate.

Polecat?

"Now, you watch yourself there, honey," Dixie said. "You're makin' a mess."

I still hadn't had a chance to say a word. I could hardly say that I was thinking it might do him more good if he stepped away from chocolate croissants or any other kind of pastry, for that matter. He resembled a heart attack looking for a place to happen. I just didn't want it to be in front of me. Then I'd be duty-bound to do something to save him. I didn't relish that thought.

Randy swallowed and took a mouthful of coffee, then turned toward my splinted arm. "What in tarnation did you do to that pretty little arm of yours?"

"Now, Randy," Dixie said, "that's likely none of your business."

"It's okay," I said. "There's no colourful story to go with it." At least none I was willing to share with complete strangers or perhaps even anyone else. "It's just a little sprain."

"Thank the lord for that," Dixie said. "I don't know about you, but I wouldn't want to get sick aboard this ship and have to be taken ashore to one of those South American hospitals." She pronounced "South American" slowly and with a grimace and a flutter of nostrils.

"Not to worry. I'm just fine," I said, wondering how I could get away gracefully.

"Well, darlin', ain't that the berries!" I must have looked confused. He translated. "That's great! Anyway, we've been busy as a one-legged cat in a sandbox on this trip and I wanted to have a chat with a bona fide Canadian doctor." He pronounced it "bona fid-ee." I had to keep from rolling my eyes.

Dear god, I thought. *Is he for real? Has he swallowed the dictionary of southern Americanisms?* I decided my best bet here was to play along and escape at the first possible opportunity for a graceful exit. "I'd be happy to provide you with a perspective. Was there something in particular you wanted to discuss?"

Randy took another bite, chewed, swallowed and patted his mouth with a paper napkin. "I've been wonderin' about that marijuana business you all have up there. Now, I don't much take to that smokin' dope business since I'm a tobacco man myself, but if there's a buck to be made, I'll be the first one to do it. My Dixie there didn't get that three-carat diamond she's sporting from me sittin' on my ass." He laughed. Dixie didn't seem to find it quite as funny as her husband did. "What I mean to say is that I've been wonderin' if there's health issues on the horizon for this marijuana, the same that we've been facing for years with the tobacco."

"Do you mean do I think that it's a good investment?" I wasn't born yesterday and knew a thing or two about issues, even outside pediatric surgery.

"I suppose I do, little lady."

I shuddered every time he called me little lady, but I didn't have the energy or the motivation to take a stand on his ingrained misogyny—a word he probably couldn't spell or define, anyway. "I'm not sure I'm qualified to give advice on marijuana as an industry, Randy, but from what I know about marijuana consumption, over the past six years since legalization, consumption has increased only marginally." Randy looked confused.

I continued. "I think I remember reading recently that something like six percent of Canadians reported using cannabis daily or close to it, a number that was hardly worth reporting since it was five percent six years ago before the laws changed. So, legalization hasn't really meant skyrocketing sales. As for the health issues, the research is ongoing, but, just like with tobacco, it's not safe."

"There you are." I looked up to see Peter standing over the table. "I've been looking for you." Peter looked at Randy and Dixie and said, "You don't mind if I borrow Claire from you, do you?"

"Not at all," Randy said. "We were just shootin' the breeze."

I got up gratefully, and as we walked out of the café into the oppressive heat on the pool deck, Peter said, "You looked like you could use some rescuing."

I liked the sound of that.

~

We walked across the deck and into the air-conditioned bliss of the corridor on the opposite side. "Thanks for the rescue, Peter."

"How's the arm, Claire?" he said. His eyes were narrowed practically into slits, and his brow so furrowed that he seemed to have aged ten years. His eyes then darted back and forth over my arm, to my face and back down to my arm. Perhaps he didn't think my injury was as much of a concern as he might have thought the day before.

"It's okay," I said slowly. "By the way, I cannot thank you enough for coming to my aid when I needed you. You've always been there for me."

"I suppose that's true, Claire. But we've both moved on. I can see you seem to have moved on in more than one direction. First, there was Jeffrey and then Dr. Ricci. I was wondering," he said as we stood there in the empty corridor, "what exactly is going on with you and Jeffrey? He's a bit young for you, don't you think?"

"Are you jealous?" I could hardly keep the glee from my voice.

Peter's head snapped up. "Jealous? You cannot seriously mean that." Then he shook his head. "Claire, I know what's going on. Maybe you need to listen a bit more to your boyfriend's lectures."

"I'm surprised *you* listened. I seem to remember more than one occasion in our past when you ridiculed people whose ideas came from any place that couldn't be reached by a probe, a scalpel or a needle."

Peter laughed. "Right back at you. That may be true for me, but it's also true for you. Now I'm suggesting you might consider opening your mind just a bit. Jeffrey asked the question are your experiences deceiving you, or are you deceiving yourself? Since it seems that experiences can't deceive, the answer is obvious."

Peter then turned and walked back out into the torpor of the Amazon day. I stood there watching him go and wondered if he might have a point. I walked across the pool deck and up the steps to the deck above where there were no guests, so I had it all to myself for a few moments at least. I stood at the railing and looked out at the dull brown water and the tops of the rainforest trees that we slowly passed on our way to our next port of call. I took a deep breath of steamy tropical air and thought about what I was doing.

Why did I really want him back? Wasn't my success enough? I'd asked myself this time and again over the years. And I always came up with the same answer. I was a fraud, and people would notice after a while.

The accolades, the promotions, the respect of my colleagues—all the things I'd once cherished—had always seemed to shimmer with an odd hollowness, as if, at any moment, someone might step in and declare it all a mistake. I could recall every compliment, every award, and every nod of approval I had ever received, and I wondered, *Do they really see me, or just the facade I've carefully crafted*?

I thought about all the late nights on call, the sacrifices, the relentless striving to prove myself. Now, the achievements seemed fragile, as though built on a foundation that might crumble under closer scrutiny. The lustre of my accomplishments seemed to be fading. How did I get here? I tried to trace the trajectory of my journey back through the years, searching for proof that my success had been legitimate, that I was not an imposter masquerading in the role of my own life.

I turned away from the water and walked around and around the deck, thinking about my life. And Peter's words. "Are your experiences deceiving you, or are you deceiving yourself?"

SEVENTEEN

Eliza

MANAUS, BRAZIL

WHEN I HEARD CLAIRE'S VOICE from behind the curtain say, "I know in my heart I can always count on you," to which Peter responded, "Don't worry, I'll be here with you," it was all I needed. I backed out of the infirmary door and closed it gently so that no one would know I'd been there.

I still didn't know what to think when I let myself into my suite a few minutes later. Here I was, stuck on this ship for almost another two weeks with a man I didn't seem to know at all. Despite how little time we'd spent together since we'd met last summer, I'd perceived a depth of feeling between us that I thought might go somewhere. I suppose I thought I was being given a second chance. Now, this. Claire was a vile woman. That much I knew. But I had no idea that Peter was that torn. He had told me there wasn't a shred of feeling left between them, and the only thing they shared were Liam and Fiona. I suppose I concluded that it was much the same as what was left between Jake and me. There was Izzy and now Mary-Catherine, my granddaughter. I smiled at the thought of her, and it occurred to me that perhaps my life was enough, just as it was. As I took off my jewellery and washed my face, I thought about what it meant to have enough—and to be enough.

There's an old line my father used to say to his three daughters whenever they whined and complained that they needed this thing or that thing. "Enough is never enough for those for whom enough is never enough." As a kid, it had gone straight over my head. In more recent years, I'd begun to realize what he'd meant.

The truth was that I had much more than enough of everything in my life. I had far more than enough money, and I knew it. This realization was one of the first things I noticed about the differing directions that Jake and I had been going for some years. No matter how much money he had (and he had enough to buy any car he wanted, to live in a three-thousand-square-foot brownstone on the upper west side of Manhattan, enough money to charter a plane for vacations twice a year and on and on), but it was never enough. He always needed more.

I also had more than enough "friends." In fact, I'd recently realized that I had far more "friends" than I needed. My closest friend was Jake's sister, Allegra, whom I'd met a few weeks before she introduced me to Jake that fateful September back in 2001. Beyond Allegra, I had "friends" that Jake and I could always count on when we were having a party—people I didn't care to see between times. I had "friends" I could sit with at charity galas while they slowly got drunk and acted like half-wits, never once having a reasonable conversation. I had "friends" who wanted me to play tennis with them despite my repeated cancellations. I wasn't that good at tennis, and I loathed the after-tennis lunches where the women in question spent their time kvetching about their housekeepers, their children, their hair salons, their husbands and their mothers-in-law. I could have joined in with those last two, but I preferred to keep my dirty laundry in-house. (I suppose I might have improved at the tennis if I hadn't been held hostage by rabid gossipers after each session. I might have learned to love it just for the game itself, but alas, that wasn't in the cards.) So, I had more than enough friends, and I knew it, and most of the ones I had, I didn't like very much. I knew I had more friends than I needed or wanted because the people Jake liked to call our "friends" were just people who needed other people to listen to them talk about themselves. To be clear, Jake needed that as well. I did not.

I had more than enough money, friends, things, career success. Although I suppose I had never considered it before, what I suddenly felt I didn't have enough of was love in my life. Then I thought about Izzy and her gorgeous little daughter, my granddaughter. Izzy's pregnancy had blindsided me (she still hadn't revealed who Mary-Cahterine's father was and probably never would if I read my daughter correctly). Still, I had embraced my new role with alacrity once I got used to the idea. I don't suppose I'll ever be a conventional grandmother, and certainly not a conventional Jewish grandmother if my mother-in-law, Esther, was any example. I would, however, be my own unique version of one.

I sat on the side of my bed and looked out the window at the dark river that was passing by. I wondered how I'd convinced myself that I was in a competition with Claire. The fact that I considered Peter to be a prize for the winner of this competition made me gag. I wasn't giving him enough credit, and I certainly wasn't giving myself enough.

I got ready for bed, slid between the soft, snowy-white sheets of the dreamy bed and then lay back, thinking about making my own life. The love I had for Izzy and Mary-Catherine was enough. Then I heard an annoying little voice in the back of my head. "But do you have enough love for *yourself?*"

~

I woke up a few hours later, and it took a moment or two before I remembered where I was. I was dreaming about being on trial for a crime I was sure I hadn't committed, although I had no idea what it was. I lifted my phone from the bedside table to see what time it was and noticed that I had missed some texts. My first thoughts went to Izzy and the baby, so I clicked open my texts. No texts from Izzy, but there were a couple from Jake. I sighed and considered not even reading them—but I did.

Been thinking about us. We're grandparents now, Eliza. That has to count for something. J. 🙁

Was Jake not aware that being a grandparent didn't require a partner? Then there was another one.

Been thinking about the time we went to Florida, and I bought you that bracelet. You said it was too much, but I bought it anyway. J.

A bracelet in Florida? If there had ever been a time in my life when I said something he bought me was too much, I couldn't remember it. I put the phone down on the bed and thought for a moment. I had a vague recollection of seeing a charge on a credit card statement some years ago that didn't ring a bell. Jake had just returned from a trip to visit his mother, who was staying at his parents' condo in Miami for the winter. It was a charge from what appeared to be a jewellery store.

When I asked him about it, I remembered him giving me some vague answer about his mother asking him to pick something up. I started to laugh at the memory. His mother had nothing to do with it, and I was not the happy recipient of that bracelet. I wondered who had been. Then I realized I didn't care, that it made me feel—nothing.

I had often wondered how long Jake had been searching for solace in some other woman's arms. This was yet more evidence that his behaviour predated the recent fling with his secretary, Eleanor or whatever her name was. I just didn't think he was stupid enough to have created a memory that he had given the bracelet in question to me. *Yes,* I thought, *I am going to cherish every moment I have on this ship by myself. I am enough.*

~

Manaus, Brazil, is a living, breathing incongruity with an intriguing history. I had done my pre-travel research and knew that Manaus was the largest city in the Amazon, with a population of over two million and that it was the farthest stop for ships of any size in the river. Despite knowing that, I was still taken aback the following morning as we approached the city to see its numerous concrete buildings rising to scrape the Amazonian sky in stark contrast to the fifteen hundred kilometres of riparian rainforest that we'd seen since entering the river. I had also read that it is an eco-tourism mecca, which made me entirely unprepared for the volume of garbage I saw floating in the water near the pier.

Some days earlier, while we were perusing the shore excursions, Peter and I had planned to take a trip ashore to see what was called "the meeting of the waters," but I now wondered if he might beg off. It didn't matter to me. I was going on the excursion anyway.

I dressed in my Amazon uniform: lightweight, long pants with narrow openings at the bottom, ultra-lightweight long-sleeved T-shirt, socks and hiking sneakers. I could hardly believe I owned anything with the word "hiking" in it. Still, after last summer on the island of Newfoundland hiking the earth's mantle with only tennis shoes, I dug deep and found my inner hiker and outdoor enthusiast. I felt she was there and had just been longing to get out. Now was the time. Anyway, I was also not prepared to get a mosquito bite. Thus, the long-sleeved T and long pants, heat and humidity be damned. Then I considered make-up.

I had never been a wildly over-made-up kind of woman, but I never left the house without lipstick, eyebrows, mascara and something to smooth out the facial skin that was aging rapidly. I remembered last summer when we'd been caught in a torrential downpour as we hiked the tablelands and the feeling of letting the water run down my face. It had been one of the most liberating experiences I could ever remember having. For at least a few minutes, I hadn't cared at all what anyone else thought about how I looked. Now, I looked at my face in the mirror, slapped on some lipstick (my youngest sister liked to kid me about my penchant for expensive lipstick and really, a little lipstick never hurts) and nodded. Who needed makeup in the Amazon?

Once I was dressed and had my hat in my hand and my cross-body bag attached, I left for the gangway, where I saw Peter standing there in his own hiking gear, waiting for me. In spite of everything, my heart did a little flutter.

"I'm so sorry to have missed dinner last evening."

I looked at him. I couldn't help it. I could not keep the skepticism out of my voice. "Are you sure you have the time to get away with me today?" Oh, how petulant that sounded. I cringed at hearing myself. I might have taken two steps forward in my personal evolution, but damn it, I'd just taken at least one back.

"There was an incident with Claire," Peter said. "She needed a medical consultation."

Incident? I bet there was. "I suppose patient confidentiality prevents you from giving details."

Peter shrugged. "Shall we?"

So, we walked down the gangway to the pier with the ghost of Claire hanging above us like a spectre of misery. We continued across the pier to board what looked like a Mississippi riverboat that would take us to an ecological reserve. Along the way, we would see the "meeting of the waters" where the River Negro meets the Amazon River, with their two distinct colours not mixing for some six kilometres. I was looking forward to it.

~

Peter and I found seats on the top deck of the riverboat where we could at least have a fighting chance at catching a breeze in the stifling heat and humidity. As we sat down, without looking at me, Peter reached over and squeezed my hand. Neither of us turned our heads to look, but I was sure he felt the same electricity. Then he withdrew his hand, and the moment was over. I turned my attention to the guide, who had picked up a microphone at the bow of the boat and was starting his commentary as the boat pulled away from the dock.

In fact, the city of Manaus is located at the mouth of the River Negro, not on the shore of the Amazon itself. Our ship had turned slightly right and into the River Negro with its clear, black waters (clear except for the astonishing sight of garbage floating by every so often) before docking. Now, the riverboat chugged its way back toward the Amazon, but before we reached the point where the two rivers meet, we headed past what seemed like a never-ending line of container piers and industrial buildings spewing smoke into the already leaden air. I had not been expecting this. If this trip had taught me one thing, it would have been always to expect the unexpected.

The boat was heading toward Lake January, part of an ecological reserve where we would disembark and take motorized canoes that, in the words of the excursion brochure, would skim through the narrow channels within the rainforest. This whole thing was so out of context for a New Yorker who thought roughing it meant not getting a dinner reservation at our first-choice restaurant on a Saturday evening—or at least that's what Izzy told us one time a few years ago. I smiled when I thought about what Izzy might say if she could see her mother now. Peter must have noticed the smile.

"I'm glad to see you smiling. Want to share? I could use a smile about now," he said. "Although, I must say you look particularly fantastic today, and that makes me smile."

I was astonished that he could say that so sincerely, given my nearly makeup-less visage. It did make me happy, though.

"I was just thinking about how different this trip is from my life," I said.

I could feel Peter shrug almost imperceptibly. "And probably different from how you might have envisioned it when I asked you to come to the Amazon with me."

Now, it was my turn to shrug, but I was doing it with a smile. "I've just remembered an important thing about life. Always expect the unexpected."

"You've got that right."

The guide was now telling us about what we could expect to see once we got into the ecological reserve. I listened with half an ear, and when he had finished, I tapped Peter on the leg. "Peter, when you asked me to come with you, you said that you'd always wanted to go to the Amazon, but you never said why."

"Yeah, it's been a bit of a bucket list thing for me for years. I've never mentioned it to anyone before, though. I had some kind of romantic notion about what it would be like. I suppose we all live within the comfort zones we've built up throughout our lives. I've never been someone who lived on the edge. The Amazon probably seemed like something that might push me to my edge and beyond. I just had no idea how."

"But you never know what's going to happen in an emergency room when you go to work. That seems edgy enough for anyone."

"Not the same thing. That is precisely where my comfort zone is. I thrive on that kind of adrenaline-induced high that comes from the sheer exhilaration of not knowing what'll come in through the door and knowing I almost always have the skills to fix it. That defines my comfort zone. This trip is something altogether different, and I'm not sure what it is."

"I suppose we fool ourselves into thinking that life is one way when it's really another."

Peter turned to look at me. "I'm not sure what you mean."

I laughed. "I'm not sure I know what I mean, either." Fortunately, Peter didn't press me for more explanation.

I was still wondering exactly what I'd overheard the night before in the infirmary. We sat together in silence for a while. Images of a long-ago television show I'd enjoyed as a child crowded my head. The show, which had already been on television for years when I started watching it as a ten or eleven-year-old, had been called "Three's Company." It was a crazy sitcom, where every show was based on a misunderstanding of one sort or another. Often, it was an overheard conversation that meant something entirely different from what the eavesdropper thought it did. That made for all kinds of zany conflicts. I was drawn back to the present moment as the guide began talking again.

He told us we were nearing our first destination. We had crossed the River Negro and had reached a clutch of rainforest-covered islands where we would pick our way into a smaller tributary toward the lake. The boat pulled up to a dock that was already occupied by two other similar riverboats. Once the crew had secured the ropes, we climbed out of our boat, into the next one, across its deck and into the third one until we clambered out and onto the small dock. Under the thatch roof was the inevitable gift shop offering all manner of indigenous crafts and I suspect, shot glasses direct from China. We had to do the mandatory gift shop walk-through to get to the other dock where our canoes awaited.

I don't know what I was expecting when the brochure said canoes, but these were not it. Each wooden canoe held about a dozen people, with a driver at the back controlling an outboard motor. Each canoe also had a flat wooden sunshade held up by eight two-by-fours. All in all, they looked like something straight out of the African Queen—or perhaps, the Amazonian rainforest. We climbed in and got ready to "skim through the narrow channels."

The sky was still low and leaden, but I could see a few peeks of blue. As enticing as seeing the sun might sound, what it would mean was that the already sizzling air would become even more sweltering—not an appealing scenario. We began our journey into the lake past twenty or more tiny, one-story wooden houses with corrugated metal roofs that floated on the water in the grasses that grew along the shore.

As I watched them go by, I was thinking about the lives the occupants of the houses led and how they would probably find our lives so off-putting in so many ways when a woman in the seat behind us loudly asked the guide, "Do people actually *live* in those huts?"

I cringed as I looked at his face because it was clear that he was probably one of those people. It was also clear that she could be a poster child for overindulged stupidity. I turned my attention to the grasses that we seemed to be floating over en route to what the guide said would be a possible sighting of the famous giant water lilies.

I had noticed a distinct dearth of wildlife all along the river for the past few days and hoped this sanctuary might be the home to some local varieties. I suppose I'd been expecting there to be animals everywhere, although I'm not sure where I got that idea. I'd been hoping for a sighting of those famously pink dolphins that Amazonia is known for, but there was nothing. This place seemed much the same. Apart from the egrets and a few other birds we could see and hear, the only movement was the myriad grasses rising from the bottom of the lake and undulating in the slight breeze. At least there were no mosquitoes.

We finally reached the water lilies. They were, indeed, bigger than any water lily I'd ever seen. As our guide reached for one to pull it up so that we could see the enormous veins on the bottom of the lily pad, he explained that they acted like giant stepping stones for the river birds. Cameras and phones clicked all around. As interesting as it was, I was a bit disappointed that, when I looked around, I could see no water lily flowers. Was that what life was like? Always looking for the prettier thing that isn't there? I sighed, causing Peter to look at me. We exchanged a glance, but neither of us said anything. I had the eery feeling that he could read my mind. The moment that thought surfaced, I tamped it down as fast as I could and refocused on the feeling of sweat pouring down the sides of my head and dripping off my forehead. *Dear god,* I thought, *I'm having a hot flash in the middle of the Amazon, and it hardly registers.*

By the time our canoe arrived back at the dock where our riverboat was now the only one left, the clouds had begun to part, and the sun was shining. As much as I could appreciate the way the sun lit up the water and the grasses, creating a different canvas of more vivid colour, all I could think about was that every piece of clothing I was wearing was plastered to my skin. I only hoped I'd be able to peel them off without taking a layer of that skin along with them.

Once back on board the riverboat, we headed out of the lake through a different passage and into what the guide said was the actual Amazon River. We'd follow it back to where it met the River Negro, and the two waters met.

It wasn't long before we could see the famed line in the water. It's hard to describe how odd this looked. The River Negro water was a clear, black, almost like translucent liquid tar. The Amazon water was a dusky light brown. Each river carried water, but the water each of them carried had a different provenance—a different background, a different place of origin, a different composition. It was those very different compositions that meant they could travel along, side-by-side for six kilometres, never mixing, until they finally did.

I looked at Peter, who seemed to be transfixed by the phenomenon and wondered if going downstream, not paddling against the current any longer, would have the same effect on people. Would they ever start to mingle?

PART 2

PETER

TEN MORE DAYS TO MIAMI. I gripped the railing on the top deck as I looked down into the depths of the Amazon River at the meeting of the waters. I had only ten more days to try to get this right. I have always been a practical kind of guy. I've always believed that what I see is what I get. But over the past ten days, I'd begun to wonder if everything I believed throughout my life had all just been one big lie—an illusion. I had never been inclined toward drama outside of my work as an E.R. doctor, but at that moment, I considered jumping into the water and letting the ship sail away without me. But that wouldn't really get me anywhere.

I knew from the first moment that I set eyes on Eliza Cohen last summer that she wasn't just anyone. There was something that crackled in the air between us when we locked eyes in the front seat of Dad's S.U.V. We had only a few days together, including that hilarious moment in my E.R. when she realized that the guy who she thought was her holiday driver across Newfoundland was really a doctor. When I looked into her eyes and saw pure candour, that was the moment when I fell in love with her. I didn't know how or when we'd meet again, but I knew we would. Then, when she ended up back on the island for Christmas, I realized I was getting a second chance—that my second chance was fated. I would be unlikely to get a second chance to grab my second chance. So, I asked her to come to the Amazon with me. How was I to know that Claire would be here? I know that Claire's presence shouldn't have made any difference, but of course, it did.

Claire was the last person I wanted even to think about, much less see. I'd had twenty years of hard slogging on that front. Then, there was that moment when we were waiting to meet the captain at that cocktail party, and I saw Claire with that Jeffrey guy.

From the first moment that I laid eyes on her standing there clutching his arm and telling me what a coincidence it was that we should be on the same ship at the same time, I knew what she was up to. I hadn't been married to the queen of passive-aggressive manipulation for twenty years without learning a few things and without recognizing a plot when I saw one. Claire, however, was so self-involved and focused on the great Dr. Claire Barrett's career that she had never noticed. The moment I saw them together, I knew exactly who Dr. Jeffrey P. Montgomery was. I just had no intention of letting her know that I knew.

Two years earlier, Claire had come back from that conference in L.A. in a strange mood. I knew something was up. Eventually, I suppose she felt guilty enough that she couldn't live with herself, and she told me about her "little indiscretion." She had slept with someone at the conference. It wasn't important. She was sorry. She would never do it again. Want to bet?

She didn't tell me who it was, and I didn't ask. I frankly didn't care. It was far too late by then. If she thought her little indiscretion was the reason for me asking for a divorce, she had her head stuck too far up her arse (as we said in Newfoundland) to realize that we'd been drifting apart for years. But the kids and how a divorce might affect them had kept me tethered to my same-old, same-old life. I guess my choice to spend so much of my time at work at least had the effect of boosting my career. It did nothing for our relationship, though. However, when Dr. Ricci, the onboard doctor, asked me to come to the infirmary to consult, I was suspicious. Medical malpractice issues being what they are these days, I was hardly in any position as a guest on board to consult on anything medical. He was insistent, though, so I went along.

The moment I walked into the infirmary on board and saw that the patient in question was none other than my ex-wife, and I looked at her lying there in the bed looking pale and pained, I knew what was going on. Claire had no more sprained her wrist or taken a "spell" than I had. I immediately thought, two can play this game. So, I let her believe that I was concerned and there to help. I must admit that when she agreed to let Dr. Ricci give her a sedative, I was mildly surprised. Then, when I told her I'd stay the night, I could see the glee in her eyes. I knew she was thinking, game, set, match. But she was wrong.

I suppose I should come clean and recognize that marrying her had been my first mistake, a mistake I was still paying for in so many ways, large and small.

Claire Barrett and I were in medical school together. She was from a family of physicians, and she was smart, pretty and very driven, as was expected of her in her family. I should have realized that her ambition and her single-minded, laser-like focus on herself and her career would be the end of us. My family was different. Yes, my father was a lawyer, so it appeared that we came from similar backgrounds, but we were a far more laid-back family. My parents were Newfoundlanders from the tops of their heads to the tips of their toes. Both of them had been brought up in fishing villages outside the city, and my father was the first in his family to go to university. Even my mother had an arts degree, making her a bit of a family anomaly among the women of her generation and her home community. So, their approach to careers and life was that they should enjoy them as much as possible. Claire's parents, on the other hand, believed that a medical career was imperative because they were saving the world. It was, frankly, exhausting to be in their presence.

When I told my parents I wanted to be a doctor, they were perplexed at first. My father had fully expected me to go to law school in Montreal as he had done and then return home to take over his law practice. Once Dad realized I was adamant, he'd simply gotten with the program and supported me through pre-med and then medical school. They never really liked Claire, though—Mom thought she was conceited and vain—and when I told my mother that we were divorcing, she said. "Peter, my son, you've not made many mistakes in your life, but this was a doozy. Get over it. Anyway, now I can die happy." And she did—of stage-four ovarian cancer a month later.

Claire had come to Mom's funeral despite the ongoing nature of the divorce at the time. Liam and Fiona needed her support because they had been close to their grandmother. I remember sitting in the front row of the church in St. John's on a cold January day, thinking about how my life might have been different if I'd resisted Claire's suggestion (push, to be more accurate) to get married all those years ago.

When I found out that I'd gotten my dream residency in emergency medicine in Toronto and would be able to learn alongside the best of the best at St. Michael's Hospital's inner city emergency room, I was ecstatic. Deep down, I probably felt a modicum of relief that Claire and I would be parted after graduation. She had other plans. Unbeknownst to me, Claire had inveigled herself with someone she'd met at a conference in Toronto the year before and had received an offer to do her residency in pediatric surgery at Sick Kids—also in Toronto. She was the first one to broach marriage.

What could I do? Sure, I could have told her that I didn't want to get married, but the truth is I didn't want to be single either. I figured it would make life easier as a resident who would be working long hours if I had a wife regardless of her own relentless schedule. I wouldn't have time to date. So, we got married. It seemed like the right thing to do at the time. All these years later, though, I knew deep down in my heart that if we hadn't married, Liam and Fiona wouldn't be a part of my life, and that would have been a shame.

I looked down again at the "meeting of the waters" just visible in the light from the ship and the moon. When we'd entered the Amazon River, the ship maintained low lights on all outside decks and even asked us to keep our drapes closed after sunset. It was an attempt to reduce the ambient light so that insects and birds of the rainforest might not be lured to their deaths by crashing into the bright lights of the passing ship. I didn't see any birds or other flying creatures. All I could see in the dusky light was the line in the water that Eliza and I had seen from a much lower perspective on that small riverboat earlier in the day.

I knew that I'd eventually see the waters from the two rivers mingle and coalesce until they became one, and I wondered if I'd thought about becoming one with Claire when we were first married. I knew I had not. Ever the pragmatist, I didn't believe that ever happened in life. Then I met Eliza.

I had never met anyone like her. Driven and successful like Claire, she was so different in that she seemed to take it in stride and had learned to laugh at herself. She was a New Yorker, all right, but her down-home, East Coast, Canadian roots still showed, even as she tried to cover them up. It was disarming. I had no idea at this point how I'd make it happen, but I knew that somehow, she and I were meant to be together. And I think she knew it.

"Hey, buddy, don't do it."

~

I turned toward the familiar voice that bled out of the darkness. Silhouetted in the dim light from the emergency lights on the ship's outside staircases, Jeffrey stood there, hands in his pockets, his linen jacket slung across one shoulder. He looked as rumpled as I felt.

I looked down at the water again as it splashed along the hull. "No, I don't really have the guts to do it, anyway."

Jeffrey came over and stood beside me, his hands hanging over the railing. He looked up at the moon. "Woman problems?"

I turned toward him in the semi-darkness. "I know who you are, you know—buddy."

I could see a smile turning up the corner of his mouth. "I figured you did. And I'm pretty sure Claire didn't tell you. I think dudes just know these things."

I winced at being called a dude. It wasn't in my vocabulary. I guess my age was showing.

"Hey, Pete, I hope our little dalliance didn't upset the apple cart of your marriage too much. Claire didn't seem all that bothered by the fact that she was married."

"Were *you* bothered by the fact that she was married?"

Jeffrey shrugged. "Not so much. I figured her marriage wasn't my problem, and since marriage isn't high on my list of things to do, it didn't matter. But I do need you to know that I had no idea she was going to be on this ship or that she was planning to use me as part of her scheme to lure you back."

I started laughing. I laughed so hard that Jeffrey started pounding me on the back to keep me from choking. I stood up straight. "That felt good to laugh," I said. "Claire and me back together? Now, if that scenario wasn't so gruesome, it might be funny. Not going to happen, man. She's all yours if you want her."

Now, it was Jeffrey's turn to look alarmed. He turned to me, and I read terror on his face. "Me? And Claire Barrett? Geezus, Pete, she's way too old for me."

I shook my head in disbelief. "So, what about Eliza, then? She's the same age, and the two of you looked very cozy over dinner the other night. She also tells me you've had a drink together."

Jeffrey shook his head as he looked out over the water. "Whoa, man, you've got me all wrong, Pete. Eliza and Claire are both awesome women, and you're lucky to have them vying for your attention, but in the long run, they're both too old for me. I am a big fan of Eliza's work, though, and we got along so well that it was like we'd met before. Anyway, I'm not looking—not now, and not ever."

"You seem a bit young to have stopped looking. You ever been married?"

"For two long years back when I was in my early twenties. I don't like to talk about it. It was a mistake, but if there's one thing I know, it's this. Letting our mistakes fester inside us and not learning from them is the dumbest way to live."

"That doesn't sound very psychiatrist-like," I said.

"I don't suppose it does. But it's a life lesson. I moved on."

"You talk a lot about love in your lectures and books. Have you ever been in love?"

"Once—and not with the woman I married, I can tell you that. But it disappeared one day and never returned."

I wasn't the kind of guy to notice when other guys looked wistful, but if I had been, Jeffrey would have. "You mean she left you?"

"Not sure what happened. Maybe it was too much for her. Maybe she got cold feet. I had never met anyone like her, and I don't suppose I ever will again. It took me a while to get over her, but I did. I've moved on, and I realize that I don't need anyone in my life."

When he said he had never met anyone like her, I immediately thought about Eliza. "Did you ever try to find her?"

"Nope."

As we stood there in silence for a few moments, I wondered how two seemingly successful and self-assured men could be so completely messed up when it came to our personal lives.

Finally, Jeffrey said, "Did you ever read that famous letter John Steinbeck wrote to his teenage son when he told his father he was in love?"

"Must have missed that one while doing C.P.R. on someone."

Jeffrey laughed. "Yeah, saving lives can be so time-consuming. Anyway, he wrote it in 1958, and one of the things he said in the letter was that there's more than one kind of love, and he wasn't talking about love of everyone, love of self or any of the other stuff we psychiatrists talk about. He said the first kind of love is selfish love, the kind that feeds the ego and survives only to support our own self-importance. He called that ugly and crippling."

"I hope there was another kind."

Jeffrey continued. "Yeah, there was. There is. Steinbeck said the other kind is the kind that exists when we pour everything good that's inside ourselves—stuff like kindness, compassion, respect—into the relationship because we know that the object of our attention is unique and precious. Precious was Steinbeck's word, but I like to think a better word might be irreplaceable. Anyway, he also told his son that the second kind of love had the possibility of showing you strength, courage and wisdom you didn't even know you had. I had that kind of love before I lost it—and her. That's why I write books and give presentations about love." He stopped for a moment. "Oh yeah, at the end of the letter, he tells his son he shouldn't worry about losing that kind of love. He said, 'If it's right, it happens,' and that nothing gets in the way." Jeffrey stopped before continuing. "And I guess that if it isn't right, it doesn't happen."

For a moment, I thought about what was right in my life—what had possibilities. I thought about what Jeffrey had said about a love that's precious and irreplaceable. I also thought again about reality and illusion and how I'd been wondering if this was all an illusion—if love was all an illusion, or maybe *life* was the illusion. In that moment, I knew it didn't matter. Reality or illusion, I knew what was going to happen. I knew what was right in my life—or would be. I now knew what it meant to see that extraordinary illusion in every ordinary moment.

I turned to Jeffrey. "So, *dude*, how old did you say you are?"

~

The following morning, I went in search of Eliza. I knew she'd be in the gleaming new demonstration kitchen on board, getting ready for her afternoon class. As I approached the vast double glass doors, I saw a large table display. The table was covered in snowy white linen and adorned with tall vases filled with pampas grass and orange flowers that I didn't recognize. Between the vases were piles of books. And there, smiling out at the world from the front cover, was Eliza sitting at an impressive granite-topped kitchen island with myriad gleaming copper pots suspended above, holding the stem of a martini glass. There were three olives in it. I'd have to remember that detail. Just the thought of her made me feel slightly off-balance.

"A wonderful good morning to you, sir."

I looked over and saw that Rebecca, our esteemed cruise director, was placing and replacing books as if she might be trying to find the best angle for future photography. The resulting photos would, no doubt, grace a cruise line ad someday in the future.

"Good morning, Rebecca. Looks good."

She looked like a delighted child. "Dr. O'Brien, you have no idea how much that is music to my ears. It is exciting, don't you think? Having someone of Ms. Cohen's calibre agree to give a demonstration class. But, of course, she's your lover, so I'm sure you would know more about that than I do." She clapped her hand over her mouth in what I hoped was mock horror.

"I could only wish," I said, thinking how terrific that sounded.

"Oh, I am sorry, sir." She seemed to take a moment to regroup. "You are, of course, joining us this afternoon for her class." It was more of a demand than a question.

I assured her I was and wondered if I could be permitted to interrupt whatever preparation was currently going on in the kitchen. She said to go ahead, so I pulled open the door and stepped inside.

The place was a monument to the modern foodie's wildest wet dream—or the female equivalent. There were three rows of glossy countertops, each boasting five shiny sinks and range tops. Those must have been the workstations for the people attending cooking classes. At the front was another impressively long counter with cooktops at each end and three overhead cameras. I counted three monitors, including a huge one behind the demonstration counter. The entire far wall was floor-to-ceiling, end-to-end windows overlooking the water as we floated downstream. It was impressive, indeed.

I looked around and saw Eliza deep in conversation with two crew members dressed in chef-like kitchen attire. The white jackets and pants and tall white chef's hats were dead giveaways. I stood there at the entrance as the doors closed silently behind me. What was it about her that made me want to stand there and just watch her work? Suddenly, as if she could feel my presence, she looked up, and our eyes locked. She wiped her hands on the apron she was wearing and said something to the young man and woman who I assumed were her helpers (possibly sous-chefs?) for her upcoming cooking class/demonstration. She smiled at them, took off her apron, said a few more words, then picked up a folder from the counter and headed toward me.

"Hello, Peter," she said. "Fancy seeing you here. I trust you slept well after our excursion yesterday. I was sorry to miss you at dinner last evening, but I just had to get some work done on today's presentation. I wasn't at all prepared. Rakesh served me dinner in my suite from the main dining room menu."

"I did miss you, but I understand."

"Did you see Claire at dinner?"

I was confused. "Why would I have seen Claire?" Although Eliza and I had spent several hours together the day before visiting the ecological sanctuary, we hadn't really had a conversation apart from our discussion about why I had wanted to see the Amazon in the first place. "Eliza, do you have time for an early lunch? We need to talk."

"I suppose we do," she said. "Just let me go and change. I'll meet you at the outdoor gill. I'm dying for a hot dog."

"A hot dog? I'm surprised that someone with your level of culinary expertise eats hot dogs."

She smiled, and I couldn't help but smile back. "My guilty pleasure," she said. "Or at least one of them."

I don't know why that made me hopeful we could get past whatever it was we were slogging through, but it did. I thought again about my conversations with Jeffrey the night before and remembered two words: precious and irreplaceable.

Half an hour later, we were settled into a table for two at the outside grill. Despite the heat and humidity, it was still nice to be able to eat outside in February. I ordered a beer, and Eliza said she'd stick to sparkling water until after her presentation. "Then we can celebrate," she said, her eyes dancing.

I wasn't sure why she seemed so happy, but I didn't care. I took a deep breath and started. "Eliza, you know when you told me yesterday always to expect the unexpected?" She nodded. "I'm beginning to understand how that might help. I need to begin at the beginning."

I told her about how unhappily unexpected it had been to see Claire on board this ship, and I explained to her about Claire's penchant for manipulation, especially when it looked like she might not get her way.

"But it does seem that Claire wants you back, Peter," Eliza said as the server placed a hot dog accompanied by French fries in front of her. She took an audible intake of breath and continued. "I suppose I need to be honest and tell you why this is resonating with me just now. It's because Jake has been texting me. He doesn't seem to realize that our marriage is over—has been over for a very long time."

I wasn't surprised that her husband didn't want to let her go. Women like Eliza were so few and far between—precious and irreplaceable. I reached for her hand across the table. "Are you over that part of your life, Eliza?"

She put down the French fry she was about to bite into and said, "I don't think it's a matter of being over anything, Peter. That's what I've been thinking. It's more about moving on. What happened over those twenty-plus years of my life will always be a part of me. What happened in the years before that will always be a part of me. It's all part of my story, and how I choose to see that story as I move into the next part of my life will be the important thing."

She was a wise woman.

Eliza bit off a mouthful of hot dog, chewed and swallowed, then rolled her eyes heavenward and said, "Deliciously divine!" Then she wiped her lips with a paper napkin and continued. "I wasn't sure how to bring this up or if I even should. I overheard you and Claire the other evening, Peter. In the infirmary. I came down to see you and heard you two talking. I heard her say how she could always count on you."

I had to interrupt her right there. "It's not what you think."

She patted my hand. "Let me finish. I overheard you tell her you'd always be there for her, and by the time I got back to my suite, my head was swimming. I suddenly felt as if I might not be able to have the one thing that I felt was completely right in my life. You." I started to interrupt again, but Eliza held up her hand. "Then I remembered my father telling me that enough is never enough for those for whom enough is never enough, and I realized how full my life would be even without you in it. We hardly know one another, anyway. And since then, after spending yesterday with you, I also realize that if anything were to develop further between us, knowing that I am content with my life, just as it is unfolding even without you, is where I need to be to begin. And I don't want to see this as a competition with you as the prize. Do you understand what I'm trying to say?"

"I think I do. And you need to know right this minute that the most unexpected thing that has happened to me in recent memory is meeting you. You were unexpected. I planned to take that new job in Toronto, leave my old life and ex-wife behind and carve out a new chapter. Then you appeared. And nothing has been the same since."

"So," Eliza said, reaching for a sip of my beer, "you and Claire are over. You might or might not be moving to Toronto. You're mesmerized by me," she smiled and batted her eyes. "There is no competition, and we are now going with the downstream flow."

I nodded. It was all I could do.

Then her eyes narrowed, and she said, "I think I need to tell you something, Peter." That sounded serious. I told her to continue. "It's about Claire. And Jeffrey."

"I already know. Jeffrey was Claire's indiscretion. Her fling. To tell you the truth, I didn't have a doubt after I saw them together at that cocktail party last week. Although Claire had never told me much about the man she got herself involved with, I'd always gotten the impression he was much younger than she was. So, I put that together with the way Jeffrey seemed so comfortable with her and *voilà*. Anyway, I'll see your revelation and raise you another shocker. Claire was faking her injury."

Eliza started to snort with laughter. Her snorting got me snorting, too and before we knew it, we were in stitches, and people were staring.

"Shall we begin again?" I said.

Eliza shook her head. "No, let's not."

"What? But I thought—"

"You thought we could start over, but there are no do-overs in life, Peter. You can't ever take back something you said or something you did. No regrets, okay? Let's take this second chance and keep that episode of our lives together always in the back of our heads. It's now part of us."

Us. I rolled the word over and over in my head. There was an "us" now. I liked the sound of that.

~

At precisely five minutes before three p.m., I arrived back at the demonstration kitchen for Eliza's class. I took my place at one of the stations, and before I even had my hands washed and dried as required, Claire was donning an apron and sidling over beside my station. I looked around to see if Jeffrey was anywhere in sight, but it seemed he was giving this a miss this afternoon. I shrugged. What did it matter if Claire and I were at the same cooking station? Eliza and I were on the same wavelength. At that moment, Eliza looked over toward me, nodded as she noted Claire beside me, and winked.

"Welcome, everyone. My name is Eliza Cohen, and I write cookbooks."

The applause from the thirty or so people attending this exclusive class was deafening. I had no idea cookbook authors were so famous. As I looked around, I could see that some of the participants had already bought copies of the cookbooks that Rebecca had placed on the tables outside in the corridor. Later, they would ask her to autograph them, but now, Eliza was turning her attention to some recipes she said would be from her upcoming cookbook. She called it a mash-up of two traditions that were close to her heart—Jewish cuisine and the culinary delights of her family's Newfoundland heritage. I suppose Claire and I might have been the only other two people in the place who had any idea how much of an odd pairing that would be.

"Let's begin with Cod Gefilte Tagine," she said. "Then we'll talk about Jiggs Brisket. We'll end the class by all making Orange Pudding." There were murmurs of appreciation all around.

The tagine sounded mildly off-putting to a regular kind of guy who loved a great pizza and a beer after a long shift in the emergency room, but before the class was finished, I'd be won over. On more than one count.

~

"You know, Eliza, this might not have been the dreamlike cruise we both thought we might be taking, but we do have a couple more stops."

It was after dinner, and Eliza and I were taking a walk outside in the heat and humidity that continued long after sunset. I don't know what I'd been expecting, but this kind of oppressive, almost choking heat was not one of them. I wasn't used to it—at all. I was used to the Newfoundland climate in the North Atlantic, where, as my father used to say, summer arrived on July 28 at ten in the morning and was over by the time we were eating supper that evening. It might have been an exaggeration, but not by much. I had a massive collection of sweaters and jackets. In spite of the heat, though, there was something that always seemed to draw us outside after dinner. Maybe it had something to do with how few people seemed to have the same idea. We had the deck almost entirely to ourselves.

The moon was enormous this evening as it shone over the water, making the dullness of the Amazon almost shimmer. I followed Eliza as she walked toward the railing of the upper deck, a kind of mezzanine that overlooked the pool that was lit from within by those aquamarine blue lights that pool designers are so fond of.

"Yes," she said, "we do have two more stops, and two of them are on Caribbean islands where we could start walking the beaches of the world."

"Walking the beaches of the world. Is that something you'd like to do?"

Eliza turned to me. "It could be our thing, Peter. But first, walk me back to my suite. Please."

I did. It was morning before I swiped my key card to let me into my stateroom. My new chapter had begun.

PART 3

EIGHTEEN

Eliza

CRUISING THE AMAZON

I'M NOT SURE WHAT I EXPECTED would l happen on this cruise with a man I hardly knew. I had tried to play down the thoughts of having sex with him. And yet, before I'd left New York, I took an afternoon out of my test kitchen where I felt safest in all the world and took an Uber to Fifth Avenue to Saks to do a bit of cruise shopping. I wandered among the bikinis (a big no) and the tankinis (what an odd name), then onto the sarongs (I haven't worn one of those for decades) and the shirt-style pool cover-ups (more my style). That was all just a distraction, though. I was really making my way slowly to the lingerie department.

Why did I gravitate toward the white lace? Wasn't that section for brides? Virginal brides? Although to tell you the truth, I don't suppose there's a virginal bride in sight outside of radical religious movements these days—or even when I was that age. Who would even want to be a virgin on her wedding night? It's such a 1960s cliché and quite dangerous, in my view. As I stood there in front of the rail of white silk and lace, I considered how awful it would have been to find that your new spouse wasn't someone you even wanted to sleep beside, much less have sex with.

I remembered that I'd sighed and stroked the cool, smooth surface of a white nightgown trimmed with delicate French lace. It was beautiful, and as I stood there in the lingerie department at Saks in New York, I suddenly felt the burning desire to have it and to wear it. That was then. That was there. Now I was here.

My cooking class had gone well, and it was now time to get ready for dinner. With Peter. What would this evening bring? As I stood there in my suite that afternoon, I plucked the delicate white silk nightgown from the drawer and laid it on the bed. I stared at it for a few moments, and then I decided to try it on.

There was a full-length mirror in the small hallway leading to the sitting area. I stood there staring. What did I see? Looking back at me was a middle-aged, menopausal woman who looked like she was trying too hard. White silk and lace? Who was I kidding? I wasn't that virginal young woman. And I wasn't what I used to be. I stared harder for a moment, seeing only the forehead lines and those marionette furrows surrounding my lips. I peered at them.

Faint lines tracked downward from the corners of my mouth. I tilted my head to catch the light and traced one of them lightly with my fingertips. I shivered as I seemed to feel the weight of years in those subtle indentations. For a moment, I convinced myself that they had been etched by a lifetime of memories that were a part of me. They spoke of a life, if not well-lived, at least lived. When I thought of them that way, they didn't seem so bad.

I stood back again and saw my wildly curly auburn hair that until as recently as last year, I used to straighten and colour. It was now shot through with more strands of silver than I could count and curled in a most natural way. I stared at the slight jowls that were beginning to drag at the sides of my face. Then I placed my hand over my stomach and felt the soft squishiness of the small pouch that never used to be there. And the boobs? Well, let's just say that they couldn't pass the pencil test easily these days.

I took a deep breath and said out loud, "Take another look, Eliza. There must be more."

So, I did.

As I looked more carefully, I saw me but not me. The reflection was familiar, yet it felt strange. I felt strange. The reality of knowing that I'm not the same young woman I was when I first moved to New York—when I first met Jake—hit me like a ton of bricks. I wasn't the same. I was so much more.

I was already in my mid-twenties when I arrived in the Big Apple—when I first met Jake. I wasn't a virgin even then, but I might as well have been. I liked to think that we're all still really virgins until we've made love to someone we really love. All the rest is just sex, isn't it? All those encounters I tried to forget for decades came flooding back to me in the moment. I had never told Jake about any of them. I didn't trust him enough. I didn't trust myself enough. As I stared at myself, I wondered where I'd even ever learned about sex.

Sex certainly wasn't anything my uptight Catholic mother had broached. The thought of hearing the word sex from my mother's lips made me laugh. Even my father, the doctor, hadn't given his three daughters any information, although I suppose that's to be expected. In our family, it was as if sex didn't even exist—as if babies materialized through virgin births. So, when I began my own search for a relationship—dare I say love—I fumbled my way along until I learned. What I'd learned, though, was that sex didn't get me to love.

So, when Jake and I met, I felt as if I might be starting over. I felt like a virgin who knew nothing. But after more than twenty years of marriage and sex with only one man, I didn't know who I was. Jake might have had his infidelities over the years, but I hadn't. I had buried myself in my work and motherhood and never took the time to come up for air. Until that moment when I told Jake our marriage was over, I'd never even considered what it would be like to be facing the possibility of sleeping with a new man. Now, I was looking in the mirror, and that was all I could think about.

I stared harder at the image in the mirror and started laughing. "Virginal white? I don't think so," I said, pulling it off over my head. I balled it up and tossed it into the corner of the drawer, thinking that if all went well with Peter, perhaps I'd drag it out someday in the future, and we'd have a laugh. I was no virgin, but I could definitely start again.

I scrambled around, pulling pieces of lingerie out of the drawer and settled on a set of black underwear. There would be no white silk and lace today.

After a fantastic dinner, Peter and I found ourselves up on deck in the moonlight. Could there be anything more cliché? Or anything more romantic? The stars seemed to be aligned just for us. When I asked Peter to walk me back to my suite, I knew he wouldn't be leaving until the next morning.

When we closed the door behind us, and he leaned into me, his lips brushing my neck, I thought I might explode. How long had it been since I'd felt like that? I couldn't remember, and I knew it didn't matter. We came together like two people who had been lost in a desert and had finally stumbled upon an oasis. We couldn't get enough of one another.

All my machinations about white silk and black lace were moot. There was no time to even think about what I was wearing because I soon was wearing nothing. We were then not more than a tangle of limbs on the bed with the moonlight shining in through the windows. I didn't even have time to wonder what Peter would think about my soft, round bits. He told me I was gorgeous, and for once in my life, I believed it.

When we fell away from one another, we both started laughing. Neither of us really knew why, but we just knew we could laugh. Then Peter said, "I wish I could remember the name of the movie where I heard the line, 'If you don't laugh during sex at least once, you're having sex with the wrong person.' I think I have just found the right person."

When we awoke the following morning, I felt happier than I had in years. I watched Peter as he slept and wondered about what the future might hold. Then, a cloud drifted over my sunny thoughts.

How was I going to tell Peter that I might not be who he thought I was? Perhaps even expected me to be. I had spent over two decades with one man, god help me, but I was no virgin when I married Jake—I had a past. It was, as I alluded to, not a past I could ever trust Jake with.

In my early years, I'd been less than the pure young woman my mother had taught her daughters to be. I had fumbled my way through my first sexual encounter before I turned twenty (I know, I know. These days, that is probably considered to be a late bloomer, but it wasn't at the time). Then, I hadn't been as fussy as I might have been as I lurched from one relationship to another, always looking for that someone who might spark something. I remembered an old quote that no one seems to know the source of, but I suspect it's from a B-grade movie. "Falling in love is easy. Having sex is easier. But bumping into someone who can spark your soul? That shit is rare." Now, Peter had sparked my soul. Even Jake hadn't done that.

When Peter woke up, he saw me staring at him. "Hey, you don't look as happy as I had hoped."

I immediately had to tell him that I was just thinking and that it had nothing to do with him.

"Then who does it have to do with?"

"Me."

Peter stared at me. "Okay, Eliza. Spill. Whatever it is, you can tell me."

I wasn't sure I could. I wasn't sure I knew him well enough. I'd never been able to tell Jake, and it probably impeded my relationship with him. But if this one was going to have any future, I couldn't bury it forever. Now that he'd asked, I knew I had to get it over with. So I did.

When I'd finished my talk, Peter said, "That's my girl!"

He truly was one in a million. I then remembered reading something Gloria Steinem once said. "Once we give up searching for approval, we often find it easier to earn respect." I didn't need Peter's approval, but I felt his respect. That was something.

NINETEEN

Claire

SANTAREM, BRAZIL

AS MUCH AS I WASN'T KEEN on spending a couple of hours in the presence of a woman I disliked so intensely while she basked in the admiration of her "audience," I wasn't going to let Peter attend that woman's cooking class alone. I texted Jeffrey to ask him if he wanted to go with me since he'd been so keen on Eliza and her cookbooks. His terse reply was that he was going to pass on this, but he provided no further explanation. He seemed so keen on attending Eliza's class when we chatted briefly about it, so I was a bit surprised. It didn't matter, though. *Perhaps this will be even better*, I thought. *Perhaps Peter and I can work side by side, and Eliza can see how good we are together*. Besides, in my one-armed state, I was going to need help. Who better to help me than the man who said he'd always be there for me? Or something like that.

When I arrived at the test kitchen, I wasn't surprised to see that Peter was already there. The space beside him was still vacant, so I hurried over. As I stood there, trying to get my apron on with one hand (he wasn't helping at all), I noticed him look at Eliza and smile. Did she wink at him?

"A little help would be nice," I said.

Peter turned to me, smiling. "Claire," he said, "As your doctor, I think you should consider using it more."

My eyes widened. Using it more? Did he know? Did that damn Rebecca say something? Or maybe it was that turncoat, Jeffrey. Where *was* he, anyway?

"I suppose I could try to use it a bit," I said, not wanting to draw any more attention to my plight.

"Yes," Peter said, "you could. And by the way, where's your friend today? Jeffrey?"

"First, if you must know, there is absolutely nothing going on between Jeffrey and me. Second, I have no idea where he is. I don't keep tabs on him." Although I was trying to do so.

Standing at the front of the room, looking like she owned the place, Eliza began talking. I was stunned by the applause for her. It seemed she was better known than I realized—not that this mattered. In the least. Peter, however, seemed mesmerized by her. This was continuing to be harder than I thought it would be, and now, I didn't seem to have Jeffrey as an ally. Just as we were told to come to the front so we could see Eliza begin preparation for something called "Cod Gefilte Fish Tagine," the very thought of which made me gag faintly, my phone pinged.

I fished it out of my pocket and clicked it on to see a text from Fiona.

Sorry, Mom. Not going to be able to meet you in Miami. Got to go on a short trip. Tell you about it later. Get some sun. You always need it. F.

What in the world was going on? What kind of short trip could be more important than meeting your mother in Miami, especially when Mom was paying for everything?

It wasn't as if Fiona had any kind of responsibility in her job. She was a ballerina, after all. She might have done something more substantial with her life if Peter hadn't lorded it over me when I wanted to veto her acceptance to the National Ballet School all those years ago. Now, I just had to live with the fact that she was a dancer. I do have to admit, though, that she's very good at what she does. So, there is that. Anyway, my plans for the big family reunion in Miami seemed to be collapsing like a house of cards, which, I suppose, some might think it was. At this point, I was beginning to consider the possibility that it might not happen at all. I sighed and returned my mind to the task at hand—learning about cooking some odd concoction that I wouldn't ever eat in a million years. I was a born and bred Newfoundlander, but choosing to eat cod, as much as it seems to go with the territory, wasn't something I had ever enjoyed. Perhaps it had been all those Catholic fish Fridays I'd had to endure as a child. Even my mother, who was a busy family physician herself, had always insisted we eat cod on Fridays and other fish in between. Now, Eliza was suggesting some mash-up between Newfoundland cod and a Jewish specialty. As I tuned back in, Eliza was talking about its origin.

"I remember the first time my daughter, Izzy, was served gefilte fish at her grandmother's—my mother-in-law's—house." Was that a fleeting scowl I observed on the sainted Eliza's face? Was she grimacing at the thought of the fish (a stance I could support), or was it about her mother-in-law? I'd probably never know. She continued. "Izzy thought it smelled like cat food and refused to eat it. I have to admit, it can be an acquired taste, but I think you'll change your mind about it when you taste this one that uses Newfoundland cod in place of other types of fish that are more traditional, like carp or pike.

The fish is cooked and ground, then mixed with an interesting combination of breadcrumbs, eggs and spices and one addition to this new version is Newfoundland summer savoury."

Now, she had lost me for sure. The name itself conjured an olfactory memory of my grandmother, who had used summer savoury on everything from cod to turkey dressing and everything in between. I could still smell its thyme-like herbal notes, but it was the peppery, earthy fragrance that made me think I was eating dirt whenever I tasted it. I was the oddity of the family, though, because everyone else loved it. And I remembered how much Peter had loved it whenever he and I had the occasion to be invited to my grandmother's house. As I said, she used it in everything.

It seemed that the majority of the participants had never smelled the stuff which one of Eliza's helpers was now passing around for the sniff test. I passed.

Eliza was cooking her recipe as a Moroccan-style tagine instead of balls, which she suggested was the norm. Either way you looked at it, we were still eating cod—and you could smell it everywhere. I was going to reek.

After the cod, we moved on to her version of what we had called Jiggs Dinner in Newfoundland—better known to some as corned beef and cabbage—but she was making it like you would a brisket. I had no idea why anyone would do that, but the people around me all seemed enthralled, especially when it came time to taste the one she'd put on earlier in the day and was now ready to eat. I watched Peter as he dipped a fork into the small plate now in front of him.

"Oh my god. This is wonderful. That woman can cook, eh?" Peter closed his eyes as he lazily chewed the corned beef brisket smothered in mustard from the mustard pickles the staff had added to the side of each plate.

I rolled my eyes. You could take the boy out of Newfoundland, but you couldn't take Newfoundland out of the boy. That much was clear.

I thought it would never be over, but it did finally come to an end. Just as I had expected, I stank of fish. I wasn't going to stay around and watch while everyone fawned over Eliza Cohen, so I slipped out.

~

Fifteen minutes later, I was standing under the shower, trying to get every vestige of the afternoon out of my hair and off my skin. I stood there, water running over my head like people often do in movies when things in their lives aren't going as planned. As the water dripped insistently into my eyes, I had only one continuous thought running through my head. *What the hell are you doing? What the hell are you doing?* I realized I had no answer, or at least no answer that made sense any longer.

By the time I was towelled off and changed into something fresh (I was considering burning the clothes I'd been wearing, but fires aren't permitted on cruise ships), I stood at the mirror in the dressing room and stared at myself.

"Who the hell are you, and what have you done with Dr. Claire Barrett?"

Dr. Claire Barrett was not someone who ran after men—not even someone as special as her ex-husband. She was not someone who had to chase after things. They chased after her. She was not someone who spent even a moment feeling confused. She was the one who straightened everyone else out.

I went to the beverage fridge and pulled out a bottle of Far Niente Chardonnay from California's Napa Valley. It was a bit fancy to drink without someone to share it with, but who cared? I rummaged through the cupboards to find the corkscrew and a wine glass and sat down on the sofa to drink myself silly. I put in a call to my butler and told him I'd be dining in this evening and could he please bring me an antipasti plate and a chicken Caesar salad at six p.m. I'd had more than enough of being around other people. I spent every working hour at the hospital with people, and perhaps it was time to take a breather. Maybe Fiona was right. Maybe I did need some sun (I knew her reference wasn't strictly literal). It was time to regroup and get back to being myself. I was comfortable with my life as it was, and I knew what I was doing. I always knew what each day and each week would be like. What was the point in changing a thing?

I then poured my first glass of wine and toasted myself. I sat back, put my feet up on the coffee table and savoured the first sip, remembering that tomorrow, the ship was scheduled to dock in the city of Santarem, where I was booked on a rainforest hike. I lifted my tour ticket from a pile of papers on the coffee table and looked at it. I was supposed to be going to the Tapajós National Forest. I rummaged for the explanatory brochure and slid it out from under the sheaf of papers, then thumbed through to find the description of my excursion.

"Trek through pristine Tapajós National Forest with a naturalist," it said. "Get fascinating insights on the flora and wildlife indigenous to this part of the Amazon," it said. It talked about this national forest as being one and a half million acres of protected rainforest. As impressive as that sounded, I wasn't sure I was up to the promised one-hour drive along the only road through that part of Brazil and then an hour and a half hiking a trail in the "unspoiled" forest to spot Brazil nut trees, rubber trees and birds. I poured another glass of wine.

I must have fallen asleep because I was startled by the ringing of my doorbell when Rakesh arrived with my dinner. I looked at my watch. It was five minutes to six, and I had no idea where the time had gone. Then I looked at the bottle of wine that was three-quarters empty, and I knew. Rakesh wanted to set up the table, but I asked him to set the tray down on the coffee table so I could eat casually. I wasn't up to linen and silverware set preciously.

When he left, I poured the rest of the bottle and went back to the wine selection to see what else was there. *Yes,* I thought as I reached for the bottle of 2008 Tommasi Amarone Della Valpolicella Classico. *Just what the doctor ordered to have with my antipasti*. Of course, I wouldn't have more than one glass of that one.

Before I fell asleep (passed out) later, I'd decided that I'd give the Amazon one more kick at the can. I set my alarm so I could get up early enough and closed my eyes.

~

To say I felt awful the next morning would be a massive understatement. I managed to down a piece of toast and a small cup of coffee that Rakesh brought to me for breakfast (did that man ever have time off?), but I could not touch the omelet. (I'd at least had the presence of mind to order my breakfast before I passed out.) I then managed to get myself to the gangway just in time to join the parade of "guests" who were moving slowly like a line of ants to board tenders to go ashore.

Dear god, I thought. *Not a boat ride. I hope I can keep my breakfast down until we reach the shore*. Of course, to make matters worse, by the time I squeezed into one of the last seats on that tender, I looked over and saw that Peter and Eliza were already there, and oddly, Jeffrey was with them. Perhaps my decision not to abort had been misguided.

The tender ride was almost twenty minutes of hot, humid pitching and rolling in the swell. I clutched the edge of the bench seat in a vain attempt for stability. I tried to take shallow breaths as if I might be able to keep out the nauseating, stomach-churning swaying of the waves. I felt every tilt and lurch of the boat for the entire time it took for us to make our way from the ship, which was anchored offshore, to the pier. I was never so grateful to step out onto solid ground, even if the temperature was soaring already. I followed the crowd to the waiting buses.

As I stood there waiting to see which one I was to board, I was thinking that these could not possibly be the transportation we were expected to spend several hours on. It was a line of what appeared to be repurposed city buses—repurposed but not refurbished in any way. Derelict was the word that popped into my mind as I boarded the one a peppy cruise line employee was pointing me toward.

I got on my bus and found myself sitting beside Jeffrey on a small bench seat that would be suitable for a ten-minute city bus ride but that promised to offer nothing but misery for a long drive into the country. I had yet to discover that the bus had essentially no suspension and that once clear of the city streets of Santarem, the roads weren't quite as smooth. Oh, yes. And the bus was not air-conditioned. Kill me now.

"Hey, Claire, what happened to your splint? Is your arm better?" Jeffrey said.

"I guess it wasn't much of a sprain, after all, " I said, protectively embracing my arm. One of the revelations I'd had before passing out the evening before was that the splint was no longer required.

As we motored along, the engine noise and the air rushing in through all the open windows made conversation impossible. It was just as well.

I was gagging for air an hour later when we finally pulled off the main road. I was still slightly nauseated, but my stomach had settled down a bit. For that, I was extremely grateful. We stopped so that our naturalist guide could join us. She was a Brazilian woman who looked to be about thirty, wearing a Tapajós Forest T-shirt, hiking shorts and boots, and a green baseball cap. She was carrying a large knapsack and a small but menacing-looking machete. I wondered why we might need a machete. She was our naturalist, but I realized that she couldn't speak English. The guide, who was with us aboard the bus from the pier, would be doing the talking.

Although we had stopped, we weren't there yet. We had to begin to penetrate the rainforest. The guide explained that we had ten more kilometres to go on a single-lane dirt road and that we should keep our arms inside the bus and not hang them out the open windows.

The bus moved along slowly, bumping over the rocky base of the road as branches and leaves smacked against the side. By the time we got to the end, my teeth were rattling.

"Well, that was fun," Jeffrey said as we got ready to disembark. I seriously hoped he was joking.

The guide was now telling us that we should use the toilet here before we headed into the rainforest on foot. Yes, the toilet. It was housed in a small wooden hut on a raised concrete platform, which I concluded provided a place underneath it to collect whatever made its way into the toilet. I didn't want the details.

As expected, by the time I got there, the lineup to the single toilet was already long. I was finally two people from the front of the line when a woman emerged. She was dressed as if she might be a seasoned hiker with her well-worn hiking boots and her neckerchief. With what sounded like a reasonable air of authority, she said, "I don't want to alarm anyone, but there's a tarantula in the bathroom." I heard murmurs of dread as women reconsidered their need to pee. "But on the upside, I think it's dead," she added for greater comfort. I decided to proceed anyway.

I stepped up the three wooden steps and opened the door gingerly when it was my turn. It was a less-than-pristine woodland toilet with a dirty sink. The air was still and even hotter than it was outside. It was suffocating. I looked around, and, yes, in the far corner, just past the toilet, I could see a mound of black fuzz with legs. I had never been this close to a tarantula, alive or dead. I suddenly felt like an adventurer in a new land. So, I pulled down the hiking pants, sat on the toilet and peed (because I really had to go), never taking my eye off the corner where the black fuzz rested. It didn't move.

When I emerged into the light, I felt oddly exhilarated. Was this what it was like to step outside your comfort zone? It was at that moment that I remembered seeing a coffee mug on the table in the overnight call room with a quote by someone named Neil Donald Walsch, someone whose work I had never had the occasion to read. I have no idea why I remembered it, but it said, "Life begins at the end of your comfort zone." Maybe he had a point—if only a small one. I did feel like I'd had an experience, though. I was ready for the rainforest.

As we began our trek, our guide started telling us about ants. Evidently, the rainforest was full of them. I had no idea. The moment he mentioned them, though, I began to feel itchy.

"Yes, the Amazon rainforest is home to two and a half million species of insects and it is believed by the scientists that ants make up 30% of the entire biomass."

I could not even imagine how many ants we might encounter. I was happy to be wearing long pants and socks, notwithstanding the itching that continued.

The guide then told us that the Amazon is home to more than a third of all the species in the world. He then started naming animals like the dart frog, malaria-carrying mosquitoes and anacondas, not to mention tigers as the deadliest pests. He assured us that we were not likely to encounter any of the above, but maybe that's what the naturalist's machete was for. I had no idea. He was moving toward the main part of his explanation. He wanted us to be aware of the ants as if the first mention of them wasn't enough to accomplish this goal.

The most problematic ant was one he called the bullet ant, whose name derived not from its shape, as I might have concluded, but from how its sting feels. According to those unfortunate enough to have been stung, for some eight hours, you would feel like you've been shot—with a bullet. Agonizing was the word he used.

Then he told us not to worry. Too late. But I'd already faced a tarantula. He told us to be careful and watch where we put our feet. Then, we were ready to proceed.

Eliza and Peter had gone on ahead, followed by Jeffrey. I was far behind in a group of people I'd never met, a situation that suited me fine. As I turned and walked onto the path through the towering trees (thank god there was a path and the naturalist didn't have to hack our way through), I suddenly felt like I was stepping into the heart of a living, breathing being. Everywhere seemed to be breathing—in and out, in and out, even as the slight breeze I'd felt earlier dropped to nothing as we proceeded between the trunks of the towering trees.

As we advanced into the forest, the air seemed to thicken, and the heat deepened. I could smell the earthiness of rotting organic material. As I looked up through the canopy, I could barely see the sun as it filtered down in slanting rays to the forest floor like light coming in through the stained glass windows of a medieval cathedral. As I walked deeper, watching where I put my feet as our guide had suggested, I saw what looked like a mosaic of greens, browns and ochres where the sun touched the floor. Each step sank slightly into the rotting fallen leaves on the pathway, and I felt myself sinking along with it. Suddenly, up ahead, there was a commotion as someone stepped on an anthill, and our guide told us all to move quickly past them. I did as I was told.

Once past the ants, I moved dreamily through the forest, not realizing that I was taking up the rear. I heard a bird call and was suddenly mesmerized. I stopped to listen. I was standing in the middle of the path, and I felt like I was in a movie where the camera begins moving around and around the person. But I was that person, *and* I was the viewer. I could see myself from all angles, a perspective I'd never had before—or I'd never allowed myself. I looked up at the grandeur of the trees, which were like natural skyscrapers blocking out much of the sun, and I was in awe of how small I really was. I glanced toward the side of the path and, for the first time, noticed bright orangey red plumes of bird of paradise flowers in the middle of a vast array of shades of green. I had to get closer to them. It was like they were trying to tell me that it was enough to be one small bright spot. I felt myself stepping off the path, my feet seeming to have a life of their own as they sank into the forest floor. As I stood a foot from the bright plumes, I took a deep breath and felt more peaceful than I think I ever had in my life.

"Claire? Thank god! We thought you were lost! This way." It was Eliza who had come to look for me.

TWENTY

Eliza

EXITING THE AMAZON RIVER

THE GUIDE BEGAN TALKING about how they harvested liquid rubber from the rainforest rubber trees. We then took turns peering closely at the parallel, sloping slices in the rubber tree trunks where we could see the opaque, whitish liquid as it trickled slowly from the incision. I considered the extraordinary effort it would have been to harvest and transport the volumes of rubber that had made Amazonia the world's biggest rubber producer at one time.

I backed away to give Peter a chance to look more closely and take some photos. As I stood there, swatting away nonexistent mosquitoes, I looked around at the group. I could see Jeffrey across the small clearing, arms crossed tightly across his chest, talking to that obnoxious Randy. I almost snickered when I considered someone from Jeffrey's perspective having a civil discussion with someone from Randy's particular point of view. I also wondered how Randy was faring in the heat and humidity on this long hike, given his ample bulk, to put it politely. I kept looking around at the group.

We looked like a ragtag army of sweaty soldiers who were losing their battle with the rainforest and its charms. Most people stood around swatting at more of these nonexistent mosquitoes and stamping their feet, doubtless trying to avoid ants crawling up their legs. One man of indeterminate age had even come prepared with one of those net things that dropped over the face, giving him the appearance of a beekeeper who had lost his way. He made me smile. As I considered how I might remember this adventure, I wondered where Claire had gotten to.

I began walking around the group and realized that she didn't seem to be among us. When Peter finished his turn taking photos of the rubber tree and chatting with the tour guide, he saw me over at the edge of the clearing and came over.

"What's wrong?" he said, no doubt seeing the frown on my face.

"Claire seems to be gone," I said.

"Gone? What do you mean gone?"

"Well, she was with us, and now she's not. We should tell the guide." I was sure our guide would want to know that we were missing a guest.

Peter began scanning the gaggle of hikers. I watched him as he made his way through the group toward our guide and the naturalist, who were on the other side of the clearing answering questions. They both immediately took on that deer-in-the-headlights gaze as they began counting hikers. We were missing one. I suspect that losing a guest was career suicide in their line of work. They immediately told us not to wander off and that they would find her.

I watched as Jeffrey went over to where Peter was. I presumed he wanted to know what was going on. Under normal circumstances, I would have been astonished to see the two of them having what appeared to be a civil conversation, but these were not normal circumstances. I turned and started to wander down the path we'd come from, but I had no desire to be the second guest to get lost, so I kept an eye on the opening of the clearing. It wasn't long before I spotted what looked like a glimpse of a white shirt. Claire had been wearing a white shirt. The dot of white was farther down the path but didn't seem to be on it. We had been specifically told to remain on the path. I hurried toward the dot of white and stopped on the path just where I could see her. I hesitated to step off the path into the actual rainforest floor, but it would be the only way to get to her, so I gingerly stepped off the path, and my feet sank into the soft detritus. For a moment, I felt like I was sinking, but it was only about an inch. When I reached her, she was just standing there, gazing upward, and she didn't seem to hear me when I called out. It was almost as if she might be in a trance.

When I reached the spot where she was standing, I tapped her on the shoulder. "Claire! Thank god! We thought you were lost."

She turned to look at me, her eyes wide and unfocused. For a moment, I wondered if she'd been stung by something. Before I could turn to call for help, she seemed to wake up, and I guided her back onto the path.

"Eliza? Oh, it's you. What're you doing here?"

"Doing here? We're all looking for you. The guide is frantic. I don't think he's ever lost a guest before, and he doesn't want today to be his first time. Are you okay?" I was genuinely concerned about her.

"Okay? Why wouldn't I be okay?" Claire suddenly sounded her usual prickly self, so I figured she was probably just doing her own thing here. Then, a cloud seemed to pass over her face, and she looked confused again. "Eliza, I think I might owe you an apology." The prickliness seemed to have evaporated.

Now I *knew* something was wrong. I had no idea where this was coming from or what was coming, for that matter. Before she had a chance to say another word, Peter and Jeffrey appeared at the end of the path, spotting us immediately. Peter called back, presumably to let the guide know we had found her, and then he quickly made his way over the fallen logs and rotting leaves toward where we were standing. Jeffrey followed closely behind.

"Claire, what the hell are you doing? Why didn't you keep up with the rest of us?" Peter's concern was masquerading as anger. I could see the unease in his eyes.

Claire shook her head. "I don't know what came over me. I was just walking behind the rest of the group when something caught my attention. I've never felt so strange. Have you seen the birds of paradise?"

She was making no sense to me, and judging by Peter's expression, I could see that he wasn't having much luck understanding her, either. Jeffrey, on the other hand, being the touchy-feely psychiatrist that he was, nodded and leaned in.

"What birds, Claire?" Jeffrey said.

"Not birds, you dolt, birds of paradise." Claire was again beginning to sound like the old Claire. I suppose that was a good sign. She pointed into the forest.

Jeffrey looked in the direction she was pointing. We all did. There, almost hidden deep in the greenery, were, indeed, three bird-of-paradise flowers in all their orange and yellow glory.

"They're just tiny little dots of colour in this sea of green, but they are enough, don't you think?'

None of us had any idea what she was talking about, but we patted her shoulder and tried to direct her back toward our guide, who was determinedly heading in our direction. He was followed by an assortment of guests, all bobbing their heads either in gratitude for us having found our wayward companion or, more likely because they couldn't imagine how someone could have been so stupid as not to have kept up. It was, after all, the Amazonian rainforest.

As we walked back toward the clearing where we had been examining rubber trees, Claire linked her arm with mine. That was the moment I knew that something weird was going on. I only hoped it was something weirdly good and not weirdly bad. That's when I realized it was often hard to tell the difference. I would have to be on my guard.

~

The bus ride back to the pier was just as bone-rattling, hot and generally uncomfortable as the one earlier in the day. And now, I was also hungry. Once we had reached the bus, Jeffrey was sitting with Claire (who I noticed seemed to no longer need her splint, by the way) at the back while Peter and I took up our seats two rows behind the driver. Everyone on the bus looked like leaves of wilted lettuce, forgotten for a week or two at the back of the refrigerator. Refrigerator? What I wouldn't have given for a cold drink right then. I had to settle for a sip of lukewarm water from the plastic bottle I'd brought from the ship. It was better than nothing.

"Well, that was strange," Peter said as we completed the ten-kilometre dirt road run and were back on the highway heading once again for Santarem and the coast. "When Claire took your arm, I thought the apocalypse must be upon us."

I laughed. I'd had much the same reaction. Perhaps the Amazonian rainforest had secrets we didn't know about, and Claire had been subjected to some alchemy. Whatever it was, I wasn't sure I felt comfortable being even slightly less annoyed at Claire.

"I was thinking that Claire might have just had a come-to-Jesus moment," I said.

Peter turned and looked at me. "Claire? A come-to-Jesus moment? That doesn't sound like the Claire I know at all."

I shrugged and decided to move on. "You know, Peter, I know you told me that the Amazon was one of your bucket-list trips, but I think I'll be glad to get away from the lethargy I've been feeling ever since we entered the river."

"It *is* a strange feeling—so unexpected. And we have a way to go yet to get out of the river. I think the guide said Santarem is eight hundred kilometres upriver from the Atlantic, so we still have a distance to cover before we turn left and sail up to the Caribbean. And we still have that crossing the equator thing to do."

I laughed. We had already crossed the equator at least twice (three times if you considered we'd all flown from the northern hemisphere), or at least we'd been hovering over it for days since it goes almost straight through the Amazon River. Just the day before, we'd received some communication from the cruise director telling us that there would be a crossing-the-equator ceremony the following day.

"What do you know about that crossing thing, Peter?" I hadn't had time to do any research.

"I think it's a kind of tongue-in-cheek festival of sorts. It used to be a rite of passage for sailors. I guess it was like a frat house hazing. Anyway, there's a lot of mythology about the equator."

"Sounds like you did your research," I said.

"Yeah. Ever since I got this notion that I wanted to come to the Amazon, I did research, read novels, watched movies—things like that."

I frowned. "You didn't tell me that."

He mimicked my facial expression. "You never asked."

I heard an echo of the day last Christmas when I realized I didn't know anything about Peter and said so. He'd said the same thing then. At the time, I thought how self-involved I'd been for so long and had vowed to be less so. I was feeling much closer to Peter now, and yet, I still seemed to be doing a lot of navel-gazing. It seemed I still had a way to go in my personal development. I would have to learn to ask more questions.

"Wow, I should have asked you about this before. I might have benefited from a bit of research myself before this trip. What books did you read?"

"Lots of novels like *State of Wonder* and *The Lost City of Z*. I also read some nonfiction like *Walking the Amazon* and *Journey of the Pink Dolphins*. I guess I might have had a slightly romanticized idea of what it would be like. But then, I've spent most of my life living on an island in the North Atlantic, so the lure of the rainforest was probably a bit like looking for the direct opposite of my life."

"What about the equator research? What did you learn about that?"

"Apart from the silliness of a cruise ship crossing ceremony?" I nodded. "I suppose it's like a rite of passage—like stepping over a line from one realm into another."

I sat back in my narrow seat as we jostled along. I was thinking about rites of passage. I'd had a few in my life. I suppose that when I was twelve and was confirmed in the Catholic church, it was supposed to be one, but it had never felt that way to me then or since. On the other hand, my mikveh, the ritual bath on the day I converted to Judaism, sprang immediately to mind as an important passage. It had meant a lot to me and clearly did mark moving from one chapter of my life into another, although now, as I thought about it, I realized that I didn't feel like a Gentile one minute and immediately feel Jewish the next. It took a bit of living in my new "realm," as Peter said, for me to really feel like I'd gotten there. Perhaps it was always like that with rites of passage.

I thought about other initiation-like experiences in my life. Perhaps equally important were my marriage ceremony and giving birth, rites of passage, to be sure, and again, movements into new roles or realms that took a bit of time to get used to. Is divorce a rite of passage? I suppose it is for those of us who have journeyed through it. If nothing else, it *is* a transition that requires a redefinition of roles that might take a bit of time, and isn't that what transitions are all about? It occurred to me that divorce might be a rite of passage, but there was no ritual, no ceremony to mark it. Maybe there should be one. Maybe I'd have to figure one out.

I started wondering if there would ever be any more rites of passage in my life other than death. I suppose I'd never given it any thought. Now I did.

TWENTY-ONE

Claire

On the Equator

I SAT BESIDE JEFFREY on the rattletrap of a bus on the way back to the city of Santarem. He tried to make conversation, each attempt feebler than the one before. Did I enjoy the rubber trees? What about those ants? I wonder what's on the menu for dinner. That was the depth of the conversation. I wasn't a chit-chatter at the best of times, and these were not the best of times in my view. I couldn't concentrate on anything he was saying, and I realized I didn't want to, either. What I wanted to do was contemplate that feeling I'd had while standing alone in the middle of a Brazilian rainforest, listening to the sound of the air, the birds in the distance and the fluttering of leaves way above me. I wanted to remember how the smell of rotting vegetation first assaulted my senses and then became like a calming aromatherapy session. I wanted to continue to feel the heat and humidity and the sweat that made my clothes stick to me like glue. I wanted to remember that I'd felt different when I emerged from whatever it was that I'd experienced. And I wanted to see where that might take me. Instead, I looked at Jeffrey and said, "I think I'd like to have dinner by myself tonight." I planned to drink sparkling water and read a book.

"No problem," he said. "I actually have a cocktail reception with the Zen and Tonic folks anyway."

He then sat back, presumably content that I had emerged as unscathed as one can from such a traumatic event as being "lost" in the woods. I rolled my eyes, but no one noticed.

We finally arrived back at the waterfront and disembarked the bus. I hoped never to be inside another bus of any kind as long as I lived. After an excruciating wait in the searing sun on the pier, the tender finally emerged into sight around the hull of one of the enormous cargo ships that blocked the view of our pretty cruise ship at anchor offshore. After a few stragglers of guests who had chosen to come ashore much later than the rest of us disembarked the tender, we clambered on board and crammed ourselves into the benches like a bunch of canned sardines. There wasn't a breath of air for the next twenty minutes until I disembarked and climbed up the gangway on the outside of the ship to the blissfulness of the air conditioning. Yes, I liked my creature comforts, and I wasn't going to apologize for that.

Once I'd reached my suite, I peeled off and spent longer than I was supposed to in the shower, given the water conservation rules we were supposed to be following while cruising in the Amazon, until I felt human again. The more I thought about the garbage that had floated in rafts on the water around the pier where we had been docked in Manaus, the less convinced I was of the pristineness of Amazonia. Anyway, that was not going to be an issue for me much longer. We were heading out toward the mouth of the river as soon as we set sail later this evening.

As I sat on the sofa drinking a tall glass of ice water (before I moved on to a lovely glass of whatever wine was still left in my bar, my plan to drink only sparkling water abandoned), I noticed the daily news bulletin. I idly picked it up and began skimming it. I noticed, with some horror, that there was an all-guest event planned on the pool deck the following day. It was something about crossing the equator. Since we'd already crossed the equator several times, it did seem a bit anti-climactic. I threw the pages back on the table and thought that if I had nothing better to do, I might watch it. But for sure, I was not participating. Then I picked up my phone.

There was a text from Liam telling me how much he was looking forward to his upcoming trip to Miami. I sighed, thinking how this "reunion" wasn't going to be as I expected—or hoped. A brief thought flitted through my head that it's not over until it's over, but then I thought that old Kenny Rogers song. It was the one about knowing when to hold 'em and when to fold 'em. Perhaps even more to the point, there was something about knowing when to walk away. Had that time come yet?

I then looked at my email and saw several of them from the surgeon who was filling in for me while I was away. He was asking me for a consultation on a patient he had on his operating schedule in a couple of days. The thought of my surgical practice calmed me immediately. I read the attached history carefully and thought about this little boy, aged eight, who needed serious surgery for a congenital heart defect. I thought about all the tiny bodies I'd fixed in my years as a pediatric surgeon and wondered if my work had made any long-term difference in the world. I had always believed that I needed to leave a legacy, but now I wasn't so sure. What I did know was that even sitting here on a cruise ship in a fancy suite was nice, but standing for hours in that operating room wielding power over life and death was so much better. I wrote my comments and sent them off to my colleague.

~

The sun was trying to make its presence known through cracks in the low clouds when I ventured to the dining room for breakfast the following morning. I was relishing this time for myself. As I took the menu from the lovely server who then hovered nearby, it occurred to me that I'd been chasing Peter for only one reason. As I looked up, I saw that reason approaching my table.

"Good morning, Claire," Eliza said. "I hope you're feeling well today."

"Why in the world wouldn't I be feeling well?" I said, perhaps a bit more testily than the situation warranted. I took it down a notch or two. "I'm just fine as it happens." I looked around her. "Are you alone?"

"If you mean is Peter with me, no, he's not. He's in the gym."

Ignoring the fact that Peter being in the gym in the morning was out of character for him (which made me wonder what he was trying to accomplish), I chose to say nothing. For a moment, I thought she was going to suggest that we have breakfast together. That would be a bridge too far.

"Well, you enjoy your breakfast, Claire. I'm off to meet with a few cookbook fans. See you later at the crossing the equator thing?"

I nodded and breathed a sigh of relief.

~

Before I left my suite later, I downloaded three new editions of pediatric surgery journals that I read religiously. Then, I gathered my things and headed out to find a lounge chair on a high deck in the shade. I'd find a waiter serving iced water and then settle in to immerse myself in the only world where I could almost always control things—surgery.

Within an hour, I could hear noise from the pool deck below me begin to ramp up. The band was tuning up, and I could hear a buzz of voices as if the crowd on the deck might be considerably larger than usual. I'd noticed earlier that the crew had cleared away many of the sun lounges, presumably to make way for whatever hilarity was about to transpire. The crossing-the-line ceremony was about to start, and people were gathering. I decided that I might as well see what the fuss was about and got up from my lounger to find a place at the railing where I could look down on the festivities without really being a part of it.

The ceremony began with an announcement from one of the ship's officers (I had expected it to be the captain, but he was nowhere in sight). The proclamation that the ceremony was about to begin was followed by a theatrical parade along the upper deck where I was standing, all around the deck and down the stairs. The main attraction in the parade was Neptune, the god of the sea (played by one of the onboard entertainers I imagined—I wasn't sure since I hadn't partaken of any of the shows) and his court—complete with tridents, tacky gold, white and blue costumes, and an entourage of mermaids and sea creatures. Given the giddiness of the guests who crowded around them as they made their way to the throne at the far end of the pool, I wondered how much everyone had already had to drink. Rebecca, in a long, sparkly purple dress and a white wig, invited guests to participate. Volunteers (some of whom were crew members and likely not volunteers at all) had to answer to King Neptune, who meted out their punishment for being landlubbers and transgressing odd seagoing "rules." Some were pushed into the pool, while others were smeared with what appeared to be whipped cream and doused with buckets of ice water.

As I stood at the railing watching Rebecca then have a turn at being drenched with ice water and pushed into the pool in her sparkly dress, the woman wedged in beside me at the railing said, "Odd how ritual becomes theatre, isn't it?"

I had no idea what she was talking about and said so.

She turned, and I noticed she was wearing a T-shirt with a line drawing of a laughing Buddha in the middle. The words above it said, "Life is terminal." The words below said, "Suffering is optional." Where had I heard that before? Oh, yes, it was a Jeffrey-ism. I also remembered seeing piles of these shirts on a table outside the theatre one day earlier in the cruise under a banner that said, "The Zen and Tonic Connection Meeting featuring keynote speaker Dr. Jeffrey P. Montgomery." I was forming a picture of this woman in my mind, and it was clearly biased.

"What I mean is that this seafaring tradition was created as a rite of passage for sailors, but it has a far deeper meaning."

"How so?"

She continued. "The equator is a symbol of balance and harmony sitting as it does on the boundary between the northern and the southern hemispheres. The crossing of the equator in mythology was and ought to still be a solemn recognition of going through a challenging journey before succeeding. At least, that is my view. It should represent that ritualistic passage into new experiences." She seemed to awaken from her monologue. "I am so sorry," she said in a distinctly upper-crust British accent. "I do hope I haven't bored you with my little lecture." She stuck out her hand. "I am Imogen."

I took her hand and shook it. "Claire. Nice to meet you. And you're certainly not boring me. Are you an expert in mythology?"

Imogen laughed. "Not at all, my dear. I'm someone who retired and found a new fascination with a subject that is far enough removed from my career that it takes me to new places—both literally and figuratively. We are always on a journey, after all, and must navigate challenges as we proceed. I have found that these stories that grow up around things in our physical world, such as the equator, often have lessons if we only drill down to the source and ask why the stories developed. Heaven knows I spent so many years thinking concretely that now it's a breath of fresh air to consider other aspects of life."

I thought about that for a moment before responding. Then I said, "I can certainly identify with being concrete." I laughed. "And the idea of a challenging journey and a passage to new experiences does resonate with me right about now. You do seem very knowledgeable about all this."

"I suppose it's something of a passion of mine—exploring new frontiers. I am recently retired from a very fulfilling career, as I mentioned, that was completely different from my interests at this juncture, so new frontiers are all I have."

Imogen looked to me to be about seventy or so with wild silver hair and an infectious smile that accentuated the lines around her eyes.

"So, is this Zen and Tonic thing a new frontier for you?" I said, gesturing toward her T-shirt.

She smiled. "As a matter of fact, it is. As it transpires, I am one of the board members who planned this little junket."

"I see you have that author Jeffrey P. Montgomery on your speaking roster." I was being a bit cagey, I suppose, but I *was* interested in what Jeffrey's "public" really thought of him. And I didn't want Imogen to know that he and I were acquainted on the off chance I might get a less biased review.

"Indeed, we do," Imogen said with more animation than I had expected. "He is something of a superstar among the Zen and Tonic crowd, you know. But, of course, you must know his work. He is rather famous."

"Aren't you concerned that his work might be a bit bogus given his age?"

Imogen looked stricken. "I cannot think what his age has to do with it. The man is a genius. And if he's been able to parlay his genius into a lucrative career at a young age, good for him, but also good for the rest of us. You should come to his next session with us. His topic for the next lecture is how to begin one's life again by learning from one's mistakes. I am especially excited because I've read some of his work on this subject, and I know he has a theory about how our mistakes play into giving up control and gaining control. I've made enough mistakes in my life to warrant a good examination, I'll tell you."

Dear god, she thinks he's a genius. Before I had a chance to contemplate the notion of mistakes and respond, Imogen reached into her back pocket and thrust a piece of paper into my hand. "It's at five o'clock. Should be over just in time for cocktails. Will I see you there?"

It was an invitation to a presentation by Dr. Jeffrey P. Montgomery titled "Begin Again."

~

I wasn't quite sure what I was doing when I found myself sidling past the boutique windows with their travel-friendly dresses and their gaudy necklaces toward the theatre entrance at ten minutes before five. I ducked behind a pillar when I saw Jeffrey standing with Imogen, greeting people who were, presumably, members of the group—the Zen and Tonic Connection—as they assembled in the theatre for the planned presentation.

I looked down at the invitation I had in my hand and wondered if something hadn't bitten me when I was standing in the rainforest gazing at birds-of-paradise. I was clearly not thinking properly. There had never been a time in my life when I'd been drawn to anything that wasn't evidence-based science, and whatever these people were contemplating certainly had little to do with anything in the real world. Yet here I was.

I was still waffling when Imogen spotted me and gestured for me to come over. Thankfully, Jeffrey had just left since I suppose he had to get to the podium to begin his presentation.

"Claire, my dear. You came! How wonderful it is to see you. Do come in and join us."

Imogen had traded her T-shirt and capris for a calf-length dress of flowy cotton with an all-over flower pattern. She looked very much like an English grandmother.

"Perhaps we can even convince you to buy one of our T-shirts," Imogen said, her eyes dancing. "If I do not miss my guess, and based on our earlier conversation, this might be just a tad out of your comfort zone. Am I correct?"

"I'm a pediatric surgeon, Imogen," I said as if that should explain everything.

"Well, my dear Claire, that *is* impressive." Her eyes sparkled again as she smiled. "I must be honest with you. I actually do know who you are, as a matter of fact."

I frowned. "That's impossible. We've never met before. I would have remembered."

"Indeed, we met briefly a few years ago, my dear. It was at a meeting in London."

I racked my brain to remember a meeting in London where I would have had occasion to meet someone like Imogen. I drew a blank. "Sorry, Imogen, I have no idea where we might have met. As I said, I'm a pediatric surgeon, so you and I would not likely have been at the same meeting."

"You are as I remember you, Claire—or should I say Dr. Barrett? I remember you as being a very intense and intelligent young woman who, perhaps, sees the world through a singular lens. It is possible to refocus that lens, you know."

I shrugged. "I doubt it." And I had no idea how she could have such an opinion of me.

Imogen continued. "Ah, but you must open your mind." Imogen looked at her watch and then took my arm as we walked into the theatre. "We must get inside, my dear. And remember that being a pediatric surgeon doesn't preclude you from having an open mind about new ideas—evidence-based or not."

I stopped just behind the last row of seats. "What kind of work did you do before you retired, Imogen?"

She smiled. "I thought you'd never ask. I was a pediatric surgeon. You may remember an old lady surgeon—who introduced you at the meeting of the British Association of Pediatric Surgeons a few years back."

My eyes widened. Imogen had been the president of the British Association of Pediatric Surgeons. I felt like an idiot.

~

Jeffrey liked nothing better than a good quote or two, even if they were ideas that he hadn't first said. Just like at the lecture he'd given earlier in the cruise, there was an enormous slide being projected on the entire back wall of the stage that Jeffrey would, no doubt, use as his backdrop. The slide had the title of his lecture, "Begin Again," on one side and two quotes on the other.

"Mistakes are the portals to discovery." James Joyce. The second one was, "Fear of failure leads to stagnation." Dr. Jeffrey P. Montgomery.

I rolled my eyes at the notion of Jeffrey giving such advice.

After stumbling over six people on my way to a single seat in the centre of the theatre, I settled in. Jeffrey came on stage, rolled up his sleeves and smiled enigmatically out at the audience.

"If you have not made mistakes, you have not lived. That's where we begin today." He began his usual schtick of walking around on stage, making eye contact with enthralled audience members as he emphasized his points. "We all know that mistakes are inevitable, and if you believe differently, it might be time to shake yourself because you are wrong if you think you have never made a mistake. You are equally wrong if you believe that *everything* you do is a mistake. Mistakes are a natural byproduct of human effort and experimentation." He stopped in the middle of the stage to let that sink in before continuing.

"From the beginning of our lives, we learn by doing things incorrectly. Think about a child learning to walk, talk, or read—they stumble, mispronounce words, and misinterpret meanings. Yet, these very missteps are what propel them forward—propel all of us forward. But for many of us, the moment we reach adulthood, we think that we can no longer make mistakes. And we fear making them because we know only too well that they can happen. So *why* do we fear mistakes? Well, many of us have been conditioned to avoid mistakes at all costs."

I had been ready to close my eyes and sleep through this, but at that point, I sat up wondering if he'd noticed that I was there. I was one of those people. I was conditioned and expected to avoid making mistakes—at all costs. I thought about my parents and how making mistakes was unacceptable to them. However, as an adult, I also knew that avoiding mistakes was unquestionably mandatory. In my line of work, mistakes were not just unacceptable but often catastrophic. I was not ready even to entertain the notion that I could make a mistake. Then I thought about Peter.

I had almost thought that allowing our divorce to happen had been a mistake. Then, I had tried to reframe it as a mere oversight, a slip-up. As I sat there in the semi-darkness, looking at my former lover (if only for a day or three) as he drilled down into my psyche, I could feel the tiny pricking of a thought at the back of my mind—a thought I wasn't quite ready to hear. It was starting to tease me with the idea that the divorce had not, after all, been a mistake, an oversight or even a slip-up. If it had not been a mistake, then what now? I turned my attention back to Jeffrey.

"Mistakes are often equated with failure," he was saying, "when in reality, they're critical stepping stones to success. Think about a mistake you've made in recent years. It doesn't have to be a major one."

As hard as I could, I could not come up with a single mistake unless I were to consider that taking this cruise had been a mistake. The jury was still out on that, and if I finally admitted that it had been a mistake, I would have to admit to many other mistakes as well. That wasn't going to happen any time soon.

"What was the outcome of that mistake? Did you learn anything? If you didn't, have you really taken the time to think about what learning might be hidden in that mistake? Know this, though, that learning is always—*always*—about you."

He then went on to talk about mistakes that had resulted in significant successes like the time Alexander Fleming discovered penicillin because of a laboratory mistake. I had a tough time reconciling this with the work I do because mistakes in my work, as much as one might consider them leading to new ideas, usually had catastrophic consequences. Then he talked about how making mistakes and learning from them will not result in an uncontrolled life but a controlled one—if that's what you want.

"A mistake is your portal to discovery. It takes you on new adventures. Let's go back to James Joyce's take on mistakes. He is inviting you to rewrite your story, to create a new narrative around your mistakes. That new story makes your mistakes crucial elements in your journey toward discovery and self-improvement. Embrace your mistakes, learn from them, and let them guide you toward discovery—of yourself."

Jeffrey then clicked on his last slide. On it was a photo of Salvador Dali, unmistakable with his bulging eyes and that mustache whose waxed ends defied gravity.

"Perhaps Dali's sobering take on our mistakes is where we need to begin our reinvention. 'Have no fear of perfection; you'll never reach it.' Just never make the same mistake twice."

Jeffrey thanked the crowd, who were on their feet, clapping and shouting "Bravo!" the moment he was finished.

TWENTY-TWO

Eliza

INTO THE ATLANTIC OCEAN

ASK ANYONE WHO KNOWS ME, and they'll tell you this. Eliza Cohen is NOT the life of the party. Eliza Cohen is the bemused onlooker who sits back with a drink and a wry smile, watching the jovial partygoers as they make fools of themselves. What, then, came over me that afternoon when King Neptune and his mermaids paraded onto the pool deck and began their mock trials? What was I thinking when Rebecca pulled me from the crowd? What was I thinking when I looked over at Peter and saw him grinning from ear to ear, and I remembered the day last summer, on a boat in Newfoundland, when I kissed a cod (another dubious regional ritual). I'll tell you what I was thinking.

The moment Rebecca pulled me from the crowd, I happened to look around and saw, out of the corner of my eye, Claire by the railing on the upper deck, deep in conversation with a woman I'd never seen before. What I knew to be true at that moment was that Dr. Claire Barrett wouldn't agree to this public humiliation, no matter how tongue-in-cheek it was. That made the prospect of humiliating myself so much more attractive. As I recall that moment, I realize how foolish that sounds. Anyway, I let Rebecca pull me into the middle of the circle.

The next thing I knew, someone was demanding that I kneel before King Neptune as he looked on with mock anger, his gold paper crown tilting rakishly and his blonde hair flopping into his eyes. The crowd was deafening, and I couldn't quite hear what he was saying. Something about being a pollywog who hadn't yet learned the lessons of the deep—or something like that. I surmised that pollywogs were the newcomers to this equator-crossing business. In any case, I was found guilty of something or other and was summarily taken off, doused with a bucket of ice water and pushed into the pool. I climbed out to great applause. Did I feel foolish? Only a little, but I discovered that being foolish wasn't the worst thing in the world. Then, when Peter came over and enveloped me in a bear hug, I thought I might be able to let my crazy side peek out again—at least for a moment.

~

As Peter and I walked back to my suite after the event, he said, "Eliza Cohen, I'm proud of you. I knew from the first minute I met you last summer that there was a fun-loving, carefree girl in there somewhere. We just had to figure out how to let her out."

"I don't suppose she'll come out very often," I said as I tried to keep my shorts from dripping onto the hallway carpet.

"Why not? We'll have to take every opportunity from now on to make sure she does," he said, putting his arm around my wet shoulder. "I love this Eliza."

The word stunned me. Peter acted like it was the most natural thing in the world to say that word. But when I stopped stock still in the middle of the hallway, he turned to me.

"What's wrong? I *do* love this Eliza—and all the rest of her, too."

"How can you love me? We haven't known each other long enough."

"How long is long enough? And who made those rules anyway?"

Who indeed? I realized that I'd loved him from the moment I met him and told him so.

"Then, it's settled," he said. "You. Me. Together from now on."

I had no idea how that would work, but the cruise was now taking on its romantic phase, and I liked that. There was little point in getting too specific. Then I remembered something I'd read years ago. Oscar Wilde once wrote, "Never love anyone who treats you like you're ordinary." Peter seemed incapable of treating anyone like they were ordinary. It was only one of the things I loved about him.

"Yes," I said, "you and me, but after the meeting I have to attend for onboard presenters."

~

After drying off and changing, I had a few moments before I had to be at the meeting. I checked my email and texts, which is when I found a new text from Izzy.

`Thought you should know Dad's being weird. ♥ Iz`

That Jake was being weird was hardly a news flash, and Izzy's text did little to illuminate the substance of this particular episode. Of course, I texted back and got an immediate reply.

Where have you been? Been waiting for you to respond. Dad won't leave the house. He says he needs to sleep over to help me. It's creeping me out because I know you told him to move out. Mary-Catherine and I are leaving for Miami in two days, and I don't think I should leave him here. Help!

I checked my cell phone service. As expected, and as usual, since the beginning of the cruise, there was none. I don't know why I expected there to be cell service, but it's just the way we're wired these days, I guess. So, I checked my phone settings to make a call over Wi-Fi and clicked Izzy's number. I had about fifteen minutes before I had to leave for the meeting. She answered on the first ring.

"Mom! I'm so happy to hear from you! Are you having a good time? How's Peter? Where are you right now? Dad is being so weird."

"Slow down a minute, Izzy. How are you and Mary-Catherine?"

"We're so great—other than this Dad thing and the fact that Grama Esther won't stop calling me to see how the baby is. You wouldn't believe the things she's been saying about you. You know how subtly catty she can be."

Subtly? I doubted that. "It's okay, Izzy. I'm sure your grandmother thinks I'm the worst kind of mother to have left you alone with your baby."

"Among other things."

I almost laughed. Esther was so predictable. Izzy was a grown woman (if at twenty-two you're grown these days) with a four-month-old baby and a new nanny to help her out (hired by me) as she prepared to return to medical school. Her father was also supposed to be on call for her—but not in the house.

It was *my* house and had been since that legal harangue Jake's company had when he put so many of our assets into my name. Too bad for him at this stage of our lives.

"Izzy, here's what I want you to do. I'm going to text you a phone number. It's for Abigail Zimmerman, my lawyer. Tell her what's going on and ask her to help you arrange to have the locks on the house changed. I certainly don't want Jake or, even more to the point, your grandmother to have access to it while neither of us is home."

Izzy agreed. "Mom, you know I love Dad, but he's making me crazy with all his talk about getting back together with you when I know you're already almost divorced. I get it."

It was so much more than I expected of Daddy's erstwhile princess. The fact that my daughter seemed to understand that Jake and I were better if we weren't together meant a lot to me. I have no idea what had happened to her while she was in California (other than the pregnancy thing, of course), but she had somehow grown up to be a wise young woman. She was going to make a terrific doctor.

Izzy told me how excited she was to be able to meet me in Miami and that we'd have the most amazing mother-daughter-granddaughter time. I reminded her that Peter might still be around, and she said, "Of course, Mom. You haven't mentioned how it's going. How *is* it going?"

I told her to mind her business, and she laughed. "That good, huh, Mom?"

This was not a conversation I was going to have with my daughter, so I told her I'd see her in Miami and wished her a safe flight in a couple of days. Then I grabbed my purse and flew out the door to the meeting.

~

In total, there were five "enrichment speakers" on board this cruise, six if you counted me. There was Jeffrey, whose presence as a general onboard speaker was sponsored by the Zen and Tonic crowd (I still thought they sounded more than a tad flakey). There was a traditional Chinese medicine doctor who gave lectures on herbal treatments, acupuncture and something I'd seen in the daily newsletter called moxibustion, whatever that was. This topic was juxtaposed with a peppy, blonde lifestyle guru who had made her fortune (?) dispensing advice on mid-life crises and how to navigate menopause (kill me now). The other two guest lecturers were "destination experts."

Both destination experts were retired professors who, between the two of them, had been on one hundred and nineteen cruises or some other unbelievable number in that vicinity. I had attended lectures from both of them. One was terrific—knowledgeable and funny—while the other rambled on into moralistic and political territory. I had avoided his lectures since he had waxed poetic on how women should stay at home with their families because it was righteous. That one made me gag.

We were all assembled in the back of Horizons lounge, with Rebecca presiding. When I arrived, I waved to Jeffrey, who was sitting across the space. He nodded almost imperceptibly to me and went back to gazing at his phone. He was acting odd. When he hadn't shown up for my cooking demonstration after being so enthusiastic about it, I wondered if something was wrong. I would make a point to talk to him after this "meeting."

Rebecca arrived and began by gushing about how wonderful we all were. It seemed the purpose of the meeting was to discuss her latest brain wave. She thought it would be a "right hoot" if we would all agree to take part in a panel discussion. I could not imagine a topic about which all six of us would have anything cogent to say. We had very little in common. She was not to be deterred even after one of the professors made this very observation—after staring at both the lifestyle guru and me.

"I have the most wonderful idea that the guests will absolutely love," she said. "We will take on the topic of Personal Reinvention." She looked around for support. There were only furrowed brows. No one was quite getting this. "At the risk of sounding just slightly ageist," she continued, "most of our guests are of a certain age, in case you had failed to notice."

I thought that most of her guests were *past* that certain age, but I chose to keep that opinion to myself—for the moment, at least.

"What I mean to suggest is that several of you have already navigated a reinvention," she said, looking at the two retired professors, "or you are at the height of your careers focused on assisting people on their journeys." She looked at Jeffrey, the lifestyle guru and the traditional Chinese medical practitioner, who, by the way, was not Chinese. That left me.

"And you, Ms. Cohen, are a cooking expert. And everyone must continue to eat even as they reinvent themselves, *n'est-ce pas*?"

"So, Ms. Bebbington-Hughes," the professor named Dr. Egerton Stevens, subject expert on Amazonian tribes, said. "You are suggesting that we all take equal part in a panel discussion on a topic not a single one of us is an expert in."

"On the contrary, Dr. Stevens—and please call me Rebecca—I believe that you all indeed are experts in aspects of the topic. At the very least, you have much to offer on the topic." She stopped for a moment, taking us all in. "And Captain Lombardi believes this to be an exciting new approach to the onboard experience."

"I was not aware that the captain took any interest whatsoever in the onboard experience, Ms. Bebbington-Hughes." My misogynist professor was now speaking. He enunciated her name with great emphasis. "It is, after all, his job to ensure passenger safety as he guides us through the seagoing itinerary."

"You would be surprised at how interested the captain is in how our guests perceive his ship and its amenities. In point of fact, he mentioned something about introducing such a panel himself. And," she seemed to take on a severe look, "he will be more than disappointed if each of you does not attend." Then she looked at me. "Of course, Eliza, since you were kind enough to do us this massive favour after boarding the ship, you would not be obliged to attend, but the panel will be so much richer for your presence. Please say you will join us."

What could I say? All for one and one for all, as the musketeers once said.

~

I caught up with Jeffrey, who seemed to be trying to get away as quickly as he could once the meeting was over.

"Jeffrey, wait up," I said as I reached him just before we reached the elevator lobby.

When he turned around (he could hardly ignore me), his face was a cross between the deer-in-the-headlights and terror.

"Jeffrey, have you been avoiding me?"

"Avoiding you? Why would I avoid you?"

"I have no idea. You said you were going to come to my cooking class, and I was disappointed that you weren't there."

"Something came up." His eyes darted around as if he were looking for an exit.

"I know it's none of my business, but what on earth came up on board a cruise ship in the middle of the Amazon River?"

Jeffrey's shoulders slumped. "You caught me, Eliza. I, um, I ..." Why was he stammering?

"Jeffrey, what's going on? Has something happened?"

"I'm not sure," he said. "Can you give me a bit of time? I need to figure something out."

I touched his shoulder. "Of course. I was only hoping that I hadn't said or done something that made you want to avoid me."

He suddenly looked stricken. "No, Eliza, it's nothing like that. No, not at all." He turned toward the elevator lobby. "Look, I've got to go. I'll see you on stage for that panel discussion, though."

I watched him get onto the elevator, his head once again buried in his phone. I had no idea what had just happened.

~

"So, how was the meeting?" Peter and I were sitting in Horizons lounge later with a cocktail in front of each of us, gazing out into the blue of the Atlantic Ocean. We had finally cleared the Amazon River and were heading north and then slightly west toward Barbados, our first Caribbean Island stop. I had studied the map earlier in the cruise. I knew that our route would now take us along the coast of South America, past French Guiana, Suriname, Guyana and the edge of

Venezuela before we veered north to Barbados and then Antigua. It was a bit of a thrill to think about where we were.

I sipped my Porn Star martini. Why did it make me want to giggle whenever I said that? Never mind. "It was interesting," I said in response to Peter's question. Then, I told him about the plans for the panel.

When I had finished, Peter laughed. "Sounds deadly," he said. "But I'll be there, and as we like to say in Newfoundland, it'll be a time."

"Something strange happened after the meeting," I said. I then told Peter about my peculiar conversation with Jeffrey. "What do you suppose he had to figure out?"

Peter looked thoughtful. "Did you ever think that he might have fallen just a little bit in love with you? After all, he did say he was one of your biggest fans."

"What? No, of course not. He's almost young enough to be my son."

"Almost," Peter said. Then he looked at me with a wicked half-smile. "Admit it, Eliza. It is flattering to have an attractive young man enthralled with you." Before I could interject, he continued. "You were the one who said how attractive he was. I'm just echoing your thoughts on the matter."

He had me there. Jeffrey was attractive, and I can't lie. Being the object of affection for a younger man like Jeffrey was as amusing as it was pleasant.

"I love it when you smile like that," Peter said, leaning over to kiss me. I didn't object.

TWENTY-THREE

Claire

BARBADOS, WEST INDIES

I HAD BEEN TO BARBADOS BEFORE. Years ago, Peter and I had spent a week at a hotel called The House on the western (Caribbean) side of the island. It had been a fraught week. We had both been working too hard, never seeing one another, so we had decided to leave the kids with my parents (more accurately, with their housekeeper since both my parents still worked at the time) and take a week to ourselves. A second honeymoon, we laughingly called it. Unfortunately, the week didn't unfold as I had hoped, and we'd spent the week arguing about just about everything, from where to eat dinner each evening to whether it was better to sit by the pool or on the beach. As I thought about it now, I realized that our arguments had been petty. Perhaps if we'd discussed more substantial issues, we might not be where we were now. But that was then.

Now, I wasn't relishing a return visit to an island with such charged memories. I could choose to stay on the ship, but what good would that do me? It was time to face the little demons that were continuing to raise their heads as if they had never been given a chance to see the light of day. I suppose I'd spent my life playing a dangerous game of wack-a-mole, never wanting to see what was raising its ugly head. Perhaps

Barbados would be my first chance to let one of them out, look it in the eye and possibly let it go. We'd see.

I was sitting on my veranda at nine a.m. on the first of two at-sea days before we were scheduled to dock for the day in Bridgetown, the capital of Barbados. I had a cup of coffee in my hand and a plate of pastries on the table in front of me while I scrolled through my iPad. I was researching private guides and things to do on the island. I supposed it might be too late to book a private guide, but I was willing to see if the fates were with me. I was also looking for places to visit—or revisit.

I remembered that Peter and I had dinner one evening at a place up the beach from our hotel. It was called The Cliff. We'd gone there after yet another argument about where to eat. He had won that round. Peter had been right to argue for dinner at The Cliff that evening. He'd chosen it because it had a reputation as one of the island's most renowned fine dining destinations. It was advertised as having a stunning cliffside location (*ergo*, the name), which offered breathtaking views of the Caribbean Sea in addition to wonderful food. Under circumstances other than those Peter and I were experiencing then, it would have been very romantic. The dining room was perched on a bluff above the water, with its various levels of open-air tables reaching down toward the sea, where there the underwater lights gave the passing sea rays and other shimmering fish an ethereal quality. Very upscale and chic, as I remembered it. If I could eat there while on the island, I might be able to exorcise some ghosts.

I continued my research, discovering that it was open only for dinner. I rechecked our itinerary and saw that we weren't scheduled to depart Bridgetown until eleven p.m. If I could get a guide, a driver and a reservation, I would have dinner there. So, that was settled. I could now picture myself dining alone at an oceanside table, enjoying my own company. Well, it was partly settled. I still needed that driver/guide.

I finished my coffee and croissants and went inside to get ready to spend a few quality hours in a sun lounge on the highest deck I could find. That would be the place where I was sure to encounter the fewest other passengers. I wanted a bit of time alone for the next few days.

Despite warnings to stop "saving" deck chairs, cruise ship guests, no matter how sophisticated they thought they were, seemed to be constitutionally unable to comply with this simple directive. So, as I walked across the deck past the pool, I noticed single flipflops, assorted paperback books, and the odd baseball cap, along with a towel laid on lounge chairs that were otherwise unoccupied. The random items designated lounge chairs that people had chosen and then promptly left, likely for breakfast or even to go to the gym, I suppose, only to return hours later. I sighed and felt sorry for people who needed to be in the thick of the group.

I was in luck. When I reached the highest deck, where there were only a few lounge chairs anyway, it was deserted. I chose one and settled in. If there was a downside to this location it was that it was also the "sports" deck. There was a miniature golf course, and what I thought ought to be a tennis court was now called a "pickleball" court. Have you heard of that game?

Dear god, I thought as two somewhat older women arrived and readied themselves for a round, *what is the attraction? Why not just play tennis?* Then they started.

Amid the loud conversation that they seemed to be having from opposite sides of the net was the infernal thwack-thwack-thwack of the damn ball. Why could they not just play tennis? The sound of a tennis ball hitting the strings of a tennis racket was so much more refined. Then I remembered reading an article about why pickleball had become so popular with the over-sixty crowd. I remembered concluding that it was intended for people who are too slow for tennis and too clumsy for ping pong. It's like someone took tennis, shrank it, added a side of midlife crisis and a sound loud enough to be heard even with declining hearing. I had no idea whatsoever what the rules were, but I had observed (on unfortunate occasions like this one where I was in close proximity to the so-called sport) that there was a lot of arguing about whether a ball was in or out (not unlike real tennis, I might add) added to the incessant conversation that suggested to me people did it just to be with other people. That certainly didn't describe one of my life goals. I popped in my AirPods and lay back to take in some sun.

I don't know how long I'd been lying there when I perceived a shadow crossing my face. It could have been a cloud, which seemed unlikely given the extraordinarily clear blue sky that had greeted me this morning, or it was a deck attendant asking me if I'd like a drink or a cold towel. I opened my eyes. I was wrong on both counts.

I sat up, popped out my AirPods and said, "Jeffrey. How are you?" He didn't actually look that well.

"Hi, Claire, mind if I join you?" he said, dragging a sun lounge closer to me before I had a chance to say a word.

I peered over my sunglasses. "Jeffrey, are you all right? You look …" (I was trying to find the right word that was neither insulting nor judgy, both activities of which I had been accused on more than one occasion) "… tired." I hoped that was innocuous enough.

"Maybe a little. I haven't been sleeping that well." He sat back in his chair, which he had pushed close to mine. He put his hands behind his head and said, "Have you ever been in a situation where you wanted to ask a question, but you knew that the answer might be one that you don't want to hear … ever?"

I sat up. "I can assure you, Jeffrey, that if I don't want the answer to a question, regardless of what that answer is, I don't ask it. And you're a psychiatrist. Can't you analyze yourself? If a patient asked you that question, what would you tell him?"

Jeffrey thought for a moment, then said, "I'd probably tell the patient to go ahead and ask the question if it was important and then reframe the answer if he didn't like it."

"Well, then," I said, lying back against the soft towel I had rolled up under my head, "you've just solved your problem. Now, I think some sun would do you good, don't you agree?"

As much as I relished some peace, quiet and rays, Jeffrey seemed to want to chat. "Claire, you're a smart woman." I had no idea where he was going with this because if I had really been a smart woman, when I met him two years ago, I would not have gotten involved in my indiscretion, but I wasn't going to discuss that with him. It was, after all, water under the bridge, as they say. So, I just grunted in agreement. He continued. "If you thought there was a chance for you to find out about something that happened, but you weren't sure if someone knew something, but part of you wanted to know while the other part didn't, which part would you listen to?"

I sat up again and took off my sunglasses, better to stare at this man who I had thought was so smart. Maybe he was, but his youth was beginning to show. As successful as he was on the surface, Jeffrey P. Montgomery was just a young millennial man who didn't know his arse from a hole in the ground, as my grandfather used to say on a regular basis. "Jeffrey, I have no idea what you just said. What's more, I don't think you do, either. What the hell is going on with you?"

"Forget it, Claire. I don't know what's going on with me either." He took a deep breath and seemed to relax. "If you don't mind me changing the subject, do you have plans for your day ashore in Barbados?"

I was very grateful for a change of subject. It was just that this wasn't a subject I necessarily needed to discuss with Jeffrey. I hesitated for a moment, then told him about my tentative plans.

"Hey, I actually have a guide booked for the day. Maybe we can use him and go to dinner at that place."

I was suddenly torn. On the one hand, I wanted to spend the time exorcising ghosts. On the other hand, Jeffrey had just presented me with a solution to my problem of unfinished plans. Finding an available guide on such short notice was proving to be somewhat of a problem. I thought about it for a moment. Perhaps being with Jeffrey might actually help me. So, I reluctantly agreed. I would spend at least some of my day on the island with him. I might even tell him about my ghosts. I might. But for now, I just wanted to enjoy the rest of my relaxing day at sea. I hoped he'd shut up.

~

It seemed like an entire lifetime ago since I booked this cruise. It seemed so important at the time because I had an agenda, but I hadn't given a lot of thought to details like where the ship was going and for how long. Those issues were not my priority. Once I got on board, though, I'd taken a closer look at the itinerary and had noted several "sea days," those days when the ship sails and there is no port stop. When I saw how many there were on this three-week trip, I was alarmed by the possibility of being at sea and having nothing to do. Once onboard, I had nightmares about bingos and shuffleboard. Now that I was in the midst of two days of transportation toward a Caribbean island, I discovered that I loved it.

I now seemed to be luxuriating in the lack of an agenda, and this both thrilled and bothered me. I had spent my entire adult life (and likely my childhood, come to think of it, given my particular parents) on a schedule. Even at the age of thirteen in the 1980s, I remember having a little black notebook that I used to keep lists of things I had to do. In the 1990s, my parents were early adopters of the PDA—personal digital assistants, which were the forerunners of the Blackberry and on and on—and in the late 1990s, they gave me a Palm Pilot for Christmas one year. I'd been hooked on digital calendars and to-do lists ever since. And now I had nothing on my to-do list. It was frightening to see how much I loved the feeling.

Make no mistake, though, I was looking forward to getting back to my life—my operating schedule, my grand rounds presentation schedule, my resident teaching schedule, my research, my international presentations—to all the things that gave my life structure and made me feel comfortable. However, I figured that since I probably wasn't going to have much of a break again in the near future, I should take advantage of the time, and so I did. I spent my two sea days lolling around, going to the spa and drinking Sea Breeze cocktails on the deck.

By the time I was waking up two days later, the ship had docked sometime in the early hours of the morning, and we were alongside a pier at the passenger cruise terminal in Bridgetown, Barbados. I stood out on my veranda for a few minutes, looking down on the dock where people had already begun disembarking for their shore excursions.

I knew from reading the brochures the cruise line had provided that some of them were embarking on "... a panoramic driving tour through the bucolic countryside and along the beautiful coastline ..." Others were going to Orchid World, where they might "... see hummingbirds flitting about from blossom to blossom." Still others would be spending a relaxing day on "... a lovely stretch of sand that rims Carlisle Bay in the southwestern part of the island." Those would be the beach people. Of course, there was also the inevitable catamaran cruise, no doubt accompanied by copious amounts of rum—dirt cheap on these islands. I also saw something about an "Atlantis Submarine" adventure. I was happy to be spending the first half of the day by myself before heading out to The Cliff for dinner with Jeffrey.

Once I was sure most people had gone ashore, I slathered on the sunscreen, slapped a wide-brimmed hat on my head and headed off for a walk into the island's capital, Bridgetown. Once off the ship, I had a ten-minute walk along the pier just to get to the cruise terminal building. It was sweltering, and the sun beat down relentlessly, but at least the humidity of the Amazon was no longer an issue. Once I reached the cruise terminal, which was really an enormous Quonset hut with skylights in its metal ceiling, there was a breath of air conditioning—but only just. I wandered past the inescapable gift shops, jewellery purveyors and liquor stores that were there solely for the pleasure of cruise ship passengers.

I had counted three other ships also at the cruise terminal, so the island would be groaning under the weight of all those tourists. I hoped that by walking out on my own, I might avoid many of them. And surely, Jeffrey and I would be the only ship's passengers dining at The Cliff later this evening. I hoped so, anyway.

As I walked toward the middle of the town, I found myself on a pleasant waterside walkway that had clearly been created for the cruisers who passed this way. I was enjoying the breeze as I passed under the shade of palm trees lining the shore. I stopped for a moment to take in the quiet lapping of the ocean against the rock wall that had been created. This was no wavey beach. I took a few photos and carried on.

It was a twenty-five-minute walk from the cruise terminal to my destination, The Bridgetown Duty-Free shop on Broad Street. When Peter and I had been here some years ago, it had been called Cave Shepherd, but after looking that one up online, I discovered it had since changed hands. I understood that it was still a department store. It wasn't that I was really looking for anything in particular, but it gave me a destination for my morning walk. And I knew it would be air-conditioned. I'd need a bit of respite from the sun before my walk back to the ship. As I made my way into the downtown area, I turned right on Broad Street and had no difficulty finding my destination.

I was mulling over the local rums that were displayed on an enormous rum wall, observing that many of them were not as dirt cheap as I remembered when I heard a voice call my name.

"Dear Dr. Barrett," came the familiar voice. "I think you might enjoy this one."

I turned and found myself looking at Imogen, who was pointing to a bottle of rum in a locked cabinet in front of me.

"I never took you for a rum aficionado, Imogen," I said as I read the label. It was called Foursquare 2004, and I had never seen it before. As a proud Newfoundlander where rum was the drink of choice for many, my father prided himself in knowing everything there was to know about rum, but I'd never seen this one in his liquor cabinet or anyone else's.

"Oh, you would be surprised by what we get up to with the Zen and Tonic crowd. That one's best over ice."

"I'm not familiar with it, Imogen," I said, leaning closer to the glass.

"It's extraordinary—and not cheap, mind you."

I wondered how expensive it could be. I peered closely at the bottle again. It was "2004 Foursquare Rum Distillery Exceptional Cask Selection Mark IV 'Zinfandel Cask Blend' Single Blended Rum," to be specific, and the price was ... no, that couldn't possibly be right. It was $450 American dollars. I felt faint. But I knew I'd have to buy a bottle.

"Dr. Barrett—Claire," Imogen said, "we were just talking about that panel discussion coming up the day after tomorrow." Imogen gestured toward the woman with her. It was one of the women who had been playing pickleball on the upper deck. I tried not to let my nose twitch.

Jeffrey had mentioned something about a panel, but I hadn't paid much attention since I hadn't the slightest intention of attending. "Yes, of course," I said.

"Well, our lovely young Dr. Montgomery is part of it. It's about reinventing oneself. An especially resonant topic, don't you think?"

Reinventing oneself? Resonant? She had no idea.

~

Winston, the driver Jeffrey had hired, was waiting in the cruise terminal parking lot at exactly five-thirty beside his black Mercedes, which must have been at least thirty years old.

I remembered my father had a similar one when I was in my late teens. Winston's car had been buffed to shiny perfection and looked like it had been lovingly cared for over the decades. What impressed me the most, though, wasn't the car; it was his punctuality. My recollection of schedules in Barbados was that they were suggestions, at best.

"Welcome, welcome to our beautiful Barbados," Winston said to me as he reached out to shake my hand. He then turned to Jeffrey. "And lovely to be with you for the evening as well, Dr. Montgomery," and I remembered that Jeffrey had probably already spent a few hours with Winston earlier in the day.

Winston was a tall, rather large Bajan with glaringly white teeth and a smile that could light up a room. He was wearing a brightly coloured shirt with a green and yellow palm tree print. He opened the back door and helped me in while Jeffrey went around and let himself into the back seat beside me. Then Winston wedged himself under the steering wheel. "We have only a fifteen-minute drive to The Cliff, my friends, so we have time for a bit more sightseeing on the west coast. Shall we?"

Once we were outside the town limits, the coastal highway was less a highway than it was a two-lane road leading past beaches and hotels on our left-hand side and fast-food restaurants and gas stations on our right. Two-lane road or not, many of the drivers seemed to believe they were on the Autobahn without speed limits, thinking nothing of whizzing past slow buses, tourists in rental cars, and cars like ours. Winston tut-tutted every time one passed by.

The Cliff was located on the northwest coast of the island, less than eight kilometres north of Bridgetown. Winston drove us past the restaurant, pointing it out as we went by and telling us we should see a beach while we were here. He seemed to think we were a couple. I just rolled my eyes and let him believe what he wanted.

When we arrived at Payne's Bay Beach, he suggested we take a walk along the sandy water's edge, and if we liked, he would take photographs. We said yes to the sandy walk and no thank you to the photos. The less documentation I had of myself with Jeffrey, the better. I supposed he felt much the same, although I didn't ask.

We took off our shoes (strappy sandals, in my case) and stepped onto the soft, beige sand. Of course, instead of fully immersing myself in the experience, I fretted about the amount of sand I'd have on my feet and legs when I finally arrived for dinner. After two days chilling on a cruise ship deck in the sun with a drink in my hand, I was still able to wind myself up about something that was of so little significance that it was less than a single grain of this sand. Jeffrey abruptly took my hand, and I allowed myself to be pulled along toward the waves that lapped against the silky sand. As I looked out at the horizon, I realized why Winston had brought us here. It was just ten minutes to sunset.

The sun was dripping toward the horizon. As I watched the oranges and pinks bleeding into the fading blue of the Caribbean sky, I wondered why we're so fascinated by sunsets. Is it just the kaleidoscopic aesthetics that human beings are drawn to, like a cat is drawn to a shiny aluminum foil ball? Or is it something deeper? At that moment, as the sun dipped closer to its nighttime resting place, Jeffrey abruptly draped his arm over my shoulder, shaking me out of my reverie.

"Penny for your thoughts?" he said.

"Just thinking about sunsets," I said.

"They're interesting, aren't they? I mean, a sunset is just a sunset, right? But have you ever seen two the same?"

I thought about that for a moment and realized I might not have paid that much attention to sunsets throughout my life, but I had a sense that he might be onto something. "No, I don't suppose any two are the same," I said.

"So, every day, the sunset is different, and it lasts only moments. That's probably why we're so in awe of them. They're fleeting. Wouldn't it be nice if we could be in awe of all the individual moments of our lives—that no matter how fleeting, we just appreciate them in the moment for the moment? But we just seem to look back and grasp."

"Are we still talking about sunsets, Jeffrey?"

Jeffrey dropped his arm from my shoulder, rolled up his pant legs and walked into the gentle waves that lapped the shore. I watched him as he stood there, staring at the sunset and wondered what was really going on in his head. Again, I didn't ask.

Once back in the car, I did my best to clean the sand off my feet with the towel Winston provided. I looked over at Jeffrey, who was doing the same thing, and for once in my life, I stopped worrying about a bit of sand in my shoes.

Less than ten minutes later, we arrived at The Cliff. Winston dropped us off at the front door and told us to text him when we were ready to leave. "And don't worry. Take your time. Enjoy the evening. I will have you back to the ship in plenty of time." I hoped so, or it would leave without us. I must admit, the thought didn't worry me as much as it might have under other circumstances.

We walked up the three steps leading to a modern entrance lit by a series of art-deco-like sconces. The street front contrasted starkly with the older-style stucco buildings that lined the road snaking along the beach.

Once inside, the maître d' led us through the restaurant to our table on the lower tier beside a railing on the edge of the water. The sun had set, but the sky and the water still shimmered with shades of purple and amethyst. The torches hanging off the railings were quivering in the slight breeze. I breathed in the slightly briny air layered with notes of floral essence that I didn't recognize.

The server, who materialized immediately, offered the cocktail menu, which Jeffrey immediately took, then turned to me and said, "Let's start with something Bajan, shall we?" His almost melancholic episode seemed to have evaporated with the sunset.

I perused the menu, considering what might truly say "Bajan" to my senses. There was something called "A Sip in Thyme," which was a mixture of local Mount Gay Silver Rum, fresh lime, raspberries and thyme syrup. That one had possibilities. Then I saw "Remy Rosé Mojito," which didn't sound very Bajan, but it did sound festive. It was a concoction of Remy Martin, fresh mint, fresh lime juice, simple syrup, and strawberries, all topped with rosé champagne. That was my choice. Jeffrey chose the "Sip in Thyme."

As the server set our drinks in front of us with the dinner menus, I remembered the last time I was here. Peter and I had sat farther back. The view from there had been terrific but not quite as spectacular as hanging over the water's edge as we were this evening. Peter had ordered a bottle of champagne. We thought we should really try to celebrate, but everything seemed so forced. Why hadn't I recognized that at the time? Perhaps it was because I hadn't wanted to. I always fell back on my rigid schedules for comfort. Now, I realized that the primary element in maintaining that comfort was my deeply held desire to prevent anything in my life from changing. Peter was one of those things. I was beginning to understand why I'd been so hell-bent on trying to get him back. Outside of my work life, I'd been flailing for the past two years since the divorce. I had never moved on, and I had never considered myself inflexible. But I was.

Jeffrey raised his glass. "To sunsets. May every sunset of every day grant us serenity and the promise of another day."

I raised my glass and said, "And perhaps every sunrise may present the promise of new experiences."

Once the toasts were over and we had ordered our food, I decided it was time to exorcise a few ghosts. Jeffrey P. Montgomery was one of them. I wanted to talk to him about his lecture I'd attended the other day.

"Jeffrey, when you were talking about mistakes not being failures but being how we learn, I was having difficulty following. In my line of work, mistakes aren't an option."

Jeffrey looked at me thoughtfully. "Claire, I get what you mean. You perform surgical procedures on tiny kids. You can't afford to slip up there. But didn't many of the procedures you learned develop from the mistakes and failures of your predecessors?" I told him I supposed they often did. He continued. "So, the truth is that every day when you're standing in that operating room, what you're doing is built on mistakes that have since been corrected. So, mistakes are indeed how we learn. But I think you're using your surgical experience as a smokescreen."

I didn't like the sound of that and told him so.

"Hear me out. We've established that your work is built on missteps or mistakes in your field over the years, and so it is with your life—which, despite what you think, isn't the same thing. You are not your career."

"Of course I am." I was insulted and beginning to regret bringing up his lecture at all.

"Of course you're not, unless you are, in which case you're not a whole person." Jeffrey looked at me, and I'm sure he could see that steam was about to begin bellowing from my ears. He continued. "What I'm trying to convey to you is that so many people these days find their self-worth only in their careers. But think about this. What would happen if you could no longer be a pediatric surgeon? Who would you be then?"

Two could play at this game. "If you could no longer be Jeffrey P. Montgomery, boy-wonder, social media psychiatrist, what would you do?"

He smiled. He actually smiled. "That's easy. I'd still be Jeffrey P. Montgomery, and I'd continue to live by being who I am. You asked the wrong question, Claire."

"Wrong question? Is there a wrong question?"

"Of course. I asked you who would you *be*. You asked me what I would *do*. And that, my dear, is the essence of your current conundrum."

"Being, doing—what's the difference? It's just semantics."

Jeffrey sipped his drink and then stared at me. "If you continue to believe that, Claire, then I'm afraid you'll always be a surgeon because it's what you do—until you don't. For example, the world of the retired is populated by so many people who couldn't let go of what they were doing throughout their lives to spend some time being who they were meant to be. And if they're no longer doing what they thought made them who they are, then they're nobody. So, they spend their lives just going through the motions—waiting to die. Sad, don't you think?"

I was fuming over the idea that Jeffrey thought I wasn't a complete person because I thought *doing* something was me *being* what I was supposed to be when the server arrived with our starters. I'd have to get back to that. Dinner was now the priority.

Jeffrey was having Miso Glazed Octopus, a dish that I found unappetizing, not being an octopus fan. I was starting with a Waldorf Salad, safe, I know, but I hadn't had one in years. I was looking forward to tasting the Roquefort dressing and the candied walnuts that looked like little jewels dotted among the greenery.

As Jeffrey started on his octopus, he tasted it and then looked at my salad as I savoured the first mouthful. "I see you're enjoying your salad."

"I am. This dressing is to die for."

He smirked a little. "So, that's what I was talking about earlier when I said so many of us can't seem just to enjoy those fleeting moments of experiences that make up our lives. We seem to want to grasp onto things. You do, indeed, have experiences that make up who you are when you're not *doing* what you *do*. What I'm trying to say is that you might consider savouring them more and thinking about how they make up your life, too." He cut another piece of octopus and said, more to himself than to me, "Perhaps I need to take my own advice."

"About that, Jeffrey. You seem to be burdened by something. Care to share?"

"Maybe. Eventually," he said as we finished our appetizers, and the server arrived with our main courses.

While Jeffrey enjoyed his Bouillabaisse à la Provençale and I inhaled my perfectly prepared Blackened Snapper, we kept the conversation lighter—more superficial. We chatted as people do about the food, the ambience, and the other diners.

When dessert arrived and the server had finished preparing our Crêpes Suzette tableside, Jeffrey, apropos of nothing, said, "What do you know about Eliza Cohen?"

For a moment, I considered my preconceptions about her versus what I actually knew about her now. Instead of voicing this thought, I said, "Why in the world are you interested in Eliza Cohen? *Are* you interested in Eliza Cohen?"

"It's not what you think," he said quickly as he took his first bite of the exquisite crêpes in all their Grand Marnier glory.

"What do you think I think?"

"Claire, I know what you'd be thinking, but Eliza is almost old enough to be my mother."

"You do realize that Eliza and I are almost exactly the same age." I wanted to ask him if he felt the same way about me (the mother thing), but I held myself back from asking. I couldn't quickly come up with any good way to reframe that one if I didn't like his answer. Instead, I said, "All I know is probably what you know. Eliza's a cookbook author who lives in New York. She was raised in Canada. I know that her grandparents came from Newfoundland. In fact, I knew her grandmother. I also know she has a daughter who's going to medical school. Oh, yes, and she's a grandmother."

Jeffrey chewed and swallowed before taking a sip of the dessert wine we'd ordered. "She mentioned that, but she doesn't seem much like the grandmotherly type to me."

"I don't suppose anyone our age is ready to be a grandmother, but what can you do?" I looked at my watch. "Geezus, Jeffrey. We better call Winston. The ship leaves in an hour. We're supposed to be on board half an hour before it leaves."

After quickly paying the bill, we waited impatiently out front for Winston to pull up. I was almost frantic by the time he pulled back onto the roadway headed for Bridgetown. I didn't relish running down the pier, nor did I really want to try to find a puddle-jumper plane to fly us to Antigua to meet the ship the following day. That's the kind of thing that happens to careless people who forget the time. That's not who Claire Barrett was.

Suddenly, Jeffrey said, "Wouldn't it be fun if we missed the ship? I mean, what an adventure we'd have trying to catch up with it. We'd have to find a hotel, a flight—or a boat. A boat would be fun."

"Ooh, that would be a long way by boat," Winston said from the darkness of the front seat. "It is almost five hundred kilometres to Antigua past the islands of St. Lucia, Martinique, Guadeloupe. A long way, indeed."

Jeffrey looked at my face, which must have been lit by the ambient light from the oncoming traffic. "Well, then, I guess we'll just have to make it back to the ship on time."

I sat back and thought about his words. Wouldn't it be fun if we missed the ship? What an adventure. I smiled. *Yes,* I thought, *it might be an adventure after all.*

TWENTY-FOUR

Eliza

ANTIGUA AND BARBUDA

SINCE WE WEREN'T LEAVING BARBADOS until eleven p.m., Peter and I opted to have dinner at one of the outside venues on board. To tell you the truth, though, I wasn't all that hungry. I'd had such a wonderful day, including a late lunch at the truly atmospheric Fisherman's Pub on the beach in Speightstown, up the coast. I hadn't had fish and chips that good since I was in Newfoundland the summer before. All that fried food, along with a bottle (or two) of the local Banks beer, kept me from feeling even the slightest bit of hunger well past dinner time. In addition to the heavy lunch, we'd also had our share of fresh beach air. We had started the day early.

After most of the other guests had departed, we left the ship and wandered into the cruise terminal. Peter immediately grabbed my hand and made a beeline for the taxi stand, where we found the affable Jackie, who was waiting beside her taxicab, fanning herself with a local newspaper. Jackie said she'd be delighted to be at our beck and call for the day.

As we settled in the back seat, Peter said, "We said we'd walk the beaches of the world together. How do you feel about starting today?"

How could I refuse? So, we spent the day (apart from our delightful lunch) visiting three of the most extraordinary Bajan beaches. We began at Carlyle Beach, the closest beach to the capital city of Bridgetown. Then we started our drive up the west coast, a coast that Jackie called their "platinum coast" because it was home to many high-end hotels.

Our next stop was Batts Rock Beach, and finally, we walked on Heywoods Beach, which was practically deserted. As we walked along the serene water's edge, the waves gently washing over our feet, I thought about beaches. I've never figured out what it is that humans like so much about a beach. Of course, they're aesthetically pleasing, especially when they're not covered with raucous sun worshippers. That natural beauty is part of what draws us in, but there seems to be more. Is it the open, uncluttered space of a beach that we love? As I stood there for a moment, staring out into the unmistakable azure blue of the Caribbean Sea, I realized that a beach offers a sense of freedom—an escape from the more structured, demanding environments of everyday life. I turned to Peter.

"What is it that you like about beaches, Peter?"

"Right at this moment?" he said, taking my hand. "Right at this moment, what I like about beaches is that you're walking on them with me."

I laughed and nudged him. "I mean in general."

We both stopped and stood there, staring out at the waves once again. Then Peter said, "I suppose it's all about boundlessness. I mean, just look out there. There's a vastness that's almost too hard to imagine. I get a sense of awe and maybe even some perspective. We get so caught up in our own little worlds that we often lose sight of the fact that there's something larger than ourselves. That's what gives us some perspective. We're just dots on the continuum of time."

"They're also romantic, don't you think?"

"I certainly do think," he said. "*From Here to Eternity*."

"What? The movie?"

"Best beach scene on screen ever."

I stared out at the ocean and said, "I never knew it could be like this. Nobody ever kissed me the way you do …"

Peter said, "Nobody?"

"No, nobody." And we both burst out laughing.

"You know the dialogue," he said.

"One of my all-time favourite movies," I said. "I'm a bit of a vintage movie fan."

"You make a terrific Deborah Kerr."

I looked at him and cocked my head as if sizing him up. "And I suppose you do resemble Burt Lancaster—if I squint."

It turned out that we had yet another thing in common. If it hadn't been for the fact that Jackie was waiting for us to continue our island adventure, I think we both would have fallen into the sand and made love right there. Grit be damned! It was time for lunch.

By the time Jackie dropped us off back at the pier, it was well past three p.m., and I was ready for a nap.

"Should we start a beach walk journal?" Peter said as we walked back along the pier to our waiting ship.

"You don't strike me as a journal type of person."

Peter smiled and shrugged. "Maybe I'm starting a new phase of life." And we both laughed.

So, we found ourselves on the outside deck a few hours later, surrounded by the lights of the cruise terminal, watching other ships depart. The dockside activity was entertaining enough and distracted us from the fact that we weren't that hungry. But it had been a good day—a great day if you must know—and I knew I'd sleep well.

~

I was right about sleeping well. By the time I opened my eyes the following morning, we were already alongside the pier in the town of St. John's on the island of Antigua. Neither Peter nor I had ever been here before. We hadn't been sure what we wanted to do while on the island, so we decided to opt for a cruise-line shore excursion and spent the first part of the day with a group. When I'd seen the "hands-on cooking class" option, how could I pass that up? Peter had agreed, but he also told me that he had done a bit of research about the capital city of St. John's, and he had been intrigued.

First, it had the same name as his home—St. John's, Newfoundland. Second, he said it had a surprise or two. But he wouldn't give me details, so I had to content myself with the brochure that described the shore excursion.

It said we would be taking part in a hands-on cooking class at an "exclusive" boutique hotel, and then we would have a chance to eat what we'd produced. I was excited to be taking a cooking class this time rather than giving one.

The class took place at a hotel in Dickenson Bay, a short drive from the pier. Peter thought it would be another good one to add to our now-growing list of beaches of the world.

When we arrived at the hotel, we were greeted by the owner, who was also the chef who would be teaching our class. Peter and I both accepted the offer of a glass of that ubiquitous rum punch that the islands are so famous for.

I took my first sip and said, "Dear god, Peter, this is powerful." It tasted like there was far more rum in it than whatever other ingredients made up the "punch" part.

Peter laughed. "Is there a better way to cook?"

I took another sip and reflected wryly that he was probably right. I'd been taking my cooking far too seriously.

Perhaps it was time to put the fun back into the whole thing. And we did.

As the class progressed and we learned that we were cooking Caribbean-Fusion dishes, the rum punch continued to flow. I had never considered that there had been so many influences on Caribbean cuisine as the chef discussed how Caribbean-Fusion meant a fusion of so many different types of cooking—West African, Creole, European, Latin American, Indian/South Asian, Chinese and others. Chinese? I'd never even considered it to be an influence on cuisine in this part of the world. I took out my notebook.

Our menu for the day was jerk pork with peas and Antigua's national dish called fungee, a polenta-like cornmeal which Antiguans use as a substitute for rice alongside many dishes like fish and stew. The chef had already prepared a fish stew for us to eat with the fungee.

When the food was ready, Peter and I and fifteen other like-minded guests settled down at wooden tables in the pink-washed stucco dining room to sample our handiwork. We found ourselves at a table with two other guests, both of whom had attended my onboard cooking classes.

"Ms. Cohen," the woman with the brightest red hair I'd ever seen (next to what mine would probably have looked like throughout my adult life if I hadn't taken measures to avoid such a colour), "it is such an honour to be cooking alongside one of my idols. You must tell me how you test so many recipes to come up with the ones that make it into your cookbooks, and you must tell us what the next book will be about. Caribbean cooking, perhaps? Or maybe Brazilian?"

Her companion, another woman of a certain age with silver hair and an eye-popping necklace of turquoise beads that looked like it might have had its provenance in a southwestern desert of the United States, added, "Oh yes, I second that!" Then she poured more wine into each of our glasses from the carafe in the middle of the table.

I told them I was flattered and described how I and my assistants tested recipes. I then told them to stay tuned for an interesting new cookbook from Canada's East Coast. They were, in fact, from Arizona, so the idea of a Newfoundland cookbook fascinated them. Then, when I introduced Peter and mentioned that he lived in Newfoundland, they turned their attention to him.

"Oh my," said the woman with the fiery red hair whose name I had missed, "you are so ruggedly handsome. Are all the men where you live as handsome as you are?"

It was the first time I'd ever seen Peter blush. I sat back and watched him chat with these two women who hung off his every word as he talked about the fjords, the mountains, the icebergs, and the food from his home province. I was thinking about how wonderful it was going to be to learn more and more about this man as the fates unfolded—because I could feel them unfolding moment by moment.

Once we had all declared that we'd done a bang-up job of creating the Caribbean-Fusion food, we had some time before we had to reboard the bus to return to St. John's. Peter and I took advantage of the time to walk on Dickensen Beach.

As we stood in the shallow water, looking out at the aquamarine that was so mesmerizing for those of us from the northeast of North America, Peter said, "Let's never stop doing this."

~

When the bus dropped us off outside the passenger area at the cruise terminal, Peter said, "Let's explore St. John's for a bit."

Of course, I agreed. As we walked around the town, I began to observe that most of it had been created for tourists. The main drag was called Heritage Quay, a pedestrian-only shopping street lined with shops like Diamonds International, Columbian Emeralds and Caribbean Beach Bums. These were not places where the locals did their weekly shopping. Beyond the tourist traps were low buildings lining a maze of streets that made up the town. We walked along on the narrow cement sidewalks and up a hill to St. John's Cathedral, where we stood under a protruding cement overhang as a brief but heavy rain shower moved overhead. Then Peter took me by the hand and said, "Let's go."

Once back down in the town proper, it seemed clear to me that he knew where he was going.

"I thought you'd never been here before," I said.

"I haven't, but I know how to navigate a town on Google Maps. We're headed to Redcliffe Quay."

It turned out that Redcliffe Quay was a street not far from the pier but outside the main tourist route. It was like walking onto the set of a period film set two centuries ago.

"Believe it or not," Peter said as he determinedly headed down the street, "this used to be a slave compound."

I looked at the little boutiques and restaurants that now populated the small street fronts of the colourful buildings. We walked for a block, and then Peter took my hand and led me across the street toward a specific shop. The sign outside said "Goldsmitty," and displayed in the arched windows that were surrounded by centuries-old stone were dazzling jewellery pieces.

"My research tells me that this store is owned by a goldsmith who designs and makes his own pieces."

I was looking at a display of earrings that resembled spun gold. One set looked like spider's webs, another like fishbones. They were stunning. My mind was starting to race. What were we doing here?

We walked into the shop, which was larger than I had expected. In front of us in the centre of the shop was a long showcase that you could walk all around. Displayed in it were eye-popping necklaces, pendants and rings. Some were gold, others were silver. Many were set with stones—rubies, emeralds, blue topaz, aquamarines, opals and more. The unique designs were not jewellery pieces you'd find in any other shop, even in Manhattan. I should know. I'd looked often enough and received enough apology pieces from Jake over the years.

Before I went any further down this path, I turned to Peter, who was chatting with one of the shopkeepers, sidled over to him and whispered, "What are we doing here?"

He turned and smiled. "I'm buying you a present."

I didn't know what to say. I wanted to say that he didn't have to do this, but he probably knew that already. Of course, he didn't have to. It did, however, appear that he wanted to.

He turned to the young woman who was standing behind the counter, smiling from ear to ear. "Give me a moment, will you please?" She nodded, and he took me by the arm so that we could stand beside another showcase lit by glittering lights.

"Eliza, I've never met anyone like you, and at the risk of sounding arrogant, I'd venture to guess you've never met anyone like me." I couldn't argue with any of that statement. "We both know that this isn't a fleeting moment in our lives. We both know where it's going." He put a hand on each of my shoulders and looked directly at me. "I have no idea how this is going to happen; I only know it is going to happen because we're going to make it happen. It's that important."

Peter then took me by the hand and led me to the counter where the young woman had placed a black velvet jewellery holder. On it were three rings. All three were solid gold—no gemstones. One resembled a golden ladder; another had what appeared to be a stylized coin on top. I reached for the third one, which looked like zig-zagged gold that might encircle a finger like a web of connection. Before I knew what I was doing, I placed it on my finger. It fit perfectly.

"We'll take it," Peter said, reaching for his wallet. "And before you can say another word, Eliza Cohen, I know there are hurdles ahead. And those hurdles are what will make the journey intriguing. I also know that our destination on this journey isn't clear, but that's what makes it fun. And we could all use a bit of intriguing fun in the final stages of our lives, couldn't we?"

Again, I had no argument.

TWENTY-FIVE

Claire

LAST DAY AT SEA

"FROM CEO TO YOLO: Navigating Your Personal Reinvention."

I stood in front of the poster, trying to remember what YOLO stood for. How I hated those acronyms: FOMO, ROFL, LMK. I often felt it would be so much more efficient just to say what you mean rather than having people ponder over what the acronym meant. Although, I do have to admit that I did enjoy a good MYOB or WTF. (In case you need to know: mind your own business and, well, who needs to be told what WTF stands for?) YOLO, however, was eluding me.

I looked around to see if there was someone that I could ask without sounding like one of those Luddites who hasn't been able to keep up with modern technologically related linguistics. Then, I remembered that all I had to do was check that I had Wi-Fi and look it up.

You **O**nly **L**ive **O**nce. I should have known. So, the panel discussion that Imogen had mentioned back in the duty-free rum aisle in Bridgetown was about reinvention after recognition of the fact that life is, after all, terminal, as Jeffrey has said—often. I could not even imagine what someone like Jeffrey would have to offer to the older among us. The moment that thought entered my mind, I remembered one time just as Peter and I were in the throes of finalizing the decision to separate. He told me that he could no longer cope with the fact that I was so judgemental that I was blinded to the possibilities of other perspectives—of different ways of seeing the world.

I squirmed a bit at the realization that the sharpness with which I had dissected others' flaws and differing opinions throughout my life might now be like the tip of a scalpel turned inward, threatening to slice open my armour of self-assured confidence that I'd worn throughout my life. Perhaps I had dismissed opportunities as I dismissed people with little more than a glance and an upturned nose. Perhaps it was time to think about that part of who I was. Maybe later.

I took a deep breath, awoke from an unaccustomed moment of introspection, and came back to the reality of today's "entertainment." I hoped that they weren't going to suggest things like dyeing your hair an odd colour, wearing a purple hat or rebranding yourself as a lifestyle influencer for the over-seventy crowd. I realized that I liked my life exactly as it had always been. Perhaps this was another of my seemingly endless problems. I had now started to ask myself if I liked the stability of it a bit too much. Was there any room in my life for adventure? I hoped so, but the answer wasn't clear. Regardless of how many times I told myself that I wasn't going to attend this panel, I knew I would. Anyway, what else was there to do on this last day of the cruise that hadn't turned out the way I'd intended?

~

The panel discussion was scheduled for three p.m. in the ship's main theatre, after which I expected everyone would retire to one bar or another to reflect on the new ideas. Sure. On a cruise, that's exactly what people do—not. What I expected was that the theatre would be packed because it was the only diversion on offer this afternoon. Many, if not most, of the audience would take advantage of the cool semi-darkness of the theatre to take a nap. There would be the requisite few attendees who would hang on every word and be sure to get in a question or two to demonstrate their superiority to everyone else in the room. And, no doubt, Rebecca would have the final word about hoping that this cruise, as it draws to a close, will have played at least a small part in everyone's reinvention going forward—or something like that. And, of course, please plan to take another one so you can be even more illuminated. Oh well, at least I expected to be able to count on Jeffrey to leave us with another *bon mot* or two. After figuring out the acronym, I was off to find lunch to fortify myself with a glass or two of wine.

I arrived at the entrance to the main dining room, hoping for a quiet, solo lunch. I almost backed away around the corner (I was even willing to brave the buffet if necessary) when I saw that Imogen and several of her friends were ahead of me in the line at the hostess's desk. I was too slow, though. Imogen spotted me and gestured me over.

"Dear Claire, won't you please join us for lunch? I've been telling Tallulah and Isadora here about you and how we met a lifetime ago when I used to be a doctor." Tallulah and Isadora? Really?

"You'll always be a doctor, Imogen," I said. "Once a doctor, always a doctor, don't you think?" The way Imogen looked at me suggested she thought otherwise. "Anyway, it wasn't that long ago—certainly not a lifetime."

Imogen just looked at me as if she were looking at a slightly daft child and said, "A lifetime can mean many things, my dear. You will come to appreciate that everything changes no matter how hard we may try to make it not so. You will have one lifetime after another, or you will remain stagnant as things change around you. Either way, it is your choice."

Well, that sounded like an auspicious beginning to a pleasant lunch, didn't it?

Imogen then looked at her lunch companions. "Well, then, the old professor has now finished ranting. Shall we?" Imogen nodded to the waiting hostess, hooked her arm through mine, and said, "Don't worry, my dear. We are not such a bad lot. I promise not to flex my old lady wisdom muscles too much more. And we could do with a bit of the younger generation's perspective."

I almost laughed at being considered a member of the younger generation, but in this company, I was.

"And wait until you meet Rowan and Ziggy," Imogen said. At that, the three of them started laughing. I had no idea what was so funny—unless it was the names.

With rudeness being my only other option in the situation, I allowed myself to be led to a table for six in the middle of the dining room. Once the four of us "ladies" had settled ourselves and each ordered a glass of wine, two older men approached the table. Imogen did the introductions.

Rowan was a tall, distinguished-looking man who appeared to be in his mid-seventies or so. When introduced to me, he lifted my hand to his lips and said, "*Enchantée, madame.* I am delighted to meet you." His accent and his entire bearing reminded me of that old film star, Maurice Chevalier. He was positively charming. Ziggy was something else entirely.

"And this, my dear Claire, is Ziggy." Imogen, who was clearly in charge, turned to Ziggy. "Be nice to Claire, Ziggy, and behave yourself for once if you can. She is a young and impressionable woman, and she is also a surgeon, as was I."

Impressionable? I doubted that, but it was fun to think that others saw me differently than I saw myself.

Ziggy then moved in to shake and kiss my hand. However, instead of that refined nod that Rowan had offered, Ziggy looked up, twitched an eyebrow most lasciviously and said, "A lady doctor, you say? I do like the smart ones." He looked at Imogen. "At least when they're not old and crotchety." Then he winked at me. Was that a cockney accent that I heard?

Imogen swatted him on the shoulder. "Don't mind Ziggy, my dear. He is an old rocker and cannot seem to forget that we are not all his groupies—if he ever had any."

I looked at Ziggy's wildly patterned shirt under a flax-coloured linen blazer that did not in any way wrinkle expensively as Peter's always did. It just wrinkled.

I looked at Ziggy as he took his seat across the table. "An old rocker? Were you in a band, Ziggy?"

"Was I in a band? You ever hear about The Beatles?" I was startled at his mention of the iconic group. Then he laughed. "That wasn't it, but I did jam with Sir Paul a few times. Ever hear tell of the Electric Kaleidoscope?"

I told him I was sorry, but that name didn't ring a bell.

"How about Fuzzy Funk?"

"More like the Polyester Players," Imogen said wryly.

"Or the Bellbottom Brawlers," Isadora, with the chiffon wrap, said. They all laughed.

Ziggy lifted a roll from the breadbasket and said, "No matter, darlin'. You're too young anyway. But don't listen to those daffy old broads. They wouldn't know good music if it came up to them and bit them on the ampleness of their butts. The Fuzzy Funk had quite a career as it happens."

I was still trying to conjure a picture of a Fuzzy Funk rock group when I saw Tallulah roll her eyes dramatically.

Tallulah said, "He's once again proving Mark Twain right. 'The older I get, the more clearly I remember things that never happened.'"

Ziggy gave her the side eye while everyone else laughed uproariously. At least lunch promised to be entertaining.

The server arrived to take our orders, and the group settled into a discussion about the cruise. They seemed to have enjoyed it tremendously, especially, it turned out, their Zen and Tonic Connection meetings and speakers. Jeffrey was the main speaker, but they had evidently had several. They were, however, interested in my take on the cruise and its onboard activities.

"Did you enjoy Eliza Cohen's cooking demonstration?" said Tallulah, who turned out to be a retired English teacher. "I have taken up cooking as a pastime in my retirement, and I do love her cookbooks."

I told them that I had enjoyed it but chose not to mention my connection to her.

"Have you noticed that dishy man she's been keeping company with?" Isadora with the flowing chiffon scarf that she kept rearranging, was a retired dancer. They were an eclectic group despite their Zen and Tonic Connection, a subject that I intended to ask them more about if I ever had the opportunity to get a word in edgewise.

"Oh yes," Tallulah said. "If I were only twenty years younger ..." Everyone laughed.

"If you were twenty years younger, you'd still nitpick at his grammar," Ziggy said.

Imogen turned to me. "I do believe I saw you chatting him up. Do you know who he is, Claire?"

I was caught. Should I say no or tell the truth? I opted to tell the truth.

"Yes, I do know him," I said as casually as I could manage. "He's my ex-husband."

All eyes at the table turned toward me and opened widely in evident astonishment.

"Good heavens," Tallulah said. "That must have come as quite a shock to you to find him on the same cruise—and for three whole weeks."

"Perhaps not quite as shocking as one might think," I said, preferring not to go into too many details.

"Well, if I found my ex-husband on board, I'd find it shocking," Isadora said.

"Shocking indeed and highly implausible," Rowan said. "Your ex-husband is dead." His comment instigated more mirth all around.

I was amazed at the way the ribbing was always considered to be good-natured. None of them took offence at a single insult hurled their way. I asked them about this. I thought they must have all known one another for decades. That didn't seem to be the case.

"My dear, we've been forced into friendship completely for the purposes of self-preservation," Imogen said.

"*C'est vrai*. That is right. We require protection," Rowan said, and for the first time, I wondered why his name wasn't Maurice or Jean or Laurent. Rowan seemed an odd name for a French man, but what did I know? Everyone snorted with laughter once again at Rowan's remark.

"What do you need protection from?" Perhaps this might help me to understand their Zen and Tonic Connection.

Ziggy spoke up. "Old people, first off."

I smiled. "Old people?"

"I know what you're thinking, my dear," Imogen said. "We *are* old people, after all. However, when you get older, you will come to understand that living in a community where everyone is old or older is not the epitome of positivity. Indeed, most of the members of the community where we find ourselves living seem to have the philosophy that they are waiting to die. That does not describe us." That's when I understood that they had become acquainted in some kind of retirement community.

"Tell the truth, Imogen. That is not the entire story, is it? It is not just the old people. It is the staff at the community centre who all seem to think that once you pass a certain age, you immediately lose all sense of the future or even the present," Isadora said. "They believe one and all to have regressed to infancy or at least infantile pursuits. Do they really think that we are all interested in bingo and crocheting?"

Ziggy snorted. "And they won't let me play my electric guitar for Saturday night socials." He lifted his glass of scotch (an odd accompaniment to lunch, perhaps).

"And let us not forget protection from our grandchildren." Isadora patted her lips with her napkin. "We are all expected to dote on our grandchildren, and I am here to tell you that it gets very old, very fast. And we are sick of listening to everyone else talk about their grandchildren as if they are god's gift to humanity and as if they have no life of their own."

"Which they don't," Ziggy said, *sotto voce,* but everyone heard. There didn't seem to be any hearing issues at this table. They were an interestingly odd bunch. I'd never met a group like them.

I was surprised that each of them expressed a distinct lack of commitment to their grandchildren. I suppose I'd thought that grandparents adore their grandchildren. Then, Imogen said something that I hadn't considered.

"Claire, my dear, we all do love our grandchildren," she said, holding up her hand as Ziggy started to interrupt (perhaps he didn't love his at all). "But we do not necessarily *like* all of them. There seems to be a rule about grandparenting that requires one to like one's grandchildren. I do like one of mine, but the rest of them are spoiled brats who I prefer not to be around." I was beginning to think I had a lot of misconceptions about what it meant to get older.

"Imogen is quite right," Tallulah, the retired teacher, said. "And we take our philosophy from something the great George Eliot once wrote. She said, 'It's never too late to be what you might have been.'"

"Here, here," Ziggy said. "I might have been a great rock musician—and it's not too late."

After the laughing subsided, Imogen said, "You may find this odd, Claire, my dear, but the topic of this afternoon's panel discussion is right up our alley. As a group, we are in the process of reinventing ourselves. You do only live once, you know."

"And if you do it right the first time," Ziggy said, "once is enough." Then he snorted again.

~

Ten minutes before the three p.m. starting time for the panel discussion, I was still waffling about attending. Then I thought about the unexpected lunch entertainment I'd had. I realized that I still was no closer to figuring out what that Zen and Tonic group was really all about, but I supposed it didn't matter anyway. I had opened my mind—and maybe even my heart—to this group of oddball individuals and realized I was in no position to judge them at all. Who was I becoming?

I looked again at the poster in the theatre's lobby. "*From CEO to YOLO: Navigating Your Personal Reinvention.*" As I considered the topic in relation to the current situation that described my life at the present moment, Rebecca saw me and immediately came over.

"How lovely it is to see you here, Claire. I do suppose even a doctor such as yourself might need a bit of reinvention from time to time, no?"

Rebecca was probably the only person on board who had even close to an accurate idea of why I was on this cruise and how events had unfolded. I was, however, not enamoured of the idea that Rebecca Bebbington-Hughes, cruise director, might be suggesting a personal reinvention for me. I decided not to engage, so my only option at that point was to find myself a seat inside and endure the hour-long festivities.

At four minutes after three, Rebecca made her way onto the stage with a microphone gripped in her right hand. With her left hand, she seemed to be gesturing to the workers to get off the stage. They were still setting up the line of chairs.

Once the workers had vacated the stage, I counted seven chairs—six presumably for panel members and one for the moderator, Rebecca.

Rebecca then began introducing the panellists one by one, who then filed onto the stage and took their assigned seats.

There were the two retired professors who had spoken about various aspects of our destinations. I had heard each of them only once. One was a terrific speaker—Dr. Egerton Stevens was knowledgeable, funny, self-effacing, a Canadian from Winnipeg. The second one, who was neither funny nor self-effacing, was called Dr. Cameron Condom, which might have been the source of his unpleasantness. Who could have grown up happy and well-adjusted with a last name like that?

I was slightly mollified to realize I hadn't completely recovered from my judgemental phase.

The next panellist, Suzette Moorehead, was a bubbly blonde from Seattle who was sixty if she was a day, despite her excruciating attempt to appear younger. From where I sat, she seemed to be desperately trying to master the art of defying time. Her hair, dyed a shade of cornflower blonde, was as convincing as the wig it might have been. Each strand glistened under the overhead LED lights like a high-gloss magazine cover, and the lack of forehead movement to go along with her enthusiastic smile suggested one too many Botox sessions. As expected, her lips were slightly plumped to a youthful exuberance, not quite overdone if she had been forty, which she most assuredly was not. She strutted onto the stage with the confidence of a Taylor Swift wannabe, waving and catching the eyes of anyone who might be staring—and there were many. I suspected that among all the so-called experts on the stage, she was likely the real deal when it came to reinvention. There didn't seem to be a single part of her that hadn't seen a reconfiguration of one sort or another.

Suzette's claim to fame was that she was a world-renowned (in the words of her P.R. firm, no doubt), best-selling author and lifestyle expert (what the heck is that?) with a special gift (?) for helping women navigate menopause. I'd recently read that the global "menopause market" now exceeded seventeen billion dollars, and there was little doubt that she was planning to get her slice of the pie. Dear god, who knew that menopause was even a business? When I was in medical school, it had been a phase of female development, one that I was navigating without the assistance of celebrity-endorsed products. According to what I'd read, it is a growing and largely untapped market. There is nothing quite as lucrative as a normal human phase that the wheels of commerce (and celebrity—Gwyneth and Oprah, I'm looking at you) have turned into a medical issue that can be solved only by employing a commercial solution. I couldn't wait to hear what Suzette had to say.

The next panellist was a middle-aged (non-Asian, more likely German) woman named Cybill Schmitt, who was a Traditional Chinese Medical Doctor. I had opted not to attend any lectures given by people with questionable medical credentials—for obvious reasons. Finally, of course, there was Eliza and then Jeffrey, who brought up the rear. Rebecca then proceeded to introduce the topic.

"Good afternoon, everyone. Isn't it a wonderful afternoon to consider the concept of reinvention? We have with us this afternoon our onboard guest speakers who have spent the past three weeks helping us to ensure you have the most wonderful cruise of your life. Now, we must look toward the sad reality of disembarking from our little slice of paradise. This afternoon, we invite you to consider how you might take a tiny bit of paradise with you and consider a possible new reality for yourself."

A tad overblown, don't you think? A new reality just because we spent three weeks aboard a ship? Rebecca might have been even more delusional than I had thought. Of course, though, it was all part of the cruise line's marketing effort, but she did appear to be sincere in her belief that a cruise was life changing. Perhaps it was for some. As I considered my own reasons for being on board, I realized that I had planned on making a change so that I could go back to things as if they had never changed. It hurt my head to think about it, so I returned my focus to Rebecca, who was still talking.

"I suppose you might be of the ilk who believes that reinvention is merely ten percent personal reflection and ninety percent new wardrobe," she waited a second for the smattering of laughs that were quite subdued in my view. I wryly considered that Rebecca shouldn't give up her day job for a life in stand-up comedy any time soon. Then she continued. "But I assure you there might be more to it than that. Let us, then, turn to our panel of experts so that we might all find a way to hit the refresh button on our lives. Dr. Stevens, would you like to start us off?"

And so the panel presentation began. Dr. Stevens told a few anecdotes about what it was like to retire from the only career he'd ever known as an anthropology professor and try to figure out who he was. He seemed to be tickled by the fact that he'd found a new way to use old skills as a cruise ship lecturer. Then Dr. Condom scowled as he spoke about not being an expert in reinvention and that it was every man for himself (his words, not mine) when it came to making something happen. Despite the fact that I suspected he didn't think he had anything to add to the discussion, I found his idea that it was an inside job to be insightful. I don't suppose he intended to be helpful, but he was.

Then the T.C.M. doctor talked about understanding ourselves holistically, balancing yin and yang and smoothing the flow of Qi. Perhaps this would, in fact, be a way to reinvent myself since it certainly wasn't how I approached life, but my eyes began to glaze over.

Suzette then took over and began talking about midlife being the catalyst for reinvention, animating her words with wild arm gestures that looked as if they were designed to clear the Qi that the T.C.M. doctor had been talking about. Suzette seemed to have a lot to say, so much so that Rebecca had to give her the time-over signal twice. I could see Eliza, who was next on the agenda, tapping her foot impatiently.

Finally, it was Eliza's turn to speak. As I considered her up there on the stage, it seemed to me that she was much more uncomfortable in this situation than she was back in the cooking classroom. For a moment, I felt a sense of kinship with her because I know how I would have felt if I had been asked to speak on a panel outside my particular area of expertise, and it did appear to me that this one was far outside hers. I thought she might talk about learning to cook when you retire, but that didn't seem to be on her mind. Eliza looked out at the audience and began to talk about writing. I thought this was an odd topic for her, but she seemed to believe that one way to reinvent oneself was to write, first in a journal and then perhaps later to write a book. I have no idea where she might have come up with that approach, but perhaps it was because she had no idea what it meant to reinvent oneself. I realized that I didn't know her at all outside of the fact that my ex-husband seemed to find her fascinating. Perhaps I did have my head stuck well and truly up my arse, as my father would have opined.

Then, it was Jeffrey's turn. I was curious to know how someone as young as Jeffrey might conceptualize reinvention. I couldn't help myself. I still thought it wasn't something he could know even a modicum about. As that thought crossed my mind, I noticed Peter sitting in the second row from the front. He was leaning forward with his head slightly turned to the left so that I could see him in profile. He was riveted to the stage.

Jeffrey talked about how he'd pursued psychiatry because when he was in medical school, he thought he was crazy, an odd turn of phrase for a professional, in my view. Then, he talked about a personal turning point but didn't specify what it was. I hadn't noticed this about him when I first met him a few years earlier, but on this cruise, he'd seemed a bit detached, as if something had happened to him in the interim.

"Reinvention, then," Jeffrey said, "is a second chance to tell your story. The object is not to leave your mark on the world, though. It is to let the world leave its mark on you."

TWENTY-SIX

Eliza

MIAMI ARRIVAL

I HAD NO IDEA WHAT I WOULD HAVE to contribute to a panel discussion on personal reinvention. I was only now facing a kind of reinvention as I learned to navigate life without Jake and all the chaos that went along with that. As I walked onto that stage, I wished that I'd had the guts to tell Rebecca that it wasn't something I'd want to do. Then, when I mentioned this to Peter, he seemed to think that I was in a perfect position to offer my insights. I hoped I didn't look too spaced out as I sat there listening to the traditional Chinese medicine doctor, who spoke immediately before me. I was having difficulty following the need for balancing things and clearing Qi, something I knew little about but thought perhaps it was something I should consider, given all that was going on in my life.

Just before it was my turn to speak, I found myself tapping my foot in exasperation. I should have been concentrating on what I would say to avoid having anyone in the audience invoke the old saying, "It is better to keep your mouth shut and be thought a fool than to open it and remove all doubt." I knew I should be keeping my mouth shut on this topic about which I knew nothing, but here I was. And instead of figuring out something useful or even witty to say, I was thinking about the text I'd received from Jake just before this event.

`Have a surprise for you. Can't wait to share it with you. Got a letter from Abigail. Her input won't be necessary. Can't wait to see you. ♥ J.`

First, I could not imagine what kind of surprise Jake would offer that would make me anything but seriously irritated. Second, if he had received a letter from Abigail, she must have an update on the division of assets so that we could put this divorce to bed, a situation I needed to have over with sooner rather than later. Third, her input most assuredly would be necessary. Finally, I was wondering if I'd be forced to block Jake if his overtures continued. These were the thoughts running through my monkey mind just as Rebecca called on me to speak.

I looked out over the audience, and I could feel the anticipation among those who had not yet fallen asleep. I noticed Peter in the second row and immediately calmed down as he smiled and nodded. Then I started speaking.

"We all tell ourselves stories about who we are, like, "I'm not creative," or "I always fail at this," or even, "I'm a cooking expert, and that's all I know." But we are all so much more, and we need to find a way to rewrite our narrative—those stories that limit who we are. I've come to realize that when people talk about rewriting their own narrative, they are usually using it metaphorically. What about literally writing? By consciously choosing to focus on our strengths, ambitions, and dreams, we can craft a version of ourselves that aligns with who we want to be. I've just begun writing in a journal, and I'm sure I'll write a book about the trip I took to Newfoundland last year, which changed my life. Perhaps you can do this as well."

Where in the world did all that come from? Why did I say any of that? It was true that I'd started scribbling in a journal that was unrelated to my cookbook projects, but considering writing a book about my trip the year before? It was only at that moment that I realized I might do just that.

When I'd finally shut my mouth and stopped babbling about ideas that I hadn't given a moment's thought to before I'd stepped onto the stage, Jeffrey took charge.

"It's a second chance to tell your story," he said, turning just slightly so that our eyes met. Had I influenced his thoughts, or had I stolen his thunder? Anyway, he was speaking metaphorically once again, so at least the audience was getting a balanced view of this story thing.

The next sentence out of his mouth slapped me in the face with its novelty and masterful sentiment. "The object is not to leave your mark on the world, though. It is to let the world leave its mark on you," he said.

I smiled as I pictured a fantasy scenario in which Jeffrey and Jake would come face to face. I could see it in my mind's eye. Jake, whose reason for existence was to do everything in his power to assure himself that everyone would remember his name, wouldn't understand a thing Jeffrey was saying. That would be a conversation worth witnessing. Alas, it would never happen, but thinking about it was a way to amuse myself as I sat there under the lights of the stage.

Then Rebecca opened the floor for questions, a situation I'd forgotten was going to occur. I was ready to jump off the stage and get on with our final day on board. I had a lot of packing to do, and I hadn't been able to get a hold of Izzy. She and Mary-Catherine flew to Miami a few days earlier, but I hadn't heard from her since her text telling me of their safe arrival. I knew I had nothing to worry about, but mothers do worry, and I was no different from billions of mothers who came before me.

"I have a question for Ms. Cohen."

The first question was for me? I hadn't expected to have to answer any questions, let alone the first one. Weren't they more interested in balancing their Qi and navigating what Suzette, in her wisdom, had referred to as the grand cosmic joke, i.e. menopause? Surely, at least half of the audience members were desperate to find out more about the hot flash apocalypse and how to journey through it, and that would be the male members if I didn't miss my guess. I was wrong on all counts. I had to sit up and pay attention.

"Ms. Cohen, you talked about writing a book." The speaker was clearly American, judging by her slightly southern accent and her high, blonde hair. She and Suzette seemed to share the cornflower blonde-from-a-bottle thing that I hadn't realized was a thing at all. She appeared to be north of seventy, perhaps even north of seventy-five if I were not such a charitable woman. "Ms. Cohen, I have loved your cookbooks, and I must say I do love the thought that ya'll might be considering writing something else. Bless your heart, I do know that my book club gals will be the first in line to buy it. But I did want to ask about this writing idea. It does seem like the perfect retirement project. I know I could pour my decades of wisdom into an inspiring memoir, but I also believe in my heart I could conjure up an idea or two that would make one of those thrillers like Stephen King writes. I mean, how hard could it be? But I want to know which of these projects you believe in your heart would be the right one for me. Should I share the story of my life, or should I write one of those mystery books?"

Dear god, what did I know? My first thought (and perhaps it illustrates how far I have left to go in my personal evolution) was that writing and sharing were two different things. *Write if you wish,* I wanted to say, *but for the love of god, do not share, i.e. publish*. I said none of that. I hadn't the slightest notion of who she was or whether her ideas had any merit at all, and I didn't give a rat's ass about what she wrote as her retirement project. Saying anything like that, though, would simply be my bitchy side resurfacing, and I knew this was neither the time nor the place to let that side of me out in full force. I immediately realized that telling someone they shouldn't write a book at all was a delicate endeavour.

Finally, I said, "Maybe you could start by writing shorter pieces in a journal or even start a blog if you want to share your thoughts. That way, you can see how much you enjoy the process before diving into something as big as a book." Well, now, that sounded sensible, didn't it?

She seemed delighted at this idea. I suspected I'd just assisted in the birth of a new blog—perhaps something the world does not need, but there you have it.

The next question was for Jeffrey. It was just a matter of time. This time, the speaker stood up at his seat in the middle of the theatre. He was a tall man with a thick head of white hair and a goatee that matched. He reminded me of Colonel Saunders of Kentucky Fried Chicken fame, but he sounded British.

"Dr. Montgomery," he began. "I have made it my life's work to assist people to leave their legacy, to, as you so succinctly put it, leave their mark on the world. In fact, I challenge your assertion that it is more important for one to submit to the world leaving marks on them. I have taught my patients—I am a counsellor of sorts—and taught them well, I might add, to make a decision about who they want to be and what they want to accomplish so they might dedicate their lives to the pursuit of that goal. For without a goal, there is no life trajectory, no purpose."

The speaker then nodded and looked around at his fellow audience members as if to determine the extent of the support for his position before sitting down. From my vantage point on the stage, I didn't see a lot of heads nodding in agreement. That's when I realized that so many of the guests were retired and that if they agreed with him and were still supposed to be focusing on getting somewhere, I (and they, I imagine) had to wonder what was happening along the way. In other words, were they meant to be still focused on achieving their life's goal? But it wasn't my question to answer.

Jeffrey stood up this time and took the microphone back from Rebecca, who had been holding it between audience questions. "Sir, I truly appreciate your perspective. It is one that has a long history. The twentieth century, in particular, was full of motivational gurus who posited that we should fight our way toward our life goals every day of our lives. Even *I* used to have that mindset, so I know where it comes from. But even Zig Ziglar, one of the great American motivational speakers of the twentieth century who often talked about focusing on our goals, said, 'Make today worth remembering.' How can today be memorable if you don't pay attention to your experiences? How is today, the present moment, which is all we ever have, going to be worth remembering if your focus is always on the future? On leaving your mark on the world? Pericles wrote that what you leave behind is not what is engraved in stone monuments—the mark you make on the world—but rather what is woven into the lives of others. I'm suggesting to you that what is woven into the lives of others isn't in any way related to living a life of chasing goals. It's having experiences and creating memories, some of which you'll share with others." There was a smattering of applause. "Give yourself permission just to experience life every day. You limit your experiences by deciding who you are and what to do beforehand. But you have to trust yourself—and the universe."

You could have heard a pin drop—and not because the audience was asleep. They looked like they'd all just been slapped up the side of the head. Then the applause began, slowly at first, then building as if gradually the whole audience realized they had just had their minds opened and it was exactly what they needed to hear. And what I needed to hear.

~

The last supper, so to speak, was elegant and low-key. It had been an exhausting three weeks in so many ways, but it was that kind of pleasant exhaustion that comes from knowing you've had an extraordinary experience.

Peter and I dined alone in a quiet corner of the specialty restaurant where steaks and caviar were the main attractions. I love caviar. I know. It's such an elitist thing to say, but caviar was something I'd never had before I met Jake, and I was surprised the first time he suggested it. It was his guilty (and hidden) pleasure since it was something Jews, as a general rule, did not eat. However, as expensive as it was—even more costly than the eyewatering price of regular caviar—caviar made from kosher fish was allowed. Whenever Esther, his mother, was around, Jake opted for that kind of caviar, which was usually from salmon rather than sturgeon. At other times, he threw caution to the wind and ate whatever kind of caviar someone was offering. I have to admit, I usually did the same. That last evening was one of those times.

Peter and I talked about the future. We would walk off this cruise ship the following morning, and nothing would be the same as it had been when we embarked in Rio three weeks ago. Then Peter made a bombshell announcement.

"You know that position in Toronto that I was so sure I'd take? I think I might take the one at Columbia in New York."

I was stunned. Months earlier, when we were first getting to know one another, Peter had told me he was mulling several job offers. The offer in Toronto was his dream job as head of the emergency room at the premiere trauma centre in Canada's largest city. In addition, it was where he had trained, and it would be a bit like going home. The offer in New York was second choice.

"I hope you're not doing this for me," I said when I finally found my tongue.

"I cannot imagine my life without you, Eliza, and you and Izzy are in New York."

I looked down at the ring of gold that zig-zagged around my finger and knew that we would move forward together if the fates allowed. However, for the first time in my life, I realized that having someone make a life-changing decision like this because of me and not because of what was right for him didn't sit well. There had to be another way forward.

"Peter, I don't know how we're going to work this out, but I, too, know that you and I are supposed to be a part of one another's lives." I pushed on. "But you want that job in Toronto. You told me this with so much conviction that I can't believe you could just throw that decision into the wind. You shouldn't choose New York just because it's close to me. We'll find a way."

Peter took my hand and squeezed it. "This is why we will be together. We can find a way through the noise."

~

The ship was scheduled to dock at the Miami Cruise Terminal at seven the following morning. Everyone was required to vacate their suites and staterooms by eight and await their turn to disembark and go through American customs and immigration. Peter and I planned to meet in the dining room for breakfast just before eight to await our disembarkation time. We were going to spend the next three days at the Fontainebleau Hotel, an upscale hotel on Miami Beach, where Izzy and Mary-Catherine would meet us for dinner later that day. I had never stayed at a hotel in Miami before because, on all previous trips, we spent our time at the condo—Esther and Louie's condo, but mostly Esther's. Louie was rarely there.

I cannot tell you how many times I've been to Miami Beach, but it was too many. From the first year that Jake and I were married, Esther would begin in October whining about going to Florida, and Louie would tell her that he was too busy. So, Esther would pack up and go, only to return in mid-December. By the first week in January, she would be back in Miami, where she would stay until March or April with the rest of her like-minded friends whose husbands had also bought condos along the same stretch of north Miami Beach. We were expected to spend at least part of any winter vacation time we had in Miami.

The condo was nice enough—four bedrooms, each with an ensuite bath—but as spacious as it was, it was never big enough for both Jake's mother and me. As a child, though, Izzy loved the beach and the enormous pool in the condo complex, so I did it for my daughter. The best I can say about those holidays is that I tolerated them. The idea of staying at a hotel was like a dream come true. The condo did, however, seem the perfect place for a young mother and her baby to stay, particularly since Esther was attending a school reunion in California and wouldn't be there. So, that's where Izzy would be, thus leaving me some free time with Peter.

Finally, our moment to disembark arrived. As we stood in the line to get off the ship, Jeffrey called out to us from the other side of the atrium. I looked over and smiled, happy that he at least seemed to have gotten over whatever it was that had been bothering him. He came over.

"Nice to have met you both," Jeffrey said. "Maybe we'll cross paths again sometime. You staying in Miami or heading straight to the airport?"

We told him our plans, and a cloud once again drifted over his face for a moment before clearing again.

"Wow, that's a coincidence. I'm staying there for a few days myself before heading home." He hesitated for a moment and then said, "I have a driver picking me up. Need a lift?"

Peter and I had planned to wait in the taxi lineup, but Jeffrey was making us a better offer. Why not?

~

When I stepped out of the terminal into the crowd of disembarking guests awaiting taxis, Ubers and buses, I felt odd. I was struck by the feeling that I'd just stepped out of an illusion and into reality. Then I thought, *maybe this is the illusion*. I had no idea.

Jeffrey, who had managed to exit the terminal before we did, waved us over to the waiting car. As the driver heaved our luggage into the back, we heard Claire's voice.

"Sorry I'm late, Jeffrey. I couldn't find my suitcase in that mass of luggage, and then someone tried to walk off with it." She wheeled her suitcase over to the driver, then turned and seemed to notice Peter and me for the first time. "Wow, this is a bit of a surprise. I guess we're a foursome. Well, I suppose there's no time like the present to bury the hatchet." Then she climbed into the back seat.

The sleek, shiny, black Suburban smoothly wended its way out of the cruise terminal and across the McArthur Causeway, one of the links between the city of Miami and Miami Beach. The drive took under thirty minutes in the Saturday morning traffic. Finally, we arrived at the front entrance to the Fontainebleau Hotel, a Miami icon since the 1950s. It exuded elegance and sophistication, at least in contrast to the rest of Miami Beach, which always seemed to me to exude artifice and a certain lack of refinement. I had always thought of Miami Beach as the land of eternal traffic jams and sidewalks that smell like sunscreen, sweat, and too much arrogance. It had always seemed to me to be more about being seen than much of anything else. I hoped this hotel would prove me wrong once and for all.

I stepped from the heat of the morning sunshine into the hotel's rarefied interior that oozed coolness and grandeur. As I admired its cream-coloured marble floor and pillars, extraordinary crystal chandeliers and famous staircase to nowhere (which these days actually leads to offices), I heard a voice.

"Eliza. You're here. Surprise!"

I stopped suddenly, the hairs on the back of my neck rising and tension descending on me, threatening suffocation.

Peter seemed to note a change in my demeanour and said, "What's wrong, Eliza?"

I turned toward the voice, and my mood of calm and peacefulness morphed into abject horror. It was Jake. What the actual fuck was *he* doing here?

TWENTY-SEVEN

Claire

MIAMI BEACH

AFTER THE STRANGE PANEL discussion in the theatre that afternoon, I met Jeffrey for a drink. As I waited for him to arrive, I ordered a martini and stared out the window at the passing white caps as we sailed inexorably onward toward my future. I was trying to remember exactly what I was thinking when I boarded the ship three weeks earlier. I had been so sure of myself with absolute certainty that I would achieve my goal. I had been so sure that by this moment in time, Peter and I would be laughing over a drink as we looked forward to a mini-family reunion in Miami with Fiona and Liam. Now, Peter, who probably thought I'd had a break from reality, was off somewhere with Eliza Cohen, who, no matter how hard I tried, I could not seem to loathe.

I wanted to despise her more than I had ever despised anyone in the world. However, I am an intelligent woman, and I knew then and know now that Eliza was not in any way that I could imagine responsible for the fractured relationship between Peter and me. He hadn't even met her until we'd been officially divorced for almost two years. But that day last summer, when I met Eliza at her grandmother's one-hundredth birthday party back in St. John's, something inside me cracked. I had immediately decided that she wasn't going to have Peter. Seeing her with him that day was what had motivated me to embark on what I now had to admit was a bit of a lunatic plan. It was like there was another person hidden inside me, and she had always been there, no matter how hard I must have tried to keep her suppressed.

She was the person who had decided that if I couldn't have Peter, then no one could. Then she had decided that she wanted and probably needed Peter in her life. After all, he was the father of her children, and we were meant to be together. That personality inside of me was the part that I'd tried for my entire adult life—and possibly even as a child—to keep hidden away. She was the insecure child and then the insecure woman. She was the one who always had to hide behind her career accomplishments and the external validation it brought. I don't know the precise moment when it happened, but I now knew that she was me, or at least a part of me that needed to be acknowledged. I realized that it was okay to be uncertain about some things. And that was when I started to feel just slightly embarrassed by my actions and my reasons for following Peter on this trip. And, worse, I realized that Eliza Cohen wasn't my problem. As much as it pained me to admit it, she was a confident, truly accomplished woman in her own field, and she and Peter seemed to get along well. I couldn't even hate her for that. I knew I needed a life of my own and not just as a doctor. So, that's why, at the end of Jeffrey's panel presentation, I sat there, allowing the tears to roll down my cheeks, not even caring if anyone else noticed.

"Give yourself permission just to experience life every day," Jeffrey had said from the stage. "You limit your experiences by deciding who you are and what to do beforehand." And he had already said, "Deciding who you are will limit who you become."

After all this time, I finally knew I didn't want to limit who I might become. I didn't want to sit here at the age of fifty-one and believe that I had already arrived. I wanted to look ahead at a life of possibilities and realize there were still so many places to go and so many experiences to gather. And I finally knew that the only way to do this was to move past Peter and all that he represented. I did love my work, and that wasn't likely to change, but it didn't have to be everything. I had never been a big believer in things like serendipity or cosmic interventions, but I had to admit that I tended to think that there had been a reason for some of the odd occurrences on this journey. One of those was that I'd met Imogen.

Imogen had been a pediatric surgeon, just as I was. But Imogen believed that she no longer identified as one, and that was okay. She no longer needed to see herself in that role—she no longer needed people to refer to her as "Doctor." It was just something she used to do. When I took the time to consider her words, I realized that she could be a role model for me. I realized that I didn't want to be just one thing for the rest of my life. I wanted to have experiences outside the comfortable environs of the hospital. I no longer wanted to limit who I might become—and the thought of that made me feel happier and more peaceful than I probably ever had in my life. Then there was Jeffrey.

"Penny for your thoughts," Jeffrey said, sitting down opposite me and gesturing to the server to bring him whatever I was having. "And, sorry I'm late. Had to sign a few books along the way."

"You do love having fans, Jeffrey, and probably always will."

Jeffrey would probably never change in that fundamental way he enjoyed the adulation of his fans, which made me wonder if he would be able to take his own advice in the future. Would he be able to be more than his success?

"I have decided to let the world make its mark on me," I said, draining my glass, "no matter what might come my way."

Jeffrey noticed and gestured for another. I didn't know if that was such a good idea. I still had a lot of packing to do, and I didn't want to be hung over the next day as we disembarked. However, I didn't stop him, either.

Jeffrey looked confused for a moment until it clicked in that I was quoting him. "Dr. Claire Barrett is going to let the world make its mark on her? Wow! I didn't see that one coming. I always thought you were the kind of person who believed that it was more important to work on leaving a legacy."

"That was then," I said. "This is now. I have to thank you, you know. Your wacky worldview has somehow touched me."

Jeffrey beamed and reached for the glass the server had set in front of him. "Well, Claire Barrett, here's to having experiences and letting the world make its mark on us!"

~

Jeffrey had asked me if I'd like to drive to the hotel with him since it turned out that we were both staying at the Fontainebleau. I had never been there before, but when I'd initially anticipated this as a family reunion, I thought a fancy Miami Beach hotel would be the perfect backdrop. Now, Fiona was on some mysterious trip to some mysterious place, and Liam had texted me just before I went to bed the night before.

Hi Mom. Hope the cruise was dynamite. Thx for the ticket to Miami. Hope you don't mind. Gonna stay in Fort

Lauderdale with the guys for a few days. Might see you before I fly home. If not, enjoy Miami! ♥

I should have been furious when I read this, but then I considered Liam's position. He was twenty-two, on spring break from law school and had a ticket to an airport a mere forty-five-minute drive from where his buddies would be having their break from reality. I'd had my own break from reality, so I could hardly begrudge my son his. Thus, I would be at the hotel alone. I was grateful for Jeffrey's offer of a drive.

When I arrived in the cruise terminal that morning, I could not find my suitcase. If you have ever disembarked from a cruise ship, you'll know that the luggage is placed in colour-coded groups in an enormous warehouse kind of place and that you have to search for yours. I had black luggage, just like eighty percent of the rest of the guests on board. As I stood there in a sea of suitcases, I noticed a woman walking away, rolling a familiar-looking suitcase behind her. I had to chase her into the customs area before I caught up with her to tell her that she had made off with the wrong luggage. By the time I finally emerged from the terminal building into the sunshine, I could see that Jeffrey had kindly offered to drive Peter and Eliza. I rolled my eyes when I saw them and thought, *What could be a more perfect ending to this idiotic cruise plan?* And, of course, we would all be staying at the same hotel for a few days. Could it get any stranger than that? I had no idea.

~

I didn't know a lot about the Fontainebleau Hotel in Miami Beach. I did, however, know that numerous famous people had stayed there throughout its storied history. And I had read about what they called the "staircase to nowhere." Evidently, the impressively curved staircase in the lobby led up to a cloakroom and nothing more. When a celebrity (or presumably celebrity wannabe) walked up the stairs to drop off a wrap or an overcoat (although it does seem odd that anyone would require such garments in this sultry climate), that person could make a grand entrance by descending the staircase. I had also read that many famous films had been shot there. *Tony Rome, Scarface,* and the old Bond film *Goldfinger* were three that caught my eye. I wasn't celebrity-obsessed and never had been, but I knew that a hotel with that kind of reputation would be something to experience. And now I could have that experience unencumbered by external objectives. I was actually looking forward to three days by myself in the lap of luxury.

When we arrived at the hotel, we all disembarked from the big vehicle. A member of the bell staff whipped my luggage onto a cart along with Jeffrey's, and we had to do a song and dance to try to explain to him that we were not a couple and that they would not be taking our luggage to only one room. I stepped into the magnificent marble lobby and was immediately transported into a glamorous past. The staircase truly was a large, floating spiral that did seem to ascend into nothing. It was magnificent.

Jeffrey and I walked into the lobby together, with Peter and Eliza bringing up the rear. As I took my time heading for the reception desk, I tried to take in the entirety of the experience. The lobby was quiet, with only a few people milling around. As I gazed around, I caught the eye of a dark-haired man in an impeccable grey linen jacket over a pale blue open-necked button-down shirt. He smiled, and I couldn't help but smile back. I was, after all, embracing new experiences. Just as I reached the reception desk, I heard a commotion behind me.

I turned and saw the man whose eye I'd caught. I heard him say, "You're here. Surprise!" He was talking to Eliza, who looked like she'd seen a ghost. All colour drained from her face. I watched as Peter took her elbow as if to keep her from falling.

Just then, Eliza seemed to come alive, "What the actual fuck are you doing here, Jake?"

Dear god. It was Eliza's husband. The man with the dark eyes was Jake Cohen. This little Miami break had just gotten a whole lot more interesting.

~

I busied myself by checking in, and Jeffrey did the same. By the time we'd both finished the required paperwork and received the news that our rooms were not yet ready (it was, after all, not yet ten a.m.), and our luggage was making its way to the luggage storage room, Peter, Jake and Eliza had moved to the side and were engaged in a heated discussion—at least Eliza and Jake were. I watched Peter and Eliza together, and I could see the future more clearly than I ever had before. I didn't know what Eliza's Jake was doing in Miami or what he thought he might accomplish (I hoped he wasn't in the same situation I thought I'd been in three weeks ago with delusions of a reconciliation). Still, I perceived that Peter was invested in *his* relationship with Eliza and that if Jake were here to try to win Eliza back, he wouldn't have a snowball's chance in hell. I turned to Jeffrey.

"I don't suppose you have any interest in dinner down the beach later? I'm looking forward to trying some Cuban food. Miami has some of the best."

"Yeah, sure." He looked over at the little group. "What do you suppose is going on ..." He trailed off as his eyes seemed to clamp onto the figure of a young woman who was hurrying from the elevator bank toward Eliza and Jake who were still engaged in what appeared to be an increasingly heated argument. She looked familiar to me. Where had I seen her before?

As she approached Eliza, Jake and Peter, who was on the periphery, I remembered. It was Izzy Cohen, Eliza's daughter. I'd seen her briefly at her great-grandmother's funeral a few months earlier.

"Good lord," I said. "The whole family is here." I looked at Jeffrey, who seemed to have turned to stone. "Jeffrey? Are you all right?"

"It can't be," Jeffrey said so quietly that I almost didn't hear him. "Claire, do you know that girl?"

I turned toward the group. "You mean the young woman who's talking to Eliza right now?" He nodded almost imperceptibly. "That's Izzy, short for Isabel, I think—Eliza's daughter."

Now it was Jeffrey's turn to look like he'd seen a ghost.

TWENTY-EIGHT

Eliza

MIAMI BEACH

THE MOMENT THE REACTION ENTERED my mind was the moment it slid out of my mouth. "What the actual fuck are you doing here, Jake?" It simultaneously occurred to me that this would be the first time Peter had ever heard me swear. But if Jake Cohen was in Miami at this very moment and wasn't planning to depart immediately, it was possible that Peter hadn't heard anything yet.

"Well, I did expect a slightly warmer greeting, but I guess we can work on it." Jake smiled as he spoke. I could not believe it.

"Eliza?" The look on Peter's face was one of concern mixed with a hefty dose of please-don't-let-me-be-right-about-this.

I suddenly felt completely out of my depth. I had no idea why Jake would be here in a hotel, especially this hotel, on Miami Beach when he was supposed to be back in New York making money—and whatever else he did. I had no idea what to say or do next. *Please, god,* I thought, *don't let him be here because he thinks there's a shred of possibility that we might reconcile.* But, perhaps most of all, I had no idea whatsoever how he might have even known I was going to be here at this moment in time. Then I saw Izzy rushing out of an elevator, making a beeline toward the three of us.

"Mom," Izzy said breathlessly as she stopped beside me, "I didn't know Dad would be here. I really didn't." Was that an admission of loyalty, or was it one of her attempts at a pre-emptive strike that she had perfected as a child?

"How did your father even know that I'd be here?" I said and then realized that was only one of a series of even more as yet unanswered questions. "Why are *you* here at the hotel? Why aren't you at your grandmother's condo?"

Izzy took my arm and started to lead me away from where Jake and Peter were sizing one another up as if she wanted to ensure they didn't hear us.

"About that. Oh my god, Mom, it's a long story."

"You better start talking," I said. I had to get this situation straightened out before it got any more out of hand.

"First of all, Mom, I wasn't the one who told Dad you'd be here. That would have been Grama Esther. When I asked her if I could stay at the condo for a week with Mary-Catherine, of course she wanted to know who I would be here with. She wasn't happy with the idea that I would be here in Miami alone, and you know what Grama Esther can be like. I mean, she literally squeezed me." I certainly did know what Grama Esther was like, although I doubted very much if the squeezing was literal. "So, I might have mentioned that I'd be meeting you here, but I told her she couldn't tell Dad."

I rolled my eyes. Had my daughter not learned anything in her twenty-two years of being on this earth as a member of the Cohen clan? Of course, Esther would have told Jake.

"Izzy, I am still in the dark. So, your father knew I'd be here today, which in itself is a whole level of hell, but why are *you* here at the hotel? We were planning to meet later for dinner if you recall." I looked around for a baby carriage or stroller. "And where is Mary-Catherine?"

"About that …" Izzy said.

Before I even had a chance to probe further about my granddaughter's whereabouts, Jake, who had been standing quietly to the side, watching the scene as it unfolded between Izzy and me, looked over and clapped his hands together. Perhaps it might be more accurate to say that he rubbed them together like a mafia boss who's getting ready to have someone whacked and sidled over beside us. I expected a henchman to appear from somewhere in the shadows to whisk me off. Why did I watch so many murder mysteries on Netflix?

"Let's all have dinner together this evening," Jake said. "We have a lot to talk about, and it'll be a great little family reunion."

What was going on inside that dense brain of his? I could not even imagine. A family reunion—which was never going to happen anyway—might just be the deepest circle of hell yet. Was I the only one who realized this? I looked around, possibly for some means of escape, and then walked back toward where Peter was standing alone, not inserting himself into the family drama. Jake followed me.

Peter, who seemed to have gleaned the basics of the current situation, reached out his hand to Jake. "I'm Peter," he said, "Dr. Peter O'Brien."

Jake shrugged. "Okay, sure." He shook Peter's hand limply and said, "Have we met? Your name sounds familiar."

Peter shook his head. "No, Jake, I can honestly say we've never met."

Jake shrugged and turned back to me. "So, dinner here at Prime 54. Remember we used to come here for dinner when we spent our winter vacations with Mom and Dad at the condo?"

How could I ever forget? I looked at Jake and then at Izzy. "Jake, I have no idea what's going on here, but I will tell you this. I am not having dinner with you tonight or any other night, and that's the last word I'll say on the subject."

Jake, ignoring me, continued to smile. "I have a present for you. You can have it at dinner."

Was he deliberately not listening to me, or had he become even more obtuse than he had been in recent years? I didn't care if he had a present for me and I certainly wasn't going to dinner with him to find out.

I almost screamed in frustration. I ignored Jake and turned back to Izzy. "*Where* is Mary-Catherine, and *why* are you here at the hotel at this moment? I want an answer right this minute." I had a feeling of grave foreboding that I wasn't going to like the answer.

Peter put his hand on my arm, which did have the effect of calming me a tad. I realized I was beginning that gradual ramp-up to hysteria when the walls begin to close in, and the air around me begins to feel heavier and heavier on my shoulders. If it continued, I knew I'd explode, and I knew that wasn't an attractive look. If Peter and I were going to have any kind of future, though, he'd have to see all sides of me.

I patted Peter's hand and looked gratefully into his face. "It's okay," I said. "I'll be okay. I just need to straighten this out."

I glanced around and saw Claire and Jeffrey standing beside the reception desk, both riveted to our little family drama. Jeffrey looked quite ill. Then I turned to Izzy. "Tell me now."

Izzy started to speak, but before she could say anything, I saw a familiar figure exiting one of the elevators, pushing a baby stroller. If I had thought I'd reached the seventh circle of hell, I'd just slid into the eighth. It was Mary-Catherine in the stroller. Esther, my soon-to-be-ex mother-in-law, was pushing it. I almost fainted.

"I've been trying to tell you, Mom," Izzy said frantically. "I tried to call you yesterday when Grama Esther arrived to warn you, but I couldn't get through. She said she ditched the reunion in California that she had planned to attend so she could spend some time with Mary-Catherine and me."

I took a deep, calming breath. It was so like Esther to manage to find a way to ruin something, especially if it had anything to do with me. This obvious scheme of hers would, however, be her last kick at the can. I wasn't going to let her have any more influence on my life. I watched her as she approached. Esther was wearing her I'm-in-Miami uniform consisting of a floaty Lily Pulitzer shift dress in all its Florida pink and neon green glory with two strands of pearls and matching pink and neon green Palm Beach sandals. She looked like every other woman in her social circle who seemed to believe that bright pink and neon green were meant to live in holy matrimony. Esther's dress resembled the aftermath of a tropical cocktail explosion. However, as mesmerizing as her outfit might have been, I was more concerned about why she was pushing my granddaughter's stroller. And I still didn't know what the hell they were all doing here at the hotel. I was now officially becoming hysterical.

"Oh my god, Eliza, you look like a fright," Esther said, whining in her own inimitable way. "Those bags under your eyes." What bags? "Have you spent your entire vacation drinking?"

I snorted. Dear god, such hypocrisy. Her remark may have to go down in Cohen family history as the first time I'd ever seen Esther without a gin and tonic at her elbow. I decided, though, to be the bigger woman and didn't mention it.

Before I had a chance to respond, Esther continued. "And isn't that an interesting outfit? I would never have chosen it for myself, but you do have your own style, don't you? And just look at those shoes. You're so brave to wear them." Esther was nothing if not the master of the back-handed, passive-aggressive compliment. She usually left me speechless. Not this time.

"What the hell are you doing here, Esther?"

"Well, my dear, if you could stop swearing for a moment—remember there are children present," she nodded toward both Mary-Catherine and Izzy, who rolled her eyes, "as it happens, a pipe in the condo above ours burst last evening so, we've had to move out. I've taken a suite here, and Izzy and the baby are staying with me." She noticed Peter for the first time as he stood there, not saying a word. "And who might you be?" She surveyed him in that up-and-down way she had of taking in everything from the top of a person's head to the tips of his shoes. She never even tried to hide what she was doing.

Peter's smile was not quite as broad as usual, but it held a tiny smirk that I was beginning to understand. "I am Dr. Peter O'Brien," he said, extending his hand to her. Esther perked up at the sound of "doctor," as she always did. "I'm delighted to meet you, Mrs. Cohen. Eliza has told me so much about you." He turned and winked at Izzy.

"Has she, now?" Esther said, looking closely at Peter. "And how do you know my daughter-in-law?"

"Ex-daughter-in-law," I said. Esther huffed.

"We're close friends," Peter said.

"How close?" Jake seemed to have tuned back into the conversation.

Peter looked at him carefully and said, "I don't suppose that's any of your business now, is it?"

"Are you sure we've never met?" Peter told Jake he was sure. Then Jake seemed to remember something. "I know who you are. You're that whistleblowing doctor we're suing for breach of his N.D.A."

"No," Peter said, "I'm that whistleblowing doctor who believes in the first tenet of the Hippocratic Oath."

The look on Jake's face suggested that he had no idea what the first tenet of the Hippocratic Oath might be. Perhaps he didn't even know what the Hippocratic Oath is, which would explain much of what I'd observed in his family's Bluestone Pharma business over the years as they raked in the money.

"In case you've forgotten," Peter said, "it's 'to do no harm.' And in my world, keeping patients in a drug trial when the drug is clearly making their condition worse is doing harm."

"The air must be pretty thin up there on the moral high ground," Jake said. Until that moment, I wasn't aware that Jake even knew there could be a moral high ground.

"Not as thin as it is clear," Peter said, smiling.

Point to Peter, or it might even have been game, set and match. I had to stifle a snort of laughter. That was the moment I heard a choking sound, as if someone were being strangled. I turned my head and saw Izzy with her hand over her mouth, staring toward the reception desk where Claire and Jeffrey were still standing. She then turned toward Esther and ripped the stroller from her. Before anyone had a moment to ask her what was going on, she'd taken the baby and run across the marble floor, disappearing into an elevator. Now what?

TWENTY-NINE

Claire

MIAMI BEACH

JEFFREY AND I STOOD THERE in horrified silence, watching the wretched Cohen family scenario play out. I felt sorry for Peter as he seemed to be peripheral to the drama until I remembered observing that behaviour in him so many times over the years. Peter always stood back, assessing the situation until he found precisely the right moment to step in. I always credited his emergency medicine training for knowing the right moment to intervene. Then I saw him speak to the grey-haired woman pushing a baby stroller.

"What do you suppose is going on over there?" I said to Jeffrey. He didn't respond. "Jeffrey?" I looked at him, and his face was a mask of confusion. "Jeffrey, are you all right?"

"Isabel. It's Isabel," he said. "She *is* Eliza's daughter."

I had no idea what he was going on about. "Yes, Isabel Cohen is Eliza's daughter. What's the problem? Eliza must have mentioned her in passing sometime over the past three weeks. You and she spent some time together, and I have to think she told you about her family."

"She always called her Izzy," he said so quietly that I almost didn't hear him. Then he said, "Synchronicity is an ever-present reality for those who have eyes to see."

"What?"

"Carl Jung said it, and he was right. I can't believe this is happening. I can't believe she's here. This is not a coincidence."

"Jeffrey, you're going to have to be a bit clearer. I have no idea what you're talking about."

We moved out of the way of a couple strutting into the lobby with their Louis Vuitton luggage that was following behind them on a luggage cart being pushed by a member of the bell staff. When I turned back to the Cohen situation, I saw Izzy, with her hand over her mouth, grab the stroller from the woman in the god-awful Florida print dress that could have blended perfectly into the background if the Fontainebleau decorators had had the bad taste to install flamingo pink wallpaper in the lobby. She then turned and rushed back toward the elevator lobby.

Jeffrey took my arm and pulled me toward the Bleau Bar just off the lobby, where he practically pushed me into a seat. "Isn't it a tad early for a drink?" I said as I rearranged myself in the round tub chair.

"It's after noon somewhere in the world," Jeffrey said as the server materialized.

"We are not officially open yet, sir," the young woman with a blonde ponytail and a forever Florida suntan said to Jeffrey.

"Can you manage a bottle of Veuve Clicquot?" He looked at her pleadingly as he was prone to do. I rolled my eyes. She complied.

"We're having champagne?" I said cautiously. "What's this all about?"

Jeffrey had morphed from zombie-like to maniacal in the space of five minutes.

"We are celebrating, Claire. Have you ever believed in miracles?"

I told him I had not.

"Then you have to believe in synchronicity. You do know what it is, right?"

"I recall you mentioning it the evening we bumped into Eliza and Peter at the beginning of the cruise—some bone-headed idea about random things happening together for a reason."

He waved his hand. "That's not exactly a great definition, but we'll go with that, and I'll forget you called it bone-headed. Anyway, Claire, do you remember me telling you that I'd never marry again and why?" I nodded, and he continued. "Well, I'm beginning to think there might be a god after all and that there are second chances at love."

"Geezus, Jeffrey. Haven't you just spent the past three weeks observing that second chances might not be a thing after all?"

Jeffrey reached into his back pocket and pulled out his phone. He tapped a couple of times and turned it toward me. I took it from him and scrutinized the photo. It was clearly of a very happy Jeffrey with his arm around a gorgeous young woman who was beaming into the camera as they took a selfie while waves crashed onto a beach in the background. The gorgeous young woman was Izzy Cohen.

"We took that on Malibu Beach back when I lived in California. It might have been the happiest day of my life."

As Jeffrey took the phone back from me, I started to understand.

"That's why I had to distance myself from Eliza for the past week. She said something one day about her daughter, and I started to put two and two together. I realized she might be Isabel's mother, but I couldn't tell her, could I? It was too bizarre and too painful."

"Izzy Cohen was the woman who disappeared from your life?" I said. I had a feeling I was beginning to understand and yet I still understood nothing.

"I was living in California before I moved to Boston. Izzy and I were taking a yoga class together. It was love at first sight." He looked at me as the server popped the cork and poured two coupes. "I know what you're going to say, Claire. There's no such thing as love at first sight."

I wasn't going to say that, although I probably should have. "No, Jeffrey. I was going to observe that she's a lot younger than you are. I thought you were into older women." Why did I say that?

He laughed. "I'm into incredible, smart and funny women. I don't much care how old they are."

"And beautiful. Don't forget beautiful," I said, laughing.

He raised his glass to beautiful, and as I sipped the champagne, darker thoughts began to cloud the happiness I genuinely felt for Jeffrey P. Montgomery at that moment. I put my glass on the table. "Jeffrey, you told me the love of your life just disappeared one day. It was Izzy, wasn't it?"

"That's right. If that day in Malibu was the best day of my life, the day Isabel left was the worst. It was right after that I decided to move back to Boston. I thought I'd never get over her. In a way, I don't suppose I have. But now I don't have to."

"Jeffrey, please don't take this the wrong way, but isn't it possible she left because she wasn't as invested in the relationship as you were?" I hesitated a moment while he considered this. "Is it possible you were in love, and she wasn't?"

"I think she was scared, Claire. We both were. It was really intense. But now that fate has put us in the same place at the same time, we have a chance to get it right, and I'm not going to miss that chance."

I tried one more time. "Jeffrey, do you think Izzy saw you back there in the lobby?"

He shook his head. "No. So, I have to figure out how I'm going to find her. But I think I might be able to get old Pete to help me out. I don't want to go directly to Eliza. She might not be as happy about this as she could, but I'll change her mind."

He had that right about Eliza. I didn't know her well, but I also had a daughter about Izzy's age, and I knew how I would feel in the same situation. I wasn't going to get involved, though. This situation had nothing to do with me. Thank god. But I was also reasonably sure Izzy had seen Jeffrey—right before she fled, looking terrified. Jeffrey had been occupied with getting me into the bar, so I was sure he hadn't seen her sudden retreat.

Instead of saying anything, I raised my glass. "Well, then, here's to second chances."

As I sipped the champagne, I realized that I finally did believe in second chances but that my second chance wasn't going to be repeating my first chance. "How can you be sure she'll want you again?"

"Because I know."

That's when I remembered the baby stroller.

~

While Jeffrey and I were still sitting in the cool of the bar, sipping the last of the champagne, I received a text from the front desk. My room was ready. I gathered my belongings and said goodbye to Jeffrey. Our dinner plans were now on hold, and I was actually hoping he might have something better to do than have dinner with an old lover again. I hoped it for him as much as for myself. I hoped things would work out with Izzy (although I had serious doubts about it), and I also hoped that I could find a few days of peace to be with myself as I moved forward from my hair-brained plan into a future of possibilities. I got on the elevator and was swallowed up by the calm perfection of the Fontainebleau.

My ocean-view junior suite, with its tranquil blue and cream décor and its small balcony, had a view over a magnificent stretch of Miami Beach. I had been here a few times (but not at this hotel) and had concluded that the beach itself was much better appreciated from a distance, like from a hotel room, than close up. Upon closer inspection, Miami Beach seemed to me to be a curious blend of contrasts. On one side were the visions of grandeur—bikinis, flexing muscles, and a perpetual air of look-at-me, look-at-me. On the other side, snowbirds of a certain age mingled, devouring their early-bird all-you-can-eat buffets at four in the afternoon, dressed in dizzying Hawaiian shirts and those cringe-worthy capris that seemed to be a staple for older women travelling in warmer climes. I preferred it from a distance, but a walk on the beach today and each of the next two days while I was here would be mandatory. I was so looking forward to the solitude.

Once I was unpacked and settled, I decided that after all that champagne, I needed a walk and some food. I was hoping not to run into anyone I knew. Once back on the lobby level, I managed to find my way out the back of the hotel and onto the boardwalk that snaked along the beach for eleven kilometres from its southernmost point at South Pointe Park, where you can watch cruise ships coming and going, to its northern end where the town of Surfside meets Miami Beach. I planned to walk every single kilometre before this little vacation was over.

As I meandered along the boardwalk, dodging baby strollers, bicycles, giggling girls with their heads in their phones and knots of older women with their backpacks and water bottles, I watched for an appealing place to nip in for a bite. What caught my eye instead was a little shop set back a bit on the street side. It was a souvenir shop, something that I usually avoided like the plague. However, I wondered if they might have notebooks. After the past three weeks of listening to Jeffrey spout off about his life view and arguing that he had his head in the clouds, I realized it was time I listened to someone other than myself (although, to tell you the truth, I probably didn't listen to myself either). It had occurred to me that I might actually enjoy writing down my reactions to all these new experiences I was going to be open to having in my life. God, had Eliza's words rung a bell with me?

When I walked into the shop that opened onto the boardwalk, a bell sounded, and a woman, perhaps my age or a bit older, materialized from behind several racks of colourful T-shirts. She was wearing a bright red bandana that was trying to keep her long, curly grey and silver hair out of her eyes and a black T-shirt with "Shit Show Supervisor" on the front.

"Hello," I said. "I'm looking for a notebook, perhaps what you call a lined journal."

"Over there," she said, pointing to the far wall.

I turned and took four steps to that wall. On a rack affixed to the wall were journals of all sizes and colours. Each one had a quote of one sort or another on its cover. Some of the quotes were intended to be motivational; others were funny. I picked up a bright yellow one that said, "I'm not old. I'm just vintage." It was not quite what I had in mind, but it was funny, nonetheless. The next one I picked up said, "I'm not bossy. I'm the boss." That one was something I would have picked up in a heartbeat, even a few months before, but now? Well, now it didn't feel quite right.

I lifted out a few more until I uncovered a navy, blue-covered journal with gold spiral binding that was hidden behind several other not-quite-right ones. On the cover, it said, "I do not exist to impress the world. I exist to live my life in a way that will make me happy. ~ Richard Bach, *Illusions: The Adventures of a Reluctant Messiah.*" I held it close to my chest and headed toward the tiny cash desk. Before I got there, I glanced at a few T-shirts and was tempted by one that said, "It's rude to talk while I'm interrupting you," and laughed. That was so me. I wondered if I should buy it. Then I saw the perfect one. On the front, emblazoned in large red letters, it said, "Hold on. Let me overthink this." Bingo!

I approached the cash register with my notebook and T-shirt. The woman in the bandana offhandedly took them from me and pressed a few keys on the old-fashioned cash register. I was staring at her T-shirt.

"Do you have any of those T-shirts?" I said, pointing to her chest.

She grunted slightly and produced three of them, all in plastic bags, from under the cash desk. "What size?"

I told her medium would probably be a good size.

She looked at me and cocked her head to the side. "This one for you or a friend?"

"A friend," I said, wondering why this was relevant.

"Take the large one. You look like the sort of woman whose friends are supervising large shit shows."

I laughed and said, "Sold!"

A few minutes later, I found the perfect lunch spot. The hostess led me to an outdoor table along the railing at the boardwalk. I could glimpse the beach through the vegetation and palm trees. There was a slight breeze. It was perfect.

I had just ordered myself a salad with prawns when I heard a voice. "Mind if I join you?"

I took a deep breath because I'd so looked forward to alone time right now. But I looked up at Peter, who was looking a bit forlorn if I didn't miss my guess, and said, "You may."

"Am I interrupting anything?" Peter had noticed the journal that I had opened on the table beside me. I'd managed to find a pen in my purse and had written a few lines.

Don't limit your experiences. Live each day in the moment and to the fullest. Look beyond what you do so that you can see who you are. That's what I'd written, but I didn't show it to Peter.

I closed the notebook and sat back. "You may be interrupting something, but that's okay. You look like you could use a friend—and perhaps a glass of wine."

"Or something stronger," Peter said wryly. He picked up the menu the server had laid beside him. "A friend, eh? We've come a long way in three weeks, haven't we?"

I smiled. "You don't know the half of it, dear ex-husband. But fear not. You are free of me. So, how's Eliza? And what about that Jake guy? Did he just show up unannounced?"

Peter told me about how Eliza had been blindsided and how even her soon-to-be-ex mother-in-law had shown up. That must have been the woman who looked like she'd just been vomited up from the innards of a Lily Pulitzer shop that had eaten a bad salad.

"Does Jake think Eliza will reconcile with him? Is that why he's here?" I'd never been much of a gossip, but I was smart enough to put two and two together, and this story was too good. For some strange reason, I also had the odd feeling that I cared.

"I actually think he does, but he's more than a bit deluded. It's over. That much is clear. Eliza just has to get him to realize that. I'm giving her the rest of the day to sort things out. We have dinner reservations at Joe's Stone Crab in South Beach." I must have looked skeptical because he said, "Yes, Eliza is Jewish, but she isn't above eating a bit of crab once in a while. Guilty pleasure, she says." We both laughed. We all had them. Mine was nachos and cheese dip.

Peter and I then went on to lighter conversation, and I have to admit it was nice to sit there with an old friend who had known me since forever. It seemed strange to think of him as a friend now, but I didn't question the feeling. I liked that I didn't have to be "on" all the time. I liked how this made me feel and intended for it to continue as I returned to my "regular" life. That made me think about Fiona and Liam.

"I bet the kids would be astonished if they could see us sitting here having a civil lunch together."

Peter smiled. "Astonished and relieved. They've both been great about all of this—very mature—but it had to be stressful. I'm sure Christmases when they're older and married, and we share grandchildren, will be much calmer now."

Grandchildren? Dear god, I certainly hadn't thought that far ahead. "You know, Peter," I said, "Liam and Fiona were supposed to be here for these few days. We were supposed to have a family reunion."

Peter started to laugh. "You and Eliza's ex-husband must be on the same wavelength. I think that's what he thought was going to happen—a Miami family reunion. Anyway, I knew you'd invited the kids. Fiona told me."

I should have guessed that Fiona couldn't keep that from her father. "About Fiona," I said. "Where is she? She texted me to say she had to go somewhere. It was all very mysterious. You don't happen to know where it is, do you?"

Peter hesitated. "She didn't tell you? Well, I don't suppose it's a secret. It must have just been an oversight. She's had a lot on her mind. She's in Monte Carlo."

"Monte Carlo? As in Monaco?"

Peter nodded.

"What in god's name is she doing there?"

"Auditioning for Les Ballets de Monte Carlo. And before you go off on a rant about the ballet world, Claire, you have to remember that she's wanted to dance in Europe ever since she was a kid. And she is a professional now."

I sat back and considered this turn of events. "I do have to admit that visiting Fiona in Monte Carlo will be a damn sight more interesting than Toronto." It wasn't such a bad turn of events at all. "I hope she gets it."

As we neared the end of our lunches, I was grappling with whether to say anything to Peter about Jeffrey—and Izzy. After all, if Peter and Eliza had any future at all, Izzy's relationship with Jeffrey could be germane—very germane. Finally, I decided I couldn't keep it to myself, and Peter might actually be able to help if he had a heads-up.

"Peter, this might come as something of a shock, but when Jeffrey saw Izzy, he thought he'd seen a ghost."

"A ghost?" He drained his wine glass.

"Did Jeffrey ever tell you about losing the love of his life?"

"As a matter of fact, he did," Peter said. "It was one of those awkward conversations that men rarely have and aren't really good at, but yes, he did tell me. Why?"

"Izzy was that love."

THIRTY

Eliza

MIAMI BEACH

WHEN I FINALLY ARRIVED IN MY ROOM an hour after the debacle in the lobby, I sat on the side of the king-sized bed, staring out the window at waves as they crashed onto the shore below. Jake's unexpected arrival was beyond ludicrous and utterly annoying. The fact that his mother was here—well, there are no words to describe how rabid I felt about that. All in all, I was facing a major cluster fuck if ever there was one. There was also the matter of Izzy's hysterical departure from the lobby. What in the world had gotten into her? I would get to the bottom of everything and straighten it all out, but right at that moment, I needed a bit of air.

I took the elevator to the lobby and asked for directions to the hotel's pool. I thought if I sat under a palm tree in the breeze for an hour, I might be able to sort things out in my head before I sorted them out in my family, such as it was. Peter had graciously suggested that he make himself scarce for a few hours at least until I could get this shit show under control.

The moment a pool attendant saw me standing there looking for a seat, he came over to ask me where I'd like to sit. I spied an empty lounge chair under the exact palm tree I was looking for. He went to the pool hut and picked up a thick, cushy mattress and three towels. I followed him to the spot I'd chosen, where he proceeded to prepare the chair. First, he placed the mattress and secured it. Then, he covered it with an enormous towel. He then placed one rolled-up towel where my neck would lie and the other one at the foot of the chair. He then stood back and said, "Now, Ms. Cohen," (how did he know my name?), "what can I bring you from the bar?"

I sat back and closed my eyes. Before long, I could feel myself drifting into that twilight zone of half awake and half asleep. Images of my family floated across my thoughts, and despite my expectation that the images would make me feel anxious at this juncture, they didn't. Peter's face then floated across my line of vision, and I knew that before this day was over, everything would be straightened out. Suddenly, I was jolted out of my reverie by something thumping against the side of my chair.

"Oh my god, ma'am," the voice said. "I am so sorry."

I took off my hat and peered over the top of my sunglasses to see Jeffrey standing above me, juggling a phone, a towel and a drink. The look on his face was one of pure horror. He stared at me like a deer in the headlights. "Eliza. Sorry. I didn't see you."

He didn't see me, or he didn't see the chair?

"Jeffrey," I said, sitting up. "Why don't you join me?" I pointed to an empty lounge chair on the other side of the palm tree. I didn't really want company, but he looked so absolutely lost. I was feeling maternal, I guess.

He took a deep breath, which seemed to change his demeanour. Then he smiled. "I don't want to interrupt your rest, Eliza. And I already have a spot across the pool." His eyes were darting around. What was wrong with everyone? Only hours earlier, we had all shared a drive to the hotel, and everything seemed to be so calm.

I shrugged. "No problem." I sat back, relieved to be alone again. "Perhaps we can all get together before we all leave."

"Yes, yes. It's likely we will." He shifted the towel under his arm. "See you soon." And he fled.

I lay back on the lounge chair and sipped the absolutely lovely lemonade the pool attendant had brought me. I was eschewing liquor until later. I wanted to be sharp.

~

I spent a lovely hour (or two) lying by the pool before my stomach began to growl, and I realized I hadn't eaten since breakfast on the ship this morning. When I checked my watch and realized it was already three o'clock, I jumped up, collected my things and headed back to my room. I had to talk to Izzy before another moment passed, but that could wait until I'd had a mini-bar snack of eyewateringly expensive cashews and a can of club soda.

When I opened the door to my room, I noticed a small package on the bed. It was wrapped in Fontainebleau paper with a note affixed to it. *Sometimes shit happens. I should know. Best of luck. In another world, we would have been fast friends. Don't let the arse fall out of 'er. Claire.*

I laughed out loud. That was the Newfoundlander in her coming out. She was channelling my Newfoundland-born father, who used to say that when things were falling apart. I could hear his voice saying, "Well, the arse is well out of 'er now."

I unwrapped the package and lifted a T-shirt from the paper.

Shit Show Supervisor.

We would, indeed, have been friends in another story. The T-shirt was perfect.

Izzy arrived in my room an hour later, after I'd texted her to tell her we needed to talk. She left Mary-Catherine with Esther, a situation we'd have to do something about, but for now, we needed a babysitter, and she and I needed a bit of mother-daughter time. I had no idea.

When she arrived in my room, before I had a chance to say a word, she said, "Why were you talking to that man out by the pool earlier?" She had her arms firmly clenched across her chest.

I had no idea what she was talking about. "What man? I wasn't talking to a man."

"You were so," she said.

I could hear the petulant daddy's princess beginning to emerge just as I was getting used to the grown-up mom who was headed to medical school. I had to find out what caused this unexpected and unwelcome regression. I thought about her question for a moment and realized the only person I'd chatted with when I was out by the pool, apart from the pool attendant, was Jeffrey.

"He was standing up by your lounge chair carrying an armload of stuff."

"Oh, you mean Jeffrey. His name is Jeffrey Montgomery. He's a celebrity psychiatrist and was one of the speakers on the cruise. Why?"

I heard a sharp intake of breath as Izzy flopped onto the couch by the balcony door. She stared out through the glass railing of the balcony to the beach below. "So, you talked to him while you were on the ship?"

"Yes, of course. I texted you after we got on board and mentioned that the cruise staff had asked me to do a cooking class and a presentation. Since we were both presenters, we had several social events together. We got to know one another a bit." I looked at my distraught daughter. "What's going on? Why are you so upset?"

"Did you tell him about me?"

I considered her question for a moment before answering. "About you? I suppose in conversation, I mentioned that I had a daughter." I thought better of mentioning that he had flirted with me shamelessly, but I had since concluded that Claire might have put him up to it. I also refrained from mentioning that he and Claire had been an item, albeit a brief one. "What's this all about, Izzy? Do you know him?"

"I guess I should tell you before anyone else does." She grabbed a cushion from the couch and hugged it close. "I met him in California."

That was all? She'd met him in California? Then I looked at her face, and it could not have been plainer. There was a great deal more to her story than that. I told her to start from the beginning and tell me everything.

Izzy and Jeffrey met at a yoga retreat she was attending as part of her work toward her yoga teaching credentials. All she knew about him was that he was a psychiatrist. It was love at first sight, according to how Izzy saw it. Soulmates, she said. Jeffrey's first book was just out and had yet to become an international bestseller, and since Izzy was on a self-imposed social media fast at the time, she didn't even notice when his fame began to grow. She heard about that later—after she'd returned to New York, pregnant and alone.

To say I was flabbergasted by my daughter's revelation would have been the understatement of the trip. I could not even put into words how awkward and bizarre it felt to discover that a man I'd just gotten to know and who I thought had at least a mild interest in me was the father of my granddaughter. So, I just said, "What happened when you told him you were pregnant?"

"I didn't, Mom. I couldn't."

This revelation made no sense to me at all, not as a woman or as a mother. When prodded for her motivation to keep such a thing from a father, Izzy said one thing. "I knew he had to be married."

"Did he *tell* you he was married? Or did you make that assumption?" As far as I knew from what Jeffrey had told me, he had been married once, years ago, when he was in his early twenties and had never married again.

"No, but Mom, you must know he's older than I am. He *had* to be married. Otherwise, why would he be interested in someone like me who was only twenty-one?"

"If he were married, that would be the situation in which *he* should not have been interested in anyone other than his wife." I could not believe my own daughter's naïvety. "And as it happens, Jeffrey did share with me that he had been married for a few years in his early twenties and had never married again." Izzy's face betrayed her anguish as only a mother could recognize. However, she was an adult, and adults need to make adult decisions. In my view, she had not. "So, you just got up one morning, packed your things and left. Did you ever say goodbye to him?"

Izzy shook her head. I could not believe the immaturity of someone who found herself in a very adult situation. We were not even going to discuss how an intelligent young woman had allowed a pregnancy to happen because it was all water under the bridge, but still. I laid out the facts for her.

Mary-Catherine was here now, and we all loved her. Jeffrey was here now, and it was clear Izzy still loved him. If I didn't miss my guess, Jeffrey still loved Izzy. Izzy had broken his heart. Jeffrey had a right to know he had a daughter and be a part of her life if he chose to, and I had a hunch he might want that very much. We were all here, and there was a lot of love going around. There was only one solution: the Miami family reunion no one saw coming.

~

I knew I'd have to talk to Jake and now we had a whole lot more to discuss beyond how he was going to have to move on. I had agreed to meet him in the bar for a drink before dinner, which I intended to have with Peter afterwards. As I stood in front of the mirror, combing my unruly hair, I said, "You've come such a long way, baby. Now it's time to see it through."

Jake stood up when he saw me approaching. As I neared the table, he lunged in, presumably for a kiss, which I dodged skillfully. I sat down and ordered a martini. I'd been waiting all day for this.

"Before you say a word," Jake said by way of hijacking the conversation, "I never signed those divorce papers, and I think you know I'm not going to."

I sighed and began explaining, as if to a child, the divorce laws in New York. I didn't need his signature to divorce him and that is precisely what was currently progressing through the legal system. If he'd been reading the materials my attorney had sent to him, he would know this. The whole scenario didn't really start to penetrate his thick ego until I mentioned that now that he hadn't signed the papers, he would be subject to whatever kind of financial settlement the judge deemed appropriate.

"We should receive the details soon, but remember that the house is in my name, and it will be mine—among other items that you and your father signed over to me during that *situation*." I couldn't help myself from using air quotes around *situation*.

Jake seemed only slightly deflated by this. Then he said, "Mom is going to blow a gasket."

And there it was. Esther was calling the shots, just as I had expected. I wondered if, in spite of her opinion of me, staying married to me was her idea more than it was Jake's.

"Jake, tell me honestly. At this stage, do you really think that you and I could still be married? And really, we've been growing apart for so many years, you must be relieved that you can be free to move on. I know I am."

Jake sat back against the plush blue velvet upholstery of his chair, swirling the scotch in his crystal glass. "You know, Eliza, I've always envied your ability to see through the bullshit. I don't really know what I thought was going to happen when Mom suggested that I meet you here."

There it was again—the long arm of the great Mrs. Esther Cohen, trying to manipulate a situation to get what she wanted. What Esther wanted was likely control over her granddaughter and great-granddaughter—and the house she gifted to us almost two decades ago. None of that was ever going to happen. All her trash-talking about me that Izzy had mentioned had just been Esther venting her frustration. Whatever would she say to her ladies-who-lunch?

"Jake, now that we're clear about how we move forward …" I looked at his impassive face. "We are clear, aren't we?"

"Crystal clear, Eliza. I'll miss you, but even I know a marriage where both parties aren't committed to one another is a sham."

"Good, then there's something else you should know." I sipped my martini and then put the glass back on the table. "I don't know exactly where we're headed, but you need to know that Peter is now a part of my life." That was the moment when I realized that although thoughts of marrying Peter in the future had crossed my mind, I wasn't there. I realized that I had just escaped one marriage, and I was certainly not ready for another. For the immediate future, at least, I needed to be free to continue exploring who I am and who I might become as I got to know myself. I was liking what I was discovering. But Peter would be a part of my life, in any case.

Jake's eyes widened, and he looked as if he might start speaking.

I wasn't finished. "You also need to know that Peter is about to take a new position in Toronto. I'm considering relocating to Toronto, at least part-time, commuting back and forth to New York only to see my agent and publisher."

Jake seemed to brighten up. "Well, then Mom will be delighted. Izzy and Mary-Catherine can live with us while Izzy's in medical school at Columbia."

"About that. Peter's new position puts him on the faculty at the University of Toronto's medical school. If I decide to relocate, he's sure they'll be only too happy to take Isabel Cohen, winner of entrance scholarships to both Harvard and Columbia. Izzy will move to Toronto with Mary-Catherine in that case."

Oddly, Jake started to laugh. "Mother is going to be apoplectic. That makes even *me* happy. I'll miss my princess if that happens, but as her father, I do think she'd be better off closer to her mother than to her grandmother, Esther."

That shocked me. Perhaps Jacob Cohen was finally growing up and severing the umbilical cord. After all, he was fifty-two years old. High time.

Now, I just had to tell Izzy that she might be moving to Toronto. And then there was the Jeffrey situation. But I had a plan.

~

I had called Peter the moment Izzy left my hotel room and before I met Jake for a drink. Peter was on board with my scheme. While Jake and I were having a drink in the bar, Peter was having a beer with Jeffrey next door at the bar in the Eden Rock Hotel, possibly even chicer than the Fontainebleau. It was all part of my plan. Peter had called Jeffrey the moment we decided on a strategy, and Jeffrey had been eager (perhaps overeager to hear Peter tell it) to join him. He probably needed someone to talk to. I was fairly certain that he'd seen Izzy in the hotel lobby earlier. While having that drink, Peter would ask Jeffrey to join us for dinner. I then called Claire to thank her for the T-shirt.

"My pleasure, Eliza. I know what these things can be like when it comes to family. I'm just glad to have a few days to myself."

That's when I asked her to beg off if Jeffrey asked her to have dinner with him. She agreed happily. Then she said, "Eliza, this is a bit of a delicate matter, but Jeffrey and I had a bit of a heart-to-heart earlier today—"

"I know, Claire. I know all the details about Jeffrey and my daughter. Izzy finally came clean. This might possibly be the most awkward situation I've ever found myself in, but we do what we must."

"And your granddaughter?"

"Jeffrey's, as you might have already concluded. Yes, it's complicated, but I intend to be the best shit-show supervisor in history. Wish me luck." She did.

Then I called Izzy and told her I had made dinner reservations at the steakhouse and that she should bring Mary-Catherine. My plan was a band-aid plan, but not the kind where you place a band-aid for a temporary solution. My plan was to rip off a band-aid as quickly as possible so we could all get on with our lives.

When Peter and I arrived at the steakhouse for dinner a little later, we sat down at our table to await our guests. Izzy arrived first—I had given her a fifteen-minute earlier slot so that she would be the one already here. I didn't want her to bolt if she saw Jeffrey at the table. She parked the stroller beside the table, and I tried to ignore the stink eye we were getting from surrounding diners. I knew the drill. A fancy restaurant, a baby stroller arrives. A lethal combination for a quiet evening. I knew it wouldn't come to that.

Jeffrey arrived right on time. When he saw Izzy at our table, I thought he would faint from surprise and, I hoped, delight. I wasn't wrong. He was, however, for the first time since I'd met him, speechless. Izzy's jaw dropped.

Peter and I both stood up, and I reached for the handle of Mary-Catherine's stroller. I leaned over toward Jeffrey and spoke directly into his ear. "Meet your daughter, Mary-Catherine."

Jeffrey looked at me and then down into the stroller, where the tiny, dark-haired cherub was sleeping peacefully. His jaw was hanging on his chest as he tentatively reached out to stroke her hand. However, my plan did not include Jeffrey getting to know his daughter just yet.

I said, "Now she's coming with us, and you two can sort things out. You, Jeffrey, can start to get to know Mary-Catherine tomorrow."

Peter and I whipped the stroller out the restaurant door, through the lobby and out to the boardwalk, where the evening was beautiful. After a pleasant half-hour walk, we took a soundly sleeping Mary-Catherine to my room, where we ordered room service and toasted to the young couple who we hoped would work things out. How they would work them out was yet to be revealed.

A few hours later, Peter and I were watching a movie when Izzy quietly knocked on my door. When I opened it, she was standing there alone. She threw her arms around my neck and said, "Thank you, Mom."

THIRTY-ONE

Claire

MIAMI BEACH

I DON'T KNOW WHAT I ENJOYED MORE: dining alone in the back of the steakhouse with a clear view of the table where Jeffrey and Izzy were having dinner or my breakfast on the patio by myself the following morning. I had to admit that they looked good together, leaning in, and talking non-stop. I slept well. The following morning, after breakfast, I gathered my notebook and my bag and headed to the beach. I had kilometres of beach walking to do.

I headed directly out of the hotel toward the shoreline so that I could walk in the waves along the way. As I made my way down, I saw a forlorn figure sitting in the sand near the water's edge. He was staring out to sea. He looked familiar.

"Jake Cohen?" I said.

He looked up, shading his eyes from the blazing sun. "Hi. Sorry, I don't seem to remember you. Have we met?"

I sat down beside him. To this day, I don't know why I did that, but he just looked like he needed a friend, and in all the family drama that was playing out, Jake might be the one who was the most left out. It must have been the compassionate doctor in me.

"We haven't actually met, but I do feel that I know you a bit," I said. "I just spent three weeks on a cruise ship with Eliza and Peter—and Jeffrey Montgomery."

Jake took a deep breath. "Geezus, that must have been some trip."

I laughed. "You could say that. Not only that, but Peter O'Brien is my ex-husband."

Jake turned to look at me and burst out laughing. When he calmed down, he said, "How could that man have left someone like you?"

Eliza had never once mentioned how charming Jake was. "Would you be interested in a walk along the beach with me?" It seemed out of character for me to invite someone I didn't know to do anything with me, but there was something about him.

I was surprised when he said yes, so we headed out. It was a gorgeous sunny morning, and the bathing beauties and muscle men were beginning to emerge. We hardly noticed them. We started talking and walking and didn't stop until we realized we'd reached the far end of the beach, South Pointe Park. An hour and a half had passed in the blink of an eye.

We walked out onto the fishing pier at the end and stood there in the sunshine, feeling the breeze. Jake took out his phone and said, "Do you mind? You look gorgeous standing there."

I was so flattered I almost fell over the railing. Of course, he could take my photo. Then we took a few selfies, and I wondered who we'd ever show them to. It was getting close to lunchtime. Jake asked me if I'd like to have lunch with him. I hesitated for a moment. This situation was awkward and so very odd. However, I hadn't had such a peaceful conversation that had no hidden agenda in a long time. Since I was inching closer to reality (my flight home) and I was open to new experiences, I said yes.

As Jake and I sat on the outdoor patio at a chichi South Beach restaurant ordering Cuba Libres, I realized that this was even better than lunching alone. Jake was funny, well-travelled and did I mention handsome? Eliza had never mentioned that.

"Tell me about that place where you live, Claire. All I've ever heard about it was what Eliza said after her trip to see her grandmother last summer, and she wasn't very detailed. I've never actually been to Newfoundland. Never had the time. Maybe I should find that time."

So, I told him about the cliffs, fjords, secluded coves, and pebbly beaches. I told him about the rugged climate and the lively music. I told him about the city of St. John's and how much it was a part of me. Jake Cohen sat there with his elbow on the table and his chin resting in his hand, staring into my eyes. I felt like he was actually listening to every word. I could not imagine what Eliza, Peter, or even Jeffrey would think if they saw us lunching together, but it made me smile, thinking about how alarmed they'd be.

~

Finally, my odyssey was drawing to a close—or perhaps a new one was beginning. After two days in Miami without children or an ex-husband (or the thought of ever having him in my life again), I was sitting in business class on my way to Montreal to connect to St. John's, sipping a glass of champagne. I was considering the past month of my life. It was like a story someone else had written, and I had simply played my part. But I also realized that I was creating my own story, just as Eliza, Peter and even Jake were creating their own. Sometimes, our stories overlapped and as I looked ahead, I realized that there might be more overlap yet to come.

Jake had told me he wanted to come to see St. John's. As tempting as that prospect was in the moment, I realized that I had this opportunity to begin experiencing more of life, or at least paying attention to the experiences simply for what they were—not for where they might be going.

I thought about second chances and realized that I would never get a second chance at anything if I weren't willing to let go of my preconceptions and just go for it. That was so not me, or at least not the me I'd let the world see in the past. That was then. I just wondered if it was all a fairy tale. But even if it was, Charles Dickens had written, "Fairy tales teach us that the path to true happiness is often filled with challenges and obstacles." Amen to that.

PETER

Conception Bay, Newfoundland

I MUST HAVE BEEN ABOUT TWENTY and in my last year of pre-med studies when I fancied myself something of an amateur psychologist and philosopher. But I was born twenty years too late. I was too late to be a beatnik and spend my evenings listening to poetry and engaging in philosophical discourse in coffee houses.

By the time I was in university, coffee houses had gone the way of the do-do bird, and Frank Sinatra was past his best-before date—at least according to the university crowd I hung out with. Bands like New Kids on the Block were popular, and the likes of Madonna, Michael Jackson, and Whitney Houston dominated the charts. Rap and hip-hop were moving into the mainstream, and I hated them. I would have happily listened to Joni Mitchell and Gordon Lightfoot—and Frank Sinatra—until the end of my days, but everything changes. I didn't appreciate that then, but I certainly did now.

I moved to Toronto two months after the cruise. Now, it was August, and I was on vacation back in Newfoundland. I was sitting on the deck of my new summer house overlooking Conception Bay. I'd bought the property a few years earlier from, of all people, Eliza's grandmother, whose centenary we'd been celebrating the year before when I'd met Eliza. I'd originally planned for this house to be where Claire and I would spend our summers, but it wasn't to be. The fates had intervened, and we'd gone in separate directions.

I stood up and walked over to the railing on the deck that wrapped the three quarters of the round house that had the best views of the bay and Bell Island beyond. I was considering the past, the present and the future. I remembered that evening when I had stood at the railing of the cruise ship, looking out over the meeting of the waters, wondering if my life was merely an illusion. I wondered if the reality I thought I'd created wasn't a reality at all. At the time, that made me question everything that was going on around me. Now, I realized that questioning it had led me to an understanding.

I now understood that everything is an illusion, and we likely write our own stories.

When I told my daughter, Fiona, about Eliza, she asked, "Are you and Eliza madly in love, Dad?"

I thought about that for a few minutes before answering. It wasn't that I didn't know the answer, but I wanted to be sure Fiona, a twenty-something young woman with stars in her eyes, understood. Finally, I said, "I don't think so. Being madly in love isn't sustainable. Being in love doesn't last. Loving someone deeply does."

Just then, I turned, and Eliza emerged from the sliding glass doors carrying two mugs of coffee. She didn't say anything as she came over and passed me a mug, then leaned her head on my shoulder as we both breathed deeply of the salt air and listened to the seagulls as they swooped over the bluff. Neither of us needed to say anything.

Eliza was now part of my story, and I was a part of hers. And because she was now a part of my story, so were her kids and even her ex-husband. Maybe we could leave out her odious ex-mother-in-law, though. My grandfather would have said she had a face like a boiled boot. Anyway, there was much more story to be written and there was no ending in sight.

I watched the seagulls wheel and dive, their pale wings flashing against the vastness of the clear blue sky, and they reminded me that I was such a tiny speck on the face of the world. I sipped my coffee and laughed. Eliza looked at me as if to ask me what I was thinking.

I was thinking about one of my gurus during my pop psychology phase. Laugh if you must, but I learned a lot, and much of what I learned stayed somewhere in the depths of my mind. Wayne Dyer, that guru, had once written, "Change the way you look at things, and the things you look at change." That's what I'm talking about. Changing the story. And second chances.

I would tell Eliza—later.

BEFORE YOU GO...HAVE YOU READ THE PREQUEL TO *MEET ME IN MIAMI*?

Short-listed finalist for the 2025 Stephen Leacock Medal for Humour

ABOUT THE AUTHOR

PATRICIA J. PARSONS has written more than two dozen books, including health and business books, a memoir, women's fiction and literary humour. Her novel, *We Came From Away,* was a finalist for the 2025 Stephen Leacock Medal for Literary Humour. She is an inveterate traveller who, after 40 years in Halifax, Nova Scotia, is a recovered academic who now lives and writes in Toronto.

Connect with her on Instagram @patriciajparsons
Join her on Facebook @patriciaparsonswriter
Visit her website at www.patriciajparsons.com

Some other books by Patricia J. Parsons

The "almost-but-not-quite-true" stories
The Year I Made Twelve Dresses (Book 1)
Kat's Kosmic Blues (Book 2)
The Inscrutable Life of Frannie Phillips (Book 3)
Something I'm Supposed to Do (Book 4)
This is the Way the Story Ends (Book 5)
It All Begins With Goodbye (Book 6)

We Came From Away: That Summer on "The Rock"
Good Housekeeping: My Unexpected Adventures in Domesticity